NOT SO LITTLE THINGS

A novel by

Kyle Ann Robertson

Published by
Hybrid Global Publishing
333 E 14th Street
#3C
New York, NY 10003

Manufactured in the United States of America, or in the United Kingdom when distributed elsewhere.

Robertson, Kyle Ann.
Not So Little Things
    ISBN: 978-1-961757-21-9
    eBook: 978-1-961757-22-6
    LCCN: 2023920927

Cover design by: Mike Quinones G
Copyediting by: Wendie Pecharsky
Interior design by: Suba Murugan
Author photo by: Yaeko Photography

kyleannrobertson.com

Praise for "Not So Little Things"

Family secrets, a budding romance, art, Victorian architecture, and lots of food! What's not to love in Kyle Ann Robertson's latest Women's Fiction novel?!

Artist and entrepreneur Tina Edwards is stunned when her estranged mother shows up at her door and announces she wants to move in with her. As Mary Jane slowly reveals the hidden truths about the family history, everything Tina thought she knew evaporates, and she questions who she is, and whom she can trust.

Readers will enjoy the colorful backdrop of the preservation of historic Georgia, as characters' pasts collide with their present. Rich with exquisite detail, this emotional tale resonates with the sacrifices and complexities of families and love.

—Tracey Enerson Wood
International and USA Today Best Selling Author of *The Engineer's Wife, The War Nurse,* and *The President's Wife.*

Robertson does it again in her sophomore novel, but this time, she hits a sweeter note. Sure, there is Mom Drama and lots of it, but we also get a sweet love story and a fascinating look at the very real world of designs in miniature. Of course, miscommunication and family secrets that refuse to stay that way jeopardize everything. But it's the mother/daughter relationship that keeps the reader's allegiances and sympathies ping-ponging. The desire for unconditional love and the need to fiercely protect loved ones sometimes appear at odds and that is a not so little thing.

—Kelly Elizabeth Huston, author of
Tex Miller Is Dead and *A Very Crowded House*

ACKNOWLEDGEMENTS

It didn't take a village to help me write this book- it took more than two! A great many thanks to all my beta readers plus friends and connections in the Women's Fiction Writers Association, especially Kelly Elizabeth Huston and Sheila Athens. A big shout out to my clan. From parents to grandkids and my siblings, nieces, and nephews in between, all have had a part in my writing -willingly or not! Their support is bulletproof and very much appreciated! Hugs to all.

CHAPTER 1

In the split second the door was open, I locked eyes with the thin woman, her hair wrapped helmet-like in a scarf. Even with dark circles around her sunken eyes, the tube in her nose leading to a white box hanging off her shoulder, and the ridiculous-looking floral housecoat-type dress, I recognized Mary Jane Edwards instantly.

"Tina, come on, open up." She pounded with more strength than I thought possible. "Is this any way to treat your mother?"

"Go away. You're good at that. Just go away," I said under my breath and leaned on my side of the door. The battle line was drawn. I refused to let the woman who abandoned me when I was nine years old walk into my life like no time had passed.

"Tina, I'm not leaving until we talk," Mary Jane said as she wiggled the door handle.

You've got to be kidding me. Stretching and loosening my jaw, I backed away from her insistence. What on earth could she want from me after all this time? I stared at the door, shaking my head as if the action itself would send the woman away.

"Come on, Christina, we need to talk," she said with a crack in her voice as she wiggled the door handle and tried to force the door open.

With deep breaths in through my nose and then eased out through my mouth, I slowed my hammering heart, a technique I'd learned through years of therapy. But the long-buried memory of being dropped off at Aunt Liddy's house for an hour, only for it to turn into forever, ached all over again. "You haven't had a word to say in over twenty years, and I certainly have nothing to say to you… and don't break my frickin' doorknob." I yanked open the door.

Holding on to the doorframe, Mary Jane took a step forward. "Thank you."

Squeezing my eyes to expel visions from the last time I saw her, I allowed one word to exit my mouth. "Speak."

"I'm not going to talk to you in this hallway." She gripped the hanging white box as if using it for balance. "May I come in? Please?"

Still, the nine-year-old in me refused to budge.

Mary Jane took a breath. With her attempt at more words, she wheezed, which led to chesty coughing.

I winced as this woman, who was practically a stranger, dug a tissue from the purse hanging off her arm. She hiked up the strap on her shoulder, swung the white box to the front of her hip and adjusted a knob. After several deep inhales, she relaxed.

Aunt Liddy would have been horrified had she seen me treat anyone like this, let alone my own mother. Truth be told, my behavior was appalling, even embarrassing, but what was I to do? With my aunt's loving parenting, strategies from a knowledgeable therapist, and emotional support from my bestie, Nissa, I had painstakingly put in place a life that honored my late father, blocked out my estranged mother, and propelled me into an existence all my own, one

I thoroughly enjoyed. I owed it to all of us not to go down this rabbit hole.

But I had already stepped on the trigger. The steel jaws had snapped, trapping me between head and heart. With thoughts of hashing things out and never having to see her again, I resigned myself. "Just this once." I lowered my shoulders and prayed I wouldn't regret letting her into my home. L'Air du Temps, the scent of my youth, passed by ever so slightly as Mary Jane entered.

With my forehead pressed against the closed door, I took two deep breaths and got ready for battle. I pulled a rubber band off my wrist, piled my long brunette curls into a bun on the top of my head, and reminded myself that my difficult childhood had very little to do with me and a lot to do with the woman sitting on my couch. I peeked at the clock: 9:30 a.m. Was it too early to open a bottle of wine? Whipping around, ready to face my past, a loose curl fell down the side of my face. So much for being Miss Tough Guy.

Mary Jane seemed out of place, sitting slumped and focused on her breathing in my living room, which reflected the mid-century home my father had built for her where she always dressed picture-perfect, behaving like royalty. Seeing her now, in her unbecoming pink floral housedress in contrast to my sleek, custom-built, 1920s-inspired, fluted-back, Art Deco couch bewildered me. Who was this woman interrupting the ethos of my condo?

Even with a mildly warming heart, I couldn't let go of my veil of protection. "Talk."

She began. "I know it's been a long time, and we have a few things to work out."

"A few? Jesus, Mother, you're unbelievable. You. Left. Me. Remember?"

"Will you sit? Please? I need to explain a few things I thought Liddy had told you long ago. I'm surprised she never..." Mary Jane's cough snuck up on her again, but I still refused to sit.

Aunt Liddy? I paced, waiting for Mary Jane to get her cough under control. She had no business bringing Aunt Liddy into this. Liddy was like a mother to me. She had raised me from the age of nine. Liddy took me to buy my first bra. She listened when I lost my first crush and cheered me on when I graduated from high school and college, then moved into my own apartment as I attempted to enter adulthood.

"Aunt Liddy?" I questioned once Mary Jane's cough subsided. "You, Mom. Let's talk about you. I saw you last year at Liddy's funeral. You didn't stick around long enough to talk to me." I paced, unclasped my tense hands, and glued my arms to my sides to keep them from flailing in anger. "You know what? This isn't going to go anywhere. You need to leave. I can't do this. I don't need you to tell me we have to talk because I know there's nothing to say." I marched to the door and yanked it open.

"Tina, I know showing up like this is a shock, but I don't know how much time I have left to straighten things out with you. I have lung cancer. I've quit my job and would like to be with you during the experimental treatment I've signed up for."

I froze. Oh, no. No way. No way will my mother do this to me. Mary Jane could not come into my home and drop a bomb of this caliber. The walls of my carefully assembled life began to crumble.

"Shut the door, Tina. We really need to talk." She pulled a large folded manilla envelope out of her purse and laid it on the coffee table.

Time slowed as I stared at the envelope with the door ajar and the door knob in my sweaty palm, my heart racing and my body numb. I let out a breath and focused on counting to ten.

Mary Jane continued, "...and I could move in with you just while I go through my treatment? I would like to get to know you. There are things, well, some family history I thought Liddy might have already explained to you. But it recently came to my attention that you know nothing about it."

My head spun around. Did she say move in? Family history? Things I didn't know? "Wait." I held up a hand. "Wait. What did I miss? Back up. You move into this apartment?"

I shoved the door shut once again and stared at Mary Jane. My stomach sank. This was such a bad idea. If only I could release myself from her snare and run to safety.

Any normal daughter would have blurted out, "Of course, Mom. I'm your only child. Where else would you go?" But Mary Jane wasn't any normal mother, and she made sure I wasn't any normal daughter. I had learned over the years that if I wanted to stay in control, if something had to be decided right then and there, then the answer was always no.

"As I was saying," Mary Jane continued, "they say I'll have some good days and some bad days, and the treatments are going to zap my strength. So, if I live here, we'll be able to spend time together on my good days."

Pacing, wanting to open the door again and push Mary Jane out, I scrambled to remember what enjoyable times we had spent together. There were none. Those memories, if they existed at all, were pushed so far out of my thoughts that they didn't exist anymore.

A disturbing giggle bubbled up from my gut. "You can't be serious?" A manic titter crept from my throat. "No, you can't move in with me. No. No. No." I couldn't shake my head any harder. My demented smile and tone of voice sickened me, but I couldn't help myself. It was as if my brain held my heart in a wrestling hold while the unstoppable words came out of my mouth like hot lava that couldn't wait any longer to flow. "It's not going to happen. There must be a million other places where you can stay. If talking to me is so damn important, I'll come visit you. You must have another husband. Other children? Why can't you stay at your own house?" My fingers dug into my scalp. "You do have one, don't you? Geez, I don't even know where my own mother lives." I whipped around and locked eyes with her. "Do you hear me? I don't even know if you own a home or rent an apartment, or what job you had to quit. Why are you working anyway? You never had to work before."

This was nuts. How had I never thought about where my mother lived or what she was up to? My therapist did such a great job disassociating me from my past, it was a shock to recall it all now as it rushed in like a tsunami. "Don't you see? You cannot live with me. We are no more than strangers."

"Please, Tina. You're an adult, and I'm an adult. I understand. I truly do, which is exactly why I need to stay here with you. We need to spend some time together and..."

"Why now? I'm not a nurse. It takes everything in me to take care of myself. In fact, look around; I don't have a pet or even a plant. Plus, this isn't just where I live. I work here too." I flung my hand in the direction of my home office and workroom. "Nissa and I work here all day, five, sometimes six, or even seven days a week. We meet our clients here. In fact, that's what I should be doing right now, preparing for a delivery. So, please…" I pointed to the door, this time as a suggestion. A plea.

Mary Jane did not attempt to get off the couch, in fact, she settled in. "I know all that, dear," she said, surprising me. "I also know you have a guest room, a spare room you use for storage. Liddy kept me up to date."

One eyebrow raised. The conversation had veered into new territory, and I certainly wasn't going to discuss what options my condo might or might not have to offer.

"Liddy was very proud of what you've accomplished. As am I. Creating a business building miniature historical replicas is pure genius. Your father would have been so proud."

My jaw dropped. I halted my pacing and tensed like a wolf ready to pounce on its prey. "Don't you dare bring up my father."

It was Mary Jane's turn to shake her head. Her shoulders dropped, and I assumed she had surrendered and let me win. But as she sat on my one-of-a-kind couch decelerating her diatribe, it seemed her shoulders lowered out of pity.

"I'm not explaining any of this very well. Liddy kept me informed until the very end. After all, we were best friends before we were sisters-in-law, and we both loved you very much."

I couldn't. I just couldn't… anything… anymore. "Mom. Mary Jane. I don't even know what to call you. I have a lot on my plate right now." I was depleted of all logic, drained of any emotion. This had to end right here and now while I could still think relatively straight. "I have a delivery, a work trip coming up."

"I won't get in the way of all that. I have a nurse, a companion. You'll love her. She'll do all the cooking and make things easy for both of us. Just think of the time you and I could spend together. I know you're upset with me. I want a chance to change that."

"You think. You want." In my exhaustion, I betrayed myself. "What about me?" My stomach burned as cigarette smoke and pearls muddled my view. Repressed memories determined to surface. But long-ago buried questions fueled a second wind. "Don't you think for one second I don't have a lot of questions of my own."

Those answers couldn't be worth having Mary Jane move in. Living without explanations for so long had convinced me they didn't matter anymore. Not until now, anyway. The give in my resolve allowed Mary Jane to circle back around to the reason for her visit.

"And no, I never remarried. There are no other children." Mary Jane scooched to the edge of the couch and placed both palms on the coffee table. Her voice softened. "So, please?"

The thought that I had brought the proud Mary Jane Edwards to begging tore at my heart, the only problem was that it was still broken from before.

As she leaned over in her attempt to stand, the white box propelled forward, almost toppling her head-first. I held back from helping her. With just one inch, I could lose control over my hard-fought life. She caught herself, lifting from a squat to straighten and swung the box behind her. "It's called an oxygen condenser, and he's a pain in the ass. I call him Bob; he's my reluctant sidekick," she said with part jest and part grimace.

Her attempt at humor was foreign to me, a personality trait I always thought had bypassed her. I picked up the forgotten manilla envelope and slid it back where it came from.

She began to pull it out of her purse, only I stepped back out of arm's reach, hinting I wanted nothing from her, so she stuffed it back in with a sigh, then a cough. On her way out, she stopped in front of me. "I understand you need time to think about this, but my time is limited. It's important, so please don't take too long."

As soon as she exited, I closed the door with just a click. I squeezed my eyes shut, releasing my curbed tears. Shaking my head, I said to my now forever-changed home, "The answer is absolutely not. No. Never."

CHAPTER 2

Salvaging what was left of my self-esteem and to diffuse the traces of Mary Jane's L'Air du Temps in the living room, I opened every window, even the picture window in the large bedroom which I had long ago transformed into an office for Nissa and myself. The view of the North Georgia Mountains' foothills grounded me as the early summer breeze warmed by the morning sun whisked in.

My focus turned to a dollhouse-size reception desk, the centerpiece of my current miniature historical project, as I settled into carving floral details into its legs.

"Good morning, Buttercup." Nissa, best friend and assistant extraordinaire, pushed through the workroom door, startling me out of my deep thoughts. The tiny desk tumbled from my hands, sending a piece of a leg skidding across the work bench.

She placed a tray with two herbal teas from SugarBeans Café onto her desk. Swinging the loaded backpack off her shoulder, she stooped and picked up the runaway desk leg.

Nissa's voice was light and airy as she chatted about a phone call with a vendor. Her fairy-like qualities: a petite frame, pixie haircut, and mischievous smile always softened my mood. But today, it brought me back to over twenty-five years ago, in elementary school, when her magical name, Anissa Fayette, had been called out and caught my attention.

It took less than a minute for us to become best friends. I went home with stories about my new friend and all Mary Jane said was, "That's nice. Good for you." She had not even asked her name.

Nissa turned out to be the one friend who was always there for me. From elementary school to middle school, through high school, and even college, we were forever at each other's sides. For eleven years now, we had operated Edwards' Historical Miniatures, my successful niche business preserving history by creating tiny rooms for clients to display.

I stared at the "Voted Best Coffee Hangout in Floral Ridge, GA" sticker on the side of the cup Nissa held as if I'd never seen it before.

Nissa waved her hand in front of my face and handed me the tiny leg for my desk. "Tina? You okay?"

"My mother came by." I removed the jeweler's headband and tightened my messy bun on top of my head.

Nissa's eyes widened as she set a tea on my desk. "Your mother? As in Mary Jane Edwards? I'm surprised she even knew where you lived. What did you do? What did you say?"

"Nothing. I don't want to..." It would all be too real if we talked about it. I slipped the jeweler's headband back on over my bun, ending the conversation. Hunched over the workbench, I did what I did best. I went back to work repairing the tiny desk's fractured leg, meticulously gluing the two pieces together. Then, to hide the crack, I used a thin, short-handled paintbrush sprouting only a few bristles, and brushed on a subtle layer of reddish-brown paint strokes, imitating the straight, fine grain of mahogany wood.

The air around me expanded as Nissa backed away and sat at her desk. I stayed focused on the job at hand, set the desk to the side to dry, and applied adhesive to a four-inch-wide Greek Revival console.

I scanned the wall of quotes I had collected over the last twenty-four years in honor of my father, Jonathan P. Edwards. I had collected torn book pages, index cards, and sticky notes of quotes he would say to put a positive spin on life, even when life wasn't going his way. If some of the words on the wall didn't come directly from him, I was sure he would have said them to me had he lived.

Sometimes I didn't even know I had a question, and I'd look up. As if I had thrown a dart, my glance would land on a phrase that made sense of my current situation. At the moment, I found *Stay true to yourself.*

I couldn't miss my father any more than I did at that moment. He always knew the right thing to do or the right thing to say. I strived to be just like him: positive, caring, and forgiving. But Mary Jane showing up had stirred the past in ways I wasn't prepared to confront, and I didn't know if I had it in me to be that person. A whiff of the slight acidic odor from the adhesive had me check the wall clock, and ignoring my twisting stomach, I returned to the next step for tacky adhesive on the console. Gold leaf application was easy but time-consuming. I carefully pressed on a thin sheet of gilded gold, then patted it with cheesecloth. Every inch needed to be as realistic as possible. That's what my clients paid for, an exact replica of the furniture in whichever historic room they wanted preserved in miniature.

After setting the console aside to dry, I stretched my arms above my head and rolled my neck. Not wanting to send an invitation for conversation, I made sure not to connect eyes with Nissa. Not quite yet. I gathered any loose curls and shoved them into the elastic, attempting to keep my bun together. Having to tuck a wayward strand behind my ear, I cursed the day I had cut my bangs.

"Okay, then. Maybe we can talk about your date last night?" Nissa asked while rummaging through her backpack.

I replied only because it was the surest way to avoid talking about my mother. "Seriously? I don't know why I bother." With no inner drive to bring someone new into my life, as per my usual, I preferred my evenings alone, reading or watching TV and imagining the fictitious miniature families interacting in whichever small-scale rooms we were working on at the time. I removed the jeweler's headband once again and sighed, "It was nice of Marge to set me up with her neighbor's cousin's son. He was nice enough, but there was no spark. In all honesty, I would rather have stayed here with our miniatures and a bottle of Cabernet for company."

"You know that's not normal," Nissa chided. She pulled the other stool up beside me at the workbench. "What are you working on now?"

"The last of the furniture for the Le Dauphin Hotel lobby. What do you think about this?" I held out a red velvet high-backed chair for Nissa's inspection.

"Perfectly 1870s." She examined the rest of the pieces of furniture laid out on the workbench.

With a gentle squeeze of the tweezers, I peeled off what gold leaf didn't adhere to the console, then rubbed and polished it, giving it a more burnished antique look. It looked great. Sometimes I even surprised myself.

Nissa pulled out her trusted Canon from college and set a tiny red velvet chair into a lightbox. As the partner who archived every project, she photographed each flawless piece of furniture and each miniature room upon completion. One day, so she swore, she would author a book of her photos.

Keeping my hands busy and my mind as quiet as possible, I created the detail in the console's faux-marble tabletop. I became lost in watching the marbling take place as I swirled black and oxblood-colored paints together. I resisted the tennis match playing in my head. I fought off every nauseating memory served to me. I wanted no part of Mary Jane now, just as she had wanted no part of me long ago.

I had to get out of the office, out of my head. I ran past the door Mary Jane had pounded on earlier, past the couch she had all but spoiled, and released my breath as I entered the kitchen. My anger toward Mary Jane for showing up unannounced conflicted with my guilt of turning her away, and yet my need for answers from questions formed long ago kept it all afloat. The clock had barely struck noon, but I didn't care. I walked back into the workroom with two glasses and a bottle of wine.

As I entered the office, Nissa sat flipping through a notebook. "Just pulled up messages, and we have a prospective client. A Mr. Jake Martin. He's renovating the old Randall mansion and turning it into a B&..."

She turned around and saw me standing with a bottle of wine and immediately dropped her notebook onto a pile of papers and cleared them off her desk. She stacked several empty SugarBeans cups onto the windowsill to make room as I set the glasses down and poured the wine, sniffling the entire time.

"She's dying," I blurted out.

"Who's dying?"

"My mother is dying." I sighed and dropped into Nissa's chair. "Lung cancer. And she wants to move in."

"In? Where?"

"Here. With me...us."

Since I had plopped into Nissa's chair, she wheeled the chair from my desk over, sat knee to knee with me, and handed over a tissue. "Enough of the cryptics. Tell me what's going on." She took a lingering sip of wine, joining my cause, while I glanced over her shoulder at the wall behind her.

I zeroed in on a lined piece of paper torn from a notebook. *Not everything happens for a reason. Sometimes life just sucks.* I agreed. Sometimes life isn't all it was cracked up to be. But imagine how sucky it would be to be Mary Jane right now. "You should have seen her, Nissa. She was so frail, so un-Mary Jane." I relayed the conversation from this morning.

We sat still and quiet until our glasses emptied. Nissa broke the silence. "I get your mother was never there for you, but how can you not…"

I cut her off. "I've worked so hard to have peace with myself. All the choices I have made to honor my childhood home, the home my father built, and…" My heart geared up again, and my hands shook.

"…and the home your mother sold out from underneath you." Nissa finished in a singsongy tone. Her subtle way of letting me know I'd repeated that particular phrase several times brought a slight grin to my face. It was something I always said to justify my muddled feelings toward Mary Jane.

"She left me with my Aunt Liddy and, yes, sold the home my father had built right out from under me. And now she wants me to share my place with her?" My heart went out to my beloved condo. "Sorry, but none of this makes sense. She's had over twenty years to get reacquainted and never bothered to visit me once."

"Not that you've ever invited her." Nissa raised an eyebrow making her point.

"I'm not the one who dumped her family. This is my space. I will not let her, or anyone else for that matter, show up and turn things upside down, ruin another home with bad memories."

Nissa rubbed my shoulder. "Okay, okay. Don't let her get to you."

Easy for her to say. I had never shared my story with anyone except the therapist Liddy insisted I talk to. Liddy knew parts of the story, and Nissa knew even less. I didn't want anyone to know, not even my best friend, the bleak and sickening thoughts I had about Mary Jane and my father's death.

Wanting to release a scream, I bolted out of my seat and out of the office, grabbing our two empty wine glasses. Nissa followed me to the kitchen with the half-full bottle of wine.

"I know I sound ungrateful, but I don't know her," I said, rationalizing my thoughts. I searched through the pantry for crackers or something to nervously nosh on.

Nissa nodded and sipped as I continued. "Mary Jane wasn't motherly. Your mom sat with you when you did your homework, made sure you brushed your teeth every night and packed lunch for you every day. Mary Jane only cared about that damn house of hers and organizing dinners for Dad and his clients. And, of course, her charities."

Nissa placed her hands atop my clenched fist. "Tina, you loved your father so much, and your father loved your mother, right? So, if you can't do this for her, what about for him? You won't want to regret anything once she's gone."

I exhaled to the count of ten and stared at the small, framed box hanging on my kitchen wall, which held my most precious possession, the miniature replica of Van Gogh's *Sunflowers* my father hand-painted for me on a piece of bark for one of my fairy houses. This one gift single-handedly confirmed the care and attention to detail he paid me when I was young.

Nissa poured herself another glass of wine and planted the bottle in front of me.

The sound of bottle meeting table rippled within my brain. The wine swished back and forth as it set me stranded at sea with no horizon, where any choice could make things worse.

The Mary Jane who entered my apartment for the first time was a smidgeon of the woman I once knew. What had become of the woman who hosted the most sought-after dinner parties for her husband's company? Where had the woman gone who orchestrated fundraisers for the largest charities in Athens? What about the woman who so confidently mothered from afar, not necessarily unlovingly, just distant? Mary Jane was undeniably ill, so how could I possibly reconcile wanting absolutely nothing to do with her while knowing I was her only living family?

I poured the rest of the wine into my glass, wanting nothing more than to be numb.

"Why don't you just give her a day or two?" Nissa asked.

"Or forget she showed up at all," I said as I sipped. "Actually, the best thing would've been to never have opened my door this morning."

"You could talk to her doctor before you make any decision," Nissa continued. "Try to figure out her angle."

Finally, a logical answer to put my indecision to rest. Surely a doctor wouldn't leave a dying woman in my care. Grateful for some sensible advice and a final decision, I nodded. "I can hear my father saying, '*It's like the weather. You can't control it, but you do have choices. You can go out in the rain and get wet, you can go out with an umbrella, or you can stay inside.*'" I gulped down the last of the smooth liquid and grabbed the box of crackers. "Come on. This is a waste of time. I don't want to think about it any longer. We have work to do."

Nissa gave me another hug. Leaving her arm draped over my shoulders, we walked back to the office. Sisters-in-arms.

As we entered the workroom, a purple sticky note on the wall straight ahead read *Do what makes you happy.* I tightened my lips against the angst that wanted to erupt and stared through the window at a large oak tree in the park across the street. It swayed and the green leaves fluttered, filtering the sunlight, mimicking the anxiety gurgling inside of me as it did when I was nine. Only this time, it escaped from my belly and clutched at my throat as I envisioned the wide-open doorway of my father's office in my childhood home.

I could still clearly see him slumped over his desk, his head turned sideways, his arms dangling by his sides. In my tiny stocking feet, I stepped into the room. "Daddy?" After no response, I followed his fixed stare. My mother sat on the couch with her legs crossed, her top leg slightly swinging, and the royal blue pump hanging off her toes. My gaze shifted up, past her matching royal blue dress, and through a haze of cigarette smoke, until I met her eyes. With flawlessly manicured fingers, she rolled her pearl necklace at the base of her throat, and I screamed, "Mama, what did you do?"

CHAPTER 3

Nissa remained working in the office while I left to nap away my churning headache. Behind my closed eyelids, I attempted to dovetail Mary Jane, the woman who showed up at my door with the philanthropist from my past in her jewel-tone dresses, matching pumps, and those damn steadfast pearls around her neck. Where had she been and what had she been doing these last two decades?

I stared at the ceiling, desperate for sleep but not able to get there. Sheep were counted, the alphabet said backward, and multiplication tables repeated, but still, I couldn't doze off. When I couldn't meditate away my visions, I put on my walking sneakers and my headphones.

I walked the three and a half miles around the park across from my condo, letting the music dictate my pace and the sun thaw my hardening thoughts. An hour later, I returned, refreshed and sweaty, and geared up for work. "What did you say about a potential client?" I asked Nissa.

"Oh, the guy that said," she read from her notes, "quote: my mother thinks it would be nice to have little rooms made like the original rooms from the 1860s unquote."

Offended at his reference to our miniature replicas as little rooms, I asked, "His mother? Who the heck is this guy?"

"On it." Nissa swiveled her chair around and Googled the possible client. She read the information out loud as it loaded onto her screen. "Jake Randall Martin, the chef-slash-owner of three Atlanta restaurants, Blue Moon Cafe, Brasstown Union, and Peachtree Steak House."

"Those are some high-end restaurants." I flipped into business mode.

"He's also the president of the Randall Mansion Foundation, whatever that is. He's involved with the Athens Downtown Initiative. And look…" Nissa lifted her laptop to show me a close-up of Mr. Martin. "Pretty cute. Brown curly hair, blue eyes. Your favorite."

I rolled my eyes. "Keep reading. And I don't have a favorite. I don't even have a general type. Do a little research on the Randall Mansion for me. I'll call Mr. Martin and set up a meeting. We need this client, and I need a serious distraction." I picked up my cell phone.

"Go get 'em, Tiger." Nissa winked and left the office.

With a thumbs-up, and in all seriousness, I had to get this right. This mansion sounded like it could be one of our biggest jobs yet. We always needed the next commission, but it wasn't like we were desperate for money. I had squirreled away the payments from my father's trust.

One thing for sure, I needed something to focus on other than Mary Jane. My sense of doing the right thing butted heads with not wanting to step into the lion's den. I zeroed in on a poster on the wall, *Worrying doesn't take away tomorrow's troubles. It takes away today's peace.* Easier said than done. That quote came from my therapist, but I knew for sure it was something my father would have said.

In the window, I caught the reflection of the messy bun on top of my head, a silhouette of a spent dandelion right before someone blew on it to make a wish. Tightening my focus, I could see my right ear sticking out a tad bit farther than my left, just like my father's.

"Hello?"

I started when a voice came through my forgotten cell phone. "Oh, hi. Mr. Martin?"

"Yes, ma'am," he said. His voice was pleasant with the lengthened vowels of a buttery-rich Southern drawl.

"This is Christina Edwards, with Edwards' Historical Miniatures. You left a message regard--"

"Yes, the little rooms," he interrupted. "I bought an old Victorian mansion in Athens. Turning it into a bed and breakfast. My mother thinks your little rooms could add a touch of nostalgia."

"So you've said." I sat back in my seat, offended a second time. "If you'd like to set up an appointment, I'd be happy to show you what we have to offer."

"When are you available? You're in Floral Ridge, right?"

"How about tomorrow morning at SugarBeans Café on Main at nine a.m.? And, yes, that's in Floral Ridge."

"Got it. See you tomorrow at nine."

"Was that him?" Nissa asked as I hung up, and she carried in a large tray with fruit salad and buttered cinnamon toast.

"Yes. I'll meet him tomorrow morning. My guess is he's not interested in our miniature replicas. I think he'll be a hard sell. He was a little condescending. Kept referring to our 'little rooms.'"

"Well, you said you wanted a distraction. I'll research the mansion. You go into our stock and dig out some gorgeous Victorian pieces to show him," Nissa said.

Saluting my orders, I opened the door of the walk-in closet filled with our craft supplies and all kinds of miniature items—my heaven on earth. I hunted through our inventory and found a miniature mahogany Victorian armchair with burgundy velvet padding on the seat, lower back, and elbow rests, with a fruit and leaf motif intricately carved in the frame. I also found an unfinished side table, its legs mimicking the curved legs of the chair, with a hand-painted faux-leather, inlaid top. With a little polish, I could show Mr. Martin how our realistic miniatures would enhance interest in the Randall Mansion B&B.

I picked up pictures of the mansion from Nissa's desk and remembered driving past the unkempt home in my youth. There were bound to be several rooms we could replicate in the enormous, multi-gabled Victorian home.

To land this project and convince Mr. Martin to order as many rooms as possible, I needed to dig up more samples to show him. Like my father and Oprah once said, *Preparedness plus opportunity equals success.*

Nissa went home early, leaving me with my orbiting thoughts. After hours of pretending to work, I made my way into the kitchen to make myself a bite to eat. I peeked into the spare bedroom and tried to imagine Mary Jane staying there. There was no possible way she could stay here. I needed the space as it was. An antique white dresser and Liddy's old steamer trunk held my winter clothes, and what would I do with the worn, faded, red, second-hand recliner saved from my college days?

I munched on a turkey and lettuce pita as I wandered around the apartment rearranging pillows, lining up the piping on seat cushions, and squaring up the corners of the *Architectural Digest* magazines on an end table. I sat on the sofa where Mary Jane had sat with that damn oxygen condenser thing, frail as could be, and I still was afraid to let my guard down. "Could anyone blame me?" I asked out loud to no one.

My father would say, "*Nothing gets done when you're doing nothing.*" With my energy slightly restored, I returned to the office to really work.

The last of the furniture for the Le Dauphin Hotel reopening, an early-nineteenth-century chair with out-scrolled arms and a leather-like seat and four tapered legs waited for me on the workbench, as well as acrylic paint tubes, brushes, and transparent glaze. I got to work stroking on the black base coat. Gold motifs would be added later. As I waited for the layers to dry, I polished the pieces to show to Mr. Martin.

The fogginess from the earlier wine faded into sleepiness, calling for a comforting mug of lavender tea. I poked around and checked my email. Nissa had sent an article about lung cancer. The subject line stated, "Fwd: Mayo Clinic on Lung Cancer—found some info, thought you'd be interested." Just like Nissa to handle a tough situation with fact-finding. Without reading a word of the email, I stared at the screen long enough for my screen saver to pop up, then looked up at my wall. *He who procrastinates in his choosing will inevitably have his choice made for him by circumstance.* I raised my mug to the computer screen then shut it down.

CHAPTER 4

After a night of little to no sleep and continual visions of smoke and pearls, I limited my thoughts to landing the Randall Mansion project.

I wrapped the tiny pieces of furniture I had chosen to win over Mr. Martin in tissue paper and cleaned out my computer bag. From the bottom, I pulled out a forgotten SugarBeans napkin. *What is meant to be will always find its way.* Hopefully, it was talking about Mr. Martin's project and not Mary Jane. With the palm of my hand, I ironed it out the best I could and taped the napkin amongst all the other quotes on the wall.

Pulling the chain on my banker's brass and green desk lamp, I shed light on my planner laying on my otherwise spotless desk; if a paper didn't have a file to go into, I put it on Nissa's desk to deal with. I shook my head in pity at the empty pages of my planner, then closed it and placed it in my bag.

Nissa flitted in, breaking through my contrary sentiments. I massaged my temples, hoping the circular movements would unscrew my coiled thoughts.

"Did you get any sleep last night?" Nissa asked.

"Not much."

"Your mother?" Nissa leaned on the edge of my desk.

My head-heart thing started tugging again, and I turned my thoughts to this morning's meeting. "I have to go throw on something relatively professional. I'm meeting with Mr. Martin in a few minutes."

"At 9 a.m.?" Nissa grinned. "Couldn't wait to meet him, huh?"

"Stop it," I said and shut the door behind me.

Pride rose as I stepped out of my lobby door and gazed down Main Street. My Main Street. I had moved to Floral Ridge right after college to be closer to the mountains and lakes of North Georgia and still be close to Liddy's home in Bluebelle, near Athens, less than a thirty-minute drive away.

Being part of this slow-paced community, as if the whole of it was my family, revamped my energy. Every time I stepped out of my red-brick corner building, I wanted to throw my arms out and sing like Julie Andrews. Listed on the National Historic Register, Floral Ridge's old town charm, where everyone knew everyone, embraced its turn-of-the-century railroad station in the center of close-knit merchants selling wares in well-maintained old boarding houses and the general store from the 1870s. I chose the second-story corner condo, above the local hardware store, for the views, the sunshine, and the cross breeze of fresh air.

I glanced up at my kitchen window with white vintage hobnail bottles and cruets displayed and ignored the spare bedroom windows with their curtains drawn. Not very welcoming. I quickly wiped away an image of the curtains opening and Mary Jane waving down to me.

I strolled next door to SugarBeans Café, my favorite spot for tea and forbidden baked goods. Zig-zagging through tables of early risers, both regular patrons and Wi-Fi-seeking customers, I managed to dodge a yoga mom dragging a screaming child by the arm who apparently wanted, but wasn't allowed, a chocolate chip cookie for breakfast. As I stood in line for a fresh iced tea, the constant *ding* from the door was testimony to SugarBean's popularity.

A woman with burnt-orange spiky hair—and if asked, she called it Atomic Cinnamon—yelled over the sound of the coffee grinder, "Morning, Tina."

"Pretty busy this a.m.," I said.

"Morning usual?" Marge asked as she grabbed a mug to fill with steaming hot water.

"Yes, please." I looked around the café, and my favorite table was just clearing out.

"You okay?" Marge dropped a sweet Tropical Green Tea bag into the oversized mug, releasing the bouquet of exotic herbs, which I preferred over the bitter smell of coffee. "You look a bit…"

"Nothing that a cup of your hot tea won't fix," I said with a wink. I wasn't sure if I was overtired, nervously anticipating Mr. Martin, or sick of thinking about my mother, but apparently, it showed. I took the cup from Marge, left three dollars on the coffee-stained counter, and blew her a kiss. Just knowing she was here and would listen as a pseudo-aunt anytime I needed diminished my tension a bit.

I snagged the table in front of the café's bay window and wrapped my hands around the warm mug. The morning sun poked between the buildings across the street and bounced off cars as they drove by, creating hypnotizing, sparkling patterns on the wall beside me.

Despite my dull headache, the excitement of a potential client geared up my creative juices. However, a 9 a.m. meeting wasn't one of my smartest ideas. When I scheduled the appointment, I didn't know I'd be awake until 3 a.m. this morning. But I couldn't let anything get in the way of locking down this upcoming project. I was uncomfortable without a project on the horizon, and right now, we had none.

Lost in the whirl of the coffee grinder, the hiss of the milk steamer, and the din of many voices, I pulled my hair back into a messy bun at the nape of my neck, missing an escaped curl that fell along my cheek. I tucked it behind my ear and took a sip of tea. "Okay, concentrate," I said under my breath and scrolled on my laptop for the file Nissa had sent regarding the Randall Mansion. *To be prepared is half the victory.*

I patted the top of my head for my reading glasses, but they weren't there. The glasses eased the strain on my eyes, and, therefore, my head. Frustrated, I rummaged through my computer bag and then my jacket pockets. I patted the front of my shirt and found them. Always the last place I looked.

"Good morning! Miss Edwards?" a powerful, deep, Southern drawl came out of nowhere.

I stumbled as I attempted to stand and pull off my glasses at the same time. I stared into friendly, midnight-blue eyes, and shook the large masculine hand presented to me. Suddenly, I became aware I hadn't put on a lick of makeup.

Almost a foot taller than my five-foot-four-inch frame, in brown leather Cole Haans, pressed jeans, a starched white collared shirt, and a tan corduroy blazer, Jake Martin stood grinning as if he'd just won a blue ribbon at the county fair for finding me. His curly auburn hair was still damp, and he smelled fresh and manly like sandalwood and bergamot.

"Mr. Martin?" I think my heart gave a little patter.

He tilted his chin and continued to shake my hand. "It's Jake. Do you need anything? Coffee? Tea?"

"All set, but thanks, and I'm Tina." I stammered, but then told myself to settle down and remember rule number one:

Never mix business with pleasure. But I did wish I had put on a touch of mascara, and maybe better shoes.

"All right then. I'll be right back with my coffee." He tipped the hat he wasn't wearing.

Once again, I pulled up and reviewed the files from Nissa. The glare from the sun, now rising above the buildings across the street, reflected off my screen. I pushed my computer around the table to the left, sliding my chair with me.

"Are you staking your claim? Where would you like me to sit?" Mr. Martin, Jake, said with a wink.

With a wry smile, I shook my head. It must have looked as if I was boxing him out of my half of the table, and maybe I should.

"No, no, sorry. It's the light." I flicked my wrist toward the blinding sun, and that rebellious curl once again fell from behind my ear. I invited him to sit for my presentation by pointing to the chair across from me.

As soon as he settled—in the chair right next to me—he angled my computer toward himself. He tapped the space bar on the laptop, lighting up the screen.

I frowned at the ease at which he took over. "Those are pictures of work I've done for the Georgia Building Authority. Their office building used to be an old bank." I angled the laptop slightly toward myself and pointed to the picture of an old brick, three-story building with a bell tower.

"Oh, sorry," he said, turning the laptop even more toward me then scooted his chair until we were thigh to thigh. "I tend to take charge. A bad habit of mine."

Stealthily, I scooted as far away as I could without falling off the other side of my chair and picked up my tea to busy my hands. "I'm sure it pays off running all those restaurants. And now the B&B?"

"That's a fact. But let's get back to you, Tina. Go on, tell me more." He gestured to the laptop.

I slid my glasses up the bridge of my nose and cleared my throat. My words came out faster and faster as I scrolled through the photos. "A couple of years ago, I created miniature replicas of the bank's original lobby and the president's office as they had appeared in 1860. See here?"

Getting caught up in what I loved most, I soon forgot our physical closeness and popped open another folder of a sizeable brick-walled room with an acid-stained concrete floor buffed so well it reflected the cast-iron beams in the ceiling. Jake scooted forward, and I ignored the arm he carefully draped along the back of my chair to get a closer look at the screen. "This is what the old bank looks like today. The lobby is an event venue that holds over five hundred people. And…"

He patted the back of my hand to slow me down. "Whoa, whoa, hold up. I've already seen these. Actually, these exact ones in real life."

As I pulled my hand away, my voice raised an octave. "You have?"

He leaned back in his chair, locking his fingers behind his neck. "I was at one of my mother's events at this very venue last month, and that's where she got the idea your work would be perfect in the B&B." He moved his coffee to the far side of the table and commandeered the computer. "May I?"

"Your mother's event?" I slid my glasses off and chewed on one tip, marveling at his smoothness.

"A showcase for local artists. It was held last month at the old bank. Great event." He pulled up his mother's website and a picture of her standing in front of one of her paintings with a miniature replica of the bank president's office nearby on her left. "So how long have you been doing this?"

I glanced at his beautiful mother, then went into my spiel about my father's architect and design career, how he built fairy houses with me and paid for my MFA from Savannah College of Art and Design. "It all started after seeing a photo of my college professor's Victorian music room. I offered to recreate it in miniature for a class project. After the music room, a church down the street asked for a replica of their original place of worship with pews and a choir loft." I unwrapped two of the Victorian miniature pieces I had brought as examples.

Jake took the desk from me, examining it with interest. "Beautiful. You made this? How long did it take? Is that real leather on the desktop?" With regard, he gently touched the top with his fingertips.

"Whoa, whoa, hold up," I teased, mimicking his earlier mode of slowing me down. My laughter lasted a second too long.

He smiled, acknowledging my subtle joke. A slight raise to the left side of his lips created a charming dimple. For a quick second, my bones liquified. I bet he got away with murder with that grin. I sat up straight, relieved not to find his hand on the back of my chair anymore and armed myself with professionalism. "Yes, of course. That's what I do. And no, it's not real leather. I painted it."

"Did you paint the miniature portrait also?" Jake pointed to the painting in the bank president's office in the picture on the computer screen.

I pulled up a close-up photo of the portrait, one that Nissa had taken in her lightbox.

The respect and admiration in his eyes softened my resolve. He really liked my work. I could only nod in answer.

"Nice work. I just recently got the permits from the town after six months of meetings and now have the budget approval from the Foundation to begin the renovations on the mansion. We started a week ago."

His fingers drew an invisible blueprint of the mansion on the table in front of us. His eyes lit up as he explained how he was moving one of his restaurants from Atlanta to the B&B.

There were so many questions I wanted to ask, but I still wasn't sure where he stood with our miniatures. Needing to stay on task, I asked, "Did you bring any photos of the rooms you would like replicated?"

"Your rooms are cute and everything, but I'm not sure what sort of investment they would make."

"Preserving history is always a smart investment, Mr. Martin."

"It's Jake, and I didn't mean to offend. I'm not quite sure how much this is going to cost me? I don't want to seem rude, but I have deadlines for this fall. I already have reservations booked."

"It will all depend on how many rooms you'd be interested in. Did you bring a real floor plan?"

He shook his head. He became that innocent twelve-year-old boy who got caught with his father's magazines. With a sly grin, he threw his hands up in apology.

I wiped the disbelief off my face. Was this man taking me seriously? Nissa and I needed this project. I needed to win him over. "I'm sure we could have it completed by the fall. But I'll need old photos of what you'd like replicated to give you an estimate."

"Well, that's the hitch. I don't have any with me. But I'm pretty sure the attic is full of them, but… we haven't gone through the attic yet. Would you want to go through the boxes in the attic with me?" His eyes sparkled with hope.

I eyed him sideways with a smirk. He hadn't prepared one thing for me. A little worried, I wondered about working for someone so charming, but I had bills to pay. "I'll have to charge you for our time."

"Our?"

"Let me check with my assistant. She's the research specialist. I'll see if, and when, we can go photo hunting."

"Deal." He stuck out his hand with that twelve-year old's exuberance.

Something made me feel as if I took this one step, I'd get pulled into quicksand. "I'm serious. You'll have to pay for every minute of our time."

"Got it." He agreed a little too readily for someone on a tight budget, but at least Nissa and I could earn some money doing what we both loved.

I closed my laptop and gathered my miniature samples as Jake remained seated. Maybe he wanted to stay and finish his coffee, but I had work to do. I'm sure Nissa would be ecstatic to treasure hunt in his attic, but as my partner, I needed to discuss it with her before I committed.

When I stood, he immediately pushed his chair back. "Really nice meeting you," he said. His dimple made another appearance.

"I'll be in touch," I said and backed away from the table.

CHAPTER 5

That night, after a tediously focused day at work, I floated in the cloud-like comfort of my bed and waded through time, reaching for pant legs and skirt hems as I gasped for air. As clearly as the day I found my father dead, his body draped over his desk crept into my dreamscape.

I fought to lift my hands and block the view, but I couldn't move my arms, I couldn't scream for help, as the day of my father's death played out before me again and again. Within the confines of my dream, a faceless brunette little girl accidentally-on-purpose kicked a soccer ball into the evil queen's lush flower bed. She needed to pick the perfect flower petals to use as blankets for the fairy beds she and her father had made from tree bark. Torn between the vibrant yellow daylilies and the soft pink roses, she ran to her land of wee folk with one of each in her gentle hands along with a large round nasturtium leaf that was just right for a rug for under the tree bark beds.

She perched on a large, exposed root of one of the many fallen pecan trees in her old backyard and peered into the hollowed-out tree stump fairy house. Reaching in to reposition the toppled popsicle-stick ladder, the young girl fell head over heels into the tiny kitchen, tumbling as Alice did down the rabbit hole, shrinking until she landed with a plop on the dirt floor.

In my sleep, I reached out and tried to grab her before she landed head-first in the hollow. She had sent all the seashell dishes flying off the upside-down cat food can kitchen table and knocked over the chairs made from matchboxes. Sparkling orbs of light fluttered in. I silently called out to her, wanting to protect her from the fairies' wrath.

She stayed calm as her now tiny body could meander freely around the fairy's abode. The little girl set the furniture straight, reset the table with its clamshell dishes, and squared up the viburnum leaf placemats. She tucked a loose curl behind her ear and glanced over her shoulder as if she heard my silent warnings.

Being small enough to wander her fairy village, she climbed out of the tree trunk, scratching knees and elbows, and tiptoed around the other tree trunk gardens and hollow stump abodes.

As she ran across her yard through seemingly shrinking grass, she surged to normal size, toppling, and flipping, growing with every tumble, until she stopped, legs sprawled out in front of her, facing the screened-in porch of the mid-century modern home her father had built for her mother.

I called for her to come back as she headed for her home, knowing she shouldn't go in there. I fought with the bindings on my arms, the cement blocks holding me under my blankets. I needed to get out of bed. I needed to stop that poor young girl from going into that house.

She sat on the stairs, took off her shoes, and clapped them against each other as loud as thunder. The young girl ducked in case the evil queen appeared upset with the noise and dust.

Once confident she didn't attract the queen's attention, she lined up her navy-blue saddle oxfords next to her green

Wellies and white Keds like little soldiers guarding the back door. She quietly peeked into the kitchen.

I screamed to stop her, but my voice went nowhere. I struggled but couldn't push through the frozen spell. This innocent child was determined to tell her daddy of her recent adventure and tiptoed down the long corridor, yards of hardwood flooring passed by treadmill-like as I wished the little girl back from entering that office. She broke from my prayer grip as the treadmill stopped and shot her forward into the office.

She stepped into the room. A faceless man lay slumped over the desk, one arm across the desk, his other arm dangling by his side, his head turned sideways staring at the evil queen, crown askew. She sat on the couch across from the desk with her legs crossed. The one leg on top slightly swung until she extended it straight out, and her royal blue pump prevented the little girl from entering any further.

The little girl shifted her gaze up the queen's long leg, past her royal blue dress to two wicked eyes peering through a haze of cigarette smoke. The little girl screamed, "Mama, what did you do?"

I rolled my head and fought to cover my ears, to break the chains holding my arms down.

Flawlessly manicured fingers rolled a pearl necklace at the base of the queen's throat. In slow motion, her gold and gemstone crown slipped off her head as she looked up and maniacally laughed.

A scream broke through my sleep paralysis as I fought off the suffocating blankets that held me down. Through panicked breaths, I sat up and turned on my bedside light. It was all too real, and I couldn't shake how that little nine-year-old girl felt and was still afraid the wicked queen would step out from behind a closed door.

Finally, I threw on my bathrobe and plodded to the workroom, leaving Wonderland behind, still fearful of becoming too small to matter.

CHAPTER 6

"No sleep again?" Nissa asked the obvious question. I had fallen asleep at my desk with my forehead on my arms. I shook off my slumber. "I never want to fall asleep again."

"Ah, jeez. I'm sorry. Here, caffeine." Nissa handed me my tea. "Nightmare again?"

I nodded and stretched my arms above my head, grateful for the freedom to be able to do so. I adjusted my mind to the activities of the day. "We're all set for the Le Dauphin. The lobby's complete. Glass panels for the front and top should be delivered today, then we're ready to rumble."

"Let me see." Nissa dug out her own jeweler's headband and joined me at the work bench. She combed over every inch of the miniature three-sided room with a fine-tooth comb. With a white glove and a light touch, she smoothed the seams of the pale pink and cream acanthus leaf wallpaper she had personally hand-painted to scale.

"So, what do you think?" I asked, knowing I'd only get the truth.

"Wallpaper looks awesome. It's perfection with the fern-green carpet. And your dad would've loved the elliptical arches in the crown molding. So perfect for the era."

Nissa reached in and flicked the tassels of a gold tieback holding open the red velvet drapes.

I grinned at her excitement. If it weren't one hundred percent accurate, I would be the first to hear about it.

"We did good," she laughed and high-fived me.

"Once again, our MFAs have paid off," Nissa said, Vanna White-ing our graduate and undergraduate diplomas on the wall.

In preparation for our upcoming trip for the grand reopening of the Le Dauphin Hotel, I bubble-wrapped a three-inch-tall gold-leaf mirror with a peaked pediment. I boxed four lyre-back armchairs and a four-inch-long curved-back velvet couch with a Greek-key design carved across its base.

"Can I ask you just one question?" Nissa handed me more tissue paper to wrap a walnut grandfather clock.

"As long as it's not about my mother." I had expected Mary Jane to call me again soon and I'd figure things out then.

"Well, okay then." Nissa zipped her mouth up with her fingers.

"Let's just focus on the project at hand and landing the Martin job. Are you sure you want to tackle Jake Martin's attic?" I asked as I sifted through the copies of the Randall Mansion photos Nissa had dug up on the internet.

"I can't wait. It's what I do best," Nissa said. "It'll be a fun way to research, and we'll be getting paid."

"I haven't given him an estimate. He's only humoring us to please his mother. He had no idea what he wanted. But he's damn well going to pay for our time in his attic." I placed a little marble-topped table on the workbench. For extra polish, I lightly sanded the swirls and veins I had brushed on in layers. The fine powder sparkled like pixie dust in the filtered light.

"Well, then I'll make damn sure we find enough info to give him an estimate and convince his city ass that he needs us." Nissa slammed her fist onto her desk ending the court session.

Through the curtain of settling dust, I imagined Jake Martin as just another wealthy businessman, moving from project to project. Going through his attic was above and beyond. Why did I ever agree? I'd have to buck up and not let his flirty, upbeat personality distract me.

"We have to leave for the B&B in an hour." Nissa pointed up and down at my bathrobe.

"Guess I better take a shower." I didn't want Mr. Jake Martin to catch me without freshly washed hair or makeup again. It just wasn't professional.

On our way to Athens, I asked Nissa to swing by Liddy's house. "I want to ask Martha if she has any ideas about what to do with Mary Jane."

Nissa veered the car toward my old stomping grounds and pulled up in front of Liddy's cracked and splintering white picket fence surrounding a small white cottage. I leaned into my seat as a slideshow of flashbacks flickered of my dad and me pulling up in front of this house, more times than I could count to pick up Liddy and her nurse companion, Martha, for one of his work trips. Liddy, Martha, and I would visit museums, historic residences, or whatever adventure they could plan for us. Mary Jane was not in any of those images.

Bitter that every thought circled back to Mary Jane, I leaped out of the car. "As much as I miss Liddy and this little house, I can't say I'd like to go back in time," I said as Nissa joined me.

"I thought Martha was taking care of the place," Nissa said and joined me as we once again walked through overgrown grass. "It looks deserted."

"She's been in Minnesota with her sick sister. I assumed she's home by now, but I guess not." I hadn't brought my keys with me, but I also hadn't used them since my first year in college, so I knocked on the front door. No answer. "You know, I don't think I've ever gone through this front door. I either used the garage, if it was open, or I ran to the back porch." I knocked again. "She must not be back yet."

Nissa pushed her way into some bushes to get a peek through the sliver of an opening in the closed curtains. "Can't see anything. What's going to happen to this place if Martha doesn't come back?" Nissa asked.

"She will. Liddy used to say she and Martha would live there forever, even if one of them left God's green earth before the other. I'll wait till I hear from Martha. But to be honest, I don't have time to manage this place for her as well as everything else going on, but maybe I'll send a lawn guy over." I took one last look around at my second childhood home and knew I'd be back to help set it right, but right now, we had an appointment in an attic.

Nissa turned into the long driveway of the large, multi-gabled Randall Mansion and maneuvered through the various construction trucks and white vans parked randomly on the graveled lot. Excitement snuck up on seeing the mansion's peeling green paint, broken gingerbread corbels, and shutters swinging from their hinges. I could hardly wait for Nissa to park the car before I jumped out. The overgrown grass scratched and tickled our shins as we trekked around to the front of the house. We sidestepped the neglected viburnum begging for trimming and the cracks in the creaky old stairs leading up to the neglected wrap-around front porch with its half-hung gas lanterns and partially missing lattice skirt. Dodging the holes in the wide-plank wood floor, Nissa knocked on the front door.

"Said he'd be here at noon?" Nissa asked.

"Yep, but I don't see our guy yet." An eerie rustling sounded from under the porch floorboards. I tiptoed backward as if I could get away from it, then flinched as one of the nearby shutters settled into its new hanging position.

"It's not like we're just going to walk in. Too bad he couldn't meet with us earlier. It's already getting steamy." My effort of taking a shower and putting on makeup was soon going to be lost. "I'll be in the car cooling off. Can I have your keys?" I asked, then headed toward the car, retracing our steps through the tall grass. I still wasn't sure we made the right decision about going through Jake Martin's attic. The more I thought about it, the more I felt I got suckered. I should be out there cold-calling other historical sites for new business.

Nissa knocked on a dirty window and peeked inside. "Wait," Nissa yelled back to me. "The house is filled with hot, dripping-wet construction workers."

I didn't let Nissa see me grin at her ridiculousness, but between the humidity curling my hair and the sweat dripping down my back, I really couldn't have cared less. It was only June, and the humidity was already building. I wanted air conditioning. As I got to the car, a truck came racing up the drive, spitting gravel at my feet. Jake stopped directly in front of me.

"I am so sorry," he said as he jumped down from the truck and pulled out a tray with three iced teas.

Nissa came running from the front porch, this time following it around to the back stairs, which was the way we should have initially reached the front door, avoiding the itchy tall grass. She reached for the tray. "Here, let me help you."

"Well, it was this or an ice-cold beer, and I wasn't sure which brand you drank," Jake said with a wink, handing the tray to Nissa.

"Aren't you the clever one," Nissa said.

"Nissa Fayette meet Jake Martin," I said.

"Nice to meet you," he said with a tilt of his head.

"Likewise," she said with a slight curtsy.

He pulled three straws out of his shirt pocket and handed them to her. "These'll make it easier to sip. Going to be hotter than a bonfire in a pepper patch up in that attic." He grinned and threw his worn leather briefcase over his shoulder. His hand slid down my back—just barely touching me—then around my waist to steer me toward the back porch.

The gesture wasn't lost on Nissa as she raised an eyebrow and abruptly turned. She led the three of us up two creaky, broken back stairs, past several weathered rocking chairs, and around to the front of the wraparound porch.

"They don't make 'em like this anymore," Nissa said in awe as we stepped over the threshold,

"She's a beauty," I said, my pulse sped up in anticipation of the rest of the house's interior.

I held my breath and circled for a panoramic view of the front entry. My heart sank, and a slow growl released through my tight lips. The light blue wallpaper in the foyer had layers of faded pink daisies screaming 1980. Peeking into the salon and dining room, I found other nauseating pastels. A man in overalls scraped coats of paint off a door frame, and two others sat on the filthy, chartreuse sculpted-carpet staircase while restoring the 160-year-old banister.

Jake began the tour as if he'd guided people through the house regularly. "The mansion's story had a tragic beginning. It's a sad story that has always stayed with this house. It starts with George Randall. He built this gem in 1861 for his new bride, Anna Westcott. She became pregnant but lost their first child shortly after moving into the mansion."

"That's heart-wrenching. I hope they had a happy ending." I offered half a smile.

"I think they did since I'm proof the Randall family continued," Jake said, leading them through the front entry. "George was my great-great-grandfather."

I walked over and caressed the stripped and sanded door casing, happy to see its original wood grain.

Jake followed me. "You can see my guys have already started to restore the old girl and bring the woodwork back to its original glory."

"Not bad," Nissa said, eyeing the men, not the woodwork. I shook my head and cuffed her on her arm.

Jake continued, "We'll restore all the historic features within the guidelines of the Historical Society, including the five bedrooms on the top two floors, each with its own en suite. The amenities will be as modern as possible." He waved his arm from the front salon to the dining room and said, "This is where I'll be moving my thirty-six-seat restaurant, Blue Moon."

As swiftly as the perspiration spotted the front of my blouse, I was sure my curls were expanding. Construction dust settled on the toes of my Victorian Lace ankle boots, and I cursed myself for not wearing sneakers.

"Be careful," Jake said as we walked past a set of sawhorses and stepped over several extension cords. "And here's the kitchen."

I wanted to puke. The last owners undoubtedly thought they were improving the property, but they had stolen the old mansion's identity. I looked from the dated sage green tiles to Jake and shook my head in pity.

"Don't worry. This is all getting ripped out and expanded into a stellar commercial kitchen."

"You'll keep the beams exposed?"

"Yes. We'll keep the beams exposed," he assured me.

Two men carrying a sheet of drywall entered the kitchen and excused themselves as they passed between Nissa and me.

"Looking good, guys," Nissa said as she winked at one construction worker and took a sip of her tea.

I leaned in and whispered into Nissa's ear, "Try to control yourself."

"You guys are pretty busy around here." Nissa poked Jake on the arm to get his attention, but mainly to ignore me.

"Well, the grand opening is set for about four months from now."

Nissa and I hurried behind as he walked away from the kitchen.

"I truly hope you can restore her and give her back her dignity," I sighed, holding up crossed fingers.

"Okay, now where's the attic?" Nissa bounced like an excited child.

We climbed up the stairs, negotiating the trail of workers. I thanked Jake again for the cold tea. As hot as it was outside, it was twice as hot on each floor we ascended. We arrived on the third floor and peeked into gutted bedrooms as we passed.

Jake took a ring of keys from his pocket and unlocked the entrance to the attic stairs. "After you," he said and swung open the door for us.

"Looks kind of spooky," Nissa said with a grin.

I jumped at the chance to go up first. The smell hit me like someone threw a dust ball into my face. I could taste the humidity-infused mustiness. With each step, the air got thicker, my heart pounded harder, and sweat saturated my shirt.

Now I knew why I agreed to go through Mr. Martin's attic. My father would never have passed up the chance. He often brought me along when he explored historical architecture and studied its structural details. I thought of those times as magical, time-hopping adventures.

At the top of the stairs, Jake pulled a single light bulb's chain, which cast more eerie shadows than brightness. In the dimness, I couldn't see the entire attic space, but what I could make out was already generating tons of ideas.

"Cell phone flashlights," Nissa called out, clicking hers on.

I followed suit. Antiques were everywhere I looked, boxes on boxes, old furniture, rolls of carpet, chests, crates, toys—a goldmine.

"Let's split up and see what's in here," I said, not knowing where to begin.

CHAPTER 7

Nissa threw her camera over her neck and headed to the left for a pile of taped-up file boxes.

I rubbed my ice-cold tea along the side of my neck and aimed for the far back corner where I could barely make out the remains of a well-worn, velvet chaise lounge. I hadn't taken three steps when, from the corner of my eye, the capital letters C-L-U-E caught my attention. I had to stop myself from skipping over to the bookcase filled with dozens of board games.

I called over my shoulder to Nissa. "Look at all the games."

She scrambled over. "Looks like Liddy's closet. Yuck," she cringed as she reached through a sticky spider web and pulled out Mouse Trap.

My heart yearned to play board games once again on Aunt Liddy's kitchen table in the small buttermilk-colored kitchen. A mix of chocolatey brownies and buttered popcorn, which we always requested on game night, wafted through the musty air.

Nissa put the game away. "We can always go get you your old Mouse Trap game," she teased and returned to her mission.

I continued to work my way to the back of the attic and tripped over a box with a dark-lidded jar sticking out of it. I dug through and pulled out a matching ashtray.

"These are from the banks of the Dead Sea and distinctly 1950. There's also an 800 series Polaroid camera still in its original box. You know, Jake, you need..." I turned and found him face to face, right behind me. Feeling heat crawl up my neck, I took a step back. "You need to get someone up here to evaluate these treasures. You have a lot of money sitting around here collecting dust."

"Check. It's on my to-do list." He leaned over and flipped open another box top.

I gasped at the items from the '20s. "Oh, my. That's a Neoclassic barometer and clock set worth thousands of dollars." I took the gilded bronze and enamel clock adorned with trumpet-wielding cherubs from Jake. "This is amazing. You know, the Victorian Age was roughly from the 1830s to 1901-ish. Still, I bet you could get away with these in the B&B. But first, get them insured. The set is worth around fifty grand."

Jake let out a low whistle. "Are you sure?"

"Maybe more."

"My retirement plan." Jake put the clock back in the box as if placing it on a dozen chicken eggs and, with his foot, carefully scooted it toward the top of the staircase.

"Same with these," I handed Jake a Coalport plate and pointed to a box full of chinaware. "Not as valuable, but you could use them as a display in the restaurant. This single rose pattern is hand-painted, I believe." I traced the outline of the rose in the middle of the plate with my fingers. Aunt Liddy served every meal on similar plates. Only hers had hand-painted lilacs, and to me, they were priceless.

Jake attempted to move the heavy box over with his foot, but it didn't budge. "I'll come back for those later."

I snickered and continued toward the back. "Oh, God!" I shouted louder than needed. My fist covered my heart as if I could calm it down. I gave Jake a you-really-need-to-get-your-butt-in-gear look. In front of me, a box of cylinders sat next to an original Victor-Victrola. My fingers dragged across the top, brushing the dust and sprinkling it onto my shoes. I couldn't believe the condition of the cabinet before me. The only thing that could have made this day any better was to have my father by my side, sharing in these beautiful finds. He would have gone bonkers.

"Can I put that in the B&B?" Jake asked.

"This cabinet looks like an earlier design, more Victorian than the later Georgian style. So, it would probably work fine on display in your bed and breakfast, but if she sounds as good as she looks, you could get a pretty penny for her."

With the back of my hand, I wiped the sweat from my brow. I pulled the elastic out of my long, dampening ponytail, then leaned over and flipped my hair. I attempted to gather all my thickening curls on top of my head, twisting them several times into a bun. I straightened to face Jake's silly grin.

"What? I'm hot."

Jake raised his eyebrows and nodded his head. "My apologies." He had a way of flattering people without saying a word, but I ignored his quip and headed into the far depths of the attic.

A nineteenth-century walnut dresser with carved wooden drawer pulls emerged from the darkness. I opened the top drawer and shined my flashlight into its depths. As if someone else controlled my arm, I reached in and pulled out a pearl necklace. I wound it between my fingers, and the gross smell of cigarettes kicked me in the gut. I wanted to throw the strand across the room, but my arms were in lockdown as my chest grew tight.

"What do you have there?" Jake asked, snapping me from my fixed posture as I released the pearls into the drawer of perdition.

"Nothing." I slammed the drawer shut, needing to put an end to the persistent reminders of my mother.

He opened the drawer and took out the pearls. "You okay?" He twisted the beads in his fingers. "I wonder if these are real?"

"Doesn't matter. They have nothing to do with what I'm looking for."

Jake placed the pearls in his pocket as I stalked away. He watched me as I continued toward the back of the attic, and when I reached the chaise lounge, I turned, sensing right where he would be standing. There would be no explaining from me.

Without looking directly in his direction, I said. "Now this you can most assuredly use in the B&B. It needs some love, but it would be great in one of the bedrooms."

"Done." Jake drew a big checkmark in the air.

I continued, my confidence returning, "Also, these Victorian parlor chairs are in good condition. If we get appropriate needlepoint seat covers and spruce up the rosewood, they'd be as good as new."

"We?" Jake asked.

I hadn't realized how vested I had become in the findings around the attic until that moment. And it just might be a good tactic in getting Jake to hire us to create the miniatures. "I mean—you, but let's face it—you need help."

"I sure do! Are you offering? It seems like you know a lot about this stuff." Jake shouted with enthusiasm.

"We know a thing or two…" I hesitated and glanced at Nissa, who had been sitting back, sipping her tea, enjoying the show.

"Well?" Jake prodded.

With a nod from Nissa, I agreed. "Okay, sure." I quoted him our hourly rate to organize the items in the boxes and to get quotes from antique dealers on the objects he couldn't use in the B&B. The business could always use the money, and anyway, we were damn good at antiques. With my degree in art history, which centered a lot around furniture because, after all, I had an interior design master's, I occasionally appraised antiques for other businesses. "I do know a thing or two about antiques," I confessed.

"I accept," Jake said and stuck out his hand. I put my palm in his, and he lowered his arm with my hand in his grasp. We both took our first steps as if strolling in a park before I pulled away, feigning to discover something significant.

I lifted a bronze Tiffany lamp base from the corner. "We're using this," I said, holding the base like an Oscar. "Look, I'm not a decorator, but I know antique furniture and art. Like those portraits leaning over there." I pointed to the many framed portraits leaning on the chaise. "You've got treasures here, and if you don't know what you're doing, you'll get screwed."

Jake put his hand on my shoulder with a big smile and said, "Yes, ma'am, I'm listening."

Heat crept up my neck, and I shrugged, taking a step back to hide my blushing face in the shadows. I sorted through the portraits leaning against the wall.

"Maybe we can figure out who these faces belong to." I oohed and ahhed over several antique, French-carved frames, American gold-leaf frames, and other oak and brass frames, all from the mid to late 1800s.

"Nissa. Could you take pictures of these portraits? My bet is we'll find a photograph of a wall full of some of these paintings."

Nissa climbed over boxes on her way to snap photos of the faces and frames.

My imagination flew into high gear as I envisioned the income from projects to come. If only I could convince Mr. Martin that he needed our miniature replicas.

"Also, please take shots of this furniture." Even if he didn't hire us, the pieces in this attic would represent the era correctly should I need to replicate them for other projects.

"Look," Nissa said, pointing to one portrait in a gilded French frame. "It's Jake."

I moved in to inspect. The man in the picture had his auburn hair, blue eyes, and the same annoying dimple. I looked questioningly up at him.

Jake shrugged. His eyes connected to mine. "Your guess is as good as mine, could be anybody. My grandmother grew up in this house. But then her family disowned her. That's why I bought it for my mother. My grandmother should have inherited it. But she didn't. End of story."

Nissa's eyes lit up; she had picked up on his reluctance, as I did. "I'll see if I can figure out who this is," she chimed in.

"Don't waste your time," he said as he walked back toward the middle of the attic. "My mother's not interested in her mother's side of the family—just the house. There's a sore spot there." Jake seemed adamant about not wanting to know anything about his mother's family, but I knew Nissa wouldn't let a mystery go.

"Did you find any boxes with photographs?" I asked Nissa.

"There are several boxes over there." Nissa slurped her tea and pointed back over her shoulder. "There's all kinds of stuff: photos, kitchen journals, bank books, receipts, newspaper articles, letters, and kids' drawings."

"Perfect," I said. "Jake, would you mind sending those boxes over to our workshop, and we'll organize whatever history you have in them. Yes, then I can come up with a proposal for the miniature replicas." Behind my back, I crossed my fingers on both hands.

"Makes perfect sense," he said. "Plus, the Randall Mansion Foundation would greatly appreciate it."

"We'll get back to you in a few days and see when we can fit you into our calendar." Starting down the steps, I signaled Nissa to follow. Nissa took one more picture of a child's broken rocking horse, then walked past Jake as he waited for us to descend first. Heat on heat rushed me out of the attic.

Once we were in the car with the air-conditioner blasting, Nissa asked, "What the hell do you mean, 'I'll try to get you on our calendar'? Our calendar doesn't have a job in sight."

"Well, he doesn't need to know that. Of course, I'm going to put him on the calendar." I slumped in the car seat. I didn't mind organizing the paperwork from the attic, especially getting paid for it, but I prayed Mr. Martin—Jake, would hire us to create his Victorian miniatures.

I adjusted the rearview mirror so I could see my face. It felt as grimy as I looked. A streak of black dust extended from the middle of my cheek to my hairline. My bun looked like it had exploded with all my tugging on it. "Great. I look like I just returned from wrestling in a pigsty."

"And yet, he still wants to work with us. Go figure."

I smacked Nissa's arm with the back of my hand. "I'm serious. Look at me," I huffed.

"Don't worry. We have established one thing; a little dirt doesn't bother him. Look how much fun you had today. I haven't seen you this fired up in years. Besides, how many times did you think of your mother while we were in that attic?"

"Um..." I thought it best not to mention the pearls. I was more upset with my innate reaction to them than actually finding the damn things. But Nissa was right. I hadn't thought about my mother while knee-deep in the antique world. If we could nail down this job, I would have to tell my mother I would be way too busy, with the tight timeline and all, to have her at my house. But I could visit her on Sundays.

"Mr. Distraction, that's what we'll call him." Nissa slurped the last of her tea.

CHAPTER 8

An unexpected early-Monday-morning doorbell erased any repose I had garnered over the last two days. Anxiety bubbled as I peeked through the peephole, having learned that lesson the hard way, then simmered after not finding Mary Jane standing on the other side. I opened the door to the smell of bacon from Mrs. Brooks' apartment down the hall and nine boxes piled in stacks of three at my feet. A man with three more boxes on a dolly exited the elevator and said, "Good morning. Miss Edwards? Sign here."

I blinked a few times to wash the sleepiness from my eyes and signed for the boxes, then the delivery man turned back to the elevator and pushed the down button.

"Hey, hold on. You can't just leave these here." I was now fully awake.

"Sorry, ma'am. I'm just the delivery guy. Consider your boxes delivered."

The elevator doors closed behind him at the same time the tinkling of wind chimes rang from my phone in my bedroom. "Geez, doesn't anyone sleep past eight a.m. around here?" I hissed as I wriggled one box into my apartment to keep the door ajar and left the other boxes right where they were so I could grab my phone. "If that's Jake Martin, he's getting an earful."

Nissa arrived in time to see me pushing the last of the boxes across the threshold with my feet. I was sweating and swearing under my breath and couldn't bend over one more time.

"Need some help?" Nissa asked in all innocence.

"Grrrrrr." I stepped around the last box and walked into the workroom empty-handed.

"Is that a yes or a no?" Nissa picked up the box and trailed behind.

"I can't believe Jake sent us all these boxes." I stepped over the coffers of history I had already hauled into the office to get to my desk.

"Well, we did ask him to," Nissa said, throwing her backpack under her desk.

"We asked him to send the boxes you had looked through in the attic, not every container up there."

"Someone has on her cranky pants today." Nissa lifted a dusty stack of papers from the box she had just brought in.

I couldn't let it go. "Seriously, I'm just saying, maybe you should be on the Randall payroll and not mine."

Nissa sneered and threw up a palm. "Seriously, who pissed in your Cheerios? Aren't you the least bit curious about this stuff and why his great-grandmother disowned his grandmother?"

I slumped in my chair like a pouty four-year-old. "My mother called bright and early this morning. I was so overwhelmed with the damn boxes I answered without looking at the caller ID."

"Yikes. And?"

"I ended up telling her I'd meet with her doctor, just to get her off the phone. Now, what am I going to do?" I swallowed my bitterness.

"Guess you're going to meet with her doctor. It doesn't mean you have to let her move in with you. You'll be able to figure out what's going on and how to say no."

"Nissa, all I can think about is how she ignored me as a kid, at least discounted me, or something. Why would I invite that into my home?"

I thought about the last two times I had seen her, and the operative word was seen, not spoken with, my mother before she showed up at my door. First, at my graduation from college—thirteen years after Mary Jane moved on without me. With a tentative smile and an impersonal handshake, she handed over an envelope with the inheritance from my father and a note that I was only to receive it once I had graduated. The second time, just a year ago, was at Liddy's funeral. Mary Jane walked straight in, knelt at Liddy's casket, and placed her fingers on Liddy's stone-cold hands. She never looked for me, never even looked around, and I was standing only a few feet across the room. Did she not think I would be there? At my own aunt's funeral? The woman who raised me?

"Be grateful she left you with Liddy."

"That's what makes little sense. Is she jealous I took care of Liddy before she died, so now she wants me to take care of her?" I took file after file from a box labeled "Randall."

"Don't be silly. This has nothing to do with Liddy. You always said you felt Mary Jane mothered you from a distance by default. Maybe she's just feeling guilty and wants to make amends before…"

"Great. So, where does that leave me now? Anyway, I told her I'd go to her doctor with her and see what's up. But I'm planning on finding her a comfortable place to live during her treatments, and it's not going to be here." I slammed the folder on my desk.

"In the meantime, we have work to do," Nissa said in her Tina-like voice.

Nissa could always make me smile. I picked up the file and pretended to read the pages. For the following half hour, the workroom's soundtrack consisted of Nissa humming to the rhythmical clicking of keyboards and the melody of rustling papers.

"Jake said he took almost a year to get the mansion on the registry for Historic Homes in Athens and he'd spent over a year raising the funds needed to renovate the house. Why on earth didn't he have someone going through that attic before us?" I rubbed my dry, tired eyes.

"Probably never crossed his mind until you asked him for some old photos. Anyway, I can do this stuff in my sleep. Give me another day or three. I've already found a great picture of the entry with several of those portraits from the attic."

"Let me see." In the photo, five portraits hung along the old staircase wall, none of which was the Mr. Jake look-alike. I dropped it back on the pile as I headed to the workbench. I'd leave the research to Nissa. I couldn't come up with a proposal until she found the rooms for me to assess, but I could start a spreadsheet with the essentials of each room.

Nissa dumped papers from another box onto a table she had set up next to her desk. "Eloise, Joseph, Alice, 1926. Look, Jake's grandmother when she was three," Nissa said, jumping out of her chair.

"Get me some pictures of the rooms. Please." I had no interest in anyone else's mother or family at the moment. I had my own to deal with. I left the spreadsheet and returned to the templet for the intricate back of the chaise lounge found in the attic. If I didn't use it for the Randall B&B, I'd use it eventually.

After tracing a floral relief pattern onto a block of balsa wood, I chiseled and gouged, chipped, and sanded. I loved spending all day, every day, in my workroom focused on nothing but the job at hand. The smell of paint, glue, and wood accompanied the tools of my trade. And there was always my wall to give me confidence. I looked up and glimpsed: *You can't live a positive life with a negative attitude.*

"Ugh," I sighed. My father had said those words to me through a closed bedroom door after I had stomped my way up to my room when my mother scolded me for pouting about not being able to go outdoors.

Carving a rose into the block of wood kept my father's and Aunt Liddy's memories alive. Both had taught me the love of miniatures through fairy houses and gardens. Not a day went by without reflecting on their influence on my life. Unfortunately, it was Mary Jane who had taken over every thought now.

Nissa handed me another photo, saving me from the edge of self-pity. "Look at this picture. The Randall family. Nice to see Anna had two more children. According to the back of the photo, this is George and Anna with Emma and Clara Randall."

I took the photo and noticed the pyramid of empty boxes in our office doorway. There were several neat piles of photos, collections of newspaper articles, journals, and other papers covering Nissa's desk and extra table.

"Wait, what time is it?" I asked. How had she got so much done?

"Three o'clock. This is only the beginning," Nissa said, patting the stack in front of her, proud of her day's work.

Where had the time gone? I picked up the frame of the chaise lounge in wonder. Details in the intricately carved frame proved that hours had passed.

"Why do you need to go through all the papers? Just pull out the photos." I still couldn't shake waking to the doorbell then answering that damn phone call.

Nissa gathered some pictures and rolled her chair to face me. "I'm organizing for the foundation. Here are some pictures of the original Randall family, the people who built the house."

"Hale Nissa, the research queen." I lifted a carving tool in salute. "They're the ones we need to focus on. They're the ones who first lived in those rooms."

"But he said something about his grandmother getting disowned. And the family is a sore spot for his mother. You're not the least bit interested?"

"We have a deadline. He has reservations for Labor Day weekend in September. We needed to start the miniatures yesterday, even if he hires us to create just a few. No time to research anything that took place after the 1890s."

"There are tons of photos thrown into the boxes with all kinds of other stuff. I found some pictures of Alice with a bunch of other kids. It says, 'the cousins' on the back. Looks like this house was the hub of the…"

"Rooms. I need photos of rooms." I was on overload and really just needed photos of the several rooms in the mansion so I could produce a proposal for Jake. The phone rang and I looked at the number. It was not the same one that trapped me in the morning, so I answered it. "Hello. Tina Edwards."

"Hi. Did you get the boxes I sent?"

I rolled my eyes. "Mr. Martin. We're going through them right now. There seems to be no rhyme or reason to the contents of the boxes, so it might take us a bit more time to sort things out than we thought."

"I don't really have an answer as to what's in them, especially since my mother never had ties with the Randall family."

Nissa waved to get my attention and mouthed, "Ask about his grandmother."

This wasn't the time for that. I waved Nissa off and pushed the speaker button so she could hear what was going on.

Nissa ran over and asked, "Can I ask you about your grandmother? Did your mother ever live in the mansion?"

I punched a fist into the air pretending to coldcock her. She knew our priority was to write up the proposal, we could worry about the history later.

"I bought the dilapidated building because Mama always said the house should have been ours. But, when Eloise Randall died, she left the house to one of her nephews, claiming she could never find my Grandma Alice. When he put it up for sale, my grandmother had already passed, and my mother couldn't afford the fight. It broke her heart."

The cadence and timbre of his voice lulled me into a hypnotic state. I listened without interrupting as he explained what little he knew of his family history. "My mom said her mother, Alice, always spoke fondly about the house, just not about Eloise, her mother. Even though she was the only child, they told my grandmother to leave because she was unwed and pregnant with my mother. Still, it seemed right that she should have inherited that house."

My gut clenched as Jake spoke about all he was doing for his mom, and I was complaining about going to a simple doctor's appointment with mine. "And now you've spent all this time and money and got the mansion back for your mom. How sweet."

"I'm happy to do it."

"I'm sure the town is happy someone will take care of the old mansion," Nissa said, approaching the speaker. "Do you know if..."

I interrupted Nissa's question. "I'll have a proposal for you by the end of today." Pointing to the piles on Nissa's desk, gesturing for her to get back to work.

"Great," said Jake. "I'll get you an answer as soon as possible. If my mother has anything to do with it, I'm sure I'll be ordering a little room."

"That'll be great. You'll hear from us soon," I said, hoping my disappointment didn't come through my voice. Only one?

I addressed my computer, rocking my head and mimicking Jake, "Yay. I might order one little room if my mother has anything to do with it." After letting out a big breath, I regrouped and asked Nissa, "I have to get on the proposal. Do you have at least one picture of each room? I want to include them all."

"I think I might." Nissa selected pictures from the several piles that had accumulated on her desk. "Here you go, there are eight possible rooms we could recreate."

I studied pictures of two identical girls' bedrooms. The furniture in each appeared to be of the same quality and design. A little girl sat on the edge of her bed with one hand on a doll-sized pram. On the back read, "Emma Randall." "Clara Randall" was noted on the back of the other photo.

"Oddly, the girls each had their own room," I said. "During that era, younger sisters shared a bedroom, if not to make it easier for the nanny to care for them, it was cheaper to heat just one room at night."

"Shows you just how much money they must have had," Nissa said.

I scanned a picture of the girls sitting at a child-size table having tea and dressed in layers of ruffles in the nursery. The woman standing near them wearing a white apron and cap must have been the nanny.

I scanned several other pictures into my computer, wondering what it would have been like to grow up with a sister of nearly the same age. I thanked God for Nissa, to whom I honestly couldn't have been any closer. I zoomed in and examined their features. Despite Emma's dark hair and Clara's blonde hair, I could see a definite resemblance. The shape of their eyes and eyebrows were the same. Their noses were different, but for sure they were related. From what I could recall from a picture of their father, their eyebrows were similar to George's.

"Nissa, do you have a clear close-up of George Randall?"

"Somewhere." Nissa shuffled through the photos on her desk.

I turned my attention to creating the proposal. Hopefully, Jake would realize our miniature rooms offered a unique marketing feature that could entice history buffs and B&B lovers to choose the Randall Mansion Bed and Breakfast over others in the southeast. I needed to send it off to Jake today because tomorrow the plan was to meet Mary Jane's doctor.

CHAPTER 9

The next morning, I pulled into Sherwood Townhomes as slowly as possible, actually contemplating throwing my car in reverse and sending an Uber to pick up Mary Jane for her doctor's appointment and avoid having to be alone with her for the entire ride to and from the doctor's office.

The neighborhood, surprisingly only thirty minutes from my apartment, consisted of more concrete than lawn. There was a dozen or more buildings, each made up of four townhouses, each door a distinctive, fading color. It was a far cry from the large, mid-century home of my childhood.

When I walked up to number 3244, a red-brick and gray-shingled townhome with a washed-out black front door, I felt nothing short of dread. The ball of nerves caught in my throat choked me. I rang the bell, but no one responded. My finger shook as I rang it again. Maybe I had the wrong address. As I turned to get my phone from my car, the front door cracked open.

"Hi," I said with a sour taste in my mouth.

A waft of fried something and baking bread beat Mary Jane out the door as she pushed it wide open. She wore another uncharacteristic floral print house dress and no jewelry, except for a thin, gold watch on her frail, patchy wrist. From over her shoulder, a long tube hooked around her ears and ended in her nostrils.

The two of us stood staring at each other. I held open the screen door. Mary Jane held onto the front doorknob—as if we both had to support the doors on their hinges.

"So, this is where you live?"

"Yes, would you like to come in?" Mary Jane asked in a not-so-inviting tone.

That was the last thing I wanted. "No, thanks. I think we ought to get going."

Mary Jane nodded and motioned she'd be right back. I leaned on the railing and wished I was back in the office organizing photos with Nissa.

A woman pushing a walker, a pink scarf tied under her chin, hobbled past with her yipping Chihuahua leading the way. Had Mary Jane lived here this whole time? Thirty minutes away from me, and she could never find it in her schedule to visit me? Did I really want her to visit me? If I were to get through this day with my head still attached, then I would have to stick to the game plan. I'd listen to what the doctor had to say, and then direct her to the facility awaiting her arrival. I had found a lovely, assisted living facility twenty minutes from my Floral Ridge apartment that would take her during her treatments. If I had to pay for her stay, I would figure it out. It would be worth it for me, and far safer for her, not to be in my home.

Mary Jane returned with her purse, and a sweater draped over her arm. She pulled the door closed behind her but had to use both hands to pull it hard enough for it to click shut. Avoiding the tightness in my gut, I took a couple of hesitant steps behind her. Should I help her down the stairs? I wouldn't be around for her to become dependent on, and she'd have to manage by herself eventually. I stood and watched, disgusted with my jadedness.

Luckily, for both of us, she grabbed the railing and handed me the oxygen condenser as she lowered herself one step at a time. I followed close behind, keeping as much slack in the tube as I could. She stopped at the bottom to take a deep breath, and then her coughing began in earnest. As she struggled to get a tissue out of her purse, I grabbed her arm, afraid she would lose her balance, and helped her sit on the bottom step. I'd rather help her than have to call an ambulance.

I looked away as her cough rattled from the core of her lungs. I couldn't let my walls down, no matter how sickly she sounded. Once the coughing fit subsided, I was uncertain what to do next. In that awkward moment, Mary Jane reached for my arm. I hesitated but offered my elbow. Together, we walked with slow deliberation to my car.

I buckled Mary Jane in the passenger seat, leaving the cumbersome white box on the floor. Reaching down for my seatbelt, I said, "I picked you up a coffee. Might not be so hot now," and handed her the cup.

"Thank you," Mary Jane said and placed it back in the console without taking a sip.

It took over thirty minutes to get to the doctor's office, twelve minutes more than it should have due to traffic. The awkward silence drove me crazy, but I was afraid to open my mouth, afraid the questions that had piled up throughout the years would come tumbling out.

Hi, Mom. Why did you desert me? Why did you call me now, of all times? Did you have something to do with my father's death?

The woman sitting in my passenger seat was a much older version of the woman I would have imagined Mary Jane to be. In her glory days, she shined bright in her solid jewel-tone, form-fitting dresses, her hair and makeup polished to perfection with a cigarette in one hand and a cocktail in the other. She never failed to make her guests comfortable and served up some of the best dinners in the county. My father said if he couldn't make the sale, he would bring his client home for dinner and Mary Jane's home cooking would dazzle them to sign on the dotted line.

A year ago, at Liddy's funeral, Mary Jane had been thin, but now she looked anorexic. Her once thick brown hair, always done up like Jackie O's no matter how out of style it became, had faded to a mousey grey and was so thin that, without looking too hard, I could see her scalp.

She picked up the warm coffee cup with two hands as if she were cold, but never took a sip. Our kitchen always had a fresh pot of coffee brewing, my father loved his caffeine. The smell brought back the mornings of the two of us having breakfast. He always sat at the head of the table with his family's copy of Van Gogh's *Sunflowers* hanging on the wall behind him. He had told me stories of how he and Liddy grew up with the gold-framed picture in their childhood dining room. It sparked many discussions about art, architecture, and design.

Having breakfast alone with my father never seemed to be an issue for Mary Jane. I guess she felt that it made up for me not being allowed to have dinner with them. I thought that was the norm, that kids ate before their parents until I hung out with Nissa and joined her whole family for dinner at their kitchen table. Everyone helped cook or set the table, and they talked at the same time. They reached over each other for whatever they wanted out of the bowls and platters in the middle of the table and sometimes took food off a sibling's plate. The first night I was so engrossed watching them, I forgot to eat.

As I pulled into the doctor's parking lot, Mary Jane had another coughing fit. I parked the car and walked to open her door but stopped short. She was still coughing, so I leaned on the back door and waited for the hacking to stop.

I'd been with my mother for almost an hour, and we didn't have two words to say to each other—more proof as to why we couldn't possibly live together twenty-four-seven. In truth, I didn't want to discuss any issue in the forefront of my mind until the right time, like after I heard what the doctor had to say. When the absence of coughing registered, I opened the passenger door and grabbed the condenser off the floor while Mary Jane inched her way out of the car.

As we entered the cold, pistachio-green waiting room, she greeted the receptionists by name. They responded with long-lost-friends-style greetings. I looked around at the sign on the glass door. Yes, this was the oncologist. How long had Mary Jane been coming here? As we sat, I shook the guilt that I knew nothing about my mother's health issues.

"Mary Jane?" a nurse called out from a door in the left corner of the room.

Mary Jane pushed on the arms of her chair to stand, and the nurse rushed over to take her purse and sweater. "How are you, honey? No Bella today?"

"No, Bella stayed home. My daughter brought me."

"I didn't know you had a daughter." The nurse gave me a quick once-over and a cramped smiled. I wanted to ask who Bella was but had the sneaky suspicion a normal daughter would have known that answer. I remained seated, fidgeting with my fingers. Soon I would have the information needed to give to the assisted living facility, and Mary Jane would be in good hands.

When they reached the door, Mary Jane turned to me. "Are you coming?"

I expected to go into an exam room and wasn't looking forward to helping Mary Jane into a hospital gown and witness her checkup. But the nurse directed us to the doctor's office. No exam today.

Listening to nothing except the tick-tock of the wall clock, we sat side by side. "Thank you for coming. It'll be good for you to hear what the doctor has to say," Mary Jane said.

I couldn't even look at my mother. Good for me? What part of any of this was good for me? If Mary Jane wasn't ill, would she even have come to my door?

"I guess I might as well know what's going on." I sounded snarky but didn't care. I felt snarky. But Liddy taught me better than this, so I took a deep breath and shook out my hands. I peered around the office and imagined how I would create it in miniature. The anatomical posters and framed certificates would be in Nissa's domain, but the L-shaped physician's desk and the two matching bookcases made of walnut would be simple yet fun to recreate.

Mary Jane crossed her legs, swinging the top one. She rolled the skin on the base of her throat, a loathsome habit with or without her pearls. My heart began to beat faster. Lucky for me, the doctor swept in, introduced himself as Dr. Perry, and sat on the corner of his desk letting us know we wouldn't be there long.

"Ms. Edwards. Nice to finally meet you. I'm sure your mother has told you what's been going on over the last eight years. I'm here to say she's been a real trouper. Even though your mother quit smoking several years ago, she had developed emphysema, which most likely delayed her lung cancer diagnosis. It's been about six weeks since we successfully removed the right inferior lobe. Now it's time to start planning her chemo. It's a new treatment and we have medications to make her comfortable. Her nurse will be with her, as she has been these many years since her last bout with breast cancer. By the way, how is Bella?"

"Feisty as ever," Mary Jane replied.

The doctor spoke over Mary Jane's cough. "Good to hear. You tell her if she has any questions to give my office a call."

Mary Jane nodded.

Dr. Perry stood and addressed me. "Ms. Edwards, your mother told me she and Bella will be staying with you. It's nice to know she will have a comfortable place to stay during this time. Do you have any questions?"

Did I have any questions? I collated the information assailing me. Had Mary Jane been sick for eight years? Last bout with breast cancer? Lung surgery just six weeks ago? She lives with a personal nurse? And, who said she was staying with me?

"Ms. Edwards?" the doctor prodded.

"Dr. Perry," Mary Jane said, regaining her voice and placing a hand on my left thigh. "This is a lot for Tina to take in." Mary Jane's crossed leg still swung. I wanted to grab it and hold it down until it stuck. The fingers on her other hand still pinched and rolled the skin at the base of her throat. "She needs time to…"

With a wave of panic, I jumped to my feet. If I were going to be a part of this, I'd be damned if anyone, this doctor, Mary Jane, or whoever the hell this Bella woman was, was going to tell me what to do, even if I didn't have a clue how to make it work. I held my hand out for the doctor to shake.

"Thank you, Dr. Perry. I'll take my mother home now. And I'll be sure to call you if *I* have any questions." I threw Mary Jane's sweater and purse over my arm, picked up the stupid, burdensome oxygen condenser, and held out my elbow to escort my mother out the door.

In the car, I placed my hands on the steering wheel, arms out straight, elbows locked. I took in a large breath, and upon exhaling, my arms collapsed, my forehead crashed onto the steering wheel, and I sobbed. I could feel Mary Jane giving me one of her don't-be-so-dramatic looks and felt the need to explain. "Look at you, you're up walking around, you look great, well a little thin, but good. So, you've got a bad cough. You're going to be okay. You're not going to—and why didn't you tell me—you had breast cancer?"

I flinched as Mary Jane reached out to rub my back, and I pulled away from her, "Let's not pretend I'm okay with all this," I said and threw my hands in the air to scoop all the madness together.

"I'm sorry this got dumped on you all at once. I didn't know he'd review my entire history, or I would've given you a heads-up on the way here. Before, when he diagnosed my breast cancer, he all but guaranteed me I'd be fine. After that surgery and a few radiation treatments, the doc said I was good to go. At the time, you were taking care of Liddy, and she told me you were traveling for business, I didn't want to burden you. This last diagnosis came on so fast. After the surgery, I knew that I had to—" Another coughing fit took over, and she was unable to speak.

Shaking off the cry, I started the car. The right thing to do was to take Mary Jane out for lunch to get some calories into her, but I couldn't even look at food right now.

"So, where to? Where do we go from here?" I wanted to know figuratively and literally. I needed someone to give me direction. Now that I know what I know, and have done what I've done, what on earth was I going to do?

"Bella, my nurse, will help me pack my belongings. I don't have much. And I have to make a few phone calls."

"Who is this Bella?"

Mary Jane's smile blossomed. "Everyone loves Bella. We have a long history. We used to work together in a nursing home. I volunteered, and she was the charge nurse. When I got diagnosed with breast cancer, she took good care of me, driving me to my appointments, and making sure I ate. Eventually, she helped me around the house and cooked for me."

I pulled a tissue out of the pack on Mary Jane's lap.

She continued, "She decided to move in to my townhouse whether I liked it or not. But I liked it. And we've been roommates ever since."

"Your townhouse less than thirty minutes from my condo?" I said, compounding my feelings of unworthiness.

"She's been a great companion. I don't know what I'd do without her."

Her silence spurred me to turn my head. She fumbled with a tissue tangled in her fingers. Her chest rose and fell as if to catch up on missed oxygen. If I could only reach out and hug her, maybe we'd both feel better, but I didn't have the slightest notion of how.

"I'll be needing nursing care, and someone to drive me around, so the only thing I could think of was to have Bella's help, so I won't interfere with your day."

"Still, why my house? Why can't you stay in your townhouse? I can come to visit you there."

"Because I want to share this time with you before it's too late."

The punch to my gut tore at my heart. I slid on my sunglasses, squeezing my eyes dry. Mary Jane, the social queen of the eighties and hostess for my father's famous office dinner parties, had to beg to share time with her daughter. What's wrong with me?

"I'm glad you understand." As if there were nothing more to discuss, Mary Jane rummaged through her purse, then handed me an order form. "I've already called the medical equipment company. All of this will be delivered to your apartment tomorrow."

"Tomorrow?" I gasped. I stared at the order form. Tomorrow a practical stranger was moving into my home. I had no words, but I knew that, as of tomorrow, my life would change forever.

CHAPTER 10

Tomorrow arrived, and I sat across from Mary Jane in my living room. Both of us sat on the edge of our seats. "Would you like something to drink? Water? Coffee?" I wrung my hands, a bit ticked I didn't know what Mary Jane preferred to drink.

"No, thank you. I'm fine. I just need to catch my breath. That's the name of the game, you know." She took two deep inhales through the tube in her nostrils. "I actually don't drink coffee anymore; never liked it."

"Really? You used to drink it every day." I avoided eye contact, not ready to engage, afraid it would pull out the brimstone in me.

"Your father liked coffee. He preferred I drink coffee. Now I drink what I like, tea or lemonade."

I focused on my breathing and curtailed my grinding teeth. I swallowed the words that wanted to spew out of my mouth at the mention of my father.

"Would you like some tea now?" I asked. Maybe I could run to SugarBeans and not come back for say, a month.

"No, no. I'm just fine." Mary Jane smoothed her cotton pastel-striped dress with a zipper up the middle and pulled it over her knees. "Thank you for letting me stay here."

My mouth fell open. Was that a challenge? I never *let* her do anything, and yet here we were. How did we get from "No, absolutely not" to "Hello, roomie" in just seven days?

"I'm sorry the hospital bed isn't here yet. I thought he said they'd be here first thing in the morning. I guess I should have asked them what time." She attempted a smile and pointed to the painting on the wall behind me. "Is that a de Lempicka?"

I didn't have to look at the large painting behind me, but I turned. "Yes, how'd you know? Actually, it's a giclée, a copy. It's called…"

"*Girl with Gloves*," Mary Jane finished my sentence.

I didn't want to be impressed. "How…?"

"Your father loved de Lempicka."

Of course, that's how she knew. If Jonathan loved it, then Mary Jane loved it. Or maybe she hates it now, like the coffee. The reality of sitting in my living room with Mary Jane Edwards consumed my nerve endings one pinch at a time. The tingling in my body was the only thing convincing me this wasn't a nightmare. "You don't like it?" I asked, silencing the roar in my head.

"It certainly fits with your decor."

I heard nothing positive in that remark. I loved my home. If it weren't for the money my father had left me, I'd never have been able to furnish my place like this. I brushed off the negative remark. My condo was exactly that—mine. It represented the same style as my early-childhood home which, did I have to remind Mary Jane, my father had built for her? Surely then, Mary Jane must love my condo.

In uncomfortable stillness, we observed each other while avoiding eye contact. I found it curious to see her without heels and pearls and considered asking her about her choice of attire when Mary Jane raised one eyebrow.

"What?" I asked.

"You're just so pretty. Your style and your hair pulled up loosely like that. It suits you."

I looked down at my cream-colored lace top and jeans. The usual, nothing special.

Mary Jane paused and looked around. "This is a beautiful apartment with these mid-century pieces your father would have loved. It's just not the apartment I pictured you living in."

Was that another barb against my dad? Or against me?

With a clenched jaw and both hands in fists, I said, "Are you serious?" I curled my toes to suck in my anger. "You, of all people, should understand my attempt at replicating the house I grew up in. The one my father built for you. He was so proud of that house."

"It wasn't my style. It was his. It wasn't like he ever asked my opinion," Mary Jane said as she flicked her fingers to brush the image away.

"Well, I liked it. I loved it. I spent many hours looking for these pieces since I couldn't have any of the furniture." I hadn't planned on bringing up past events in our first moments together. But there you have it.

Mary Jane's voice cracked. "The people who bought the house bought all the furniture inside." She paused a moment, then added, "I had to sell it. I had to get out of Bluebelle."

I bolted to my feet. I'd heard enough. "Of course, you had to move. Daddy died in that house. And you left me down the street."

"I didn't mean..." Mary Jane's cough caught in her throat.

She leaned forward to stand up but got stuck midway. With three large steps, I got to her as she fell backward, arms flailing. I grabbed one arm but to no avail.

"Ouch," Mary Jane cried as her head hit the hard, rolled armrest. "If you let go of my arm, I'll attempt that again."

I rested Mary Jane's arm across her stomach and backed away from the couch. She rolled on her side and pushed up with her left arm. "I don't know why I keep forgetting to slow down when I clearly need to," Mary Jane said with a strained attempt at a smile.

I exhaled through pursed lips. There was everything and nothing to say. It was even too distorted for a Lifetime movie. I hoisted the suitcase the taxi driver had helped get onto the elevator into Mary Jane's soon-to-be bedroom. Already feeling better having something to do, on my second trip, I grabbed the brown-paper-wrapped package off the coffee table that Mary Jane had carried in. I shoved it under my arm and dragged an ungodly pink carry-on roller behind me. I couldn't get out of the suffocating living room fast enough.

I abandoned the suitcases in front of the closet. As I tossed the package onto the old recliner, my finger caught on a wire attached to the back. Blood smeared across the brown paper. Obviously, a framed picture, I tore off the wrapping to find a painting of mine from my freshman year in high school. What was Mary Jane doing with this?

My knees caved as I sucked my bleeding finger, and I barely caught the edge of the old red recliner as I stared at my painting that had won Best in Show at the All-State Art Show.

With my fingers, I traced the intricate details of the pea stone walkway meandering toward a fairy-sized footbridge that led to the gate of a tiny white picket fence. Large-seeming but scaled correctly, life-size pecans showed the perspective of the fairy garden at the base of a pecan tree. An elaborate stone-grey filigree garden table with four matching chairs were another finer point that had won me such a grand award. The last place I saw this picture hanging was in Liddy's living room. The fact that Mary Jane had my painting with her baffled me.

Mary Jane stood in the doorway. "Tina?" she asked with both hands gripping the door frame.

I stood, embarrassed to have unwrapped Mary Jane's possession, and pointed to the recliner. "Here, sit." I didn't like the way my manners delayed showing themselves around Mary Jane. Somehow, the weight of her presence slowed my thoughts and reactions as if they were being sifted through mud.

Mary Jane took a few labored steps before I took the oxygen concentrator off her shoulder. She backed up to the recliner and collapsed. "That's another thing they keep telling me not to do—plop into a seat. Old bones can break, you know." With a great deal of effort, she scooched herself into the chair and leaned back on the headrest, then said, "I know this is awkward for you."

I tilted my head, restraining myself from saying something I'd regret, and grunted, "Yup."

The words *The devil makes work for idle hands* ticker-taped in front of me. I gave a silent nod to my father for his nudge and pulled my winter clothes out of the drawers to be dealt with later. I dumped them onto my bed with the sweaters from the old chest and the few items I had hanging in the closet.

"As you can see," I began saying from the living room, "your bathroom is the closed door across from you. The dresser has six drawers, and you can store stuff in that chest…" I startled Mary Jane awake as I entered the room. "Oh, sorry."

I dropped to my knees and unzipped the larger suitcase. "Where do you want these pants?" Every piece of clothing screamed at me that this stranger was actually moving in. I avoided looking at her. Eye contact was too personal. Was I afraid to see what was there or fearful of what she'd see in my eyes?

"Doesn't matter what you do, Bella's going to redo it anyway. That's just the way she is."

"Hmm, Bella." Starting with the first drawer, I stuffed in her underclothes.

"Bella's the best. Wait 'til you taste her cooking."

"She's not coming here to cook for me." If Bella the Best wanted to come over to care for Mary Jane, leaving me with minimal to no duties, I was okay with that. My privacy would be all but nonexistent, but I'd make sure my time was my own. I could cope with five or six months of this. I would leave any health-related issues and Mary Jane's comfort to Bella, leaving me the time, and hopefully, the space to continue working. I'd have to suck it up.

While Mary Jane rested in the recliner, I made us a fruit salad sliced chicken breast from last night's leftovers. Thinking the worst, I asked her out to the dining room for lunch. Surely, it would be safer if she sat at a table to eat. "Is Bella coming today?"

"She's running a few errands, then will head on over," she said, hanging Bob on the back of her chair.

As I pulled out my chair, I wondered if I should have cut the grapes in half when the doorbell rang. Time to meet the famous Bella. I was grateful she'd be here in case Mary Jane choked or something.

Through the peephole I saw two large men and a huge metal bed frame. When I opened the door, the older of the two handed me some paperwork and asked, "Mrs. Edwards?"

"Come on in." I backed up and dropped the paper on the console. I already knew exactly what was on the delivery list, having stared at Mary Jane's copy for hours last night. "Follow me."

With four trips up and down in the elevator, they carried in the bed frame with all its bells and buttons; a mattress; a pile of linen wrapped in plastic; a shower seat; a walker; a rolling table; a large, square oxygen generator on wheels; and an IV pole. The room was changed from a storage room to a hospital room in less than an hour.

Glancing around Mary Jane's new bedroom, I checked off the inventory. As I signed the delivery order, a voice came from my front doorway.

"Yoo-hoo, Miss Mary Jane? Yoo-hoo. Where y'all hiding?"

CHAPTER 11

After meeting Bella, a jovial, full-figured, bleached blonde in her sixties, rocking bright orange Bugs Bunny scrubs, and undoubtedly proud of her ice-blue eyeshadow, bleached-blonde eyebrows, and bright cherry-red lipstick, I hid in my room. I spent the night listening to the tumult taking place as she overtook my kitchen.

Not up for a morning meet and greet, I took my time making my bed with perfect hospital corners and smoothed out every wrinkle of my white-on-white cotton duvet cover. I fussed with the two pillows until the grey and white geometrics were perfectly square. Next, I sorted through the folded pile of clothes from my storage room, figuring out how many bins I could fit under my bed, all the while stalling until I heard Nissa's keys jingling in the hallway.

"Good morning." Nissa's eyebrows furrowed as I rushed out of my bedroom, intercepted her by the elbow and dragged her down the hall toward the workroom.

"Thanks for coming in on a Sunday. We have a lot of prepping to do for our trip."

"No problem. David went to a..." Nissa stopped and turned an ear toward the back of the apartment.

"...and I know a thing or two about eating breakfast. Just look at me!" Bella's cajoling erupted from the kitchen.

"What? Who?" Nissa asked and pointed toward the kitchen.

I yanked her arm and jabbed my pointer finger toward our workroom.

As soon as we entered, Nissa stopped mid-stride and pulled her arm from my grasp. "Who is…"

"That's Bella. She came with my mother. Apparently, my mom has known her for years, ever since before she had breast cancer," I said.

"Breast? Who?" Nissa cocked her head in confusion and followed me around the workbench. I wished I had time for a hike so I could do something with my nervous energy.

"Long story," I said, then explained Mary Jane's past medical history. All of it.

"Bella, what about Bella?"

"She's quite the character. Bella told me she was," my quote-unquote fingers flew in the air, "caught with her pants down when my mother asked her just to move in with her as part of her pay." I tried to make my voice as hearty as Bella's. "And did you know my mother plays a mean old game of gin rummy?"

"Your mother plays cards?" Nissa asked, grinning. "Damn, you can sure get into a mess when I'm not around. What made you change your mind?

"I didn't. I never stood a chance. It was like getting pelted with snowballs, one right after the other. 'What a trouper Mary Jane was during her previous cancer,' the doctor told me. Plus, how 'she just recently recovered brilliantly from lung surgery,' and how much he approved of Bella as her nurse. Plus, he was thrilled she had my comfortable home to retreat to, 'it could make all the difference in the world.' It was like they were in cahoots. They rolled right over me. She—and apparently now Bella—moved in yesterday morning."

"Is that why you asked me to come in? Do we really have work to catch up on?"

Flustered, I stammered, "Of course, we do. But don't you get it? I never really said okay. Yet here they are." I stayed stuck on the fact that I had two new roommates. "Or, at least, I don't remember ever saying sure, come on and move on in. I had no defense. After the doctor's appointment on Friday, she handed me an order form for the medical equipment to be delivered yesterday morning, here, at my address. I'm flabbergasted. I've been hiding in my bedroom waiting for you to get here."

The doorbell rang, and I looked up at the clock. ten a.m. What now?

I got to the door at the same time Bella arrived. I glared at her. This is my door, my condo.

Bella stepped back. "I'm sorry. I'm just so used to answering the door. I've got some learning to do."

"No problem," I said. We both had a lot to learn.

The doorbell rang for the second time as I opened the door.

"Sorry," Jake said, pulling his hand away from the button he was still pushing.

My brain stuck in second gear. I couldn't think past my grinding teeth. "It's okay. I was just…" Was just what? Tossing a coin to see if Bella or I should answer my very own door? "Nothing. Never mind." I shook my head and swept my arm toward the office. "Please, come on into our workroom, my office." I said the last two words loud enough for Bella to hear.

"I was in the area, and I wanted to—Oh hi, Nissa. Didn't expect to see you on a Sunday."

"Neither did I," she responded and pushed a box aside with her foot so he could enter the office.

"I wanted to bring you the contract you emailed me, along with a check."

With fingers crossed behind my back, I glanced at Nissa and said, "Thank you. Have you decided to have us create a room for you? We've already become quite wrapped up in your family history." I pulled a chair over to my desk for him, but instead, he walked over to my collage of Jonathan-isms on the wall.

"*Art enables us to find ourselves and lose ourselves at the same time*," he read out loud. He turned and looked at me with softening eyes. "Thomas Merton."

I wasn't expecting that spark of knowledge.

"My mother says it all the time." He pulled his chair close to my desk, knocking my knees with his.

I rolled my chair a bit away and gestured to the proposal in his hand. "The proposal?"

"All of them," Jake said and handed me the papers.

I looked down, panicked, and blindly thumbed through the pages. I had wished for all eight, but I figured he'd go with a couple at most. In reality, we only had time to make four. Five, if we were lucky. I was pretty sure my face turned green.

Nissa flew to my side. "All of them? As in all eight rooms?" Nissa slid the papers from my hands.

"My mother pointed out that the beauty of your miniature replicas is not only in their fine, detailed likenesses, but how you build the souls of the families right into them. It's as if you create the rooms just as they were left one morning, way back whenever."

That's what we do. I never had the words before, but I knew that was what we do. I'd have to thank his mother and hope that one day he'd feel the same about my "little rooms."

"You'll have them all done by September?"

A tinge of panic preaching, "be careful what you wish for," smacked me upside the head. It usually took us up to six weeks to put together one of our miniatures because of delivery time for parts and accessories. We'd have to be very efficient. Could I even make this commitment? I was about to tell him we couldn't guarantee every single one of them, but we'd do our best.

In my hesitation, Nissa jumped in. "We have a trip to deliver our latest project this weekend, then we'll clear our calendar for you." Her voice squeaked as I squelched my fluster.

"Great, let me write you a check so we can get the ball rolling."

I hated this part of the job, the money stuff. In the beginning, most clients didn't want to write a check until the miniatures were tangible, something they could hold and see, but there were usually weeks of research and planning before that.

"Usually, we take a $500 deposit per room." Nissa automatically took over as she usually did with the financial matters. "So, $4,000. The balance upon delivery."

"Four thousand, huh?" he said with a frown that turned into a half-smile. That dimple. "That's what I calculated. And what do I owe you for the research?"

"Well, normally, some research is part of the project," I said.

Nissa interjected, "We've separated all the photos from the boxes. I'm sure your foundation will be able to archive all the other items using my spreadsheets. I charge $50 an hour."

Jake raised an eyebrow toward me as if needing confirmation.

I nodded in agreement. "She's the boss," I said, giving credit where credit was due and knowing Nissa wouldn't let me forget I said it.

The two of them made payment arrangements for the hours of organizing and tracking the paper items in the boxes, while I calmed my nerves by repeating over and over, "We can do this. We make this happen."

"You couldn't find anyone with better organization or research skills than Nissa," I said, trying to sound professional and suppressing the urge to immediately begin work on the miniature blueprints for each room.

"Those boxes are ready for pickup," Nissa said, pointing to eight boxes to the right of the doorway. "I've kept all of the photos I could find that pertain to our replicas. I'll get those back to you later."

"No problem," Jake said and picked up the top picture off one of the piles on the table as he passed. He flipped it over to read the back. "Eloise," he said. "Don't spend too much time on unnecessary information. We're really only interested in the original Randall family, George and Anna Randall, and their daughters, Emma and Clara, right?"

"Yes, but I have to sort through everything to get what we're looking for, so I might as well organize it for you."

Jake could tell Nissa not to bother, but I knew she would dig for every nugget she could.

"I guess," Jake said. "I'll send a couple of guys over to pick up the boxes you don't need."

"Why not the Martin Mansion B&B?" Nissa was determined to get some answers. "Why call it the Randall

Mansion B&B if your mom and grandmother have broken ties with the family?"

He ran his hands through his hair. "The house has been called the Randall Mansion since the day they broke ground back in the 1800s. That's how people know it. Mom and I talked about it. She can't deny her lineage, but she can damn well ignore it. You girls have fun."

As soon as Jake was out the door, we race-walked back into the workroom, and Nissa let out a loud, "Whoop!" She twirled in circles, kissing the check Jake had just turned over to them, then lifted her hand in the air for a high-five.

I moved past her and opened my laptop. "I hope we can keep the promise we just made. It's going to be a lot of work. We'll celebrate when it's all done. Let's get to it." I circled a finger in the air to rein in our excitement.

It took a few moments for us to settle down. Nissa slipped her spreadsheets into the correct boxes packed and ready for the foundation. Neither one of us could erase the smile from our faces. I picked up the raised-panel walnut armoire I had been polishing for the Le Dauphin Hotel. We'll get the miniature lobby replica delivered this week, then focus on nothing but the Randall Mansion.

As a whistled version of Hank Williams' "Jambalaya" filled the hallway, Bella backed into the workroom with a tray of blueberry muffins and two iced teas, reminding me I had other things on my plate.

"Well, ain't you just a pip of a thing?" Bella said to Nissa as she placed the tray on the workbench.

I cringed as she broke the unspoken rule of no food or drink on our workbench.

"Who, me?" Nissa chuckled, fanning her hand in front of her chest, and batting her eyelashes.

"How do you do, missy? I'm Bella, Miss Mary Jane's nurse and companion."

"Great to meet you, Bella. I'm Nissa."

"I knew that, darling." Bella winked.

I wrapped my arms around my waist and tapped my foot, waiting for the charade to end.

"I waited until your gentleman friend left before I brought you some sustenance. It seems Miss Tina likes only tea for breakfast," Bella said, as if drinking tea for breakfast would send me to hang.

I rolled my eyes. "He's not my gentleman friend. He's a client."

"I'm thinkin' you might want a nibble or two to keep up your concentration," Bella said, handing Nissa a muffin.

"Yes, ma'am." With a slight curtsy, Nissa took the muffin. "I'm not one to turn down a warm muffin."

"Traitor," I exhaled under my breath.

Bella put her arm around Nissa and faced her directly in front of me as if she'd just discovered a new sidekick. "I'm going to like this one."

I picked up a muffin and stuffed it into my mouth. Take that, Bella.

Satisfied, Bella left the workroom and said, "I'm fixing to sit on the balcony with your mother to get some fresh air. She's full as a tic from eating her entire breakfast. If y'all need anything else, just holler."

As soon as Bella left, I swallowed my mouth full of deliciously warm blueberry muffin, and promptly removed the tray from the workbench and placed it on my desk. "And that, my dear friend, is my mother's companion, Bella. Now we are three."

Nissa took another bite of her muffin as if she had never had a muffin so delicious. Her eyes and head rolled as she moaned in delight. "How much fun are we going to have while she's around? And these muffins . . . they're to die for."

"Traitor," I said, this time out loud.

"You've got to admit it's hard not to smile around her."

"That's not the point."

"Lighten up. She won't be here forever."

"But she's here for now."

I turned away, not wanting Nissa to see my eyes well up. There was a fine line between sharing my space and *wanting* to share my space. I quickly swiped my tears and bellied up to the workbench.

"I'll start making some sense out of all the photos," Nissa said as she ripped the wrapping from around three new shoebox-size plastic containers. "I'll pull out photos we need before I organize the rest for Mr. Martin."

I was excited to begin the Martin project but couldn't give it the attention it deserved until after we delivered the hotel lobby this upcoming weekend. Just thinking about Mary Jane and Bella occupied the "multi" in my usual multitasking abilities.

Nissa handed me a picture from her pile of photos. "Here's one of the girls' rooms. It says Emma and Clara with Baby Jane on the back. Baby Jane must be the doll Emma's holding."

"Looks like she was well-loved," I said, taking the picture from Nissa. "She's beautiful, or at least was before losing a few of her long blonde curls. Her cloth body and porcelain head, hands, and feet date her to the late 1800s. I wonder if

I could create or find a miniature doll like her. Can you blow that picture up for me?"

"Can do, boss. Oh, yeah, I'm the boss," Nissa said, and I wondered how many more times I was going to hear it.

CHAPTER 12

The next day, sunk deep into our study-focus playlist, we divided up our hours, Nissa on the Randall project, me, checking details on the Le Dauphin Hotel lobby. Bella's fortissimo, "Girls, come and get it." fractured our concentration.

Nissa jumped up in response, but I grabbed her arm and held her back. "Where are you going?" I asked.

"Didn't you hear Bella call us for lunch?"

"Yes. But no. We're not going to sit with them for lunch. We'll eat later." I picked up a picture and poked it into her abdomen, hinting at getting back to work.

"That's ridiculous."

"Mary Jane is here like she wants to be. Having meals together wasn't part of any deal I made. Anyway, we have work to do."

"She's here so you two can get to know each other. How are you going to talk if you're never in the same room with her?"

"We'll talk… we'll talk when I'm good and ready to talk."

"We have to eat. Which, by the way, we would do if they weren't here. Think about it. We'll save time not having to prepare lunch."

If there were stories Mary Jane had to tell me, I would most certainly address them, just not at the moment. "I'd like to get New Orleans off our plate and a better handle on the Martin project before she turns my brain to mush."

"Okay, let's keep it casual. I'll cut her off if she brings up anything..." Nissa guided me by the shoulders toward the dining room "...anything sensitive," she finished and didn't let go of me until she dropped me in a chair at the end of the dining room table.

"Did you say lunch?" Nissa asked with a grateful smile as she pulled out her chair, blocking me in. Mentally, I duct-taped my legs to the chair to prevent me from retreating.

A pile of pimento cheese sandwiches cut into triangles and a garden salad occupied the center of the table. As she served her new guests, which is how she was making me feel in my own home, Bella continued her conversation about something happening at the nursing home she and Mary Jane had worked at. I kept my head low and ate the delicious sandwich, wondering how Mary Jane and Bella, and Nissa for that matter, could appear so comfortable in this awkward situation they've all put me in.

Mary Jane smiled as if she didn't have a care in the world, as if the four of them were out for a girlfriend's lunch, and added, "Cranky old Mrs. Kane said, 'Go ahead and give him the damn shoes, just get the bastard out of here.' Then she held her cane in the air like she had shot off a dozen rounds at a passing goose."

"Literally, raising Cain," Nissa chimed in as she got caught up in the story.

I shot her a look of betrayal. Whose side was she on?

In between bites, Bella picked up where Mary Jane left the story, "And I had to stay back and console poor Mrs. Kane. She was fit to be tied. I promised I'd get her shoes back, and she made me swear to bring her a vanilla ice cream with them." Bella laughed out loud, and Mary Jane snickered, trying to keep her cough at bay.

"Did you both work at the nursing home?" Nissa asked.

My blood simmered as I tore through the duct tape and delivered my plate to the kitchen sink. I betrayed my allegiance to my father by having Mary Jane in this house, sitting at my table, and having lunch with her—something I had to remind myself Mary Jane rarely did with me in our home in Bluebelle. And I wasn't going to pretend I liked it.

I balled up a dish towel and soundlessly screamed into it. I was going to have a coronary if I didn't get my resentment under control. I needed to find time to talk to Mary Jane so I could get it over with and clear my head, but I wasn't ready. I leaned on the counter and reminded myself this was my home, I had let them in, and I can survive anything for a few months. I folded the dish towel in half and half again, then laid it on the counter with a pat and returned to the dining room to let everyone know I had work to return to.

"In the beginning, Mary Jane volunteered, and I was a nurse. We had some good times. Of course, that was way before Mary Jane got sick the first time." Bella piled her plate on top of Mary Jane's in time to hand them to me as I entered.

Confused for a second, I looked at Nissa, who hid her giggle with a napkin and picked up her own plate and added it to the pile in my hands. She gave me the go-ahead nod toward the kitchen and said, "I'll meet you in the workroom."

"Can I ask what you are working on?" Mary Jane directed her question to Nissa as I left the room.

I dumped the plates in the sink. Why can't I stick to my own rules? Mary Jane can stay here, but I didn't have to play her way. But there were only two ways to get to the workroom from the kitchen—through the living room, but I'd have to pass the opening to the dining room, or through the dining room itself. So, I stayed in the kitchen, rinsed the dishes, loaded them into the dishwasher, and listened to the conversation between my runaway mother and my betraying best friend.

"We've been researching the Randall Mansion in Athens. Jake Martin is turning it into a B&B. He hired us to create miniature replicas for his grand opening."

"I remember that place. Is there anything I can do?" Mary Jane asked.

I froze. A plate slipped out of my hand and sunk to the bottom of the soapy water.

"I'm sure there is," Nissa said.

Crap. What was she thinking? We were on a tight timeline.

"Want to go through a box of photos and pull pictures of the mansion?" Nissa asked.

"I'd love to," Mary Jane's voice lit up.

I shoved a plate into the dishwasher, then the next, and the next.

"That sounds like a perfect job for you, Mary Jane." Bella pushed her chair from the table with a loud scrape. "I'll clear the rest of this stuff up, and you can sort through pictures right here on the dining room table. I'll have it all cleaned up in a jiffy."

As Bella entered the kitchen from the dining room, I slammed the dishwasher door shut and took off through the living room and rushed past Nissa and Mary Jane at the table. Nissa followed one step behind me.

Once in the workroom, I hissed through clenched teeth, "What was that?"

"If you don't want her to help, you should've said something."

I glared at her, huffing like a bull aiming its horns. Did I really have to explain myself to my best friend who should know exactly where I was coming from?

"Give her this box," Nissa said, handing me one of the clear shoeboxes full of pictures.

"Me? You take it to her. It was your idea. Whose side are you on, anyway?"

"I'm on your side. You can't avoid her forever. This will give you something totally random to talk about. Just have a meal with her once in a while, talk about the project every now and then, or Liddy, or the weather. Anyway, how can you pass up Bella's food? Didn't you just melt over her pimento cheese? Consider her cooking as part of her rent."

I refused to yield, even though the sandwiches and the homemade poppyseed dressing on the salad were to die for.

"Just bring this to her." Nissa pushed the box into my hands and walked away, dismissing me.

As I turned and stomped out of the office, a purple piece of paper on the far wall caught my attention, *If you can't beat the fear. Do it scared.*

Shit. I wasn't scared. I was pissed. Damn it all. How had I lost all control over everything? My head rolled back and forth as I leaned up against the hallway wall, delaying the inevitable. This was Nissa's idea. Why the hell wasn't she bringing the box to Mary Jane? "Shit."

We were leaving for New Orleans soon, and I had a boatload of work to do. I didn't appreciate wasting my time playing these unwelcomed games. When I got to the dining room, Bella waited for me all cheery-eyed and a little too triumphant.

She took the box from my hands and placed it in the seat of the chair next to Mary Jane. "Better for you to reach into," she said. Bella thought of everything.

I flipped one photo over to show Mary Jane the writing on the back. "You can pile them by people or by the room. I'd prefer by the rooms if they're discernable. There are eight different rooms in all."

"Is there anything in particular you girls are looking for?" Mary Jane took the first photo out of the box.

I retreated a step but didn't turn around. "I don't know. Mostly pictures of the rooms, so I can draw accurate floor plans. But if you come across something interesting, let us know."

"You know, your father used photos of that house in some of his presentations. He…"

My stance shifted, my base of support widened, and I readied myself to defend my father. But instead of completing her thought, Mary Jane's cough snuck up on her again.

Bella stepped in and leaned across the table to hand me a glass of water, and nodded toward Mary Jane, as if she couldn't possibly take the five steps and give the water to Mary Jane herself.

I dropped my shoulders, reached for the glass, and handed it to Mary Jane.

Bella returned with a bowl of grapes and picked up the picture Mary Jane was questioning. She pulled out a chair and joined in, "So, is this interesting?"

"I don't know." I fiddled with the cuffs of my shirt. Bella wiggled the picture in front of me. I took the bait in defeat and snatched the picture from Bella. The desire for a young girl to please her mother began to soften something inside me, and I reluctantly sat.

"I'm not sure without my glasses, but maybe. It has both of the young girls in it. Just try to put them into piles per subject, preferably location." I went through a few more pictures pointing out details we might be interested in and started piles for Mary Jane, catching her eye on occasion, but quickly looking away each time as not to invite any extraneous conversation. I soon left the room before Bella could cast another lure.

On the way to the office, I detoured and grabbed the keys off the credenza to go down and get the mail. When I reached the ground floor, I instantly relaxed. The eight-foot by eight-foot lobby contained twice the oxygen as my 1,200-square-foot apartment.

Mail forgotten, I drove out of the parking lot with nowhere particular in mind. I just had to leave. With my windows rolled down, I followed the back-country roads that led to Liddy's old house, avoiding the route past my childhood home. I pulled up in front and parked. It looked old and lonely with its drawn shades and overgrown lawn, but the dragonfly wind chime still tinkled like broken glass, and the relaxing harmonies brought me comfort. I leaned on the headrest and closed my eyes. If only Liddy were here now.

I walked around to the backyard and up the wheelchair ramp to the porch, where I usually found Liddy sitting. I peeked through a beveled glass panel into the kitchen. The house seemed abandoned with all the window shades drawn. Martha was still up north taking care of her sister, and I made a note to reach out when we returned from New Orleans and see if there was anything she needed me to do until she returned.

I meandered through the overgrown lawn in search of signs of my old fairy village in Liddy's back garden and found the old stump where I had built a pink fairy house. With the rose petals curtains and homemade stick furniture long gone, I rested one palm on the outside of the stump and peered into its center. I recalled all the cookie and brownie crumbles I had left on the stump's edge to attract the sweets-loving fairies to that spot. Remnants remained of doors and windows on the north side of trees where moss defined my fairies' yards. I wondered what remained of the fairy gardens my father and I had created under the pecan trees at our house down the street, but I didn't have the guts to go find out.

Needing to pack for our trip tomorrow, I tore myself away from the tranquility and started the car. I could get through one more night, then, hopefully, the trip to New Orleans would give me time to regroup. Before I drove out of Bluebelle, I decided to drive past the mansion since it was nearby. I slowed on my approach, noting the aluminum exterior siding had been stripped away.

Jake and a slim woman with curly blonde hair stood in the front yard looking up at the house. The blonde laughed at something Jake said and punched him in the shoulder. He threw his arm around her and pulled her in for a big hug.

I hit the gas and reprimanded myself for driving by. What was I thinking? Of course, he had a girlfriend. Had I ever asked? Did I just assume he was single because he never mentioned anything different? Why did it matter anyway? I should have jumped out of the car and said hello. He's one of my clients, after all, and I would have loved to see what progress had been made on the mansion. My confounded thought process convinced me I had lost my mind.

Having rushed home to get back on schedule, I stepped into my lobby and piled packages from the lockbox in my arms and tossed the envelopes on top. Armed with something to keep me from having to talk to Nissa about my mother, I pushed the elevator's up button.

The workroom was quiet as I entered and dropped two bills on Nissa's desk then headed to the closet to put away the new supplies. An old familiar book cover caught my eye as I passed one of the boxes ready to be picked up by the foundation. "Were these in with all the papers and photos?" I asked and picked up an old hardback copy of *Twig* by Elizabeth Orton Jones.

Nissa didn't look up. I didn't blame her.

I sat cross-legged on the floor and opened the book's cover. "I know this book. Aunt Liddy read it to me when I was little. It's about an elf who wants to hang out with the fairies. It was one of my favorites."

When no response came, I continued. "Liddy had a collection of her mother's books, and I used to love when she read them aloud to me." Instead of packing for our trip, I pulled out one book after the other, wiping the dust off the covers with the back of my hand. I recognized many titles, remembering the days I spent with Liddy, before and after I moved in with her. Seeing the familiar books filled me with both delight and sorrow. I'd have to ask Martha if Liddy's copies of these same books were still in the cottage. "*The Doll's House* by Rumer Godden," I said to no one. "It was Liddy's favorite because it was her mother's favorite." Making sure not to tear any pages, I opened the book and imagined sitting in Liddy's lap, in her wheelchair, on her back porch, smelling her rose oil perfume as I read the words out loud.

CHAPTER 13

This morning's seven and a half-hour drive from Floral Ridge to New Orleans started shortly before sunrise. Once we got there, Nissa and I had several hours to relax in our French Quarter boutique hotel across the street from the Le Dauphin Hotel before the night's events.

I wrapped a towel around myself as I stepped out of the antique claw-foot bathtub after an exquisite thirty-minute soak. Walking into the brick-walled suite, with its shuttered windows wide open, I combed out my wet curls, embracing the luxury.

"Don't know what made me think of it now, but have you heard from Martha since you called?" Nissa asked and handed me a glass of wine.

"Now that you mention it. I haven't." I dug my phone out of my purse and scrolled through my texts. "Not like her."

"Maybe she's still with her sister?"

"She probably doesn't want to be involved since I asked her about facilities for Mary Jane. Doesn't want me to ask her to care for Mary Jane." I wasn't much of a worrier unless there was something to worry about, so I put it aside, figuring I'd contact Martha after we returned home. "Too late now anyway. Mary Jane and Bella have already planted roots. I'll let her know."

Nissa pointed to the dress I had laid out on my bed. "Is that what you're wearing for a New Orleans reception?"

"Hush. I don't need a fairy godmother, thank you very much."

"Says who?" Nissa rummaged through her suitcase. "Here, wear this. It has less…"

"Fabric?" I took the black spaghetti-strap dress from Nissa and eyed it skeptically.

"I was going to say it has less of a chance of being seen at a funeral."

"Your skirt is black, too. Plus, this looks tight, and I'll freeze in it. I don't do sleeveless." I threw the silk dress onto the bed and slid my perfectly acceptable black tailored dress with laced bell sleeves over my head.

"Come on. Just try it on." She threw her dress back at me. "It's more—cocktail-y. That's what tonight's all about." She pulled the invitation out of her purse. "'You are cordially invited to a cocktail reception in honor of the grand reopening of the blah, blah, blah.'"

"What's wrong with the dress I have on?" I truly wanted to know.

"Seriously? You look like a schoolteacher. You won't catch anyone's eye wearing that."

"I'm not here to catch anyone's eye." But I caved and pulled off my comfy black dress, then reluctantly slid on Nissa's slinky one. I rolled my eyes in submission as I did when we were roommates back in college and I followed Nissa's orders for our nights out in charming Savannah. I enjoyed the nights full of fun and friends, but my priority was to study hard to make my father proud. I wasn't the least interested in what I wore where.

"There. How's this?" I frowned at Nissa, lifting my wide visible lavender bra straps with my thumbs like a farmer in overalls.

"Well, duh. You'll have to borrow this too." Nissa threw a strapless bra across the room.

Once we approved of each other's appearance, me in the black, slinky, spaghetti-strap dress, and Nissa in a silver metallic silk top with a black leather pencil skirt, we headed across the street to the Le Dauphin. We had dropped our miniature display off before checking in to our hotel, and now we had just enough time to make sure every piece of furniture and accessory was in place.

"Hi, I'm Phil." A tall, well-dressed, well-built man greeted us at the entrance.

"Hi. I'm Nissa. This is Tina. We're Edwards' Miniatures." Nissa pointed to the historical replica on the round table in the center of the lobby and headed toward it.

"My father and uncle are the ones who renovated this hotel. I guess you can say you and I are in the same business."

I half-listened. "The same business?" I wanted to follow Nissa but didn't want to appear rude.

"Yeah, the construction business." He all but slapped his side as he laughed.

"Oh, yeah." I forced a small guffaw. We were, but we really weren't. "There's a little bit of a difference," I said, bringing my thumb and forefinger together to emphasize "little" and laughed for real at my own joke. "Nice to meet you. I should really go check on our display."

As I headed for the center of the near-empty room, my heels clicked and echoed in my wake. A breeze from the air conditioner blew past marble columns and crystal chandeliers, chilling my bare arms. The center staircase conjured images of my perfect father and perfect mother, always the most gracious hosts, together on our front porch stone stairway, drinks in hand, toasting guests as they arrived. The image of the woman changed to the thin, ailing patient lying in a hospital bed in my storage-now-guest room. I gasped and startled myself back to the hotel lobby.

"You okay?" Nissa asked. "You're awfully pale."

"It's nothing. Just got a chill. How's our little lobby?"

"She's all set and ready for her reveal," Nissa said and draped a black velvet blanket over the display.

After the presentations, thank-yous, and giveaways, I wanted to head back and enjoy our hotel room, soak in another hot bubble bath, this time with a glass of wine, and dissolve the past week into the soothing bathwater. But Nissa had other ideas. She handed me a cocktail in a tall, shapely glass and said, "Drink up."

"I can't drink this. I'd rather have a glass of wine. And I'd rather have it in our hotel room."

"Come on, Tina. You're in New Orleans. Home of the hurricane. It's a bit sweet and a bit tart. Kind of like—never mind."

I'm pretty sure she stopped herself from saying, "You."

"Drink it. You'll love it."

I took a sip and cringed as it went down like pickle juice. If I took my time and got something to nibble on, I could drink it and humor Nissa for half an hour. On my way to the hors-d'oeuvres table, I caught Phil staring at me. I didn't look away fast enough, and he took it as an invitation. Before I could react, he was at my side.

I would have shaken him off but he offered to hold my drink so I could use both hands to fill my plate to overflowing with several slices of glazed andouille, two creole crab cakes, and several cold shrimp. "Let's set down your drink so you can..." he indicated my plate, "eat all of that."

If he was trying to make me feel guilty. He didn't. I was starving.

Talkative, yet polite, he described detail after detail of the newly designed lobby and led me by the elbow to the bar. His conversation was light, and his smile pleasant enough. I smiled and nodded as I focused on my food choices. I leaned against the bar in the modern, blinged-out lobby of the hotel. What girl wouldn't feel sexy talking to this handsome, confident, and funny man in such an elegant setting?

Me, that's who.

Uncomfortable looking into Phil's eyes for any length of time, I shifted from one leg to the other as I fought with my stupid dress riding up my hips and the one strap that continually slid off my shoulder. I gulped down the last of my drink as a sign I was taking my leave, but Phil had already motioned to the bartender for two more.

"Oh, no. I can't. But thank you." I waved off the drink.

"Open bar. Take advantage," he said and slid a tall pink drink my way.

I accepted the unwanted libation with half a smile and let it water down on the bar while Phil's humor became ramblings. My phone rang, and I fished it out of my small evening bag. By the time I answered, Jake had hung up. I checked my watch. It was almost ten p.m., surely it was a butt call.

For a split second, Phil had morphed into Jake Martin. What was he doing tonight? Was he with his blonde friend? What would he think of this shiny modern lobby? Pretty sure he'd hate it. What would be the first thing I create for his miniature replicas?

I snapped to attention when I caught Nissa heading toward us out of the corner of my eye. I again made my excuses to leave, but then she disappeared behind a column. Always the class clown, her arm extended as she spied on me using her cell phone as a side-view mirror.

I laughed and said my final goodbyes to Phil and the bartender. This time I was walking out the door, with or without Nissa. I couldn't wait to chill in our hotel suite, wine in hand, far away from my apartment. Nissa took a few sips of my watered-down drink then grudgingly followed behind me.

In the morning, after a quiet, relaxing night, we wheeled our carry-ons onto the bumpy sidewalk of Canal Street. Streetcars passed as we waited for the valet to deliver Nissa's car.

"That's one beautiful hotel," I said as we stood across the street from the Le Dauphin, watching the busy doorman welcoming overnight guests for the first time in over two years.

"I wish we could have stayed there. Too bad it was booked solid." Nissa shrugged. Her car pulled up in front of us, and the valet loaded our suitcases into the trunk.

"I would definitely come back." I slid into the passenger seat.

"I bet you would, Miss Double Hurricane," Nissa teased and tipped the valet.

"What? Oh, no. I never drank that second one. You drank more of it than I did."

Nissa rolled her eyes. "You spent all evening with tall, dark, and chatty, while I mingled, trying to drum up some more business."

"And did you? Anyway, I tried to avoid him, but he was always right behind me. He ordered that second drink without even asking me if I wanted another."

"Well, clearly he thought you needed another."

I refused to keep this conversation going. With all her teasing, Nissa made me feel like I was a lush and a flirt. Her joking hurt only because she hadn't a clue how much I wish I had both in me.

On our way out of the city, we passed multitudes of hotels, restaurants, and pedestrians. Once we hit I-10, we settled back for the seven-hour drive home. "That was one of the most fun trips we've been on together. And I'm including spring break our senior year of high school," Nissa goaded.

I poked her arm. "Ha-ha. Not funny. I'm pretty sure Liddy never forgave me for that." We had fun. We had lots of drinks, and there was lots of sand wedged in my teeth and other places. A cute guy had dragged me out to the bonfire to dance, and I was so tipsy I fell face first in the sand. Nissa had gotten a kick out of it. But what we put Liddy through…

"You okay?" Nissa broke into my thoughts.

I shifted in my seat, tucking my left leg under me, and wiped my eyes with the back of my hand. "Just thinking of Liddy. If she hadn't taken me in, I'm not sure what my life would have been like. Mary Jane couldn't get out of Bluebelle fast enough after my dad's funeral. Why didn't she take me with her?"

"Be glad she didn't. We had some great times in Liddy's house. I loved hanging out there," she said. "Just imagine how your life would have been different if Liddy wasn't in that wheelchair."

The few times I had brought up Liddy's horrific car accident when her fiancée died and she became wheelchair-bound, my father would just say it was terrible and sad. Other than that, no one ever talked with me about it. "I can't believe she's gone… almost a year now." I pictured myself sitting in front of the house yesterday and willed myself to hear the tinkling of the wind chimes. "I used to wish Liddy was my mother, and I'd feel guilty for not missing Mary Jane. I wonder if other abandoned children truly miss their mothers or just feel like they *should* miss her, like it was expected? I feel guilty either way."

The cornfields hypnotized me as each row passed by. I imagined Mary Jane peering out the kitchen window, watching a young me play in my fairy gardens in my old backyard. There was Mary Jane setting dinner plates for two after my teddy bear and I ate alone in the kitchen. Next, a streak of light entered through the crack of an opening door as a young me pretended to be asleep when she checked on me at night. Next, visions of exquisitely designed wrapping paper torn off a birthday present floated in the air, only by the time it settled, my mother had left the room. Then finally, Mary Jane, sitting on the couch, twisting her pearls at the base of her neck, staring through cigarette smoke at my dead father strewn across his desktop.

I understood things as I saw them as that young girl, but I couldn't make sense of them as an adult. "I'm glad you had fun on this trip, but I'm looking forward to the Randall project." I feigned perking up.

"Sure. But there won't be another event like this past one in New Orleans. The music, the food, you drinking hurricanes."

"I only had one," I again insisted.

"And the people at the event were fun. You were fun. We should've stayed longer."

"Are you saying I'm *not* usually fun?"

"Listen, Tina. I know you work hard, and I know how much you feel you have to hold it all together. But, girlfriend, I'm here to say, you're not getting any younger. That guy Phil liked you. I could tell, especially when he bought you that second hurricane."

"Get over the second hurricane, will you? I never drank it. I should have, then we wouldn't be having this senseless conversation."

"We'd be having a much more interesting one, I'm sure. You have to start putting yourself out there, or you'll have a long and lonely life."

"That's a bit dramatic," I said, crossing my arms.

"I know, I know… and you don't mix business with pleasure." Nissa shifted her focus to the road ahead. "I'm just saying, I love having David in my life, someone to go home to. I just wish that for you."

"Oh, but I do have someone to go home to. Two someones." I withheld a huge sigh.

"You know what I mean. You have to try, have to make an effort if you want a happy love life." Nissa began humming along with the tune on the radio, her cue she was done with the conversation.

I didn't have the energy to argue with her anyway. But she had a point. I'll never be happy in love. Such situations, like Phil in New Orleans, only proved I wasn't cut out for small talk or even dating. It's not that I didn't want romance in my life. I discovered through the many dates I had in the past that I wasn't comfortable enough with myself to be comfortable with someone else, and now was definitely not the time to practice. I hung on to what Liddy used to say to me, "You just haven't met the right person yet."

I lowered the seat back and thought about the Martin project. And Jake. And Jake's dimple. His natural flirtatious nature was just a front since he obviously had a girlfriend. And of course, I could admit I was more interested now since I knew he wasn't available. But I most certainly didn't have time to find out what was beneath his flirtiness if anything. Anyway, a relationship was the farthest thing from my mind. It would be like putting ice cream on a loaded baked potato.

Needing to get out of my snit, I texted Martha to check up on her, and she responded, "Don't worry. All's well here. We'll chat soon." It was good to hear she was well, but I don't think I made it clear what a shambles, with its overgrown lawn and closed-up windows, the cottage was becoming.

The quiet rest of the ride lulled me to sleep, and I startled myself awake with a snort just as we passed the farmer's market, which was two minutes from my downtown condo, I slipped on my sandals. I pictured Nissa excited to see David after two days of absence, whereas I would be going home to Mary Jane and Bella. "We still have a few hours of daylight left. How about I get us something to eat, and we work on the Randall job?" This way I could spare myself the possible chance of a conversational ambush from my roomies.

"Tina, no," Nissa said. "I'm going home."

"Drop me off out front anyway."

Nissa pulled up to the curb, and I jumped out of the car in front of SugarBeans Café. She popped the trunk open for me to collect my suitcase. I knocked on the side of the car twice and waved Nissa off.

The "ding" announced my arrival in the cafe, and three faces looked up from their laptops. Simultaneously, as if choreographed, they returned to their typing.

"Hey, Marge. Green tea please."

"Iced or hot? Here or to go?"

"Iced and to go. I'll take a turkey wrap, too."

"Weren't you just in New Orleans? How was it?" Marge slid a carry tray across the counter, wiggled my iced tea into a corner, then set my dinner next to it.

"Great. The hotel was beautiful. I'd like to go back one day." I tucked the wrapped sandwich into my purse.

"I went to New Orleans once," Marge said. "Remember little about it." She lifted her hand as if drinking out of it and said with a laugh, "Hey, have you seen that tall, good-looking guy again? The one who had morning joe with you the other day?"

"Which one?" I teased and lifted my chin to wave goodbye.

Just as someone entered, I rushed through, dragging my suitcase behind me and managing not to let the door hit me on the way out.

I sat on the bottom step of my apartment lobby and unwrapped my sandwich. I would have eaten in the café, but with it being not so busy, I wasn't in the mood to chat with Marge. I've known her long enough to know she would have asked a lot of questions about Jake, my next project, and probably point out I couldn't avoid going up to my condo forever.

CHAPTER 14

It had been over three weeks since Mary Jane moved in, and everyone involved seemed to know their place. The day after I returned from New Orleans, Mary Jane had begun her treatments. She and Bella had a routine, and things seemed to be going smoothly without me being entangled. So, I stayed in my corner of the condo and only crossed paths out of the necessity to eat.

Bella's jovial laughter came from the kitchen, mixed with the smell of bacon, eggs, and toast, my new morning norm. Mary Jane was served a full breakfast every morning, even though she'd only nibble a few bites. And when Bella left to run her daily errands, she always made sure Mary Jane was comfortable in bed, taking a nap. She'd leave some homemade soup or sandwiches for Nissa and me, which was something she didn't need to do, but Nissa insisted it would be rude not to enjoy them.

I didn't know what Mary Jane paid, or even *if* she paid Bella, but it wasn't enough. She was, for sure, worth her weight in gold. And that's a lot of gold. She made it easy for me to like her despite not wanting to.

In her colorful nurse scrubs covered in beloved Looney Tunes characters, Bella baked homemade treats of some sort, like blueberry pie or coffee crumb cake, every day. She fixed dinner for three, which most nights I brought in my office to eat. She would then help Mary Jane get ready for bed, and that sometimes included a shower. I knew when they watched *Dancing with the Stars* because it sounded like a party in Mary Jane's bedroom. And to top it all off, I assumed Bella went home every night, I had given her a key, but she had been sleeping in the old red recliner to keep a close eye on Mary Jane at night. I owed her big time.

That very sentiment boggled my mind. Why should I feel grateful for Bella doing her job, when her job included taking care of a woman I never had any intention of having in my home, ill or healthy? I felt like a horrible human being thinking these thoughts. Still, the memory of sitting on the top stair in my old house, sneaking a peek at my father and mother eating at the dining room table, just the two of them, with napkins in their laps, listening to classical music in the otherwise silent room, reminded me that Mary Jane didn't want me at her table.

I had one leg in my pants when Nissa came in through the front door. I focused on buttoning the waist of my jeans as I walked out of my bedroom and straight into Bella, who had greeted Nissa as she came in. Bella now resided comfortably in the apartment as if it were her own, and I decided not to fight that battle.

"Good morning." I curtsied as Nissa led the way to the workroom, and I fell in line behind Bella.

Bella, at Nissa's heels, had two homemade biscuit egg sandwiches and two homemade iced teas. She had made it quite clear that she would tan Nissa's hide if she "brought in that tea from outside when she makes perfectly fine iced tea right here in our kitchen."

"Tina, your mother had a rough night last night," Bella said a bit sheepishly as if she intentionally waited to talk to me once Nissa arrived. "I've got an extra errand to run today, a doctor's checkup of my own, and I'll be gone most of the afternoon, so you best keep a close eye on her. She'll be all settled before I leave, and I'll put her bell real close, so she can call you if need be. Try to get her to eat something. Lunch is in the fridge. Don't worry if she's of no mind for eating. I'll be back well before supper."

"You're leaving… for most of the afternoon? But you… I…" my voice caught in my throat. I'd become used to having Bella there twenty-four-seven except for Mary Jane's nap time when Bella ran to the grocery or some other errand. Sixty minutes tops.

"No worries. We got this," Nissa said with her mouth full of biscuit. "We'll be fine."

Bella nodded her thanks and, with a big smile, pulled two napkins out of her pocket and left them on the workbench next to my untouched, delicious-looking egg biscuit.

"What is wrong with you?" I sniped, pulling Nissa in by the shirtsleeve and shutting the office door.

"You've got to get over yourself," Nissa said while licking her buttery fingers.

"Sorry. I just don't want to be left alone with Mary Jane. I'm afraid I might say something to upset her. I don't need to be the cause of a medical emergency." I plopped in my desk chair.

"You're not alone. I'm here. And talking to your mother about what she came here to talk to you about should hardly upset her," Nissa said in a comforting tone.

Ignoring the egg biscuit Nissa held out, I paced. Once I broke the wall of silence and avoidance, there'd be no turning back.

A torn-out magazine picture of a coastal wave breaking on rocks stuck out on my wall, *The ultimate act of power is surrender*. Was I ready to put out a white flag? "I'm a mess. I don't know how I feel about anything anymore. Aunt Liddy's gone, and Mary Jane's here. I know I should be over it. But it's all so unfair. I would've given anything to have spent more time with my father before he passed. But—no. I get extra time with my mother instead."

"Yup, your world is upside down. But it's not coming to an end." Nissa took another bite of her biscuit.

The front door slammed after Bella called out her goodbyes. Time to focus my energy on the Randall project. Supplies and items were arriving daily. I asked Nissa where we stood with the family's story.

She handed me more photos of the mansion's interior. "George Randall owned South Georgia Printers. I found an article from 1869 in the Georgia Printer's Association archive about George and Anna Randall and their daughters, Emma and Clara."

"Beautiful family," I said, "More importantly, this photo was taken in their parlor. Look at the English-style Chippendale corner chair. I'll need a pic of that blown up."

"Then you'll probably want to see this pile of pics. These were taken in the parlor, and there's a pedestal mahogany tea table with three feet and a bookcase with leaded glass doors."

"I wonder where these pieces are now?"

"Ask Jake. Maybe there were pieces in the house when he bought it."

"By the look of the place when we saw it, I can't believe the people who updated the house understood the value of hanging on to antique furniture. But I'll ask him." I didn't mind having a reason to reach out to him.

The images spread out before me gave me the confidence to begin designing each of our miniature replicas for the Randall Mansion B&B. There were four bedrooms, the nursery, the kitchen with its oversized fireplace, the parlor/living area with the beautiful staircase, and the elegant dining room, our most involved project ever.

Most of the framed portraits from the attic showed up in either the parlor or staircase photos. I typed their exact measurements into a spreadsheet and let a program figure out the dimensions for the miniature versions of the portraits.

As I set out a small miter box and razor saw to build the little frames, a distant noise splintered my concentration.

"Did I hear the bell?" I asked.

"I didn't hear anything," Nissa replied, not missing a beat with her filing.

"I better go check." I figured I'd check on her before I delved into a project.

"You're going out there?"

I wished Nissa didn't think so little of me, but I certainly couldn't blame her, considering my behavior of late. "She's too stubborn to ring that bell, and I don't want anything happening to her on my watch."

"Okay, go on." Nissa shooed me out of the room.

I rounded the corner to the living room and came to a halt. Jake Martin sat side by side with Mary Jane on the couch, sipping from a tea cup and chatting as if they'd known each other for years.

"How… what…?" I stumbled over my words.

"Well, hello there. Your charming mother and I were having a nice conversation. Did you know she has tons of stories about Athens and the Randall Mansion?" Jake asked, standing.

Looking at Mary Jane, who didn't look a bit like she had a rougher night than usual, I said, "I was just checking in on you. I thought I heard your bell." I looked around. It was nowhere to be found. She had pink in her cheeks, making the dark circles under her eyes less apparent. I turned and questioned Jake. "And I never heard the doorbell ring either."

"Bella let me in on her way out. We've been engrossed in conversation ever since."

"You've been here for over twenty minutes?" I asked. Mary Jane sat looking at the two of us and smiled when Jake gave her a wink.

"Guess so. Time flies and all that." Jake looked at his watch.

"Okay, so, did you come over for a specific reason?" I asked, picking up the empty cups and walking them to the kitchen, trying to get out of earshot of Mary Jane.

He excused himself and followed behind me. "I've been checking out the restaurants near Athens, so I know what I'm up against when mine opens."

"Floral Ridge is over forty minutes from Athens," I stated.

"Ha. I know." Jake looked at his feet. His awkwardness rattled me. Sensing a bit of nervousness in the confident Mr. Martin, I looked away.

"Since I was out and about, I wanted to see how the project is going. And I thought I could get some of those boxes out of your hair since I have my truck with me."

At least that made sense. But still, I could only respond with a squint.

"Okay, coming clean." It seemed he couldn't stand his own duplicity. "I thought, maybe, you'd like to go check out a restaurant or two with me?"

I could imagine Mary Jane in the other room stretching her neck to listen. So, to keep our conversation professional,

I said, "I wouldn't know the first thing about the value of a restaurant." I placed four chocolate chip cookies on a plate and scooted around Jake returning to the living room.

"But certainly, several boxes can go back with you," I said, completely sidestepping the restaurant question. "Let's go talk to Nissa. She'll want to go over what's in each box." I rambled as I placed the cookies on the coffee table in front of Mary Jane. "Construction of the replicas has begun, but I'd like more pictures of the early kitchen and pantry."

"What about dinner?" Jake asked.

Persistent bugger.

Mary Jane straightened up a bit on the couch.

"How about if you come here for dinner?" I glanced at Mary Jane, not for approval, but to make the point that nothing about her living in my apartment would interfere with any plans I wanted to make.

"That would be a great idea. I haven't had a dinner party in years." She nibbled on a cookie.

I gave her a sideways glance, but not wanting to be rude in front of Jake, I added, "It's business, Mary… Mother. I have a lot of questions about furnishings for the mansion." Taking the opportunity to prove my point and find out about any significant other, I said, "You're welcome to bring a date."

"Now, why would I do that?" Jake asked. His dimple instantly disappeared.

"Just putting it out there." I hoped my scheming didn't sound in my voice. By inviting Jake over, it seemed I could break the ice with Mary Jane, and through Mary Jane, I could learn a little more about Mr. Jake Martin. For the miniatures, of course. Perfect balance.

"Sounds good. How about this Friday?" He asked both me and Mary Jane.

"Friday's fine with me," I said before Mary Jane could reply. "I'll invite Nissa and David, too."

Once Nissa explained the spreadsheets and tucked them back inside their corresponding boxes, we helped Jake load the unnecessary items into the back of his truck and sent him on his way.

"See you on Friday." He waved goodbye.

"What's Friday?" Nissa asked, raising one eyebrow.

"Dinner. Here. With you and David." What was I thinking, saying I would cook dinner two nights from now for a four-star chef and the 1980s queen of hostesses in attendance? I was out of my mind.

"Sure thing." Nissa waved to me as she walked toward her car on the other side of the parking lot. I hadn't noticed her purse slug over her shoulder.

"Wait. Where are you going?" I said as I caught up with her.

"David just called. I'm meeting him for lunch."

"Since when do you and David go out on a weekday?" I asked Nissa. She couldn't leave me alone with Mary Jane. What if something happened to her? "We've got a lot of... "

"Since he asked me."

"I'll be alone at lunch."

"No, you won't. You'll be with your mom. Anyway, Bella won't be much longer."

I stood in the parking lot and watched Nissa drive away, sure the ice was going to break today.

How could she do this to me?

Mary Jane was no longer in the living room when I returned, but I could hear her rummaging in her bedroom. I tiptoed to the workroom, paced back and forth, wiggling my fingers by my side, attempting to dry my sweaty palms. I knew this day would come. All I had to do was stay calm. If I'd had any notice at all, I would have had time to prepare.

Who was I kidding? If I had any warning, I would have run as fast and far as I could.

With as much courage and confidence as I could conjure up, I ducked into the kitchen. In the refrigerator, Bella had left three Saran-wrapped turkey and cheese sandwiches on plates and a spinach salad with sliced Canadian bacon and hard-boiled eggs.

I grinned. I had asked Bella to lighten up on the fried bologna and real bacon, and she let me know she did not think that deleting the sixth food group, food that wasn't necessarily healthy but tasted delicious, was a good idea. Funny that she used Canadian bacon on a day she wouldn't be here to eat lunch. "Variety is the spice of life," she had said and snuck in items like chicken-fried steak or a Hot Brown once or twice a week. I honestly couldn't say I minded. Bella, indeed, was a doll. She had set the table with silverware and glasses before she left and put out a pitcher of iced tea.

Taking a deep breath, I knocked on Mary Jane's door. The television inside the room quieted. "Come on in."

"Lunch?" I asked, staying in the doorway.

Mary Jane unhooked her hose from the larger, square oxygen generator near to her bed and hooked it up to her portable condenser. The rest of the room looked the same as the day Mary Jane had moved in, except for Bella's pillow and a blue and white quilt folded on the seat of the recliner. When Mary Jane reached the doorway, she handed me her tank and smiled her thanks. She had such an excellent way of making me feel like an unmannered numbskull.

CHAPTER 15

Iscooped salad onto Mary Jane's plate, "How are you feeling?

"Fine."

"It's nice out today. Are you going for a walk with Bella later?"

"It depends when she gets home," she said.

I grimaced at not being able to hold a conversation with her.

Halfway through our meal, she broke the silence. "If you aren't sick of looking at photos, I brought a couple of old albums we could go through together. They're in my closet."

"Albums? Albums of..."

"Us. Our family," she said.

I sat for a moment. One step at a time. I could do that—get through some photos and try to enjoy our time together so we could put some pleasant new history behind us. As long as she didn't dis my father.

"There are pictures of Liddy and me from early on," Mary Jane said.

"Pictures of you guys in college?" I found it hard to believe the stories my father and Liddy had told me about how she and Mary Jane were best friends. Courteous, as sisters-in-law, I could understand. Friendly, maybe. But best friends?

I cleared the table and retrieved the albums I didn't remember unpacking. Bella must have brought them from Mary Jane's townhouse for a surprise attack such as this.

Mary Jane pulled one of the books toward her and opened it to the first page. "Our first holiday together."

I wanted to make this time with Mary Jane enjoyable, but the more pictures I looked at, the more my legs shook under the table, and the more I had to control my breath. "Liddy, with no wheelchair," I murmured.

There she stood, on her own two feet, with Jonathan and Mary Jane. The three of them posed in front of the Louvre in Paris, the British Museum in London, and other museums throughout Europe.

"Since their parents had died years before I met your father," Mary Jane said, "he oversaw his and Liddy's finances. He made sure every trip we went on was as educational as it was fun. Back then, he was the light of my life, as well as Liddy's." Mary Jane's breath rattled.

My scalp prickled with protection at the mention of my father "back then." I readied my defenses.

But then Mary Jane flipped to the front of the album. Pictures of Liddy swimming, playing tennis, running track, and cheering at a football game had me forgetting I didn't want to talk to Mary Jane. "Are these from high school?"

"Yes, before I met Liddy." Mary Jane smiled, "She was so much fun to be around. I met her on my second day in our freshman year of college." She pressed her hand on one page to slow down my page-turning.

Liddy had mentioned Mary Jane had gone home with her during spring break and met my father, who said it was love at first sight. My parents looked like the perfect couple. But the stories of fun and laughter shared between Liddy and Mary Jane were a little harder to swallow. I just never saw it. When my father was out of town, I was with Mary Jane or Liddy, but very rarely both at the same time.

There was a picture of the co-eds hula-hooping, caught in mid-laughter. Mary Jane smiled, her eyes glistened, and as the pages turned, she told me tidbits of their past together. Snapshots of Mary Jane peddling a bike with Liddy sitting on the handlebars and several photos of the three of them horseback riding in the mountains and visiting the Mayan ruins in Mexico.

I stared at Mary Jane's wedding pictures with my dapper father smiling, holding up a glass of scotch. There was a picture of Mary Jane holding hands with Liddy, her maid of honor, dancing, center stage, having the time of their lives. Mary Jane seemed a happier person before I came into her life. And seeing the pictures of Aunt Liddy swimming, playing tennis, and traveling on her own two feet, sunk my heart. I took a deep breath. "Why did she never marry? I mean even after the—you know—accident."

"Liddy?" Mary Jane shook her head with pinched lips. "After her accident..." Mary Jane closed the album as if sealing the answer within the pages.

"Liddy told me she had been in a wheelchair since the age of twenty-five," I said, "right after I was born. She said her boyfriend died in the same car accident that put her in the wheelchair." I watched as Mary Jane's eyes filled with tears. "She said Dad had taken care of her and built her the Victorian cottage right down the street from us so she could focus on her health. He also employed Martha as her full-time nurse and companion for her." He had done so much for her, and I loved him all the more for it. Liddy even assisted him doing research for some of his projects, giving her purpose. To me, it proved the man he was.

Mary Jane lowered her gaze and said in a low tone, "We were best friends, and I miss her."

"You went to Liddy's funeral," I said wanting to ask many questions but didn't think I could get the words out without tears, and I was dammed if I was going to cry in front of her.

"Yes, I did." Mary Jane said. She reached over and took my hand. My toes curled. I wanted to know why she didn't search for me at the funeral. "It was complicated."

I jerked my hand away and stood. As emotions welled in my chest, I raised my voice a pitch, "What's complicated is that we haven't spoken in over twenty years. What's complicated is that we've never discussed how Daddy died." The floodgates were now opened, and I fought against the tide.

I catapulted into the day of my father's death, revisiting the image of him stretched across his desktop while Mary Jane sat cross-legged, smoking a cigarette. I pulled my hands through my hair, the pressure in my fingers attempted to calm the thoughts below my scalp.

Mary Jane's coughing added to the stress. She pushed her chair away from the table, grabbed her condenser and turned up the knob. She pivoted away from me as her cough took its time settling.

I stared at her back, focused on my own breath. The overhead fan spun off-kilter, *clickety-ding*, like a pickax on a stone in a faraway mine.

Finally, Mary Jane turned to me, and as if I were a child, said, "Sit down. Please."

I took my seat. The sooner we got it all out, the faster it would be over.

"Your father had a heart attack. What is there to discuss?"

Ire prickled up my spine. "You let him die." This is not how I wanted to discuss the past. I knew once the pin was out, I would explode.

"He was already dead, Tina."

I squeezed my eyes shut, trying to erase the terror of that day. But I'd been replaying those images, frame by frame, for most of my life. My father awkwardly slumped across his desk, head turned sideways, one arm reaching out, the other hanging by his side. "You should have called someone."

"I did--"

"Or pulled him onto the ground and started CPR."

"I... I didn't know what to—" Mary Jane wiped her eyes with her tissue.

"But you knew he was dead?"

"I— I—" Mary Jane stuttered, reaching for answers out of thin air.

"Answer me," I growled through clenched teeth, then hissed out, "Please?"

"I don't know. I—" Mary Jane sobbed.

I covered my wet face with both hands. I wanted answers but wasn't quite sure what mattered anymore. I ran to my room and sobbed into my pillow.

The day of my father's death was as clear to me as if it had happened yesterday, and even if I could go back and change that one day, I wouldn't be able to make us a family again. I could see that now. I splashed water on my face and returned to clear the table, hoping I could keep my resentments at bay.

CHAPTER 16

As I passed by the dining room, Mary Jane looked up from the photo album with pleading eyes. "Tina, please, there's more to tell," she said.

Not in the mood for forgiving, but willing to bury the hatchet, I rubbed the back of my neck, trusting the deep pressure would calm the tension feeding my anger, and took a seat at the table.

"Please understand that this is hard for me," I said. "Dad was a good man. But you—"

"You only saw what your father wanted you to see."

My jaw dropped. "I saw plenty," I said, scowling. "He loved us, and he cared for us. You never had to work, yet he spent more time with me than you ever did. While you were off with your charities and bridge club, he helped me with my fairy villages. I wouldn't be who I am today without him."

"No." Mary Jane wrinkled her brow and slowly shook her head. Lost in her thoughts, as if I weren't right in front of her, she said, "He didn't love me, just the image of me." She turned to the window; her voice grew weaker with each word. "He loved the way I completed his version of the perfect family. But it was never enough."

My words were tangled up with my emotions. I couldn't form a rational sentence. What was Mary Jane saying?

She turned around and pulled over the second photo album. She opened it to a photo where Jonathan had his arm around her. It was taken on a beach. Liddy sat on the sand at his feet close to another man on all fours building a sandcastle.

"In the beginning, your father was so sweet. No, that's not true, he was sweet for a long time, just not always sincere. That's how he controlled his surroundings. No one wanted to disappoint him. It took a lot of energy to be with him, even more to protect you."

I shook my head. "Protect me? From what? His attention? His love? How can you say such hurtful words?" I blurted. Lies, all lies. Her words sounded as if they were spoken underwater, and I was drowning. Yes, my father was a perfectionist, but he was patient and full of love. I didn't see that as a bad thing.

"When your father and I got married, he didn't see the need for me to finish college. He needed me tending to our home. He handled the responsibility of his family, including his own father's legacy, with great knowledge and skill. He ran his father's architecture company as if he started it, regardless of the partners who came with it. That's why he couldn't have Liddy—well, he had to make sure he took care of Liddy."

Mary Jane held her breath to stave off a coughing fit. "Liddy dropped out of college, which upset him. Note his double standard. He didn't see the need for me to finish, but he felt Liddy should have."

Mary Jane wriggled in her seat, adjusting the pillow behind her. "Then, after her accident, she lived with us until your father couldn't handle the wheelchair and felt the nurses coming in and out throughout the day disrupted our household. His perfect-picture life wasn't perfect with her wheelchair around."

"That's not true!" I yelled and slammed my fist on the table, but then I calmed down. This was a conversation, not a trial... yet. "Liddy told me Daddy built the cottage for her to help mend her broken heart since her fiancé died in the same accident that put her in that wheelchair."

"She told you he was her fiancé, that they were getting married?" Mary Jane's eyes widened, and her breath caught in her throat.

"She said they were discussing their wedding when the accident happened. Is that her fiancé in the picture?" I pointed to the shirtless, well-built man on his knees, digging a moat around a detailed sandcastle. I liked the idea of Liddy and this playful man messing about in the sand together.

"Umm, no..." Mary Jane fumbled again. "Maybe. I don't remember..."

"Well, Daddy loved Aunt Liddy. She was his only sister, and you can't tell me anything different," I said, not willing to hear anything different.

"Of course, he loved her, but your father... he didn't want... it's hard to explain."

"Dad loved Aunt Liddy. He'd take her and Martha on business trips with him. I know because I went on some of them, too. They are some of the best memories I have. He wasn't ashamed of her." I contained another growl. I couldn't believe I had to defend my father's love for his own sister.

"You're right. She did a lot of research and permit work for him, sort of as an assistant. He didn't regard her as his sister when she worked for him. Can you understand that?"

My mind spun out of control. What the hell was Mary Jane insinuating? If I doubted my father, I'd have to challenge who I was at my very core. I didn't want to hear any more.

My heart ached for Liddy and my father. I missed them now more than ever.

I stood up and put one album on top of the other. "I think we're done here." I dropped the photo albums on the coffee table on my way through the living room and stormed right into Nissa as she walked through the front door fanning three single red roses.

"What's the matter?" Nissa said, dropping the roses to her side. "You look terrible. Oh, no, you didn't…"

"Yeah, I did, and it wasn't pretty. Let's not talk about it."

Nissa held up and wiggled her roses like some kind of trophy.

"Nice," I grumbled and stomped into the workroom.

"Three years ago today, David and I met at a Frisbee tourney. I guess he still loves me," Nissa said in a light, breathy tone.

"Lucky you." I approached the workbench not knowing where to begin. My mind had yet to cool off.

"Are you really not going to tell me what happened at lunch?" she asked as she closed the door behind her.

"I said I didn't—you wouldn't believe—" I paused to collect my scattered thoughts. "Mary Jane tried to convince me my father controlled and manipulated us." I shook my head. "Or something like that, maybe worse. I don't know. I can't believe what she said."

"Okay, I can see controlling," Nissa said as she arranged the roses in a large plastic SugarBeans Café cup.

My eyes bugged out, and I threw my hands up in the air. "What are you talking about?"

"Tina, surely you remember how your dad used to take us to the Country Club? He smiled, surveyed our appearance, and told us not to forget to put our napkins in our laps.

And if we started to talk or giggle, he shot daggers at us. He'd raise an eyebrow and give us his let's-not-do-that-here-in-this-fancy-country-club-in-front-of-all-these-fancy-people look. You'd whip right into shape, and then it wasn't fun anymore. I hated going to dinner with him."

"You never said a thing." I flicked a hand as if to brush away Nissa's words.

"We had to be picture-perfect as if he was expecting Annie Leibovitz to come around the corner any minute." Nissa clicked the button on an imaginary camera.

That struck me silent. Nissa used the same phrase as Mary Jane. Perfect picture. Well, what was so wrong with wanting things to look good? My father worked hard. He had a reputation to uphold. I didn't see a problem with any of that.

"Too bad Annie Leibovitz wasn't around. I'd at least have a great photo of my perfect family." I tried to make light of it and threw the proverbial dart at my wall. My eyes fell on a little sticky note, and I walked closer to read it, *If it's too good to be true, then it probably is.* "Humph," I returned and slumped in my seat.

I loved everything I could remember about my father. I had to. I was just like him. We were both stubborn and, yes, maybe a bit controlling, but not manipulative. What's wrong with wanting what you wanted?

Look at me now. I'm being flexible every day with Mary Jane in my house. I'm kind of mixing business with pleasure by having Jake over for dinner. If I questioned my father's behavior, I would have to question my own. I thought about that beach picture.

"I'll be right back," I told Nissa.

I peeked around the corner. Mary Jane was no longer at the dining room table, and her bedroom door was closed.

I sat on the couch and leafed through the top photo album until I found the picture of my mother and father on the beach. I unstuck it from under the plastic cover. and looked at it more closely. Mary Jane's young expression came across as content with Jonathan's arm draped around her, his hand cupping her shoulder. What a handsome couple they made. Barbie and Ken. Mary Jane's haircut framed her face with a short modern style. On the beach and not a hair out of place, typical Mary Jane.

Everyone always said they were the perfect couple. How could Mary Jane tell such untruths about my father? And Liddy? My father adored Liddy.

I only ever saw my father treat Liddy with kindness. He wasn't embarrassed or ashamed of her. Regret, apologies, explanations, that's what I had expected from Mary Jane, not jealousy or accusations. Nothing made sense anymore.

I recalled traveling with my father and his sister often. Around eight years old, while my father lectured in some hall, I pushed Aunt Liddy around in her wheelchair through the Museum of Modern Art in New York. Over three days, we stopped and read every plaque in every gallery and hovered long moments staring at paintings then deconstructed the image paint-stroke by paint-stroke as I pushed Aunt Liddy's wheelchair closer and closer to the masterpiece. The image would reappear as we backed away, always surprised every time the image popped back into view. It was all about perspective. Life was about perspective, apparently.

I tucked the perfect picture of the ideal couple away in my dresser drawer. Was Mary Jane just trying to hurt me? Well, she wouldn't move into my home and get away with negative talk about my father. I would rise above it all and avoid her the best I could. I would explain to Nissa how much I needed her to stick around and provide cover for a few more months. No more escaping at lunch time.

My phone chimed, and I scooped it up. "Hello."

"Hello, I am looking for Mrs. Mary Jane Edwards."

"This is her daughter, Christina Edwards. Can I help you?"

"I'm your mom's real estate agent, Linda McDermott. I got an offer on her townhome. I just need her approval, and it'll be sold."

Sold? I clenched my jaws shut. Mary Jane was selling her house? Where would she go after her treatments?

"I'll have my mother call you back. Thank you." I hung up the phone. Is there something I didn't know about Mary Jane's prognosis?

CHAPTER 17

Friday came sooner than I fancied. On several occasions, I found myself wishing I had agreed to meet Jake at a local bar. The most time I ever spent in the kitchen was when Liddy and I created tiny fairy dishes, pots, and such with polymer clay and baked them in a 350 degrees oven. Assuming my guests didn't want polymer clay for dinner, I made a phone call.

"Silvio?"

"Tina, *cara*. How are you, my darling?" Silvio, the owner of the local Italian eatery in Floral Ridge, answered in his heavy Italian accent. "I'm-a hoping everything *è buono* with you."

"I invited friends over for dinner Friday night, and I forgot I didn't know how to cook. Can you help a girl out?" Silvio and I had become fast friends when I moved into my condo. I had eaten at The Italian Eatery at least three or four times a week during my renovation.

"But of course, *amore mia*. What would you like?"

I knew I could count on him. I ordered the most popular items on the menu and a couple of bottles of wine.

Mary Jane had informed Bella of my plans, and Bella offered to cook anything I wanted. But Bella wasn't there for me. I appreciated the offer, and as much as I would have loved her to do so, it felt like I would be throwing in the towel. No, I would do this my way.

"Bella, by all means you're invited to dinner, but it could be a good night to take off and visit your sons," I said confidently since I wouldn't be home alone with Mary Jane. We hadn't really spoken since our ill-fated lunch when I left her at the dining room table.

"Those boys won't want nothin' to do with me on a Friday night. Their wives will have them all tied up in daddy duty. But maybe I'll take advantage and run a few errands. Don't you worry, I'll be home in time to get Mary Jane settled by eight p.m. for the Friday night classic movie."

Since I knew popcorn would be on their Friday-night schedule, I popped and bagged some before beginning my dinner preparations. The food delivery arrived right on time, thirty minutes before Jake, Nissa, and David were expected to show up. I removed the Parmesan chicken breasts from their round tins, placed them into my own baking dish, and slid them into a low oven to keep warm. After that, I dumped the red sauce into a pot, threw in some fresh basil Bella was growing on our windowsill, and let it simmer. Italian bread was slathered with garlic butter then wrapped it in aluminum foil to warm up later, and I put a large pot of heavily salted water to boil.

I berated myself one last time for thinking it would be a good idea to have Jake over for dinner. Not only could I not cook, I could barely reheat. I'm definitely not my mother's daughter, especially when it came to dinner parties. I didn't have a hostess bone in my body. I was more of a maker and sharer. Friends came over knowing my events were always pot-luck, self-serve affairs, where I would supply a green salad or chips and dip.

Tonight was to allow myself to feel as if I was moving forward with life even though, in reality, I held my breath, waiting for that proverbial "other shoe" to drop. The distance between mother and daughter was a massive abyss, a space of unknown width and depth, which I was afraid to hurdle because of the obscure landing.

"Tina, would you mind bringing me a cup of water?" Mary Jane called from the living room.

Exhaling, I wiped my hands on a dishtowel and tossed it onto the countertop, ignoring it as it slipped to the floor.

"Be right there." I filled a plastic cup with room-temperature water, the way Mary Jane liked it.

I placed the cup on a coaster on the end table closest to her. Mary Jane looked tired, although she had tried to dress up by wearing a nice pair of slacks and a loose blouse. And her cough was getting worse and worse. The treatments seemed to be harder on her than the cancer. No matter what, I didn't like to see anyone suffer. At least there was that.

Mary Jane took a small sip and mouthed her thanks. "By the way, my realtor will be by in a day or two for me to sign those papers."

My pulse began to rev up. This was not a good time to start an incendiary conversation, but I went ahead and asked, "Where will you go after your treatments?" My insides began to itch, and my breath sped up as I forced myself not to flee.

"We'll figure that out when and if the time comes," she said and settled back on a pillow.

"But we should make a plan, right? We need to make a plan." Something inside me began to spin.

"We will in due time. Go ahead with what you are doing. It'll be fine."

I could do anything for a couple of months. But without a deadline, a time limit… that's not the way I worked. I needed a plan. But Mary Jane was right, we have time, and I have dinner guests arriving soon. "Will you need anything else? Everyone will be here in a few minutes, and I still have to decant the wine and finish making a salad."

"I'm fine. Thank you."

I wished Bella would hurry and return. I regretted letting her feel I would be fine without her. Her absence now reminded me of how grateful I was when she was present.

"Whatever you have cooking in that oven smells delicious." Mary Jane reached over and placed her cup on the coffee table in front of her.

I scooped the coaster off the end table and put it under the cup. "I'll be in the kitchen if you need me."

I set the plates and silverware on the end of the counter, buffet style. David and Nissa were used to my dinner parties. Here's the food, fix your own plate, and I'll meet you at the dining table.

"You're not going to set the table?" Mary Jane startled me. She squatted to pick up the dish towel which had slipped to the floor. Her sidekick, Bob, swung forward, almost pulling her into a tumble. "This is dirty. Where do I put it?"

I pulled it from her grasp and threw it on the counter. It was my house, my party, my dirty dish towel. Why can't the queen hostess let me do my thing? My jaw was clenched so tight, I worried I wouldn't be able to eat or talk when my guests arrived. How could I get through the evening knowing there was no plan to when my home would be returned to me? I poured a glass of wine, deciding I deserved an early start.

I pointed to my buffet-style layout and said, "This is just as easy."

"But not as charming." Mary Jane glanced over at the dining room table.

I looked at the empty table and took a large sip of wine. Setting places at the table was something my mother always did for my father, not for me.

"I thought Dad was the one who wanted the perfect picture," I snipped and continued getting glasses out of the cabinet above.

"Tina, don't be flip. A dinner party is a dinner party. It won't hurt to look prepared for your guests. Here, let me help." Mary Jane adjusted her oxygen tank on her hip then picked up the plates.

"I'll do it," I said and took the plates from her. I not-so-gently placed the five plates around the table.

"Now, get salad plates," Mary Jane said as she left the kitchen.

I huffed, grabbed the smaller salad plates and silverware, and left them in a pile on the dining room table.

I worked in the kitchen, listening to dishes clink as Mary Jane set the table. Sip. Exhale. She's just trying to help. Sip. This is what Mary Jane does best. Sip. Let it go. Gulp.

I loosened my jaw by the time I finished making the salad, then filled five glasses with ice and hung a slice of lemon on their sides. I slid the bread into the oven and filled a pitcher with water. Prepared to put the pitcher and glasses on the table, I hesitated when Mary Jane held up two glasses waiting for them to be filled. I filled them, then the other three, and followed Mary Jane into the dining room. "Pick your battles," echoed in my head.

As Mary Jane placed glasses at the two closest place settings, she said, "There, now doesn't that look nice?"

Each place setting had a small white plate in the center of the larger floral one. Solid white linen napkins, which Mary Jane must have dug around for because I couldn't remember where I even kept them, were neatly folded to the left of each plate with the silverware placed according to the Emily Post Institute.

I retrieved the spinach and green apple salad and placed it between the set of lit candles in my vintage hobnail milk glass and brass candlesticks, which were usually atop the credenza by the front door. Apparently, Mary Jane could move quickly and quietly when she wanted to.

The door opened and loud laughter entered from the hallway as I set the timer for the fresh pasta I had just dumped in the boiling water.

"…and I just knew you'd love a piping-hot cobbler, so I rushed here to get it into a warm oven." Bella never entered the apartment in silence.

I shook off the mixed feeling of wanting to pile the plates up at the end of the table, not wanting to come across as someone I wasn't, but the table did look welcoming.

Bella walked in, wreaking havoc. She dropped her overstuffed purse and her cooler bag, a large, insulated bag she always brought back from her errands filled with all kinds of goodies in the entryway followed by Jake with his leather satchel over his shoulder, flowers under his arm, and a peach cobbler in his hands. He had to step over the cooler to greet me and hand me the cobbler.

"You shouldn't have," I said.

"I didn't. I met Bella getting out of her car." Jake slid his satchel off and set it on the credenza, then greeted Mary Jane, handing her the flowers. My heart fluttered a little as she brightened while accepting the oversized hydrangeas. I could tell she liked Jake and that he liked her. He sat next to her on the couch, and they talked as if they picked up the middle of a conversation.

I brought the cobbler to the kitchen and returned with a vase of water, two bottles of opened wine, and six glasses on a tray.

Mary Jane rearranged flowers and Jake poured the wine as Nissa and David let themselves in, and the evening began. I set a place for Bella, a setting that matched the others, and got a nod of approval from Mary Jane.

"You set the table?" Nissa asked.

"She did," Mary Jane answered after I stared at Nissa a moment, thinking she surely knew better. "And doesn't it look nice?"

I stared at Nissa, daring her to answer.

Dinner went off without any drama. The conversation revolved around the mansion.

"Jake, how is your mother doing? Is she excited about the B&B?" I asked.

"By the way," Nissa jumped in. "We never found a family bible."

"Random." Jake raised his eyebrows at Nissa's statement.

"Not really. It's a very common thing to expect from that time. I find it hard to believe there wasn't one. Would your mother happen to have it?"

"I'd have to ask, but I doubt it. She didn't spend any time in that house, but her mother, my Grandma Alice, had many stories from her youth until, of course, she was no longer welcomed there."

"No longer welcomed?" Mary Jane asked.

"My Grandma Alice, well, found herself pregnant at sixteen in 1952. My great-grandmother, Eloise, wanted to send her to a home for unwed mothers, but Grandma Alice refused to go."

"Guess your mother wouldn't have the bible then," Nissa said sadly, sulked, and sipped her wine.

"Your grandmother sounds like a very strong lady," Mary Jane said.

"So how did she survive on her own?" Nissa asked, always the dig-deeper type.

"Actually, her boyfriend, well, my grandfather was in the military stationed abroad. His mother took Alice and the baby in. His family was more of a true family to Grandma Alice than her own family ever was. My mother grew up around his family's restaurant, where I ended up hanging around when I was young. They are all the family I know. By the time I was old enough to hold down a job, my uncle had taken over, and he showed me all the ropes."

As my guests kept the conversation going and laughed at each other's jokes, they passed the salad and the red sauce and requested seconds of wine and garlic bread. I held back the tears wanting to fall from the normalcy of it all. Mary Jane's composure, albeit less flamboyant than I remembered, had an ease that ensured comfort for my guests and me, as if she cast a spell. I could see a bit of the old Mary Jane in her content demeanor overseeing the dinner party.

I passed around a few miniature pieces I had created for the B&B, the two twin beds for the girls' rooms and a simple vanity with a tilting mirror for the nanny's room. Seeing them in Mary Jane's hands as she examined each piece, I tensed like a four-year-old hoping for a pat on the head from her parent. I was afraid to look at her face.

"These are beautiful," Mary Jane said. "The detail is remarkable. You made these?"

I could have taken her comment as doubtful, but her expression showed sheer delight. My four-year-old self was proud. As the pieces completed their rotation around the table, I returned them to their boxes.

Bella asked, "What did your mother do at the restaurants? Did she cook?" Bella wanted to know.

"No, She kept the books. Between that and raising me, she had her hands full."

"I'm looking forward to meeting your mom and seeing the progress you've made on the B&B," I said and stood to clear the plates. With dinner completed, I suggested to everyone to bring their wine into the living room where I'd serve Bella's famous peach cobbler.

"Thank you kindly, but your mother and me only have a split second to get ready for bed before our show is on. And thank you for thinking of our popcorn for movie night." Bella opened her mouth wide, bent over from the hips, and gave me a big wink.

I almost spat out my wine. Jake laughed and helped Mary Jane to her feet. He followed her with the glass of wine she'd barely touched—what a charmer he was.

"You did something nice for Bella and your mom?" Nissa asked as she picked up a couple of water glasses on the way to the kitchen.

"I just made popcorn. Wanted to keep Bella out of the kitchen tonight."

"Well, I'm glad to see it didn't kill you."

"Ha," I smirked at Nissa's comment.

Nissa finished clearing the table and stacked the dishwasher while I cut generous slices of the peach cobbler.

"I'm impressed you set the table. Was that for Jake or your mother?" Nissa asked.

"Pretty sure my mother set it for Jake." I fixed a wide fake smile on my face. "Ready for dessert?" I lifted the tray of plated cobblers and brought it into the living room.

Nissa said, "It was a great dinner, Tina, thank you, but David and I need to head out." Nissa said.

"Really?" I eyed David, who scrambled to get in his first bite.

"We can wrap up the rest of our cobbler to take home," Nissa said.

She followed me back into the kitchen and helped pack up our two slices, leaving two for my mother and Bella. "You don't have to leave, you know," I said.

"I have a tough boss, and I have a lot of notes to get in order before the morning." Nissa half-joked.

We joined David at the door as he shook hands with Jake. I waved goodbye with the roll of plastic wrap I brought with me from the kitchen to wrap up Jake's slice of cobbler.

"How about I eat my cobbler now?" he said, picking a plate off the tray and took a bite of the tart goodness before his rear end hit the couch.

CHAPTER 18

In the quiet, after David and Nissa said their goodbyes, the peach cobbler occupied our attention as we enjoyed the creamy sweet-tart bites. I took my last bite as Jake lifted his empty wine glass, "To a great dinner," he said.

I tapped my glass to his.

"Tasty vittles. I'd love to do it again sometime," Jake said.

Heat rose up my neck, and I confessed, "Then I better fess up. I didn't cook dinner. I only heated it up. I ordered it from The Italian Eatery around the corner."

"I knew it was too good to be true. How can anyone as pretty, smart, and artistic as you and also be a great cook? Way too many talents for one person."

I slapped his arm with the back of my hand and giggled like a silly schoolgirl.

"Next time, let's go to the restaurant. Then you won't have to clean up the dishes. But we'd have to come back to your place for Bella's dessert." He licked the back of his spoon.

The laughing and coughing had quieted from Mary Jane's room, and I could tell from the lack of light coming out from under the door Mary Jane and Bella were down for the night. They must have been too tired to finish out movie night.

Our conversation remained light and easy until Jake mentioned Mary Jane and I quickly changed the subject back to his mother.

"My mama is the best. For years, she did the same thing five days a week and sometimes Saturdays. She would drag me to and from the restaurant. Once I started school, I would walk to the restaurant and do my homework. Eventually, she took over collecting receipts and balancing the books so Grandma Alice could bake desserts and the staff would give me little jobs. At 4:30, we would leave for the bank with the final deposit. Sundays were for the two of us. She made every Sunday special, even if we just went to the library and then go for ice cream. I lived for Sundays."

"I'd love to meet her." How had I never noticed the intensity in his sapphire eyes? "I Googled some of her artwork. It's so fresh. Colorful yet subtle. True to life, yet not realistic. When did she start painting?"

"She always sketched and used watercolors for fun. She took lessons about fifteen years ago from a local artist, and now she's a bona fide artist in her own right. And I'm the lucky guy who gets to make one of her dreams come true by buying the mansion and turning it into a B&B."

"Well, she sounds lovely," I said.

"You'll have to come to one of her shows."

"I'd love that."

"Your mom's a doll," he said. "She can tell a great story. She was in Athens when the schools were finally desegregated in 1964 and around all the Navy families transferring in and out of the Navy Supply Corps School, which no longer exists."

He told me things I never knew about Mary Jane and was bemused how she could hold an enjoyable conversation with Jake but couldn't say two words to me without ticking me off.

Change of subject.

"We've made copies of the photos we're using for the replicas. The original photos, to the best of Nissa's ability, are in chronological order. Would your mother like them?"

Silence surrounded us as he stacked one empty cobbler plate on top of the other. "Do you have any bourbon?" Jake asked as he placed them on the tray and stood.

"In the hutch in the dining room," I said as I brought the tray into the kitchen and returned with a rocks glass.

Jake held up the Makers Mark he dug out of the bottom cabinet. His dimple caught my attention as he focused on his pour.

I nestled into the couch with a pillow on my lap and my wine. I felt him juggling his thoughts and wondered why it was so hard for him to discuss his family.

"My mother feels she's betraying the family that raised me, my father's family, if she shows any interest in anyone or anything except the mansion itself. She thinks I'm doing all this for her mama, Grandma Alice, but really, I'm doing it for her."

It was nice that we were comfortable enough with each other to finally talk about his family. I sipped, he reminisced and confessed.

"She and I got just as screwed as her mother in the deal. If Grandma Alice inherited the mansion, I would've grown up there." Jake adjusted the pillows and sunk back into the other corner of the couch.

"Good or bad, they're still your family," I said.

Did that just come out of my mouth? Who am I to give him advice about family?

Jake leaned back and sipped his bourbon. "Your condo doesn't look like you."

And bam, there went my peace of mind. I stopped mid-sip and stared straight ahead, waiting for the punch line.

"It's unexpected, like that painting," Jake said, pointing to the Lempicka.

"I happen to love my condo. I worked very hard finding and paying for every one of these pieces."

He opened his mouth, then shut it. "Ah… I'm sorry, did I say something wrong? I didn't mean it wasn't pretty and nice. It's just not what I expected."

My mother had said something similar. "What did you expect?" I asked, pursing my lips, twisting them from side to side, keeping the tension there so the rest of me could relax and take the hit.

"Oh, I don't know. I expected it to look like you, you know Victorian, I guess."

"What, straitlaced and prudish?"

"No, soft and romantic."

I followed his eyes as he took in the room. My father loved Art Deco and all things Frank Lloyd Wright. Why am I defending my choices again? It's how I grew up. It's what I know. For myself, I just happened to like lace and ruffles. They went with my long brown curls. Not knowing how to respond, I didn't say anything. Everyone's entitled to their own opinion.

"There's a restaurant I'd love to try, not too far from here. The head chef is a friend of mine. Would you like to go?" Jake added, "with me?"

"Geez, I don't do social events with clients. Maybe some other time," I said, trying to sound polite, honest, and professional.

"And what do you call this?" Jake asked a little too smugly.

He'd caught me. But in my defense, I wanted this dinner for several reasons. Jake and Mary Jane seemed to enjoy each other's company, Nissa and I did have a few questions, and I wanted to remind my roommates that it was *my* kitchen.

"I'll tell you what," he said. "How about you meet me for a drink? We'll talk business, I'll update you on the progress of the B&B, and you update me on the little rooms?"

I gritted my teeth. "They're called miniatures or replicas, or miniature replicas." But then, my mantra of not mixing business with pleasure collided with the thought of getting out of the house for a bit. "I'm busy this week. But maybe sometime next week I can come up with an hour or two to meet you for a drink. And talk business."

"Great. Let me know which night, and I'll make sure my calendar is clear."

Our conversation continued with ease, and we finished our drinks. After he helped me load the dishwasher, there was little more to say but goodnight.

"Thanks again for dinner," he said, throwing his satchel over his shoulder. We walked to the door, and after an awkward pause, he leaned in and hugged me. I stiffened, remembering Mary Jane across the room behind the closed door.

I stepped back, waved my fingers goodbye, closed the door, and bolted the lock. I didn't want to fall asleep thinking about Jake Martin, so I poured another glass of wine and continued working on a Victorian pedestal side table I was staining.

It wasn't until I got ready for bed that I recalled Jake saying I looked "soft and romantic."

CHAPTER 19

The doorbell shattered my focus and instantly the faint smell of garlic and basil wafted through the air triggered a growl from my stomach as Bella reheated the chicken Parmesan leftovers for Mary Jane's lunch.

"I'll grab us something to eat," I said. Nissa focused on painting floral patterns as she replicated wallpaper in just the right Victorian colors from a black-and-white photo.

As I walked into the dining room, my thoughts lost in a heady scent, the scent of a Southern sultry summer evening, Bella rounded from the kitchen with a large vase of white-and-cream peonies and gardenias, my favorites.

"What beautiful flowers. I could smell them over the garlic." I leaned over and savored the scent.

"They just arrived. Let's set them right dab in the middle of the table. I bet they're from that Mr. Jake. He's sweet on ya," Bella said, wiggling her eyebrows. She whipped out the message card and handed it to me.

I opened the card and read it to myself. "Tina, these flowers reminded me of you. Thank you for a wonderful dinner. Till next time, Jake."

"Flowers?" Mary Jane questioned. She dragged her newly purchased oxygen tank pull cart behind her. I cringed as the wheels left a light smudge in its trail through the cream-colored carpet. It wasn't even that bad, but she knew better, and I felt she was doing it on purpose.

"Please, you can't use that cart outside for walks and inside on the carpet. Could you please carry your tank or ask one of us to when you're in the house?"

"Really, Tina? You can have the carpets cleaned after I'm gone." Mary Jane plopped on the couch and parked her tank by her side. Was Mary Jane referencing her leaving my home once she recovered or something else?

"I apologize if that came across as mean," I said, reprimanding my behavior. "But you never allowed any dirt in your house when I was little. I'm surprised you're treating my home this way."

As a child, Mary Jane insisted that my friends, and I, if I even bothered to invite any over, remove our shoes if we stepped one foot into her house.

"It wasn't me who didn't want shoes worn in the house."

"Oh, here we go…" I rolled my eyes. This was precisely why I didn't want to start a conversation with her. It was always about my father and unfailingly turned into a battle. "Are you going to blame that on Dad, too?"

"Blame? What are you talking about?"

"You don't ever have a nice thing to say about him."

"It's not about having a nice thing to say. It's about the truth. About who he was. He had a powerful personality. He inherited not only the responsibility for his family's name and reputation but also a certain lifestyle. He was very controlling, which, according to Liddy, was their father's personality. He chose my clothing, my hairdresser. If I weren't best friends with Liddy, I probably would never have—" Mary Jane paused to catch her breath.

Bella walked into the dining room, drying a pot with a dish towel. She leaned her shoulder on the wall and prodded Mary Jane with a nod.

I looked back and forth between Mary Jane and Bella. "Listen, I see what's going on here." My volume rose as I spoke. "You two believe what you want to believe. But I was there, Bella. I was there. I know what I saw. You never met my father. He was the best. He was a good man and…"

Nissa, having rushed out of the workroom, shoved her face in front of mine until she registered in my gaze. I blinked, turned, and stared at Mary Jane through watery eyes, then at Bella, who faintly shook her head.

"You've got it all wrong." Mary Jane stiffened. She seemed to have gained strength with both Nissa and Bella in the room.

"Enough," I all but barked. "If you're going to stay in my house…"

"Why don't you two agree to disagree for the moment," Nissa interrupted.

I pinched my lips and squinted. That would be hard to swallow.

"For now, that's a fine idea." Bella shuffled her feet as if confused as to which direction to go. "Nissa, I believe Tina's mother has a story to tell you girls about the Randall Mansion. Isn't that right, Mary Jane? The one about Miss Eloise Chambers, Jake's great-grandmother, and a fashion show."

Nissa nudged me with her hip, but I refused to play. I couldn't just turn off my outrage. I didn't know why Mary Jane insisted on bringing up my father when she knew it was a sore spot.

"Tell me, Mary Jane," Nissa said and took a seat across from her after she sat my reluctant butt into the only other chair in the room.

Bella held up a finger as if to say she'd be right back.

"My mother was one of the models for the Athens Elk's Hall fashion show and luncheon to raise funds for the local school," Mary Jane said. "I remember participating in it, but I forgot it was Miss Eloise — that's what she wanted everyone to call her — who sponsored it and put it on. The other day I found a picture of Mama and me all dressed up, standing in front of the stage with Miss Eloise. It was the fanciest event I'd ever seen. I must have been six or seven."

Bella returned with a yellowed brochure and handed it to me. Since I refused to look at it and be part of this plot to make everything seem just fine, Nissa took the papers.

"That's the brochure from the event. I'm not sure why Mama saved it. But there it is," Mary Jane said.

Nissa flipped through the pages, and a photo caught her attention. Miss Eloise sat in the middle of her nieces and nephews, who attended the event. Each name was listed.

"Can we keep this for a while?" Nissa asked Mary Jane and slapped my arm with the brochure, and insisted I look at it.

"Sure, I don't need it. Maybe you can give it to Jake for his foundation."

"That would be great. We can bring it to him when we visit the mansion," Nissa said.

Mary Jane sat up. "When will you see him? Are you going to the mansion? I'd love to see it."

I winced, my mind ready to detonate, one minute calm, the next ballistic. "If we go, it will be for work."

"I could pack us all up a little something to eat," Bella said, "and Mary Jane and me... we'll stay out of your hair. It would be good for her to take a little outing." The sugar-sweet tiptoeing in her voice surprised me. I prepared for Bella to flutter her eyelashes.

I looked from Bella to Mary Jane, then to Nissa, all eyes bright with anticipation of a road trip.

With a huff, I grabbed the brochure and headed back to the workroom. With my back to the group, I said, "Okay. I'll see if I can set a date the next time I talk with Jake." I wasn't about to tell any of them I was meeting him for a drink next week.

I just wanted to get lost in my miniatures. I'd rather be dealing with their little issues, than my not-so-little problems of real life. I walked into the workroom and threw the brochure onto Nissa's desk. It landed open to the picture of Miss Eloise, Mary Jane as a little girl, and the grandmother I never knew.

I took a closer look. "You know?" I said when Nissa came in the room. "I'm all Edwards. I don't look the slightest bit like my mother or her mother."

"You're the spitting image of your father, that's why. There is no room for any other DNA. He was very proud of that," Nissa said. "By the way, did you get us anything to eat?"

I threw the brochure at her. "If you're that hungry, you go out in the lion's den and fend for yourself."

CHAPTER 20

The following week, Nissa and I buckled down, verifying the blueprints of each of the rooms for the B&B and checking our inventory list for every item, accessory, and tchotchke so we could stay on our tight schedule. As soon as we had everything on hand for the eight miniature replicas, the easier it would be to manage the project.

We kept to ourselves and kept quiet. Mary Jane was sicker and weaker than usual after her latest treatment, and she spent a lot of time in bed. It was hard to feel good about not having to see or talk to her when she wasn't doing well. I tried to take the time to build up my resolve and learn some patience.

As I closed up shop late one afternoon, I returned my lunch plate to the kitchen and found Bella sitting at the dining room table, staring out the window. I looked at my watch. I had some time before meeting Jake for a drink. "Got a minute, Bella?"

"Let me get us some tea, and we'll chat," Bella said and rushed into the kitchen, continually talking as if this opportunity would disappear if she stopped. "Miss Tina, one thing you need to know," Bella called out from the kitchen, "is that your mama is one of the strongest persons I've ever met."

"Great. But how are *you* doing?" I asked and pulled out a chair. She settled at the end of the table with two iced teas and a plate of Snickerdoodles.

"Oh, Honey, I'm just fine. But I do better when Mary Jane is fine. Which she will be, we've been through this before."

Knowing that Bella knew much more than I did about my own mother, I didn't remark.

"She needs her rest, that's all," Bella said.

I nodded, knowing it hurt Bella that she couldn't do more for Mary Jane. "Tell me about you and your sons."

"Oh, yes. The best two boys the good Lord handed out. And I got 'em. They're both hard-working with kids of their own. I have lunch with them once or twice a week, that's one of my errands. When your mama was all good, we would all gather for Sunday dinner at the townhouse. That was very important to her."

Really? She insisted on gathering for a meal? Thinking of the townhouse, now sold, made my heart take a quick dip. "When did you move into the townhouse?"

"I met her at the nursing home where I was a nurse, and she volunteered. But you know all that. After the first time your mama got sick, I would come in a couple of hours a day and take care of her, but I had a full-time job. I couldn't do all that was needed. Since my kids were grown, we decided if I gave up my apartment and moved in with her, I wouldn't have to pay rent, and she wouldn't have to pay me. That was over eight years ago." She took a sip from her tea. "Ya' know, things are never quite as scary when you have a friend. My boys were happy that I wasn't alone, and I was pleased to have someone to cook for."

I rested my chin on my palm and grinned. I liked Bella. She was nothing but good. I stood and side-hugged her as she sat. "Well, she's lucky to have you. We both are."

Bella grabbed my hand as I walked away to put my glass in the sink. "Your mama's doing her best, ya' know. She's happy to be here and knows this ain't easy for you. In time you'll understand why all this is so important."

I contemplated Bella's sweet face, wondering what she knew that I didn't. I nodded and said, "I'm doing my best, too." I left her to get ready for my meeting with Jake.

As I sat at my vanity applying my makeup, I wondered if I truly was doing my best. A whisper came to me, *Things are only as bad as you make them.* Could I make things easier for all of us?

I played with my loosely spiraled banana curls, freeing them from their usual mess-bun on the top of my head. I very rarely wore my hair down, and if I were a betting woman, I'd put money on my hair being up in a mess-bun within the hour. My honey-brown eyes, passed down from my father, sparkled within the smokey grey eye shadow I applied, something else I didn't have much practice with.

Because this wasn't a date, I could easily brush away wondering if my father would have approved of me going out with Jake. And even though this was a business meeting, I hoped my father would send me a sign, positive or negative during this one drink with Jake.

I added a final layer of mascara and brushed on a bit of lip gloss. Done. I opened the closet's mirrored door to peek at my entire ensemble. Usually, when I went out for drinks I was with Nissa after work. We would wear whatever we had on for the day, sometimes just one step up from pajamas. My typical style was a pair of jeans or leggings and a simple lace top. Nothing special.

Tonight, I had on my dressed-up version of normal. I upped the ante by adding high heel nude pumps to my best jeans and a slightly sparkling dove grey blouse with a lace peplum, a gift from Nissa I'd yet to wear. This was as good as it gets. I grabbed a shawl and switched off the lights.

I checked the time. I still had thirty minutes before I had to leave. Jake had offered to pick me up, but me being me, I told him I would prefer to meet him at the restaurant. What I didn't tell him was I wanted to be able to leave at my convenience and not feel bound to his plan. Also, Nissa had agreed to a "rescue call" thirty minutes into the meeting in case I needed an out.

I inhaled a touch of southern humidity in the idyllic summer breeze as I closed the workroom windows for the night. The horizon offered the beginnings of a beautiful sunset with pinks and purples taking over the blues and whites.

My hands shook as I cranked the window closed.

Geez, it's just a drink.

Okay, then why did I dress up? The tennis match proceeded in my head, and neither side won.

I'm going to have this drink with Jake because it would help take my mind off my mother, and I really did have a few business items to discuss. So, this wasn't a date. The very idea of dating added more to my plate. And that, I couldn't handle. I lifted both hands and watched my fingers tremble. "This is ridiculous," I said aloud, shaking out my hands and dropping them to my side.

I grabbed the jeweler's headband. Not wanting to mess up my hair, I peered through the left lens and inspected a miniature portrait I had left to dry. This Randall family member had similar blue eyes and auburn hair as most of the others. But her skin appeared darker, more olive, most likely married into the family.

I had to admit, the Randall family was growing on me. Nissa did a great job putting the family tree together, and soon we could put a name to each one of the portraits we've chosen to put in the miniature parlor. All frames matched their originals to perfection. About half of the paintings on the workbench were complete, except the ones in need of gold leaf. Those would be finished soon.

"Shoot!" I had let the time get away from me. I should have left ten minutes ago. As I raced out of the room, I couldn't help but glance at a torn magazine page stuck on the wall, *Life is a great adventure or nothing.*

"Okay, Dad. I hear you."

Twelve minutes later, I pulled up to the Blackwater River Grille. A valet greeted me and opened my door. As I stepped out of my car, he handed me a receipt that slipped out of my fingers. I stretched, trying to catch it mid-air, and smacked the valet on his arm. The ticket fluttered into the gutter. When he handed it to me again, I had to give a slight pull for him to release it.

"Sorry," I said hoping my klutziness was over for the night and entered the dark-paneled, men's club styled restaurant.

Straight ahead at the end of the leather-edged bar, Jake sat on a high stool. His auburn hair picked up the alternating shadows from the lights and fan above. With relaxed shoulders and a three-fingered grip, he stared into the center of his swirling bourbon. Not wanting to disturb the image, I stayed near the front door. He seemed pleasant enough, but I wondered what kind of man he actually was.

"Just one?" the hostess asked, startling me back to my senses.

"Oh, no. I'm meeting someone." Just then, Jake looked up, and I waved pretending to see him for the first time. I walked forward and met him halfway.

"Hello," he greeted me. With a presumptuous arm around my waist, he led me to my seat. "Aren't you a sight for weary eyes? Nice to see you with your hair down."

The double entendre wasn't lost on me. He squeezed me with a quick side hug. Since he had hugged me before, I knew to brace myself, not to resist.

"You look like you're covered in pixie dust," Jake said, one finger lifting the sleeve of my glittering blouse.

I smiled, appreciating the comment. It had to be a sign from my father. Why else would a beefy, almost-cowboy bring up something from my past fairy world?

"I'm certainly looking forward to a glass of wine," I said as I jockeyed up onto the high stool next to him.

"What's your usual?" Jake asked, handing me the wine list.

We discussed our favorite Cabs, and I chose my drink of choice, a bold but smooth one, nothing too fruity.

"You made a great choice of wine for the Italian food the other night."

"Well, that, too, my friend, was sent with the food." I shrugged and offered a cheesy smile.

"Well, it was a great choice. What, pray tell, is your second favorite drink?" Jake smiled.

"Bourbon. Hence, the Wild Turkey and Maker's Mark in my hutch. I prefer it on ice. Melted ice. Well, ice and maybe a large splash of water."

"Watered down? No, ma'am! Straight up and barrel-aged is the way to go."

I laughed. He reached over and picked up my Cabernet. "Do you mind?"

"Help yourself."

He swirled the glass, inhaled deeply, then took a drawn-out sip.

"Nice and smooth. If I'm going to eat a steak, medium rare, of course, then I want a nice bold Cab to go with it. This one would do nicely."

My phone chimed. Excusing myself, I reached into my purse hanging on the hook underneath the lip of the bar. Nissa's face lit up my cell phone. Crap, I forgot we had decided on a rescue call, and I should have let her know I was running late. I haven't decided if I wanted to hang out longer or not.

"Hi, Nissa, what's up?" I hoped my tone didn't sound rehearsed.

Nissa bombarded me with questions, "You okay? What's Jake drinking? Has he asked you to stay for dinner? Does he look hot?"

"Just got here. I ran a bit late." I did my best to come across as if Nissa had something serious to say. "Nissa says hi," I said, giving Jake a little wave.

"We'll figure it out in the morning, Nissa. See you then." I hung up. I never claimed to be an actress, but I trusted Jake didn't notice anything amiss.

"She's a lot of fun," Jake said.

"She is. But in all seriousness, I'd be lost without her. We've been best friends since we were eight, went to the same schools and college. Been together ever since. What about you? Where'd you go to school? How did you become a chef?"

Jake held up his empty glass. "I'm going to have another. How about you?" He called the bartender over as I quickly finished the last bit of my wine and slid the glass toward him. I could always Uber home.

"I was born and raised in a small town in Alabama. My dad, James Paul Martin, was the head chef at the family restaurant when my mom took over the books for Grandma Alice."

"So, Alice never remarried?"

"She never married to begin with. My mother never met her father. Grandma Alice found out she was pregnant just after he deployed, and sadly he never returned."

"I'm so sorry. So, you never met your grandfather?"

"Nope, he never returned from Vietnam. But if he was anything like his brother, my great-uncle, the one who ran the restaurant, my grandfather would have been a great man. Grandma Alice loved him, gave up her own family for him and his baby girl, yet never saw him again. His family took in Grandma Alice before my mother was even born. They became her family. Together, they waited for him to return. It's the only family my mother knows, and me too actually. Alice gave my mother their name, Williamson, when she was born. She didn't want her to be a Randall."

"And so, you grew up in the restaurant business."

"When I was three, my job was to crawl under all the tables and pick up items people dropped like napkins and chicken bones."

I laughed and held up my glass. "Here's to your start in the business."

Jake picked up his glass and said, "It doesn't count if it doesn't clink." He tapped mine with his own.

I hid my gasp. My father used to say the exact same thing. Another sign?

"How about I tell you the rest over dinner? I'm starved."

I nodded. A girl's got to eat. Why rush into business and have to go home before Mary Jane and Bella settled for the night? One night for myself couldn't hurt.

"Is your chef friend in tonight?" I asked as the waitress led us to a cozy table in the corner. He soaked in the décor and stopped by a partially set table with a reserved sign on it and checked out the silverware tucked away in a folded linen napkin.

"Not tonight, but you had tonight free, so… I wanted to see what all the hype is about."

He set his bourbon on the table, then pulled out my chair and handed me a napkin before the hostess handed me the bill of fare.

Peeking over my menu, I watched Jake study his. He read every word, back to front, and scanned the wine list with his finger. I assumed he was seeing if his friend had competitive pairings. I was ready for a refill of wine by the time he set down both menus.

When the waitress arrived, I settled on the black and blue salad—mixed greens with blue cheese crumbles with sliced filet mignon on top. Jake ordered a New York strip, medium rare, with a horseradish topper, two sides to share, and a bottle of wine with two new glasses. Then he returned to our previous conversation.

"So, Peachtree Steak House used to be Peachtree Diner. My uncle took over the front of the house and hired my father to focus on the kitchen. The two of them built it up to the finest steakhouse in Atlanta. It was my dream to follow his footsteps, so I went to CIA in Hyde Park, New York."

"CIA?" I almost choked.

"Culinary Institute of America. I graduated, then worked in a top New York restaurant for two years. When my uncle passed, I came home to help with Peachtree. Then my father passed, and I took out a ton of loans, worked twenty-four-seven in the kitchen and the front of the house to buy the restaurant outright. About three years back, I bought Brasstown Union Cafe from a buddy who wanted out of the business. I have general managers who run those two restaurants. But my baby is Blue Moon, my four-star restaurant I started that from scratch."

"That's the one you're moving into the B&B, right?"

"Not moving, just opening another, smaller, more intimate version. I want to do something farm-to-table, and there's not as much competition in Athens. I've built up a great team, but I'll be the executive chef for a while until we see how it goes. It'll have a Southern theme, and we'll serve seasonal menus. Whatever I find at the market."

"Sounds awesome. I was raised outside Athens, in Bluebelle. I haven't been back in a while, except, of course, to browse through your attic the other day. I'm looking forward to seeing your progress."

"Two different crews are working six days a week. One crew is working on the restoration, and the other is updating the bathrooms and kitchen. I'm hoping we'll be finished by the end of August. You are more than welcome to come by anytime. Visit next week if you'd like; bring your mom if she's up to it."

"Well…" It was as if my life was scripted.

"I know, I know. You have to check your calendar."

"Actually, I do. But I'll let you know as soon as I can."

"Boy, you must be one busy lady with a calendar like that."

I laughed it off. "Not so busy, just a lot of moving parts. My mother did mention wanting to see the mansion."

"Anytime."

I pictured Jake working with his father as the waitress returned with the bottle of wine and presented it to Jake. I mourned the opportunity to work with mine. As soon as the waitress poured the approved wine, I asked, "What was it like working with your father?" I asked.

"Ah, a mixed bag. I miss him now that he's gone; he had cancer. But the glass was always half empty with him." Jake once again stared into the center of his swirling bourbon.

"Sorry, that stinks. My father was almost too positive."

"Well, I say a glass half empty still has at least two fingers left." Jake lifted his glass and gulped down the last of his bourbon.

"Hear, hear." I raised my glass to meet his empty one—clink. That's a good one for my wall. Another sign from my father?

"What about you? Inquiring minds want to know."

"Okay, one question. What one question would your inquiring mind like answered?" My mind raced to all the subjects I didn't want to address.

The restaurant began to fill up and the acoustics became muffled. Jake slipped into the chair next to me. The waitress rushed over to adjust his place setting. "There, that's better," he said, rubbing his chin with two fingers feigning deep thought. "Let's see... one question... what's your favorite childhood memory?"

My heart skipped a beat. Childhood memory and favorite really didn't go together in my world. "Hmm, a childhood memory? Random."

"I know where you live, where you work, what you do for a living, and who you work with. But you said your father was positive, as in past tense."

I rarely let little utterances like that slip. But kudos to Jake for picking up on it. Dinner arrived, then I continued.

"My father passed away when I was nine. Heart attack. But my favorite childhood memory…" To keep the mood light, I mocked Jake by rubbing my chin with two fingers in thought, although I knew which memory was my favorite.

"Yes?"

"My favorite memory was my twelfth birthday when Aunt Liddy took me to Fayetteville, North Carolina, for a Fairy House Festival. We meandered for hours admiring over fifty fairy houses and gardens hidden throughout three acres of forest."

I paused as I sliced the steak on my salad then continued. "Liddy's nurse—Liddy, my aunt, was in a car accident when she was twenty-five and lived the rest of her life in a wheelchair—so she had a live-in caretaker, Martha. I had never, before nor since, spent so much time alone with my aunt than on that day. And I've always been grateful to Martha for excusing herself and staying back at the registration house 'in the air conditioning' so I could push Liddy's chair myself."

Jake topped off my wine glass, and I took a sip. His silence encouraged me to continue.

"I pushed Liddy's wheelchair up and down the well-worn paths in those woods until my calves cramped up. Twinkling lights shone throughout the treetops as we searched for fairy doors along the base of the trees. We chose the perfect spot for a picnic among the fairies, near a little creek and next to a fairy garden quite like one my father and I had built in my backyard. Pure magic."

"Sweet."

"Sorry, that's it," I shrugged, apologizing for not having a more exciting story to tell.

"Hence, a miniature business in the making." Jake leaned forward, looking deep into my eyes.

I should have felt more uncomfortable than I did, and that made me uncomfortable. I needed to get to business. "About your replicas…"

"Can I ask you one other question?" Jake interrupted. He placed his knife and fork on his plate and leaned back in his chair.

"I said one question." But to be nice, go for it. "I wiped the corners of my mouth with my napkin.

"The pearls?"

Caught off guard, my mind raced for a good story to explain why I had recoiled from the pearls I found in the drawer in his attic. I'm allergic? I thought I saw bugs crawling on them? Pearls carried the soul of the past, and I didn't want anything transferred to me? "Pearls? I just don't like them." I put my fork down. I knew I sounded ridiculous and instantly lost my appetite. Who doesn't like pearls?

"That's a thing you know—oystersartisphobia."

"You're making that up." I picked through my salad and let Jake stare at the top of my head.

"I looked it up later that night. A very rare form of OCD. A scientist from the early 1900s had a fear of pearls. He couldn't tolerate them."

"Well, I don't have oyster… whatever." I separated lettuce from blue cheese. "It's just my mother used to wear pearls every single day."

"And?"

I couldn't shake the heaviness in my chest. I wished I could have explained and talked with him about what I was going through, and about how I felt like an awful human being when it came to my mixed feelings about Mary Jane, but it wasn't the time or the place, and actually, he wasn't the right person. He was my client, and I really needed to keep it that way.

I couldn't eat anymore with my stomach clenched from thinking of Mary Jane. A female laugh caught my attention, and I glanced at the couple with their heads leaned in, elbows on the table, holding each other's hands. Then across the room, a heavily built man laughing with his friends distracted me. Squinting my eyes, I strained to hear their muffled voices. A car alarm went off in the distance, snapping me out of the din enveloping me and back to the conversation with Jake.

"…the Randall Mansion Foundation said to give the pearls to my mother. I guess they…"

I interrupted. "I'm sorry. I missed all that. What were you saying?"

"Just talking about the foundation. You okay?"

"I'm fine." I wish he hadn't brought up the pearls. We were having such a nice time. "I just realized how late it was, and I have to drive home, but maybe I should call an Uber."

"How about I drive you home? We can get your car tomorrow. Would you like dessert first?" he asked with a touch of concern as if he was afraid not to offer.

"Let's just finish up here," I said, lifting my nearly empty glass. "After all, it couldn't beat Bella's peach cobbler."

After a few minutes of finishing our wine in silence, I stood. My napkin slipped off my lap, and I stupidly tripped, grabbed the arm of his chair, and almost landed head first in his lap. He steadied me by holding my shoulders until my balance was in check.

"Oh gosh, I'm so sorry," I said, brushing off the arm of his shirt as if I spilled something on it. "I'm good. Just tripped." How many glasses of wine did I drink? Hard to tell since every time I took a sip or two, Jake or the waitress topped off my drink.

Convincing myself it wasn't the wine—Nissa and I could down a couple of bottles in one sitting—it had to be the lack of food or the abundance of stress. Probably both. My nervousness about this evening preoccupied me, and I never thought about eating lunch. The salad I ate for dinner didn't cut it. I needed to go home and eat a loaf of bread.

"Okay?" he asked and pulled out my chair.

"Really, I'm fine." Not really. I didn't like the feeling of not being in control. Between the wine and the conversation, I cursed myself for letting the pearls set me off track.

Jake drove me home, and we agreed to deal with my car in the morning.

"Thank you for dinner and thank you for sharing your stories," he said when we reached my front door.

"You bought dinner, I'm supposed to thank you. So, thank you." I pulled my keys out of my purse.

"Let me know when you can make it out to the B &B."

"Will do."

"And here, let me have those," Jake said and unlocked my door. He stuck his foot out to hold it a bit ajar, then removed just my car key off the ring and tucked it in his pocket. "I'll need that to get your car tomorrow." He handed me the rest of the keys and placed an arm over my shoulder, nudging me toward him.

I closed my eyes out of reflex, inhaled the musky scent of him, and gave into his kiss. This was just what I needed, and he didn't even know it. I knew it was wrong, he had a girlfriend, but it had been a long time since I let myself melt into the arms of another, and I liked it. When I pulled away, I backed into my apartment with one arm straight out, barring him from following me. "We'll talk in the morning," I said and closed the door.

CHAPTER 21

In the morning, Nissa had questions. Lots of questions. But I wasn't in the mood to answer any of them. Bella had taken Mary Jane out for a treatment, and I was grateful we were alone in the house. I wanted only quiet for my throbbing head.

"Hand over the juicy details," Nissa begged.

"I'll think about it but thinking hurts at the moment."

"Well, at least you have a hangover. I'm proud of you. Drink pickle juice."

"What?" I cringed as the words sloshed in my stomach.

"They say pickle juice will cure a hangover."

I dropped my head into my folded arms on my desk. My mornings lately felt as if I had spent the night running a marathon in a wind tunnel. I was as sleep-deprived as I was hungover and didn't know which made me feel worse.

"At least drink plenty of water," Nissa said, "and take several aspirin."

I groaned, "Stop. Shuffling. Those. Papers. And don't talk." Nissa laughed.

I stood up, not lifting my head until the last moment. "I've got to lie down." I crawled into bed and managed another couple of hours of sleep. When I woke, my head was foggy, but not throbbing.

"I made us something to eat." I dropped a paper plate with cinnamon toast and a few bunches of grapes onto Nissa's desk.

"You're quite the chef." Nissa popped a grape into her mouth. "I completed the entire Randall family tree," Nissa said, holding up a multicolored chart. "Jake's mother has a ton of cousins. I wonder if she even knows. I found letters Eloise had saved, and I think a cousin in New Jersey has the family Bible. I might reach out."

I took the folder as the doorbell rang and squeezed my eyes shut, as the throbbing began anew. For a split second, I wished Bella was here to answer it. With one eye open, I handed the chart back to Nissa and rubbed my temples. Maybe I'd take one more short nap after lunch.

"Good morning." Jake handed me a large iced tea from SugarBeans. "Marge says hi."

"I bet that's not all she said, and I bet the rest of it wasn't appropriate."

"How'd you know?"

I attempted my best smile, the pain minimized after I took a large sip of the ice-cold drink. "Thank you, kind sir. This is just what I needed." I beckoned Jake to follow me into the living room and offered him a seat. "And thank you again for dinner last night."

Jake held out my car key. "I should run, one of my guys is out there waiting for me."

"Oh yeah and thank you for driving me home."

"Next time, I'll pick you up, too. How's it going with our little project?" he asked.

"We have plenty of photos from 1861 to 1863 to create the miniatures. The wooden room-boxes have been built, and the floorplans are all designed. So now, we're either in the middle of building furniture and creating accessories, or I've ordered them and am awaiting their delivery."

Nissa came out of the office waving a file. "Did you know your mom has a boatload of cousins, and you have a ton of second cousins?"

"Jake brought you an iced tea." I handed her the tall cup.

"Thanks," Nissa said. "You're sure you and your mom don't want this family tree?" She handed Jake her discovery.

He opened up the file. "She would say they're all strangers, and their parents did nothing to help out my grandmother. My mom used to tell me that Grandma Alice picked out our family, so we didn't get stuck with hers." He handed the file back to Nissa with hardly a glance.

"Thanks for the tea," Nissa said. She waved the folder at Jake and added, "Not interested in the least?"

"Maybe some other time," he said.

As I walked Jake to the door, he asked, "Can I ask you a favor? I need to go to an auction in a few weeks and thought you could help me with the furnishings for the B&B. You'll get paid for your time and expertise, of course."

"Which auction house?"

"Luther Buckley's." Jake handed me the catalog for the upcoming auction.

Nissa and I grinned at each other. "We know it well. It's out in the boonies, but I'd love to help you out." The words were out of my mouth before I knew it. I couldn't help myself, but if I weren't in the world of miniatures, I would be a full-time antiques and art appraiser.

"Great, then come by the mansion sometime this week so we can figure out what I need." Jake reached over my head and waved to Nissa, then squeezed my arm goodbye.

"You two are getting chummy." Nissa grinned.

"It's work."

"Whatever you want to believe," she said, and I followed her to the workroom. "So, he drove you home last night, and you have a hangover…"

"Okay, okay. He kissed me. And I liked it."

"Woot! Woot!" Nissa shouted. "So, it was a date."

"Not really. If I were dating him, I would have been more honest about what was going on in my life. And I couldn't do that. But it was nice to have someone pay attention to me like that."

"So proud of you," Nissa said as she settled back into work, "so proud."

I heard keys jingle in the hallway. Bella, decked out in Elmer Fudd and Porky Pig on florescent-yellow cotton scrubs, met me upon opening the door. She appeared to be holding up the wall with one hand. Four shopping bags hanging off the wrist of her other hand as she stretched to the floor, searching blindly for her keys, which were not near enough for her to grab.

Behind her, Mary Jane leaned on a walker, drained of all color. I didn't know who to help first. In my exhaustion, indifference couldn't raise its wiry head, so I gave Bella a boost to standing, handed her the keys, then slid the oxygen condenser off Mary Jane's shoulder. I guided her through the too many steps to her bed, leading her like an old, weakened dog on a leash.

"What happened to her?" I asked Bella as we covered Mary Jane with a blanket.

"Nothing. This is how she gets when she runs clean out of energy. I keep telling her to slow down." Bella winked at an exhausted Mary Jane.

"What did you guys do today?" It came out so casually, a pang of betrayal for my father almost stopped me mid-question.

"She insisted on going to the grocery with me after her treatment. Said she was feeling just ducky. Well, the duck went kaput." Bella fluffed pillows and pulled the covers under Mary Jane's chin.

I backed out of the room as Bella sat in her chair, picked up Mary Jane's hand, and squeezed it. The compassion Bella shared with Mary Jane wasn't unfamiliar to me. I felt that tenderness for Aunt Liddy while she was ill before her death. I closed the door quietly, feeling Liddy's hand in my own.

I could still hear the beeps measuring Liddy's pulse as it slowed. Sitting bedside in the hospital, I held her hand and watched her chest rise and fall for hours. Pneumonia got the better of her and she barely had the strength to cough. Her eyes hadn't opened for hours, and I knew they likely never would again. Every half an hour, a nurse came in and listened to Liddy's chest and checked her blood pressure.

"It won't be long now," the nurse had said with compassion in her eyes.

I held on to Liddy's hand tighter than ever before, glad her struggle would soon be over. I missed her more and more as the beeps grew slower and slower until they stopped.

"I love you, Liddy," I whispered My shoulders shook, and I hadn't strength left to breathe. The ache of compassion I felt for Liddy, and now for Mary Jane, weighed heavier than any anger I hung on to.

I curled up on my bed for another nap, comforted to know Bella and Mary Jane had returned home safe and sound.

CHAPTER 22

Mary Jane regained most of her energy by the middle of the following week and contributed to the morning chaos. Long gone were the days I could read the local paper and review my morning notes over hot tea at my favorite table in SugarBeans. Now, Bella insisted on brewing fresh tea and whipping up breakfast for anyone around. If Nissa showed up early, which occurred increasingly more often, Bella had breakfast ready for her. Today, Nissa wouldn't be coming for breakfast. She would meet us at the Randall Mansion.

Bella, in Marvin the Martian purple scrubs, had not only cooked breakfast this morning, but she had also packed enough food and drink for a family of six going on a long weekend road trip. I pretended not to see her sit on the top of the massive cooler to shut and lock the lid.

"It's 9:50. We have to go," I sent the alarm from my bedroom doorway as I brushed my hair. Impatient and antsy, I wanted to get going. I had a job to do. I didn't organize this trip for Mary Jane and Bella to have a play date. I only agreed to them coming to show Nissa, Bella, and Jake that I was capable of including Mary Jane in my busy schedule. They had all expressed interest in getting her out of the house and going on a road trip to the mansion. See… I'm flexible.

I had a simple plan: Figure out what Jake needed from the auction house while checking on the progress of the B & B and get Mary Jane out of the apartment for a few hours. As long as Bella came with us, it would be no sweat off my back. I wouldn't have to watch over Mary Jane nor carry the conversation. And hopefully, I'd receive brownie points for my good deed.

Mary Jane had had a couple of good days, so with fingers crossed, the outing seemed promising. I figured it must have taken a lot of time and energy for her to get dressed in a blue-and-white seersucker dress, cinched at the waist. Her low-heeled pumps matched the blue in her dress, a touch of the old Mary Jane. It still looked odd for her to not be in one of her solid jewel-tone shift dresses, but I appreciated her effort.

I half expected to see pearls resting on her collarbone, it was daytime, after all. In the past, the pearls went to the grocery store or spent the day in the garden. It didn't matter. If the sun was up, Mother had pearls around her neck. I was glad not to see them. Did she sell them, like she did the house? Did she give them away to distance herself from the memory of Jonathan?

I really had to get over the pearl thing.

She reached out and took my hand as I helped her stand. Today was the first day she earned points for an attempt at preening. I applauded her attempt at makeup: fuchsia-pink blush and black mascara. Nothing like the days of my youth when Mother's perfectly made-up face could have appeared on a magazine cover, but she tried. To save Mary Jane the steps through the parking lot, she waited with Bella outside the lobby door for me to pick them up. "It's great to get Miss Mary Jane out of the house and into the fresh air," Bella said when I pulled up to the curb. "She sits inside like a chicken in a coop—a nice coop, but a coop all the same."

It took over ten minutes to situate Mary Jane and her oxygen tank in the front seat of my compact Prius, plus squeeze Bella, with her cooler, into the back. I then had to cram Mary Jane's folding walker, just in case she needed it; two sweaters, in case the mansion was too cool; two umbrellas, even though there wasn't a cloud in the sky; my computer case; and three packed purses into the trunk. I should've borrowed Nissa's SUV.

Once all doors slammed shut, and after a dramatic but much-needed exhale, I started the car and wished for a glass of wine. "Everyone good? Bella? Mary Jane?"

"I'm fine, dear. Don't worry about me. I'm the one with the extra oxygen, remember?" Mary Jane said.

I hid my grin. I had grown to appreciate Mary Jane's personality and humor, but I didn't trust her just yet. Her playfulness still seemed a bit foreign.

Behind me, Bella's knees poked into the back of my seat, and she huffed and puffed while she dislodged herself. "Somebody's gone and made this seatbelt too short."

"You okay?" I asked, turning around as Bella settled down with the seatbelt clasp in her hand.

"I've seen photos of the steps going up to that mansion, and I might be needing to borrow that there oxygen tank," Bella said.

"We'll all be fine," I replied to the rearview mirror. "I can drive to the back door. There are only two steps onto the porch."

"Thank the Lord," Bella said with a few grunts as she worked up a sweat, still struggling to get her seatbelt hooked around her ample girth.

Bella kneed me one too many times before we left the parking lot, and I hit the brakes. "This isn't working. Mother, how about if you sit in the back, and we'll let Bella up front? Her legs are…" I caught Bella's eyes in the rearview mirror, "longer."

Bella's seatbelt recoiled with a slam. I got out of the car and went around to help Mary Jane exit. Bella had miraculously jumped out and was attempting toe touches and stretching her limbs as if she had been bound for hours.

I slid the cooler behind my seat then held Mary Jane's arm as she slid into the back seat with her portable tank.

"Lordy me. This is straight out of one of those Three Stooges episodes." Bella dabbed her glistening face with a pink hanky, then stuffed it down her more than ample bosom.

I smiled but wasn't quite as amused as Bella.

Mary Jane laughed, which led to a coughing attack. In between her last few coughs, she said, "Bella, you know better than to make me laugh."

Once we were all settled, I said, "Let's try this again." I started the car at the same time Bella's seatbelt clicked.

Worried Bella would barge into the mansion's construction site giving orders to the workmen about their mess or their fluid intake, I said, "When we get there, I'll need to make sure it's safe enough for you two to walk around. So, expect to wait outside a few minutes for us to figure things out."

"When we get there, I'm going to put out lunch." Bella was clearly thinking about other things.

"Lunch? We just ate breakfast." I shook my head. My simple plan turned out to be anything but simple now.

"Sugar, it's been at least forever since me and your mama had a picnic. Breakfast was almost two hours ago. By the time we get to the mansion, and I get all set, believe you me, it'll be lunchtime. If you don't want to join us, you can go sit with the old lady who fell out the wagon."

"Okay, I'll bite. Who is and what happened to the old lady who fell out the wagon?" I asked as we pulled onto the mansion's street.

"She's the lady who's no longer in the wagon, and therefore, she's staying out of our business," Bella explained.

A coughing fit started in the back seat.

Getting out of the car was a lot easier than getting in. It turned out that Mary Jane's walker, her oxygen tank, and Bella's big cooler were the only things needed for the afternoon.

Nissa skipped out of the back door of the mansion with energy to spare. "What can I help with?" she asked.

I signaled toward Mary Jane. "Can you help Mary Jane up the stairs? If you don't mind, I'll stay here in the car and take a nap."

"Excuse me?" Nissa's head popped up.

I handed the walker over to Nissa. I dug my notebook out of my purse, then walked around the car, having to close all the doors. "Only joking. It's just that it's already been quite a journey. I'm going inside to assess how much of the mansion those two can see."

Nissa elbowed me in the ribs. "Jake is looking especially fine today."

"Stop it. I'm here to work." I hadn't spoken to Jake over the last couple of days, and my simmer had died down. I had thought about our kiss, and then about the blonde I saw him with on his lawn. What kind of man kisses a girl like that when he's seeing someone else? Glad he straightened me out. All business from now on.

With a jerk and a bump, Bella pulled the cooler up the stairs managing to keep all four wheels intact. I was happy to withdraw and look for Jake after watching Bella make a Goldilocks-like ordeal over which Adirondack chair Mary Jane should sit in on the front porch.

Upon entering the kitchen, my heart leaped at seeing Jake's accomplishments. Gone were the avocado-green appliances and floral wallpaper. In front of me, the stainless-steel commercial kitchen sparkled. Above, an exposed-beam pine ceiling framed out the new kitchen ceiling. Wide-plank, natural-looking pine ceramic tiles graced the floor in homage to the original kitchen. An entire wall of exposed brick framed the oversized fireplace, modernized as a wood-burning pizza oven.

Moving on through the dining area and into the front entry, my hand flew up to my mouth. The carpenters had unveiled all the original wood trim. The restored nine-inch baseboards, crown molding, gingerbread fretwork in the archways, and stair rails were all glistening walnut.

"There you are." Jake tucked a small notebook into his back pocket, and a pencil behind his ear. He shot out his arms, ready for a hug.

"It's all so beautiful. I love it," I said with a slow, disbelieving shake of my head and turned sideways for his one-arm hug.

"Yes, I believe we will bring back the old girl's charm," he said, and I could tell he was a little miffed at my greeting.

"And I, for one, am glad you are. Her original beauty warms my heart," I said, still awed by the transformation taking place. "I hope we can find furniture to match the quality of all this wood."

He grabbed a measuring tape off a makeshift sawhorse and plywood table and led me up the stairs. The elevator had yet to be installed, so Mary Jane's and Bella's visit would be limited to the first floor. "The auction is this weekend. Are you still available?"

"Sure. I wouldn't miss it. I printed their newest brochure. They have a lot to offer." I brought a copy of my own blueprints from my miniatures and confirmed my measurements as Jake measured each bedroom, not only the floor space but the wall heights and window frames. I wanted to cover all bases, not knowing exactly what we might find at the auction house.

He handed me a folder. "Here's the file from the interior decorator. These are the Victorian colors and fabrics she'd like to use. But Mom said I should get your opinion for authenticity. Let me know what you think."

"I'm flattered your mom trusts me so much," I said.

"It's obvious you have zeroed in on the time period. Don't be afraid to tell me if you don't like what she picked."

I skimmed through the file. Jake's interior designer seemed to be updated on a modern Victorian design, but Nissa and I could go through it and make sure all was on point.

As we walked into the final bedroom, I remembered an article Nissa showed me the day before. "I read there was a fire in the mansion," I said, "and that's how Eloise Randall died. Rumor had it her husband came home drunk and pushed her into the fireplace. Was that when the family sold the house?"

Jake sat down on the window seat he had just finished measuring. "I knew there was a fire in the house, but it was contained to the parlor. We saw signs of it when we checked behind the walls, and the inspector knew the history. Yes. My great-grandfather came home drunk. And yes, there was a fire, and my great-grandmother died that night. But she wasn't pushed into the fire."

I continued to measure every space I could think of where he might like a piece of furniture as he shared his story.

"He came home, threw another log on the smoldering coals, and passed out nearby. At some point that night, he pulled his shirt off and tossed it. The sleeve caught on fire. Eloise must have smelled smoke because, somehow, she woke up and got him out of the room. Her dress caught on fire, and the two of them ran out of the house. Probably, she rolled on the ground, and by the time the fire department came, my grandmother had had a heart attack right there in the front yard. They took her away in an ambulance, barely conscious, and she passed away later that night."

"Oh my." I recoiled at the thought of it then realized he knew more about his family than he had let on.

"I know, right?" he said. "I'm sure if any passers-by saw them, it looked like my grandmother died in a fire because her dress was burned and all."

"Does your mom know?"

"I told her, and she said it was just part of our sordid family history. Proves how crazy they were, and that Grandma Alice knew what she was doing when she never went back."

"It's all so interesting because your family's history is right here under one roof. Too bad you didn't grow up under it."

"I'll be here from now on, making new, hopefully less sordid family memories."

"Are you planning on living here in the B&B?" I had never thought about where he actually laid his head each night.

"Right now, I stay in my old bedroom at my mother's house when I'm in town. She's right around the corner. But before you go judging me, I own a beautiful condo on Phipps Boulevard in Atlanta."

"They say be wary of thirty-year-old men living in their mother's basements," I joked.

"No worries, my bedroom's on the second floor."

"Well, in that case, good thing!" I said, laughing at his quick humor. "Let's go check out lunch. Bella packed a boatload."

As we rounded the corner of the wraparound porch, Bella was serving lunch to not only Nissa and Mary Jane but six rugged, tool-belted carpenters who were all commenting on her unbelievably delicious dill-infused deviled eggs.

After we all enjoyed a delicious lunch of chicken salad sandwiches on rye, and old-fashioned jam bars with a hint of rum. Mary Jane and Bella peeked into the kitchen, dining room, and parlor. Several hours later than I had initially planned, we packed up and filed back into my car.

With dual snoring as my background music on the ride home, I mentally scheduled what needed to be accomplished in my workshop over the next two days. I had to finish five miniature bed frames and insert glass panels into the matching set of curio cabinets for the parlor, all so I could take time off to help Jake at the auction.

CHAPTER 23

The ride to the auction house was comfortable as Jake and I traveled past cloud covered fields and forests with a country music backdrop. To keep my excitement down, I played the alphabet game with the few billboards and license plates we passed. I percolated with impatience, anticipating the activity at Luther Buckley's warehouse. I told Jake about my findings in the catalogue which were hopefully as perfect in person as they looked online. He just nodded, whistling to whichever song played on the radio and went along with whatever I said. I wasn't sure if he was clueless or if he couldn't care less.

The rusty warehouse smell and the rhythmic jumble of the auctioneer's chant over the din of want-to-be buyers flooded my senses. Heaven, sweet heaven. Oh, how my father would have loved this. He would have been scouring for mid-century items but would have been just as excited as me about the Victorian pieces.

The sounds drew me in as I drifted around the corner and peeked into the showroom. The many white rectangular paddles with black numbers randomly popping up above the heads of anxious bidders ramped my eagerness. From behind a podium at the front of the large room, a tall man in a rumpled grey suit stood pointing in all directions encouraging buyers to up their bids on a 1972 Ford Bronco.

Fond memories of traveling to auctions with my father, usually to buy artwork, rushed in. I stood immersed until the gavel hit the podium, and the auctioneer shouted, "Sold!"

Adrenaline pumped through my veins. I turned to speak to Jake, only to find he wasn't behind me. Back in the lobby, I spotted him at the registration desk, laying down his credit card and getting our two paddles. I rubbed my palms together in anticipation.

"Hi, Miss Edwards. Is Miss Fayette with you today?"

Jake regarded me with questioning eyebrows as the man behind the desk addressed me. "You two know each other?"

"Hi, Sam. I'm not here on business today. Today, I get to spend his money." Without thinking about it until after I did it, I introduced Jake then grabbed his hand, dragging him away toward an entrance labeled FURNITURE. "Nissa and I work as appraisers for several of the Georgia auction houses. They hire us to research and appraise antique pieces from time to time. You didn't think my major was in dollhouses, did you?"

"Now it makes sense why you knew so much about what was in my attic."

"Exactly."

I pulled out my auction catalog with the notes I had written the night before after Nissa and I scoured the internet for information on pieces I was interested in. I had only twenty-five minutes to race through the sections, find the lot numbers I had circled in the brochure, and show them to Jake. "Come on, slowpoke. We haven't got much time."

"Okay, okay. Give me the list." He laughed.

I handed him the brochure and found the first lot. No. 104. It contained two separate bedroom sets; one was mahogany with a four-poster, canopied, queen-size bed alongside a matching armoire and vanity. The second was a distinctly Victorian walnut headboard and footboard embellished with carved floral reliefs, which took my breath away. It coordinated with a man's wardrobe, which wasn't a perfect match but made from the same beautiful walnut. It had a burl wood in-lay on its flat-panel doors with the letter "A" intricately carved in each one. I reached up and brushed my fingers across the letter. It didn't matter that it wasn't an M for Martin or an R for Randall, it was an A for the original family who took obvious care of the closet that contained their belongings.

"This wardrobe has a history, well, they all do, but this family initial is special. I love that. This lot is in great condition and would be perfect for the B&B."

"That's why I brought you along. And this one lot covers two of the five bedrooms."

"The chaise lounge, the one we found in your attic, would go perfectly with the walnut set. Once we, I mean, you, have fixed it up."

"And provided we catch the winning bid."

"I'll make a note, so your decorator knows which bedroom set the chaise should go with." There was no doubt in my mind we would win the bid for that particular set. "Come on, we've got to get a move on and check these other items before they go on the block."

Figuring it was the best way for him to keep up with me, I hooked my arm through his as we raced through the rest of the lots.

I gave some items the once-over and carefully inspected others to determine which furniture would fit best in the last three bedrooms to make each room its own Victorian experience. With five minutes to go until they started auctioning off furniture, we raced through a room full of original artwork and figured out there would be more than enough pieces to choose from.

I bubbled with energy. I loved the vivacity of an auction and hurried to get seats near the back. "The best spot to see who's up front bidding against me."

Jake followed close behind, carrying a cup in each hand and a giant pretzel between his teeth. I glanced over my shoulder at him, excited for the bidding to start. He shook his head at my excitement.

"What?" I asked.

"Having fun, aren't you? Like spending other people's money? Sorry, no tea." Jake said as he handed me a coffee.

I took a swallow, not loving the cream and sugar, and wishing it was tea, but appreciated its warmth as thunder echoed throughout the warehouse, silencing the crowd.

"I'm having a ball. Usually, when Nissa and I get a request to audit incoming antiques, no one's in the building, and the silence lends itself to the imagination and the ghosts who come with the furniture. Now with all the people, all the energy… I forgot how much I loved live auctions."

"Glad to accommodate you, but remember, we have a budget," he laughed. He stretched his legs out under the chair in front of him. "I'll just sit back and watch the pro."

"Go right ahead." I sat on the edge of my seat with both paddles in hand. As excited as I was to bid on these beautiful pieces, I wished my father was by my side. I imagined his discussion of the wood's beauty and the quality of the workmanship from the previous century. "But you'll miss out on all the fun."

"Somehow, I don't think so. It will be fun just watching you in action," Jake said, extending his arm over the back of my chair and leaned back in his.

For the next sixty minutes, paddles popped up and down, some waved in the air for attention. The crowd thinned out as people won or didn't win the items they came to bid on.

I explained to Jake that things were getting serious. "The more expensive and larger lots are coming out now. The bidders still here are hardcore and know what they're doing. Watch how quickly the auctioneer raises the bid increments. He'll slow them down and narrow the increments as he gets to the true value of the items. He knows that we know what's what and will respect our time and intelligence."

I sat on the edge of my seat, focused and determined to get what Jake needed for the B&B. When the last lot came out, I was exhausted and happy I didn't need to bid on it. Silence signaled the end of the furniture auction. Taking the pen and brochure out of Jake's hand, I scanned my notes.

"We got some great deals," I said and leaned back, fanning myself. "I'm so glad we got that double lot. It was my favorite."

"You surprised me when you let Lot 223 go, the walnut vanity with the tri-fold mirror? I enjoyed watching that battle."

"It would have matched the walnut armoire, but that old battle-ax would have gotten in the last bid no matter what I did. So, I thought I'd drive the price up and stick it to her."

"Bwahaha, you're evil."

"Well, I had to get revenge for her screwing me on that gorgeous, four-piece mahogany set. I wasn't planning to bid over $4,500, but she pushed it to $4,800. Still a good deal, though."

"Five thousand for the one desk was a bit much, don't you think?" He pointed to the circled sideboard in the brochure.

"Are you kidding? That's not just any desk… It's a mint-condition, seven-foot-long Smith and Kentor rosewood sideboard with boxwood and satinwood inlays. It's the perfect hostess desk, the pièce de résistance to greet your guests when they enter your four-star restaurant. It's gorgeous! Anyway, we made killer deals on most of the other pieces."

"If you say so. Get ready for round two. The art is coming out next. We have a lot of walls to fill." Jake gave my arm a quick squeeze. I was glad he was enjoying himself because I was having a ball.

I got into my bidding position—sitting on the edge of my seat, paddle gripped in my lap, ready for action. I watched the auction team set out a large easel and bring out the next item up for bid: a large, semi-abstract painting of a Hawaiian coastline in muted colors by Reuben Tam.

"Shoot!" I said as my cell phone chimed. I wasn't bidding on the Tam painting, but I didn't need a distraction. I dug through my purse and pulled out my phone. Bella? What on earth would Bella want? She knows I'm at the auction and wouldn't be home until late tonight. If she had a shopping list for me, it would have to wait until tomorrow.

The auctioneer yammered, and people around us bid away when I half-heartedly answered my phone. "Hello?"

I dropped my paddle into my lap to cover my other ear. Between the auctioneer and the pounding rain on the warehouse roof, I heard only a portion of what Bella was saying. And though I couldn't tell from specific words, I could tell from her tone that something was wrong.

My panic must have shown on my face because Jake immediately snapped up the paddles and stood. He reached behind as he turned and clasped my hand, then guided me out the row. He made excuses as we sidestepped over a few slightly peeved people trying to get in a bid.

"Hold on, Bella," I said and held the phone by my side as we hurried out of the auction hall. Once in the registration lobby, I found a bench and plugged my left ear with a finger. "Tell me again, Bella. What happened?"

CHAPTER 24

Unsure of the feelings Bella's phone call conjured up, I took a moment to catch my breath, then found Jake confirming our purchases and informing the auction house manager he would call to make arrangements for delivery. Wrestling with my coat as I approached them, my mind raced through the stark possibilities. I gathered from Bella's phone call Mary Jane had been admitted to the hospital, but I thought I also heard her say she was going to be fine. But was she, or was Bella trying to placate me?

Anything medical was Bella's domain. It's not like I could do anything for Mary Jane, nor do I think she would want me to. Why should I feel as if I should drop everything because of one phone call? Bella's with her. My mind resembled the inside of a tumbling dryer.

Jake thanked the man then helped me pull the sleeve of my jacket right side out and slipped it over my arm. He hooked his elbow with mine as we raced past the corridors of rooms filled with beautiful antiques.

When we reached the front door, I wished I hadn't left my umbrella in the truck. I harrumphed at the downpour the parking lot's streetlamps highlighted like sheets of glass. On a good day, with no traffic and no rain, we were well over an hour away from the hospital. Tonight, it could take forever.

"Maybe we should wait it out? It's a torrential downpour and look at those trees blowing." I said, pulling Jake back from the door.

"Thought I heard you say your mom's in the hospital?" He raised an eyebrow in question.

"She is. But Bella's a bit of a drama queen. I'm sure Mary Jane's okay. What can I do for her, anyway?"

He turned me by the shoulders to face him. "Where is this coming from? Your mom is being treated for lung cancer. I doubt she's okay. I saw how alarmed you were when you got that call. Are you just trying to be polite?"

Having concern for Mary Jane surprised me too, but then, reality set in. Mary Jane didn't need me. She had Bella. She hadn't needed me for over twenty years. How can I explain that to him? I knew what he was thinking—how could a daughter not worry that her mother's in the hospital? His look bore through me as if I were the serial killer Rhoda Penmark in *The Bad Seed*. I had avoided talking about my mother with Jake, so I understood his confusion. But I'm not a bad daughter. I had let my mother move in with me, hadn't I?

I cast my eyes down to my Ferragamo ballet flats, an expensive treat I had bought myself after a project earned us a bonus, and they became my excuse not to go out in the rain. With humor, I said, "But my shoes..."

"Listen, I have a big truck with big wheels. It can handle this weather." Jake took off his shoes and held them inside his coat under his arm. He stroked a hand down my coat sleeves.

I laughed and the deep pressure calmed my nerves. "Okay, Mr. Monster Truck, but go slow."

I tucked my shoes under my arms, buttoned up my coat, and pulled my collar up over my head. The two of us ran out into the pelting storm, our shadows like characters on stilts in a Mardi Gras parade. By the time we reached the truck, our pants and jackets needed wringing out, but my Ferragamos and his Cole Haans were dry.

We shook off what raindrops we could as we jumped into the front seats. My eyes met his, and I nodded my thanks, still feeling bad we had to leave the auction. He was a good man.

"At least our hair is dry. Buckle up," he said and started the truck.

Before I could buckle up, I pulled a dented, sopping wet folder out from beneath me.

"Oh shit. I ruined your decorator's folder."

"Well, if she's any good, she didn't give me the only copy." He took the folder from me and tossed it on the floor behind us with our shoes.

I stiff-armed the dash when the truck hydroplaned, even though the already flooded parking lot limited our speed.

"We got this," he said, patting the dashboard and navigating through the rising tide.

"Yeah, a four-wheeling adventure," I said with no enthusiasm at all. I would have waited out the storm in the auction house if I were here by myself. I wouldn't have rushed out. I would have stalled, so I didn't have to go through what I felt now— unwillingly feeling closer to and caring about Mary Jane only to have her reject me when I showed up at the hospital.

The streetlights were few as we inched our way through the muddy, pot-holed country roads. The wind whipped and whistled, and Jake's white-knuckled grip on the wheel proved he was fighting competing forces.

He leaned over the steering wheel and squinted, trying to see through the downpour. The wipers swished back and forth so fast they created rooster tails as if nine-foot waves hit us. Up ahead were the tail lights of a car traveling at a snail's pace. He raised his voice over the deafening lashing of the storm. "Sorry. Can't go any faster."

Leaning forward, I also squinted straight ahead, trying to see beyond the limited brightness of our headlights. A knot grew in my throat as we got closer to a town and crawled through each of its three blinking red lights. This was ridiculous. I grabbed my phone to call Bella. Unless Mary Jane was on her deathbed, we needed to pull over and wait out the deluge. I dialed Bella several times, but none of the calls went through. Either she had shut off her phone, or this storm was far worse than I thought.

The coffee I drank earlier turned rancid in my stomach. Why on earth would I pick today to start drinking coffee? And with cream, to boot. My left leg bobbed Elvis-style as I drummed my fingers on my thigh. I kept my right hand on the passenger door handle, just in case.

"This is silly," I said. My head and my heart were at odds. Opposing thoughts tore at my gut. I didn't want to care about Mary Jane, and yet, something inside me did.

"What's silly?"

"Sorry, thinking aloud." I settled back into my seat, pressing my knees together.

"No, seriously. What's silly?" He raised his voice over the hammering rain.

"I'm sorry our shopping spree got ruined. And it's silly we are driving in this storm."

"But it's an emergency."

"I know, but... you don't understand. Why should I be upset about an already-dying woman going to the hospital?"

Jake gave me a curious look, making me feel like the mean girl I was. "Maybe because she's your mother?"

"I didn't mean... she didn't care about me for twenty years," I said and mumbled the rest of my sentence with my face in my hands. "I don't want to start caring about her now."

With false confidence, I crossed both arms across my chest. In the window, reflections of my tears blended with the raindrops sliding down the other side of the glass.

"Your mother told me it took some convincing to let her move in with you. She also said you two hadn't been very close. I waited for you to bring it up, but you're whopping good at not talking about yourself."

"You don't understand, Jake. There are specific reasons we don't have a relationship."

"I'm sure there are. But it seems she's trying to make amends." He slowed the truck down from a crawl to a creep.

"She more or less guilted me into letting her move in. And it's hard to see her so sick when we have a lot to sort out. It's complicated. Can we please talk about this later?"

Silence took over. My nostrils flared. How dare Mary Jane talk about my private life to a client. What gave her the right? I leaned my forehead on the side window and doodled in the condensation formed by my breath. What else had Mary Jane told him? She better not have said one bad word about my father. This is my story to tell Jake, not hers.

I glanced over at him. The set of his jaw made it clear he respected my request for silence. "I'm sorry. It's just that—"

Headlights glared from the street to the right as a sedan whipped in front of us, fishtailing, cutting us off.

"Watch out!" I screamed.

Jake bored down on the brakes as the menacing taillights took off down the road in front of us.

I froze solid with fright. Bands of bright colors flashed through the windshield as our truck spun in circles. I squeezed my eyes, anticipating the crash.

Jake jerked the wheel to the right, and the passenger side hit a guardrail, scraping and screeching until he brought the truck to a stop facing the direction we had just come from, staring straight into headlights of oncoming cars. "What an asshole! Are you kidding m—"

Dizziness, weakness, and nausea struck me all at once. I shoved open the truck door, smashing it into the guardrail. I leaned out, the seatbelt tightened on my chest, and I heaved, unable to avoid the running board. By the time I finished, the rain had soaked through my hair and saturated the inside of the truck. Closing the door, I sat up, my heart pounded as though it would explode, and I squirmed from the water streaming down my back.

Jake pulled a hand towel out from underneath his seat. "Are you all right?" he asked wide-eyed.

"Yeah, a little woozy." I wiped the corners of my mouth with the edge of the towel. Tears trickled down my wet face. Driving in the storm wasn't a good idea to begin with, and now it was because of me Jake had wrecked his truck.

"Sure you're okay? You don't look so good." Jake asked again as he shut off the truck and unhooked his seatbelt. He twisted and arched, reaching into the back. "I've got another jacket back here somewhere."

The sound of three loud raps made him jerk back into his seat. An older man in a bright yellow Gorton Fisherman slicker and rain hat stood with his hand shading his eyes, peering into the driver's-side window.

Jake lowered his window down an inch.

"You all right in there? Anyone hurt?" The man asked and held up his cell phone. "Should I call an ambulance?"

"No, no, we're fine. Thank you," Jake rolled the window down a bit farther even though the rain spit in at him.

"You sure?" The man stood on his tiptoes and peered deeper into the truck cab. "Ma'am?"

"I'm good," I responded with a little wave and a fake smile.

"No worries, sir," Jake said, pulling the seatbelt over his chest. "I made hamburger out of one side of my truck, but we're both okay. We'll take it easy from here on out. You best get yourself out of this rain."

The man saluted Jake and ran across the street to his car.

"Where do you find people like that?" I wondered aloud.

"Yep, nice of him to stop in this storm." Jake started the truck and turned the heater on full blast. With no cars in sight, he made a U-turn and got back on the roadway.

The starless night was of no help when sections of streetlights weren't glowing. With no taillights to follow, we had to trust that the road existed beyond our headlights. We passed several cars pulled over to the side, but Jake kept a slow and steady pace, watching out for cross traffic.

The drive took forever. It was well over two hours since Bella had called me from the hospital. I had no new information about Mary Jane's condition. Once again, exhaustion allowed my emotions to overtake my logic, and my heart heaved. I tried to call Bella again, but to no avail.

The rest of the drive was silent except for the pummeling wind and rain. My concern for Mary Jane made me anxious. Never had I any feeling for Mary Jane other than indifference and contempt. What was I supposed to do with concern?

I would betray my father if I gave into the worry, but I'd fail myself if I didn't. Liddy would not approve of the way I treated my mother, that was for sure. I had never been an unkind person, nor even raised my voice to anyone. Putting more energy into not being myself around Mary Jane was costing me.

Jake pulled into the hospital's well-lit parking lot. With my shoes in hand, I jumped from the car as he pulled under the canopy in front of the emergency room. I flew through the squealing automatic doors, attempting to don my shoes as I ran. The reception desk was straight ahead. I spat out my mother's name before I even reached it.

"Mary Jane Edwards?" I asked. I removed my dripping jacket as I approached the desk validating the bright yellow WET FLOOR signs scattered throughout the lobby.

"ID please," a nurse with cat's-eye glasses said and held out her hand, palm up.

"Shoot! Didn't bring my purse in. I'm her daughter, Tina, rather, Christina Edwards."

"Yes, ma'am, you're right here on the list." Nurse Cat's-eye peered over her rims.

"Well?" I asked.

"I still need to see a license or something. Hospital policy. Can't be too careful."

"Ugh…" I did an about-face and slid. I regained my balance by throwing my arms in the air and my coat across the lobby. The electric doors scraped open in time for a dripping-wet Jake to watch my coat settle near his feet. He scooped it up and held my purse over his head like a winner's trophy.

"My hero." I grabbed the purse and pulled out my wallet. Other items tumbled out as I rushed back to the registration desk.

I headed toward the doors Nurse Cat's-eye pointed to, and Jake handed me the pen, travel pack of tissues, and tube of hand lotion that had been in my purse.

"Breadcrumbs," he said with a quirky grin.

I stuffed the items back in where they tumbled from. "This way."

Jake followed me through the heavy door, into an elevator to the third floor. As the door slid opened, Jake grabbed my hand, and we headed down a long hallway.

CHAPTER 25

"Room 324... 3-2-4... 3-2-4..." I scanned the numbers on each door, looking for Mary Jane's room.

I took a deep breath before we entered the low-lit, pale green hospital room. The room was empty. "Oh, no. No. No." My knees weakened, and I hung onto Jake's arm, almost pulling us both to the floor. My heart raced toward panic.

He quickly threw his other arm around my waist and held me up. "Maybe we have the wrong room."

"She said Room 324. I'm sure it was 324." I was too late. Mary Jane never got to tell me what she so desperately needed to tell me, and it was all because of my stubbornness. All these weeks living together, and I never gave her a chance. I reached for the wooden chair next to the vacant bed, and Jake lowered me into it.

"Let me go find a nurse," Jake said and tried to release my hand.

"I'll come with you," I said. The last time I was in a place such as this, with Liddy, I had never felt so alone. "I don't want to be—"

Bella's laugh came barreling from down the hall.

"Laughter's good," Jake said.

My body softened, and I agreed. "Laughter is always good." My tears flowed in relief as I ran up to Bella. "Where's Mom?" I asked, wiping my eyes.

"And here's the young missy now. Miss Tina, Mr. Jake, this here's Candice. Nurse Candice. She's been taking good care of your mother."

"And where is she?" I held my hand out to greet the nurse.

Candice had a welcoming smile and a comforting bedside voice. "They took your mom for X-rays. She'll be back any minute."

"So, what the heck happened?" I asked.

"It's raining harder than a cow pissing on a flat rock," Bella said, pointing at the ceiling.

"You don't have to tell us," Jake agreed and grinned at me apologetically. "But what did happen to Mary Jane?"

"She got up in the pitch dark 'cause her big old oxygen tank was dead. Guessing that's when we lost the electricity. She tripped and fell. I couldn't get the light turned on and had to rummage up a flashlight. Sorry for the dumped-out drawers when you get home, Sugar. Don't you fret none, I'll pick it all up and organize things better when I get back."

"Mary Jane?" I said, rolling my wrist to get Bella back on track.

"Oh, yes. Well, Miss Mary Jane was hollering like a stuck cat by the time I got back with the flashlight. So, I called 911."

"How hurt is she?" I asked and realized my legs still felt shaky and returned to the chair.

"She banged up her shoulder good and got a few other scrapes and bumps. But she'll be fine," Bella said.

"The cancer? Did it cause this?" I asked the nurse.

"Her cancer is her cancer. This was an accident. One that could've been a lot worse. But, no, the cancer didn't cause this, but it could cause a setback in her healing."

I nodded my head, then caught Jake's eye and tilted my head toward the door. Out in the hallway, I said, "If you want to go home, I understand. I can get a ride home with Bella or call Nissa."

"It's late. Better not call Nissa," Jake said. "Let's wait until your mother returns. Then we'll decide. You still might not have any electricity at home."

He had a point. I shivered in my damp clothes. "I'm so sorry about this, about your truck, about missing the rest of the auction. I'm so sorry you got dragged into my family drama."

"Let's get you a blanket." Jake scanned the hallway for anyone in the vicinity. "None of this was your fault. We're both okay. Accidents happen. It's just a truck, and I can get it fixed. And there'll be many more auctions. You were a big help. We still have time before the B&B opens. As far as family drama—" Looking over my shoulder, Jake raised his hand as a nurse's assistant approached, and asked for a couple warm blankets. Turning back to me, he said, "As far as family drama, you don't own the market share. We all have skeletons in our closets."

"You're sweet for saying so. I'll wait here for Mary Jane. You find us some hot tea. No coffee, please."

He picked up my hand and squeezed it. "It's all going to be fine," he said and let his hand linger in mine a moment.

Voices grew louder as Mary Jane was wheeled into the room in a wheelchair appeared from around a corner. Relieved to see her, I stepped out of the way as they rolled into room 324. Her eyes, rimmed in what looked like a dark pink eyeliner, lifted at the corners when she saw me. The orderly locked her wheelchair in place and gestured an "all-yours" to Nurse Candice.

Bella wedged herself between Candice and the wheelchair and helped Mary Jane to her feet. As soon as Bella finished fluffing pillows and tucking in the sheets around Mary Jane, Nurse Candice took over. She checked the IV, hooked up the monitors for Mary Jane's heartbeat and blood pressure, and placed a clamp on one of Mary Jane's fingers.

"This is to check the oxygen level in her blood," Nurse Candice explained, even though no one asked. She hung a clipboard of stats on the foot of the bed. "I'll go see what I can find out. You got her, Bella?"

The nurse's assistant appeared with two warm blankets and threw one around my shoulders. Not wanting to interrupt Bella spoon-feeding Mary Jane one chunk of crushed ice at a time, I hung back in the corner. She removed a strand of hair stuck to Mary Jane's thin, dried lips and curled it behind her ear. My heart skipped a beat.

"You'll be all right, Sweetie," Bella spoke into Mary Jane's ear. "They got you all doped up, so you don't feel much. But you're going to be just fine."

Again, witnessing the care Bella showed for Mary Jane left a lump in my throat. I wished I could provide the same tenderness and was sad that it wasn't naturally inside me to offer.

Jake returned with a hot tea for everyone. "And I brought you some saltines. I expect your stomach is empty."

I didn't need the reminder, but the crackers were just what my raw stomach called for, along with the warm tea.

Mary Jane sputtered and lifted her right hand, signaling she had had enough ice chips. "Thank you," she whispered in a dry, tired voice.

"Good news," declared Nurse Candice as she joined the group surrounding Mary Jane's bed. "Nothing broken. A dislocated shoulder, a few big bruises, and a bump on her head."

"Nothing we can't handle at home," Bella said and slid her hand behind Mary Jane's upper back, lifting her forward to fluff up the pillows she had sunk into. Mary Jane thanked her with a nod.

I cleared my throat, feeling I'd interrupted something very intimate and asked, "When can she come home?"

Mary Jane's eyebrows raised, and Bella's lips twitched. The two exchanged a glance then returned their attention to me and I realized what I said.

Bella broke the awkward silence. "She'll be home in no time, Sugar."

CHAPTER 26

Bella had gone to see her cousin in Valdosta, and I took it upon myself to visit Mary Jane in rehab where she was working on her balance as well as her shoulder. Each evening, even if it was for just ten minutes at a time, I stayed long enough to say hi, but short enough not to delve into any real conversation. I planned to get as much done on the B&B miniatures as we could while they were gone.

"It's awfully quiet around here without Bella and your mom," Nissa said.

"Especially without Bella," I said. A pink piece of paper on the wall caught my attention: *The quieter it becomes, the more you can hear.*

"How is she doing?" Nissa asked.

"Bella?"

"No, silly, your mother." Nissa threw a paintbrush at me.

"I saw her last night. Her arm is much better, but she's still a bit weak. She should be back in a few days." I slid a baking sheet toward Nissa. "It's been great having my kitchen back so I could bake some miniature polymer clay pots. I'm not sure when I could have gotten a chunk of time long enough in the kitchen between Bella cooking meals and cleaning up."

The mini carpets, which I designed and special-ordered from a woman in Omaha who made them to scale by hand-hooking or weaving wool, arrived. I spread them over the wide pine plank floors in each of the replicas. With the interiors of the room boxes almost complete, I could focus more on the accessories and furniture—the first being a two-and-a-half-inch-wide walnut blanket chest needing staining. Once it dried, I cracked open the lid of the chest, placed a little woolen blanket inside, leaving just a corner hanging over the edge. It was beyond adorable.

"Thank God we're ahead of things." We had only a few weeks until the grand opening, and time was becoming a factor. "Sounds like Mary Jane might need a little more help when she gets home than before she fell. I'll be glad Bella will be back to help."

"You sound like you miss her," Nissa said as she touched up the wallpaper where the seams met.

"I feel bad for her. To fall and get hurt in the middle of cancer treatments must suck." I forced my mind to focus on the job at hand. "Jake sure got more than he bargained for when he hired us."

"Mr. Distraction? What do you mean?" Nissa baited.

"I've become quite the handful, plus now he has to get his truck fixed. Anyway, he said he's gotten a lot accomplished in the last couple of days."

"Like what? Wait, you've been talking to him?"

"He called to check in on Mary Jane. Anyway, I guess it doesn't hurt to have friends in Athens. He got the last of his permits super-fast. I can only assume City Planning and Zoning is very interested in Jake bringing one of his restaurants and its commerce to town. It'll be beautiful. The other day he gave me his interior designer's plans." I hunted through my file drawer and pulled out the remains of the sodden folder.

"I thought *you* were his interior designer," Nissa teased.

"Ha. I'm just helping him with some furniture and accessories per his mother's request. The interior designer is doing wall colors and fabrics." I handed over the torn, wavy, and crinkled, water-stained file.

"What the heck happened to this?" Nissa pulled out the wrinkled papers, pictures, and paint samples, then tossed the manila folder in the garbage.

"The decorator calls her design Modern Victorian."

Nissa pulled out one wallpaper sample. "I love this one. This oversized antique floral print is gorgeous. And this one here has a repeat in grey and white on velvet. These are great modern examples of the Victorian era." Nissa flipped through the rest of the swatches." I'd say she's pretty good at what she does."

I handed Nissa a wallpaper sample of grey and cream heirloom roses that had slipped out of the pile. "I can picture this room. Imagine the natural pine floor and whitewashed trim, the ornate bedroom set in walnut, and all the textiles in dove-grey and white—rugs, drapes, cushions, and pillows. Wait, and JW Waterhouse's first *Ophelia* hanging on the wall."

Nissa let out a low whistle. "I know Jake's putting a lot of dough into this B&B, but I'm pretty sure he can't afford a Waterhouse."

"A girl can dream, can't she?"

In typical Nissa fashion, she organized all the samples in clear sheet protectors and in a floppy three-ring binder, then placed a large, thick dictionary on top to hopefully flatten out the papers.

Getting back to touching up the miniature geraniums, ferns, philodendron, and maranta plants made from felt and nylon fabrics, I glued them into the terra-cotta or hand-painted porcelain-like pots I had created from the polymer clay. There were also two small glass and lead greenhouse terrariums, which I had ordered from my favorite miniature shop in London, displaying the tiniest plants I'd ever created. "What do you think about these?"

"They'll do," Nissa said without even a glance.

"They'll more than just do." I hit her on the shoulder.

Nissa poked through the plants. "Kidding. I love them all. The blue-and-white vases look like real Chinese porcelain." She placed two of the potted plants in the corner of the miniature parlor. "Liddy would have loved these."

That pleased me. The weekends spent making miniature accessories and objects d'art with Liddy, back when my life revolved around fairy houses, warmed my heart. I missed her so much and the days we spent forming polymer clay into vases, flowerpots, dishes, lamps, and whatever else was needed for my fairy houses. I don't remember missing Mary Jane when she left all those years ago. I was young, angry, and confused. Did I not miss her, or had I not let myself miss her? "I keep thinking how much longer," I said, leaning back in her chair.

Nissa put down the miniature potted plant. "Longer?"

"I'm drained. My life's a roller coaster. Every morning I wake up thinking today's the day Mary Jane and I will have the talk. I start out thinking, it's okay, no big deal, I can handle it. But the same hostility keeps bubbling up every time I see her. We've been so distant for so long. It's all I know how to be." I snapped the hair elastic on my wrist, making sure I could feel something. "And now, I don't know... now that I know her a little bit, I think it's all going to be much harder on both of us."

"Maybe you should take the time to hear her out and just get it over with."

"When she was in that hospital room, lying on that cold, uncomfortable-looking hospital bed…"

So far, the arrangement of Mary Jane managing her treatments while in my apartment worked out okay. What an odd conflict. To have my mother, ill, here in my own home, and there was nothing I could do to help her. Yet, the millions of times I accused her of not lifting a finger to help my father when he lay across his desk dying echoed in my mind. But this was different. I was doing something. I was doing a lot. Mary Jane was living in my house, wasn't she? My moral compass kept my anxiety alive and well. "Never mind," I said. "Part of me feels that whatever she has to say to me she can bring it up or not."

Nissa pulled out a tissue and handed it to me. "What about looking at it from the other side? Won't it be better if you two can have a few peaceful weeks or months together now rather than regret not having them after she's gone? What if she doesn't make it through her treatments this time?"

I looked at my wall, hoping for an answer from beyond. *You can never go back and start a new beginning, but you can always start today and make a new ending.* My wall never failed. Thanks, Dad.

"Well, you have a couple of days to think about it anyway." Nissa grabbed her paintbrush and went back to her wallpaper.

I stared straight ahead out the window into the bright, endless sky beyond. I'd had my life under control all these years, but only because I'd never had to face my mother. I didn't have the resources to deal with the challenge of her coming back into my life, only strategies to deal with her absence. Strategies for her return never entered the discussion in any of my therapy sessions. Years of therapy had failed me.

I cradled the perfect image of Baby Jane, the doll in the photos, in the palm of my hand, which I had brought into existence. I had squeezed her with charcoaled fingers, lightly stepped on her dress in the asphalt parking lot and swung her by her wavy blonde mohair curls until loose strands fell out. I was determined my Baby Jane would look as real and well-loved as the original.

How I wished I was sitting at Aunt Liddy's kitchen table, adding a history to this tiny doll. Life played out so much more simply back then. The contrasts between Liddy and Mary Jane ping-ponged back and forth in my mind. When I thought of one, the other wasn't far behind, as if both haunted me. Some of the tears on Baby Jane's pinafore were real.

Over the next several days, Nissa and I painted, sewed, hammered, and glued. The parents' bedroom, two little girls' rooms, a nanny's bedroom, the nursery, a parlor, a kitchen, and a dining room materialized on our worktable, each a replica of the photos dug out of the boxes from the Randall Mansion's attic.

The doorbell rang. I asked Nissa to answer it so I could continue to hold a stained-glass Tiffany-style lamp shade to its base as the glue dried.

"Look who I found loitering in the hallway," Nissa said as she entered the workroom with Jake at her heels.

"Hey," I greeted him. My wave consisted of lifting both arms with a tiny lamp between my fingers.

Jake walked to the workbench. "Look at these. Unbelievable. I can't wait for my mother to see these."

"She can come by anytime," I said.

"Oh, no. I'm not letting her see any part of this until they're set up at the mansion when everyone else sees them. Now, I get what you meant about history adding value." Jake leaned over to inspect the portraits. Did he just say something nice about the replicas without referencing his mother's input?

"Is there something you needed?" I asked as I set down the lamp, slowly freeing my hands in hopes the pieces stayed together.

"I was nearby and thought I'd see if I could take you girls to lunch," Jake said, still scanning the boxes.

"Thanks, but I have plans for lunch," Nissa said. She grabbed her purse and winked at me. She left so fast, I wasn't sure what happened.

"Did she just leave?" Jake's head whipped around. His dimple distracted me again.

My stomach pinched, and for a second, I wasn't sure if I was more nervous being alone with Mary Jane or Jake. "I was planning on eating lunch with her here at the apartment, you can have her portion."

"Works for me."

Thankful once again for Bella, and her love of cooking, I reheated the ham and sweet onion quiche I had taken out of the freezer that morning. I handed a salad to Jake, asking him to bring it to the dining room table.

"I order what mini furniture, parts, decorations, and accessories I can from very talented vendors," I explained, answering Jake's many questions. "A lot of the antiques I need aren't readily available in the dollhouse world. Sometimes, I carve legs or backs out of balsa wood and place them on a premade chair or table. Sometimes I repaint pieces. And there's always polymer clay."

"Wow, that seems like a lot of work."

"We pride ourselves on each piece being as authentic-looking as possible. I have people who will make rugs, drapes, and other fabric pieces like bedspreads and such to my specifications. Nissa hand-paints all our wallpaper."

"No wonder y'all aren't cheap."

"You get what you pay for. These boxes will be remarkable. And, for the record, no one's ever called me cheap."

As the quiche and salad neared their end, Jake seemed uncomfortable in his chair. He placed his fork across his plate. "Tina, since we're alone, I'd like to ask you a question."

I didn't like the change of tone in his voice.

"I know you weren't happy to hear your mother had mentioned y'all's relationship to me. But she did it out of concern."

I sat in silence. What did he want from me? Nothing had changed since he asked me about my relationship with my mother right before the truck accident. Why would he want to bring it up again? Exhaustion filled every nook and cranny. My arms grew heavy, and my body numb.

"She's your family," Jake added.

"How can you lecture me on communicating with my family when you and your mother won't even consider anything concerning the Randall side of her family?"

"That's different. My mother never knew them."

"No, that's where we're the same." Anxiety surged inside me. I'd never even told Nissa the whole truth. Scratching my palms, I considered Jake. This poor guy came into my life at the same time my long-lost mother chose to reappear. On the one hand, he was a client, so I shouldn't say anything about my personal life. On the other, it might be easier to talk it out with someone who knew nothing about my past, someone who would listen to my side of the story.

I stood up and paced. How much should I tell Jake? Could I say the words aloud that had been mostly in my head for the past twenty years?

"My mother and I, we've never had a normal mother-daughter relationship." I paced. "I haven't spent any time with her since I was nine. And my memories are of just wanting her to hug me." I stopped in front of Jake and shuffled my feet.

He remained silent and poured more tea into my glass as if expecting I needed it.

"My father died when I was nine. He was my life. It crushed me. When he died, I found him sprawled over his desk in his home office…"

My voice faded as cigarette smoke and pearls muddled my view and sickened me. "I've never talked to anyone about the details outside of therapy, not even with Nissa."

I sat and closed my eyes. My heart pounded in my ears, and I struggled to breathe. In my mind's eye, I took two steps toward my father's desk and saw those properly crossed legs, the one on top swinging and blocking my advance. I saw the royal blue shift dress through the haze of cigarette smoke and the delicate fingers twisting the pearl necklace.

"Hi, you two," Nissa called from the door. "I saw Jake's truck still here and figured he was eating my—Did I interrupt something?" She stopped and looked back and forth between Jake and me.

"We, um, we're just finishing up." Jake stood and picked up the half-empty plates.

I rested my hand on his arm, suggesting he put the plates down and sit. "No, it's okay, Jake. Nissa needs to hear this too," I said. My mind was set to get the words out and saying them might finally take some weight off my shoulders.

"Hear what? What's going on?" Nissa stepped in closer. I could see the concern on her face, ready to defend and lash out at Jake to protect me.

"I think my mother had something to do with my father's death." There, I'd said it.

Nissa's eyes widened. "What? You don't mean that. That's not rational. Your father had a heart attack."

I held my breath in an effort to stay in control.

Jake stood and pulled a chair over for Nissa. She ignored him and stood between us.

"About thirty minutes before I found my father, he had come out looking for me. I was in my fairy garden." I turned to look out the window. "He wanted me to come in and pack a bag. He said we were going on an adventure. I told him I'd be right in, but I rode my bike over to Liddy's to tell her I was going on a trip with my dad, and we couldn't make our curtains for the fairy house that weekend. When I got home, I heard Mom and Dad arguing so I stayed on the back porch until things settled down." I dissolved into my seat.

"Then I went in and found them. He lay across his desk, staring at her. She was on the couch, smoking a cigarette. In the house. Perfect Mary Jane Edwards sat smoking in her immaculate house, staring at him and twirling those damn pearls. She didn't raise a finger to help him." I rested my forehead in my palms. "We were going to go on an adventure." Tears fell.

"Tina?" Nissa clutched my shoulder.

Jake cleared his throat. "I'm so sorry. I was just concerned about your relationship with your mom. I didn't mean to—"

Nissa slid into a chair with a sigh.

I looked at Jake with a half-smile. "Aren't you glad you asked?"

"Does your mother know how you feel? Have you ever talked to her about it?" Jake asked.

I looked him straight in the eyes. "She knows what I saw. I walked in on my dead father, and she was sitting right there on the couch when I found him.

"The pearls," Jake said under his breath.

I twisted my lips and raised my eyebrows then bowed my head in embarrassment.

"I ran in. I think she had just hung up the phone, but my dad… I didn't think about that call until much later, but I remember she wasn't upset, or crying, or anything."

The phone call showed up in some of my recalls and didn't in others. Did I not want to remember if she reached out to 911 so I could keep her the villain? Or was there no phone call at all?

Nissa removed her hand from over her mouth. "My God! I can't believe you never told me. All these years?"

"What was I supposed to say, 'I think my mother might be a murderer'?"

"She may have been a not-so-great mother, but she did not kill your father," Nissa said.

"I'm not so sure. But that's why, even when I'm in a good mood, and Mary Jane and I are getting along, my mean girl comes out. I know better, but I just can't help myself."

"Have you ever talked to her about any of it?" Jake repeated his question.

"Liddy and I went to see her in the hospital the day after my father died. The doc said she was in shock and under stress, something like that. She wouldn't talk to either one of us. That only confirmed my suspicion."

"But all these years?" Nissa was trying to make sense of the facts.

"I don't know. Liddy said it wasn't the first time my mother found herself hospitalized for shock. She said my mother was stronger than I knew and for me not to judge how she handled things. I guess I didn't want to set her off by asking questions. Doesn't matter anyway. She dumped me on Liddy and moved away."

Jake lifted my chin with a finger. "Tina, you're strong. You and your mother can get through this. Just tell her how you feel."

"Mary Jane said she had things she needed to share," Nissa said, agreeing with Jake. "I bet she can clear all this up for you."

"She knows how I feel. Why did she want to stay with me now when she's so ill and when she could die? Is this some kind of sick joke? She sat and watched my father die, and now she wants to make me watch her suffer?"

CHAPTER 27

Ithought Mary Jane would come home from the hospital, and we'd pick up where we left off. But when she arrived, she had aged another ten years. Staying in the rehab, even if only for six days, had taken a lot out of her. The paleness of her skin contrasted with the newly acquired dark-gray circles around her eyes. The evidence of not eating Bella's food showed in the hollows of her cheeks. My heart couldn't help but feel for her. I assisted her to the dining room table and adjusted her blue arm sling while Bella hauled her overstuffed overnight bag to the bedroom and set off to do her laundry.

"Lordy, Lordy, woman." Bella draped a shawl over Mary Jane's shoulders. "I'll have to cook up a boatload of lard to put some meat back on your bones. You stay out of the wind, hear? You just might blow away."

Bella's hearty laughter erased the silence of the last few days. The bustling energy the two of them brought to the apartment was now the new normal, and I had missed it. I didn't like that I had missed it, but I missed it all the same.

Mary Jane gave a weak smile and said, "I might not look good, but I feel okay. But I think I'd rather go lie down than eat anything right now. It's good to be home."

Home. The word struck me like a taser.

"Of course, Sugar," Bella said, and with one hand, grabbed a handle of the wheelchair Mary Jane now required. With her other hand, she hung the oxygen tank over her shoulder.

I stood helplessly in the dining room, quelling my guilt. I was beginning to understand how Bella's faithful devotion to her friend was based on history. It took a lot of time spent together to develop a relationship as close as theirs, and I wouldn't want to take that away from her.

After a couple of relatively slow days filled with Mary Jane and Bella playing rummy at the dining table or watching television game shows in her bedroom, I peeked in to see how she was doing. Bella was helping her sit up in bed. Her eyes were wide and bright, her back against several pillows, and her injured arm supported by her sling. With her good arm, she waved me in.

I sat on the corner of her bed and asked, "How are you feeling?"

"Not too bad, considering." She took another sip of water. "Not looking forward to my treatment next week."

"I would think not." I picked at a pulled string on the bedspread, weighing whether or not it was a good time to start a conversation.

"Is there something you need, dear?" Mary Jane asked.

"You probably don't feel up to it, but I was wondering if you wanted to talk."

Mary Jane choked out her laugh with a cough. "I've got nothing but time on my hands."

Bella leaned toward Mary Jane. "Honey, I think you should stop piddling around. There's only so much time to mend fences."

The thought wrenched a cough from Mary Jane. Bella handed her tissue after tissue until Mary Jane's cough came to a simmer.

I turned to step out and give her privacy. In a few short months, I had become accustomed to my mother living in my home but still wasn't comfortable sharing space with her. Mary Jane called out to me with all she could muster. "Sweetie?" she said between coughs and patted the bed, signaling me to come back.

As the coughing subsided, I sat on the corner of the bed.

"What is it you want to know?"

Where to begin? I had practiced for days before, wanting to keep things calm and simple. But now my brain was mush. I didn't know where to begin. I focused on slowing down my breathing. "I need to understand why you never came back for me. How could you leave me with Liddy and never come back?" I held my breath. I had to remain calm and just listen.

Mary Jane turned her head toward Bella and gave her the slightest nod.

Bella placed the cup of water she was holding for Mary Jane on the windowsill and walked over to the dresser. She dug under several nightgowns and pulled out an 8 x 11 manila envelope, the envelope Mary Jane tried to leave with me the day of her first visit. She handed it to me, then walked around to the head of the bed, squeezed herself between it and the recliner, and helped Mary Jane sit up even straighter, propping her arm with extra pillows.

"What's this?" I asked as I got up and paced, turning the envelope over several times; both sides were blank.

Mary Jane began wheezing.

Bella adjusted the cannula in Mary Jane's nostrils. "You have a tough enough time breathing without choking yourself on all this tubing," she said as if it were just a regular moment in a regular day.

I knew it wasn't. The tide of anxiety rose. My palms became clammy, and I could hear the distant roar of panic.

Once Bella fluffed the pillows to her satisfaction, she slipped out of the room without a word.

Oh, no. Here we go. Stay calm, Tina. Breathe.

"Come. Sit." Mary Jane patted the bed closer to her. "There are things... I need to tell you."

Even through the raspiness of her voice, I could hear a nervous tone. The light dimmed in the room as a cloud covered the sun, and the air took on a stifling quality.

The tick of the clock grew louder. I took a deep breath and scooted closer to Mary Jane, my legs and feet still pointing toward the door. There would always be *this* moment, a time when Mary Jane and I would have to face our past. I was as prepared as I could be, at least I hoped so. Having already said how I thought Mary Jane had something to do with my father's death out loud had calmed me a bit, although I wished I had told Nissa my true feelings long ago. With all the grit I could muster, I met my mother's eyes, blue fading to grey. Eyes that slowly filled with tears.

"I..." I looked away.

"Tina, I need you to know... one thing. I have always loved you with all my heart, the best way I knew how." Mary Jane took a slow bubbly breath.

As she spoke, a knot built up in my throat. I sat too close to her and too far from the door. I walked around the bed to the window, fanning my face with the manila envelope to cool my stress.

Through water-filled eyes, I clung to the darkening clouds as they rolled past, distancing myself from whatever was headed my way. "If this is too hard for you, it's..."

"No, no, Tina. We have this moment. This is important." Mary Jane patted the edge of the bed again.

I sighed through tears and settled onto the bed.

With several starts and breaks to breathe and cough, Mary Jane explained.

"You know Liddy and I were best friends since the first day of college, and that's how I met your father. I dropped out of college, and we got married…" She paused as if she'd lost the words.

I remained silent, waiting, hoping it would help Mary Jane stay on track.

"A month after we got home from our honeymoon, I found out I was pregnant. When I told Liddy, she gave me some shocking news—she was pregnant, too."

"What? No, that can't be."

"Yes, it's true. We were afraid to tell your father about her pregnancy. We knew he wouldn't be pleased, but she and I were secretly excited. We would raise our babies together. Two naïve women, what did we know?"

"Aunt Liddy? Pregnant? But who, where is—" My heart raced, my hands shook. A cousin? The forgotten envelope slipped from my hands to the floor. Aunt Liddy pregnant? "That's why she was planning her wedding?"

Mary Jane held up her hand to silence me and continued, "I assumed your father would be angry with Liddy, but he went ballistic. You wouldn't believe the damage he did to his library. Back then it wasn't the end of the world to not be married and pregnant. Not like twenty years prior. But he was irate. What would people say? Their parents would have been so humiliated. She should be embarrassed for herself. He wanted her to get married on the spot. There would not be that kind of 'blemish' on his image or their family's name. He told her if her parents were alive, they'd have disowned her. He demanded the name of the father."

"So, so I have a cousin? An uncle?" I backpedaled through a lifetime of memories looking for what I had missed.

Mary Jane shook her head.

I burrowed through my thoughts. "The accident? Did she lose her baby in the accident?"

"No, honey, no," Mary Jane said. She gazed out the window for what seemed to be an eternity.

"Liddy wouldn't tell us who the father was. Anyway, when she refused to produce a husband, your father sent her away to have the baby and give it up for adoption."

"Away? Where? So, she had the baby before the accident?" I asked, already making plans to track down my cousin.

Mary Jane seemed to pick through her words with care. "She and I stayed in touch by mail. Liddy planned to keep her baby, no matter what her brother said. We wrote every week, sharing when we each felt those first flutters, the little kicks. We wrote about our hopes and wishes for the future, our children's birthdays, their graduations, and weddings." Mary Jane drifted off in thought.

"So, I have a cousin? Where is she?"

"Well, no. I'm sorry. I'm not telling this very well. But I want you to know what that time meant to Liddy and me. The time we wrote letters to each other and watched our bellies grow. We were both deliriously happy."

"Okay. Go on," I said. Unable to follow the path of her story, I tried to maintain my patience. My right leg stuck straight out as if putting brakes on my spinning mind.

"Could you please—my water?" Mary Jane asked pointing to the cup Bella had left on the windowsill.

I picked up the cup, trying to remember the way Bella angled the straw for her to take a sip.

Settling on the bed once again, I picked at the hem of my shirt, waiting for Mary Jane to continue. Breathe. Breathe.

"I… went into labor, and it was tough…" Mary Jane pulled a tissue out of the box Bella had left by her side. She looked at the ceiling, her face twisted in agony.

"I lost… my baby, my little girl." A pool of tears settled into the hollows of her cheeks. She coughed, but this time she couldn't get her breath under control.

I froze in a stupor and watched my mother struggle for air. Lost her baby girl? I had a sister? I struggled for air too, trying to absorb her story.

Bella burst through the door, leaned Mary Jane forward, and with gentle taps, rubbed her back. She encouraged Mary Jane to calm down and cough into a tissue. Once her throat cleared, she breathed in deep, rhythmic breaths.

I hadn't moved a muscle since receding from the bed. I stood with a rigid back as my only defense.

Once Mary Jane quieted and drank a few sips of water without coughing, she grabbed Bella's hand and quietly pleaded, "Please stay."

Bella looked at me, waiting for permission.

I dipped my chin.

Bella returned her gaze to Mary Jane, who nodded toward the recliner, then again patted the bedside, inviting me to sit. I sat, but not one muscle in my back gave way.

"I had an older sister?" I asked. My fingers tingled as the blood drained from my arms.

Mary Jane shook her head.

"I couldn't accept my little girl was dead. In fact, I wouldn't accept it. And when they told me I wouldn't be able to have any more children—"

"What do you mean?" I couldn't make sense of the words coming out of Mary Jane's mouth. The room spun. I inhaled and focused on Bella's face to maintain my grasp of reality.

"After they told me I could never have another child, I couldn't get out of bed. I stopped eating. My entire being froze, and I wanted to die. Your father and the doctors admitted me to the Georgia Mental Health Institution. I was there for six weeks."

I looked at Bella for some clarity, and she offered encouragement. "You're doing fine, both of you." Bella looked from one to the other.

"By the time I got home, Liddy had given birth to a beautiful baby girl. She convinced your father to let them come home, convinced him that she and her three-week-old newborn would cheer me up. If we couldn't raise our children together, at least together, we could raise... you."

I stopped breathing. I gasped for air and blinked, washing away the black shadows floating in the back of my eyes.

"Me? What do you mean, me?"

Mary Jane struggled to sit up with Bella's help. Then she reached for my hand. I let her hand rest on mine but did nothing to welcome the gesture.

"Several weeks after I returned home, Liddy asked me to watch you for a couple of hours. And that's when the car accident happened. I took care of you while she recovered in rehab. You brought me so much happiness. You were our reason to want to keep on living. Especially for Liddy, after learning about the death of your birth father, after learning she'd never recover the use of her legs, you were her reason to fight."

The tsunami arrived. The roar filled my ears as I struggled to keep my head above the series of waves pushing me under. My motionless body drowned in someone else's dream as I sat on the edge of the bed.

"Your father allowed Liddy and her baby to stay with us. As my mental health improved, Liddy's physical health deteriorated. She needed full-time care. She still hadn't gotten over the loss of—"

"Her fiancé. My real father," I whispered.

"Liddy never told me they were planning on getting married. I swear I didn't know until you told me," Mary Jane said.

As if that mattered. I rocked back and forth, torn between needing to hear the rest of the story and running away fast and far.

Mary Jane found the strength to continue. "Poor, dear Liddy. So much had been taken away from her. Jonathan couldn't tolerate Liddy's wheelchair, nor the nurses that came in and out to help get her ready every morning. She really needed a live-in nurse. Liddy and the baby disrupted his household. He wouldn't have it. He built that cute little Victorian cottage down the street for her to get her out of his house and hoped it would make her happy.

"Liddy's my—" I couldn't get the words out of my mouth. I lived with her until I left for college, and she never told me. Why did she never tell me?

"When you were a little over a year old, and the new house was ready for Liddy to move into, your father decided we would keep you as our own. After all, you were still an Edwards. Liddy agreed. She thought it was best for you under the circumstances. She could hardly take care of herself let alone a toddler. And for the first few years taking care of you kept me busy. But I always felt I was just taking care of you until Liddy could. I was so afraid I'd lose you to her that I fought falling in love with you."

My numbness turned into sharp bee stings as I listened to the drama play out before me as if on a movie screen.

"I never dreamed she wouldn't tell you she was your birth mother. There had to be a reason she didn't tell you, but for the life of me, I don't know what it could be. All these years, I assumed she did tell you, and that's why you never reached out to me. Liddy had directed her lawyer to contact me upon her death once Martha was ready to move on from the cottage. She has moved away to live with her sister."

Liddy's seemingly abandoned cottage flitted across my mind. Martha wasn't coming back? But all that had to be tucked away for another day. I couldn't add to the undeniable pressure building in my chest. Puzzle pieces floated in front of me, trying to connect. If I could have inhaled, I would have screamed for her to stop. The movie screen decreased in size as my conscious mind retreated.

I slid off the side of the bed. My legs trembled as I fought to keep them from giving way beneath me. Taking two steps backward, I slipped on the manila envelope and backed into Bella. She put her arms around me, and I struggled for release. Like the sleep paralyzed in my nightmares, my limbs were locked, and my head filled with silent screams. The deep pressure of Bella's arms calmed me, but only long enough to breathe. Then I broke free and ran out of the room.

CHAPTER 28

I fled from Mary Jane's bedroom straight out the front door of my building and bolted to the right. When I got to the corner, I stopped. My arms wrapped and unwrapped around my waist. Unable to breathe, submerged in the crashing waves of truth, the pull of the undertow of disbelief had me walking in circles. I retraced my steps, and not until I scraped the hair out of my eyes, did I take in an efficient breath and felt the pouring rain drenching my body.

"Shit!" I said, looking for a place to take cover. My car keys were in my purse. My purse was up in my workroom. Dragons couldn't pull me back there.

I ran across the street toward the park to a covered bus stop and plopped onto the bench. The humidity mimicked the sludge in my brain. Sitting slouched with a pool of water surrounding me, I pulled my knees up to my chest. I squeezed my feet onto the bench, wrapped my arms around my knees, and rested my forehead on them. I made myself as small as I could make myself. The roar in my head subsided as I swallowed air, gulping down my pain and confusion.

Squeaky boots slowed down in front of me. I never looked up, and the boot owner sloshed on his way. A few minutes later, a woman rushed in under the bus stop cover, shook out her umbrella, and sat on the bench. I slid over to the far end, turning my back to the waiting woman, sending a clear message to leave me be.

Aunt Liddy was my mother.

The depth of that statement cradled me in a warm hug. The love and deep affection we had for each other now made sense. I smiled at my seven-year-old-self, visiting Liddy on her back veranda, eating the cookie of the day, and drinking sweet tea.

But why didn't Liddy tell me? My tears were now for our lost mother and daughter time, although grateful for the years we had together. Thanks to Mary Jane. Really? Thanks to Mary Jane? What did she say? She felt she was taking care of me until Liddy could. She was so afraid she'd lose me to Liddy that she fought against falling in love with me?

Fragments of memories of Liddy blended. The dusty smell of polymer clay baking, the rhythm of *"This Is How We Do It,"* the taste of fresh basil in Martha's red sauce at a Sunday dinner, the squeak of Liddy's wheelchair as she took a right turn, the song *"I Want It That Way,"* a warm kiss on my forehead before bed. Jumbled memories came flooding in of times spent together, every new thought a warm hug from Liddy.

As I reshaped my memories from aunt and niece to mother and daughter, the shadow of a faceless man stood in the distance. My father. My real father.

I squeezed my eyes, wishing I had a time machine to go back and ask Liddy so many questions. Had she ever mentioned her fiancé other than the accident? I dug with intention for files in the back of my memory. As a kid, would I have paid enough attention to save such information? I had nothing. Did Liddy not tell me because she was ashamed of me? Please don't let it be that Mary Jane was afraid to love me and Liddy refused to love me.

Oh, so many more questions. Would Mary Jane have the answers to my questions? Would she give me those answers?

Mary Jane was not my mother. She couldn't keep pretending, so she stayed clear. I got that. We never had a mother-daughter connection. No matter how hard I tried as a kid, I could never gain her heartfelt affection. She would pat me on the head like a good puppy. I never understood why, but Mary Jane always knew.

She was distant because she didn't want to love me and lose me to my own mother. Now that's a kicker. My indifference and contempt toward Mary Jane before she moved in with me were tangible, now the emptiness and confusion left me numb. A new guilt.

Questions bubbled up inside me, but I couldn't put words to them. My thoughts all hit a dead end. I needed to pace again, shake out my nervous energy. I walked back and forth between the glass walls of the bus stop, ignoring the lady with the umbrella.

The bus arrived, and several people got off. The lady gathered her belongings. On her way out she turned and said, "Sometimes, when things are falling apart, they may actually be falling into place. I'll pray the good Lord will help you, dear." Then she stepped onto the bus.

Anger surfaced as the message reverberated in my head and I pictured it on my wall as one of Jonathan's quotes. I cackled. "Falling apart?" I said out loud to no one. "How about imploding?" And Jonathan. Jonathan was no longer my father. Jonathan P. Edwards was not my father. "Daddy isn't Dad. Dad is... Uncle? Dad is Uncle Jonathan. Uncle Johnny. Uncle JP."

The last screw loosened, releasing any control I had over my emotions. I began hysterically laughing. Not caring who heard me or watched me spin with my face to the spitting rain, I twirled until I smashed into the stone wall on the other side of the sidewalk.

Giggling as if the devil himself were tickling me, I sat back on the bench, legs stretched out in front of me crossed at the ankles, I watched the rainwater drip from my clothes and wash away blood on my legs. I hadn't even felt the rocks scrape my thighs and rip my skin.

Jonathan. The biggest liar of all. Everything I knew, everything I was, I credited to my love and reverence for that man. Had I not had the first nine years with Jonathan, who would I be now? Tears dripped, and the salt burned my skin.

Who was my real father? Did Mary Jane mention a name? I couldn't remember. "Dad is not my dad. Dad. Is. Not. My. Dad." I repeated it over and over. It echoed and circulated in my head like a freight train coming at me faster and faster, louder and louder. Then silence hit. I was empty all over again.

I recalled the facts of Liddy's accident as I knew them. Liddy's fiancé died in the car accident that put her in a wheelchair. My real father had died in that car. Was he one of the men in my various dreams who passed through my mind's eye without a face?

The photo of the man on his knees building the sandcastle came to mind. Did Mary Jane say who he was? I stood, wanting to see that picture again, but then sat down, not wanting to enter my home.

Slumped with my head between my hands for the longest time, I stared at a pecan tree on the other side of the stone wall through the summer downpour wanting it to be one of the trees that housed the fairy villages of my youth. I wanted to shrink and hide there forever.

Nissa stepped out of the rain and into the bus stop. "Your mother called me."

I put my head on Nissa's shoulder and said, "She's not my mother."

CHAPTER 29

The rain had not let up as Nissa and I walked across the street arm in arm. And even though we had her umbrella overhead, we drenched the floors of the foyer as we entered my building. Nissa shook like a dog, splattering me, and I laughed at myself for ducking from the spray as if I weren't already saturated. I, too, shook off the droplets. Both of us giggled like schoolgirls as we took seats on the bottom step leading up to my condo where Mary Jane undoubtedly waited.

"I don't want to go up there," I said, staring at the ceiling. The thought of facing Mary Jane, a stranger all over again, was daunting.

"Okay, then we won't."

Nissa had clearly heard enough from Mary Jane or Bella to know the gist of what was going on. The two of us sat in silence, listening to the drumming of the rain. I watched the blood dripping off the front of my scraped thighs as if it were a living art installation.

Nissa looked at her watch. "Let's go to SugarBeans and get you cleaned up. If we run, we can get something hot to drink before Marge closes."

Nissa grabbed my hand, pulled me up from the now swamped step, and dragged me out the door. We ran through the rain, setting foot in the café door as a crack of lightning struck behind us.

"I'm about to close up shop," Marge called out from somewhere behind the counter. As we stood on the entryway carpet, stamping our waterlogged shoes, she popped up from behind the bakery window.

"Hello, girls. What the hell are you two doing out in this weather? What happened to your legs? Come on in. Lock the door behind you. What'll you have? Something warm, I bet."

"Yes, please. Two teas, our way," Nissa said.

"What the hell happened to you?" Marge asked, coming from around the counter with a clean dish towel. "Sit. Here." She sat me in a chair and gently patted the shallow but extensive scrapes on my legs. Still numb to reality, the stinging pain made me cringe, but it was good to feel… something, anything.

"Did you get attacked by a dog?" Marge asked as she gently patted the cloth on my legs.

"Nope, fell on some rocks," I said and took the cloth from her.

Marge returned to behind the counter and placed a tray of goodies on the countertop. "Come and get what you'd like off this tray. It's Saturday night. We start fresh tomorrow at 4 a.m. These have to go."

"I'm in." Nissa grabbed a lemon poppy seed muffin and an apple Danish.

"I'm not hungry. Thank you, though."

Marge brought me a cold wet towel, which helped relieve some of the pain from my thighs. She carried three mugs over to the table, placed a napkin in front of each of us, and pulled up a third chair. "Okay, what's up, Hun? You look like shit."

I looked over at Nissa and caught her stuffing her face with a muffin as if it were a piece of wedding cake. Yet, instead of laughing, a tear slipped down my face. Nissa dropped the food, swallowed the dry crumbs, and scooted her chair next to me. "Aww, Tina."

"Is it your mother?" Marge asked, reaching out to grasp my hand. "Did she… is she gone?"

I took Marge's hand with both of mine, the same way I used to grip Liddy's when we had serious discussions. "No, it's not that."

If the words came out of my mouth, they'd for sure be real. They would be my new truth. A truth replacing twenty-four years of beliefs. "It's just—"

"Spit it out, child." Marge said, placing a sticky cinnamon roll next to the muffin on her plate.

"Mary Jane isn't my mother."

Marge opened her mouth, looked at Nissa who nodded with raised eyebrows, then said, "Come again?"

I took a deep breath, then let it out as if to expel my demons in one slow exhale. "As I sat on the corner of that bed, up in that bedroom, the room I let my supposed mother stay in, even against my better judgment—because it was the right thing to do—even though no one else in my family knows right from wrong, nor when to be honest, I learned Liddy gave birth to me." As I gestured and rambled, my heartbeat raced faster and faster. "How could they all keep me in the dark? Why would they?" My rant escalated from sorrow for the life I missed out on, confusion as to whether anyone truly loved me, to being pissed at all the lies and secrets.

Thirty minutes into listening to me rant, watching me pace, wrap and unwrap the tea bag string around my finger, and pick at my muffin crumbs on my plate, I still grappled with the information bequeathed to me by my no-longer mother.

Nissa and Marge's silence gave me permission to let my emotions evolve, just as Liddy would have done. I talked in circles until I zeroed in on the question that bothered me the most. Who the hell am I? "My whole life, my whole career, is based on keeping my father's memory alive, showing appreciation for the talent he gave me, and living as the person he would have wanted me to be. So, where does that leave me now? It's as if I just woke up from a coma and have no memory of the past, and now I had to start over. Pick up from nothing, with absolutely no memory of a life before blacking out."

Once I sat down, semi-calm, the three of us picked through the goodies on the tray, destroying most of the leftovers. I managed a few bites of a sweet, sticky cinnamon roll, but mostly I played with the crumbs on my plate between postulations.

Marge grabbed both of my hands, looked straight into my eyes, and said, "Good or bad, this moment will not last forever."

I laughed, "That's something my father… well, Jonathan, would have said. This too shall pass."

"Tina, Johnathan was still the man who brought you up, no matter how your mother feels about him. He did right by you. You said so yourself. You spent more time with Liddy and your father than Mary Jane. She wanted you to share a life with Liddy. That's more than most kids might have gotten in your situation. Sure, the three of them handled it in a screwed-up way, but is it really the end of the world? Johnathan wanted a real family; he found a chance to have one, and for whatever reason, Liddy let it happen. I'm sure she thought it was the best thing to do at the time—giving you a whole family, something she could not."

"And Mary Jane?" I asked as if that situation could change.

"Mary Jane is upstairs," Nissa said, piling six mugs onto the counter, "waiting to make amends for how the three of them screwed up."

"I need to think," I said, still not wanting to face my rewritten life.

"No, you don't. Your life isn't some fairy tale. You can't click your heels three times, and everything will be okay. You have to go find your glass slipper by yourself," Marge said, pulling me toward her as she stood. She put her arms around me. "You need a hot shower and some sleep. Things will be better tomorrow."

The sun had set, the rain had stopped, and the tray held only crumbs. "But who's my real father—?" I rambled on, wanting to avoid the inevitable.

CHAPTER 30

Nissa and I tiptoed into the condo and slipped off our wet shoes. Across the living room, Bella's voice and flickering lights came from Mary Jane's wide-open bedroom door. The manila envelope lay on the coffee table, for sure placed there for me to see when I entered. I grabbed it and threw it on my bed. I took a hot shower and got into some dry clothes. As Nissa changed into borrowed sweats, I wrapped both thighs with witch hazel-soaked gauze and ace bandages in hopes of controlling the seeping.

Sitting on the edge of my bed, I combed my hair. "I don't know what to do next. The life I've known is based on lies and hidden truths." It surprised me all over again.

"All families are a melting pot of miscommunications and misperceptions. It's all about perspectives." Nissa pulled out the vanity chair and sat facing me. "Perceptions of life are based on what we think we know—what we were taught to grow up believing. True or false, good or bad, everyone has their own truth for each situation. And Tina, all families have secrets."

"But some are bigger than others. And my family's issues are not so little. What if I knew then what I now know?" I asked as if we could make that happen.

"You can't change the past," Nissa said. "And you're not going to kick your sick mother—Mary Jane—out, so let's focus on something else like who your real father is. That's something constructive we can do. Let her get some rest. Then we'll ask her some questions."

"So why now? Mary Jane— We'll just call her Mary Jane from now on. She could've come and gone without ever telling me she wasn't my birth mother. Why did she feel like she had to tell me?"

"What would it have changed if she told you before now? Would your story be so different?"

"I don't know." I twirled my damp hair with my fingers. "I would've known, that's all. I just would have known. Why didn't Liddy tell me? That's what hurts the most."

"She must've had her reasons. Tina, you spent every spare second with your aunt. I was with you a lot of that time. That cottage was your home after your father died."

"Well, only because Mary Jane dumped me on Liddy."

"Dumped? Are you sure? Think about it," Nissa urged.

I could hardly thank Mary Jane for the favor of leaving me with my own mother. The absurdity of it all was painful, yet that was the truth. My whole take on Mary Jane was that she was a distant, unloving mother. And now I find out that she was protecting her own heart and had returned me to my rightful owner. "So, what now?" I couldn't control my bitterness. "All hail Saint Mary Jane?"

Nissa slid off the chair and onto her knees and grabbed my fidgety hands, holding them still. "Bingo. She felt it was the right thing to do. She even said she was surprised Liddy didn't tell you. She spent the last twenty years waiting for you to reach out and thought you didn't because you knew she wasn't your mother. You need to go back in there and talk to her. Not now, but soon."

I turned so Nissa could comb the length of my hair. I stared past her, deep into the vanity's mirror, and saw the envelope on my bed. "Go get us some wine. I'm pretty sure they won't be surprised to see you and not me."

"Is wine strong enough?" Nissa joked.

My mind played a continual loop as I crawled into bed with the envelope and pulled the covers over my head. I wanted to stop thinking and stop asking questions that had no answers.

The betrayal sickened me the most. All those nights I felt lucky spending the night at Liddy's when Mary Jane and Jonathan were out for an event or special occasion, they knew they were leaving me with my own mother. But no one ever told me. Even though I loved living with my aunt, I grew up with a sense of abandonment—a shadow of neglect. The distance made me feel like a third wheel in my own family. Jonathan was there for me, but looking back, he was there on his terms. They all lied. They all betrayed me. Why did no one ever tell me the truth?

Nissa pushed the door open, a bottle of wine in one hand, swinging two glasses between the fingers of her other. "Here's our liquid courage."

I nodded in agreement, sat up, and stacked my pillows up against the headboard. I took the glass Nissa poured for me as I turned the envelope over and over. Another Pandora's box: once I opened it, I could never unopen it. "I can't. You open it."

Nissa climbed into bed next to me. She ripped open the envelope as if pulling off a Band-Aid and pulled out several pieces of paper. She dumped a set of keys onto my lap.

I picked up the three keys attached to Liddy's pewter rose keyring. I examined each one as Nissa skimmed through the paperwork.

"Well, now we know," Nissa said, dropping her hands and the papers into her lap.

"Know what?" I asked, fearful of the answer.

"I can't tell you why Liddy didn't tell you before, but I can tell you why Mary Jane needs to tell you now," Nissa said, handing me the top few papers. The first was a handwritten note from Liddy. She wrote of her desire to allow Martha to stay in the house as long as she wanted and then asked the attorney to contact Mary Jane for her to personally hand over the deed to the cottage and other belongings.

The rest of the papers were from Liddy's attorney. A letter presented Liddy's daughter with her trust: "Last Will and Testament of Lydia Coretta Edwards names her daughter, Christina Ann Edwards, her sole beneficiary… Liddy wanted to make sure Mary Jane was with me when I found out who my real mother was?" I questioned out loud.

"Mary Jane said she didn't know that Liddy never explained things to you until she got that call from a lawyer about three months before she asked to move into your apartment."

"So why didn't she?" It made no sense. We could have lived as mother and daughter for over twenty years.

Nissa handed me the signed-over deed to the Victorian cottage at 35 Cranberry Lane in Bluebelle, Georgia. There were several bank forms, one for a checking and savings account in my name and one that looked like it would open a safe deposit box. As I read through the documents, my jaw loosened, and my grip became less tense as I handed the rest of the documents to Nissa, who tucked the papers back into the envelope.

I sighed. "Mary Jane's been sitting on these papers for months. Once she got her diagnosis, and Martha wanted to move out, she couldn't put it off any longer." After a moment of thought, I said, "The cottage. We have to go back there. It's been neglected for a few months."

Nissa handed me a small white envelope with pictures of Liddy's cottage. "We will. But look at these. These are the rooms of our childhood. Remember when we spent Halloween night here? The scary movie? We screamed and knocked over the whole bowl of popcorn. Martha got so mad because we made such a mess."

"And we ended up sleeping on the floor in Liddy's bedroom," I said, glad for the memory.

"I loved all the game nights and movie nights. We had fun in that house, and it looks like we'll have more. That is, if you're going to keep it."

I lifted my wine glass and met Nissa's. The thought of moving into Liddy's cottage, where I felt most loved, was intriguing. But once again, I needed to shelve an idea until I got through what faced me daily in the near future—Mary Jane and Bella living here and the Randall Mansion project.

"Slap some fairy wings on and make the best of this," Nissa cheered.

"I'm damn well going to try." I wanted to hang onto the warm, cozy feelings emanating from each picture. I scrutinized every photo, rounding up every memory I could.

I jumped to high heavens when my door burst open, and Bella pushed through with her bright turquoise backside covered with a Road Runner and Wile E Coyote robe. She carried a tray full of chips and sandwiches cut into triangle quarters.

"Thought you two might want a bite since I saw Miss Nissa here sneak out of the kitchen with that there bottle."

"Bella, it's after midnight," I said, throwing the blankets over my legs, making sure my bandaged legs were covered up. I certainly didn't need Bella going into nurse mode on me.

Nissa jumped off the bed and helped Bella with the tray.

"You doing all right?" Bella asked. She tightened her bathrobe sash.

"I guess so," I said.

Bella leaned over and kissed me on the forehead. "Nothing needs to change, Sweetie. But remember, nothing ever stays the same, either. Holler if you need something."

"Thank you, Bella, but we won't. Please, go get some sleep."

"I will if you will," Bella winked.

"Seems we're all thinking the same thought. Nothing has to change." Nissa took a bite of a turkey and cucumber sandwich and licked her lips. "Bella's the best."

I held up the pictures of Liddy's house, now my house. "Maybe nothing has to change, but for me everything is different. I'm the only one who didn't know the truth. To survive all this, I'm the one who has to change. It's scary to think everything I know, the foundation of who I am, is based on lics or at least unknown truths." I took a bite of my sandwich, and for the first time all day, I was hungry.

"Will you help me figure out who my real father is? And will you go with me to Liddy's house?"

"Before or after you talk to your—Mary Jane?" Nissa asked.

I shrugged, We finished the sandwiches and wine with the photos splayed out across the bed, prompting memories we shared. The giggles lasted well past 2 a.m.

Once Nissa left, after I asked for a day to myself, I changed into my pajamas but couldn't entertain sleep. I threw on my bathrobe and paused across from Mary Jane's closed door. My aunt lay in that room.

Entering the workroom, my sanctuary, I searched for my reading glasses and found them on the corner of my desk. I turned and faced my wall of quotes and pulled off a previously wrinkled but presently flattened out Post-it, one I must have deemed important after throwing it away. I laughed out loud as I read it by the brightness of the moon: *After all, tomorrow is another day.*

I folded the thought in half. Another day of what? More unanswered questions? I folded the paper in half again. Another day of wondering who I was? Lost in a clash of emotions, I folded the paper in half, and in half again, then tossed the tiny, consolidated notion into the garbage can.

Reaching to pull another profound revelation from Mr. Jonathan P. Edwards off the wall, I read: *A man cannot be comfortable without his own approval.* I hope he was very uncomfortable, because if not… I crumbled up the no longer needed snippet and dropped it in the nearby trash can. I peeled one voice of encouragement after the other off the wall, realizing each one had prepared me for today, the day I would become my own person.

I pulled the garbage can even closer, read each quote out loud, then tossed it. *Only in the darkness can you see the stars.* Crumble. Toss. *Life is tough my darling, but so are you.* Crumble. Toss. *Success is not an accident.* Crumble. Toss… Pull. Read. Crumble. Toss… Pull. Read. Crumble. Toss…

As the sun rose, its bright warmth spread across my face and woke me. I stretched on the office floor and stared at my mostly empty wall. One more quote remained stuck in the top right corner. I jumped up and pulled off the last yellow sticky note, the last remnant of Jonathan's credo: *You never know how strong you are until being strong is your only option.*

"I don't need a piece of paper to tell me that." I crumbled and tossed the last quote I would ever need from my not-father.

CHAPTER 31

I hadn't experienced sleeping like a baby for a long time. Taking yesterday off for an all-day solo hike did the trick. As refreshed as I may have been, I was still too chicken to run into Mary Jane without backup. I sat on the corner of my bed, waiting to hear Nissa's keys in the door. By nine a.m., Nissa had yet to arrive. I tiptoed from my room to the workroom and faced the empty wall. A blank slate. Permission to start over.

I would begin today with who I now knew myself to be, Lydia Edward's daughter. From now on, I was the woman Liddy had brought up, not the daughter of a woman who had left me behind. Accepting this recent truth allowed me to easily find the new woman inside me. I was now the daughter of a mother who loved her and a father who left this world too soon.

Relieved when Nissa let herself in, I rushed out into the hallway, but Bella was at the ready. She snatched Nissa's arm as if she had been hiding out waiting for her.

"Y'all, I got whole wheat pancakes and fresh-squeezed orange juice." Bella smiled extra big as she hooked my arm as in a do-si-do. The three of us headed to the dining room arm in arm, although one of us was more reluctant than the other two.

"I'm starving." Nissa smiled and took a step forward.

"I know you two'll be busy," Bella said, "so, you best eat a fine breakfast."

Nissa pulled her hand from my grasp and whispered, "She's trying to break the ice here. And she's not wrong. We should eat."

I lowered my shoulders and followed Nissa to the dining room. A bowl of fresh fruit sat in the middle of the table, but more importantly, there were only two place settings with silverware, napkins, and orange juice. With a sigh of relief, I deduced no one else planned to join us.

Nissa grinned and mouthed *thank you* to Bella.

Stubbornness wasn't a trait I liked in myself. I appreciated what Bella did for Mary Jane and me, not only the caretaking and cooking but the unexpected housekeeping and moral support. But still, I couldn't stomach seeing Mary Jane. Not just yet.

We ate while listening to Bella sing as she cleaned the kitchen. When I placed my fork across my empty plate, Nissa still had half her pancakes left.

"Sorry, we've got to get to work." I swallowed the last of my orange juice while standing.

"You just don't want to run into Mary Jane."

"She needs her rest. And I need more time." Leaving my dishes, I walked away, trying to stay positive. "I'll meet you in the workroom."

"Chicken," Nissa said in a loud whisper.

At the end of the day filled with touching up pieces of furniture and gluing them in place in their rooms, Nissa left for home. On her way out, she put her hand on my shoulder. "Talk to Mary Jane. Ask her about the stuff that's eating at your insides. You want to know the truth… ask her."

"But what if she…"

"Just ask her."

After a warm shower where I rehearsed many probing questions, I got up my courage and walked straight to Mary Jane as she worked a crossword puzzle in the dining room. I pulled out the chair beside her and rested my clasped hands on the table.

"Well, hello, dear," Mary Jane smiled. "What's a five-letter word for fibers of cellulose pulp?"

"Can we talk?" I asked, hoping Bella would take the hint and leave us alone, which she did. "Paper."

"Excuse me?" Mary Jane asked.

"A five-letter word for fibers of cellulose pulp. Paper."

"Oh, thank you," Mary Jane cheered as she filled in the spaces then put her pen down.

With her one good arm, she maneuvered her wheelchair around to look at me. I was ashamed to find her eyes were bloodshot and red-rimmed. "I'm sure you have a lot of questions," she said.

I exhaled to stay in control. "I'm angry. I'm hurt and confused. I have been for a long time now, ever since Dad, well, Jonathan, died. Please, no more secrets. I'm sorry you lost your child, but it seems he wanted to make you happy. What was so wrong with him wanting to have a nice family? Why did you have to leave us—me and Liddy? I always felt like I didn't quite belong; now I know why. But why didn't Liddy ever tell me who she was? That she was my mother? I feel betrayed. By all of you."

"Honey, I've always loved you. I'll tell you the truth. But first, you must tell me your truth. Tell me all the good you saw in your father. Make your case. And I want you always to remember that's how you felt about him before I tell you the rest of the story." Mary Jane sat up straight in her chair and turned the knob of her oxygen up a notch. "Do you understand?"

"Not really." There was more to the story? My insides cowered.

"I want you to remember you said that nothing I could say about your father would make you think badly of him."

I now fostered doubt about Jonathan but certainly wouldn't come around to admit it. Where was Mary Jane leading me? I stared into her eyes, wiggled my butt into the back of my chair, and crossed my arms. I sensed some kind of trap. I took my time before I answered in defense mode.

"I loved my dad. I loved our breakfast time together. There was not one moment in my life I didn't feel his love. He paid attention. Sure, it wasn't perfect. He was strict and didn't have a lot of extra time, but when he did, he spent that time building my fairy houses and teaching me his love for the arts. Those times, sitting in the dirt with leaves blowing around us, carving furniture out of tree bark or gluing moss on the inside walls of a stump…"

I continued my monologue with Mary Jane as if it were a closing statement in defense of my father. "The two of us on hands and knees, looking for acorn caps to use for bowls or gathering tiny pebbles for the walkways leading up to the many fairy doors he had attached to the base of all those trees in our backyard… those are the times I remember."

I excused myself to step into the living room and grab a tissue. I needed to gain control, not let anger or confusion or even exhaustion deplete my reserves. As I spoke of the memories of the man who raised me, I couldn't align him with the man who took me from my birth mother and lied to me my whole life. I needed it all to end. And it wouldn't end if I didn't allow it to start. I paced in front of Mary Jane, not able to sit.

"Is that it?" Mary Jane asked.

I stopped pacing. "All the trips we took to the museums, and with Liddy…" I swallowed as the disbelief that Jonathan wasn't my birth father wriggled in my belly. There were many more good things I wanted to say about him. And I tried to keep the good thoughts of him from fading. But he betrayed me, just like Liddy and Mary Jane. "He pretended all those years, and I never had one inkling, not one clue he wasn't my biological dad. I guess you could say he was a great actor."

"He wasn't acting," she said. "He truly loved you. You were the apple of his eye. The daughter he always wanted. The child I failed to give him. He wouldn't have changed one thing about you or our situation."

"Except that I be his real daughter." I threw my arms in the air. "And you, what's your excuse? You kept your distance from me. I had assumed you just weren't the motherly type. Okay, you gave me back to Liddy. You knew I'd be happy there, but that changes nothing. You could have come and visited."

I reached into the many corners of my mind as I stood in front of Mary Jane, challenging her. "You watched him die. Don't deny it. I might not have heard your exact words, and I think you called someone, but you weren't the least bit upset. Please tell me the truth." I scraped my hands through my hair and gripped my head so tightly my fingernails dug into my scalp. Taking a deep breath, I plopped down across from her and whispered, "Please. Tell. Me. The truth."

"I will. I will." Mary Jane's chin fell to her chest.

"We had met the young man Liddy was dating."

"The man in the picture building the sandcastle?" I interrupted. "Is he my birth father?"

Mary Jane angled both palms to slow me down. But her silence confirmed my query.

"When your father found out Liddy was pregnant, all hell broke loose. He sent her away to a women's home in Pennsylvania. He said she absolutely couldn't marry Bobby Canton. When Liddy returned with you, she convinced us the whole Bobby Canton thing was over. She convinced your fa... Jonathan that it would be good for me to have her and her baby living there at home when I came home from the hospital." Mary Jane took a sip of water.

Bobby. She had said Bobby Canton. But before I could ask any more questions, Mary Jane started back up.

"One night, Jonathan ran into Bobby and Liddy at a restaurant, and Bobby had you in his arms. He was furious with Liddy for breaking her promise about not seeing Bobby anymore. He dragged you and Liddy home. She was terribly upset. She and I stayed up all night trying to figure out what Jonathan had against Bobby and about how we could bring Jonathan around."

I couldn't shake that Jonathan must have had a good reason to eliminate Bobby, unless he just wanted me to himself.

"The following day, Liddy came to me. She put you in my arms and said Bobby had asked to meet with her and for me not to say a word to Jonathan. She told me Bobby was leaving town, and she was just going to say goodbye."

I was more confused than ever. "But Liddy told me they were engaged. He was her fiancé, and they were going to get married."

"By morning, Liddy was paralyzed from the waist down, and Bobby was dead." Mary Jane doubled over in spasms of coughing.

Confusion circled as I tried to make sense of what Mary Jane was trying to say.

But she wasn't finished. "I didn't know it then, but that very morning, Jonathan had given Bobby a $50,000 check and an ultimatum. He told him to stay away from you and Liddy and never to return or ask for any more money. He assured Bobby he and I would take good care of you both."

I sat rooted to my spot. The hair on the back of my neck rose, and my arms tingled as goosebumps formed. "No, no, no," I pleaded for it not to be true.

Jonathan had *paid* my birth father to have nothing to do with me.

"I swear to you I knew nothing about any of it until Jonathan wanted to keep you for our own, well after the accident." Mary Jane put her hand on my knee. "He told me what he had done the day of Bobby's death, and once I knew, I became an accomplice to his dirty little secret. I couldn't tell Liddy the truth. She had never mentioned it, but I didn't know if she knew about her brother giving Bobby the check or not. Do you understand now? If your father didn't give Bobby that check and the ultimatum, they wouldn't have met that night. They wouldn't have been hit by that truck. And Liddy…"

Mary Jane paused, and in the silence, something inside me died.

"I loved Liddy and could never forgive Jonathan after that. He said Bobby's family was dangerous and threatened Liddy's reputation, her inheritance, and so much more. But I don't think he could ever forgive himself. That's why Jonathan built Liddy's house for her. Out of sight, out of mind."

I looked away and rubbed the back of my neck. I promised myself to practice patience. I needed the whole truth, and I wasn't going to get it if I ran away.

Mary Jane pushed ahead. "Jonathan took away the only chance for Liddy to be happy, and he expected me to play along. That truck hit them when they were saying their goodbyes. At least I thought Bobby was saying goodbye, but maybe they talked about running away or getting married. If she found out about the bribe in that car before he died, and she ended up in that wheelchair..." Mary Jane wiped the tears from her eyes. "If Liddy knew and never mentioned it, she's a stronger woman than I am. Maybe that's why she never told you; she didn't want you to think badly about her only brother, the man who raised you. It all just makes me so sick."

I dropped my shoulders and rocked in my chair. The rhythm comforted me but didn't silence the screams in my head. Liddy went to the grave with so many secrets, and I was in the middle of all of them.

Mary Jane continued, "I tried to be a good mother and a good wife after that. And Jonathan tried to be a good father to you."

"No, no, no, no, no." I grabbed at the sides of my head, covering my ears. "This can't be. You can't tell me... My whole life's a..."

"Tina, please." Mary Jane reached for me, "You wanted the truth. Please, I am not trying to hurt you. I'm telling you what happened."

"You're not done? Are you saying there's more?" I sat up, ready to vomit.

Bella came around the corner and leaned in the doorway, drying her hands with a dish towel.

"I'm trying to explain," Mary Jane pleaded.

I held my breath.

"I tried to be a good mother and wife after that. And a friend to Liddy. But it was hard. The truth was eating me up inside, so I tried to stay out of the picture so you could turn to Liddy. Your father turned to other women."

I covered my ears. I didn't want to add disgust to my resentment of the man I once adored, but as Mary Jane spoke, I grew to detest him.

"I expect he couldn't find another woman as well trained as I was. He kept me around for window dressing, the perfect family picture, and to host those perfect dinner parties. It was all business to him. Our love disintegrated years before he died, mine from heartbreak, I guess his from guilt."

My insides melted. Nothing I remembered from my childhood was real. Jonathan? Other women? I needed that to be a lie. "When I noticed you two looking at each other, all this time I thought you were so much in love that I wasn't even relevant."

"That wasn't love, Tina, dear. What you saw was us sharing an ugly secret, one we depended on each other to keep. It was far from love. Your father turned to other women because I couldn't give him what he needed, not anymore."

I couldn't stop shaking my head. How could I ever trust anyone or anything again?

"That secret, our skeleton in the closet, was why I never traveled with you and Liddy and Jonathan. It's why I never had Liddy over while he was home." Mary Jane took a moment, lost in thought. When she returned to her explanation, it was as if she needed to pry the words out. "It's why I could no longer be her best friend. I didn't know what she knew and what she didn't know. Your father convinced her that keeping you with us was all for the best. And, when I sold the house and left you with Liddy, I felt you deserved to live with your real mother. I never dreamed she would not tell you the truth. She must have kept the secret, like all the rest of us, to protect you. Once her lawyers called me and told me you were named on the deed as her legitimate daughter, and I got my diagnosis, I knew I had to tell you the truth."

I stroked my arms as if wiping my palms clean. "But what about when Dad died?" This was always my one haunting question. I didn't even know to question the rest until after Mary Jane told me the truth.

Her eyes searched mine. "Yes, Tina, I watched Jonathan die. He sat at his desk telling me he was in love with another woman, someone who loved him back. He wanted a divorce, and they were moving to Washington, DC." Mary Jane took in a big breath. "And he was going to take you with them."

It was all too much. I didn't know the man at all. I had revered Jonathan with every bone in my body, and I was nothing but a pawn to him. He had come out that day and told me to pack for an adventure, but he planned for us to never return. My gut wrenched.

"I was not going to let that happen." Mary Jane's fist hit the table with determination. "I was not going to let him take you away from Liddy—again. He didn't want to hear my objections. That's when I got angry. I had held my peace long enough. I told him he could go to hell. I told him if he tried to leave with you, I would tell Liddy everything. I would create a messy divorce and make sure his bribe was all over the newspaper."

My heart softened toward Mary Jane as I listened to the strength in her voice.

"I had never been so angry in my life. I grabbed the statue off the side table and lifted it over my head to throw at him, but he stood up and lunged over the desk to stop me. He reached for my throat and grabbed at my pearl necklace." Mary Jane's fingers twisted at her throat. "That's when his face got red. His fingers loosened, and he began pulling at his shirt collar struggling to breathe. He sunk down and fell across his desk. At first, I panicked, I didn't know what to do. But when he stayed there, staring at nothing, it all became clear."

After a long pause, Mary Jane continued, "I guess you could say I watched him die, but understand, I did call emergency, and then I called Liddy," Mary Jane sobbed. Bella leaned in and gave her a shoulder to cry on. "He would have taken you away from Liddy forever. I couldn't let him take you away from Liddy."

I drowned in my visions of that day. I sat speechless. This was too much information to process. My mind shattered from overload. How could the Jonathan I knew be this man Mary Jane described?

Mary Jane went into a full-blown coughing fit, and Bella sat her up, patting her back.

"Miss Mary Jane, sweetie, slow it down. It's okay now." Bella patted Mary Jane's back and whispered calm sentiments.

I looked at Bella for some measure of sanity.

"So, sad, Sugar, but it's all true," Bella said.

Mary Jane sobbed, "I couldn't let him take you away from Liddy; he had already taken so much from her."

My tears were no longer for me. They were for Mary Jane and Liddy and Bobby Canton. "So, when I heard you on the phone before I went into the office?"

"I had called Liddy. I told her you were all hers."

My stomach clenched. I didn't move in with Liddy because my mother sold our house. My mother sold our home so I could move in with Liddy. Had I been older, would I have seen more, known more?

"I figured Liddy needed time to sort out how and when to tell you. I am so sorry Liddy never shared the truth with you. I thought she had. I assumed you knew the truth and refused to reach out to me. I never asked if she told you, and she never brought it up. She must have had her reasons, or it was her way of getting back at me, keeping me wondering if you knew the truth. If that were so, I guess I deserved it. I went to Liddy's funeral out of respect for her. I left the funeral out of respect for you."

The pressure within forced my frozen body to crack as the pain of truth pushed through my pores. I had it all wrong. My whole life, I assumed the worst of Mary Jane.

"I didn't realize Liddy never told you until her lawyer contacted me per her directives. I was as shocked as you."

I found that hard to believe, but I couldn't fight it any longer. My heart gained understanding, where before I had none. It all made sense, and nausea took over. I ran into the kitchen and vomited into the sink. If nobody allowed this secret to take over their lives, things would have been different. What had Nissa said? Families were a melting pot of miscommunication and misperception. That was putting it mildly.

Several minutes passed before I dropped to my knees in front of Mary Jane's wheelchair. I covered her cold, shaking hands with my own and brought them up to my forehead.

"I'm so sorry. I'm sorry for everything," Mary Jane murmured.

CHAPTER 32

The following morning, after lying in bed all night, staring at the ceiling, afraid to shut the lights off, I waited for the sun to rise so I could walk around the park across the street. I had to move about as the surrealness shifted inside me. I had to swallow my past beliefs and digest all I now knew.

After walking and running, then sitting on a bench considering my next move, then walking and running several laps again around the shaded park, I headed to SugarBeans for some much-needed iced tea. As I passed The Italian Eatery, Silvio called to me. *"Ciao, Bella."*

As soon as he saw my face, he opened the door wider and shuttled me in. He sat me in a dark corner booth and brought me an Italian breakfast—a glass of wine and a basket of bread and cheese. Multiple Chianti bottles wrapped in straw hung from the ceiling, casting shadows onto the dark paneled walls and well-worn red leather benches that contributed to the cinematic scene I felt a part of. I texted Nissa, who was already at the office wondering where I was, then rested my forehead on the red-and-white-checked tablecloth and waited for her to bring her laptop and my backpack.

I should be home in the workshop working on the Randall Mansion, but I needed one more day to sort things out.

Nissa tore into the restaurant as if she owned the place, and Silvio pointed at me in the back corner. "Are you okay?" she asked.

"Last night, I asked questions and got more than I bargained for." I scooted the bread basket over for Nissa to put down her laptop. I relayed Mary Jane's version of events as the overwhelming garlic scent from the kitchen kept me in the here and now, preventing any unwanted memories to come up. "Understand, my life unfolded in front of me; a life poles apart from what I remember, like I was watching a movie, someone else's story."

Nissa hissed like a slowly deflating tire. "I don't know what to say."

"Say you hope that's everything, that there are no more secrets." With new inner strength, I dragged a not-so-warm piece of bread from under the white napkin covering the basket. My appetite took over once the words were out. A waitress appeared with two bowls of hot minestrone. Silvio was telling us it was time for the two of us to eat.

Between spoonfuls, I continued, "Mary Jane's a lot stronger than I thought. She's my hero."

Nissa flopped back in her seat.

"Liddy never allowed me to say a bad word against her, and now I know why—and she didn't know the half of it. I really hope Liddy went to the grave thinking her brother took care of her out of love, not guilt."

"Well now Mary Jane's a hero in my book, too."

"Liddy might have given me life, but Mary Jane spent her whole life trying to make my life story a better read. And in the end, she's the one who had to break my heart and tell me the truth. That wasn't fair to her. I don't know how I can make it up to her, or even if it's possible. I hope we get the time to get to know each other."

"How do you feel about Jonathan? About his death?"

"I'm ashamed. For all these years, I thought Mary Jane was so cold-blooded. And to find out every negligent, uncaring, unemotional thing she ever did or said was my warped perception of her not liking me. She did her best to keep a horrible secret. It's tragic. And now she's so sick. Keeping all that guilt inside her has made her physically ill. I don't think I can ever forgive Jonathan for that." I tapped the base of my wine glass with intention as if calling up my confidence. "I can't worry about him anymore."

"The truth shall set you free," Nissa said and lifted her wine glass.

"Now, I just want to spend the rest of the time I have with Mary Jane in a positive light." I sopped up the last of the soup in my bowl with the homemade focaccia bread, not wanting to waste one drop of deliciousness. "Open your laptop."

"What exactly do you want me to look up?" Nissa pushed her untouched minestrone aside and opened her laptop.

"Here, you need the Wi-Fi password." I handed her Silvio's business card with the unique code written on the back. I also slid the black-and-white photo of my parents across the table.

Nissa picked up the photo. "Hmm, Mary Jane and Jonathan. Perfect as usual."

"Look at the other couple."

"Liddy before the accident?"

"Yep, and I believe that's Bobby Canton, my birth father." I pointed to the man digging in the sand, building a sandcastle.

Nissa held the picture closer to the sconce on the wall. "I can't see his face. Did you ask Mary Jane about him?"

"She said she and Jonathan had come home from their honeymoon and met Bobby at the beach, then Mary Jane announced she was pregnant and found out Liddy was pregnant, too."

"I wonder what was so wrong with Bobby Canton that Jonathan didn't want him dating Liddy?"

I pointed to the laptop.

"Okay, Googling Bobby Canton, is it Robert?"

"Not sure," I said. "Last night, I Googled Bobby and Robert but found nothing. Not even about his death, which is weird. I know it happened after my birth and somewhere around Athens. There should be an article or police report. I need you to look deeper."

"No problem. You know I'm always here for you. You don't have to do this on your own. What do we know about him?" Nissa pulled out a notebook and wrote *Bobby Canton* on the first line, then handed me the pen and pad across the table.

"Mary Jane mentioned something about his family ruining Liddy's reputation. That's all I know." I pulled my reading glasses out from my backpack and slid into Nissa's side of the booth.

People were beginning to arrive for lunch. The waitress topped off Nissa's glass of wine, emptying the bottle, then asked if we'd like water or a couple of iced teas. I told her we'd order food shortly, knowing we were going to take the booth up for another hour or so.

"Give me a few minutes," Nissa said as she sank into the corner of the booth, pulling the laptop with her.

I drifted into an imaginary tableau of Liddy, Bobby, and a youthful me picnicking in the park, playing soccer in a field of grass, laughing and enjoying the day. If they had married and the accident never occurred, would Liddy have had other children? Would I have a brother or sister? Would I have spent holidays with my Canton grandparents? And cousins? Do I have cousins? I had visions of a Christmas tree surrounded by gifts wrapped in holiday colors with children running around the house playing hide-and-seek while aunts and uncles set the table and cooked the Christmas meal. I pictured a quiet Christmas in Liddy's cottage, ripping open my presents with only Liddy and Bobby, my mother and father, sitting side by side on the couch, holding hands, content to watch their one daughter open the American Girl doll of her dreams.

"Tina. Tina, wake up." Nissa shook my arm.

I lifted my head off my forearms and rubbed my eyes. "Sorry." I shook off my nostalgic dreams. I couldn't miss what I never had. "Did you find anything?"

"I think I did. Robert, Sr., his father, went to prison for extortion and murder."

"Murder?" Had Jonathan found out this same information?

"Here's an article about him," Nissa said and slid the laptop over to me to read.

"Robert Canton Sr. was not a very nice man," I said as I skimmed the article. "He took part in a decade-long extortion ring in the jewelry industry, which ended in several murders." A chill ran up my spine. "Is this why Jonathan didn't want Liddy involved with Bobby Canton?"

"More importantly," interjected Nissa, "is this why Liddy didn't want you to know who your father was?"

I continued summarizing the article out loud. "Robert Sr. got out of jail a few years later. He appealed his sentence on a technicality. A judge declared his trial a mistrial. Robert Sr. claimed he was out of the country, they found no weapon with his prints, and everything else was hearsay. Three other men went to jail for life for the same crime.

"That means Bobby was about fifteen when his father got out of jail."

Nissa reached over and clicked on another window. "I can't find much more about Bobby or the accident, but here's his obit."

I stared into the eyes of my father at the age of about twenty-six. It was definitely the man building the sandcastles. "Interesting. Maybe Jonathan was right keeping Liddy away from that family." I wondered how much Mary Jane knew and wasn't telling.

"This might be why Liddy never told you she was your mother. She'd have to tell you about him. I bet she wanted to keep you away from his family. Do you want me to keep digging?"

I wasn't sure I needed or wanted to know any more. "Jake just might have been right when his mother said she might have to accept her lineage but had no problem ignoring it."

CHAPTER 33

With the air clear between Mary Jane and myself, I forged a new commitment to our relationship. Since she was nearing the end of her treatments, she stayed in bed most of the time, but every once in a while, she insisted we enjoy a game of rummy in the evenings with Bella. It was a satisfying way to wrap up a full day working on the miniatures for the B&B.

"How are you really doing?" Jake asked when I finally returned his many texts and messages several days after I had last spoken with him.

"Fine. Well, not perfect, but better." How do I explain I had become a whole new person and my mother and father were not my mother and father? My aunt's my mother, and my birth father is the son of a murderer. It sounded like a punchline for a joke.

"That's all I get? Did you talk to your mother? Did you get some answers?"

"Yes, and now I have many more questions, but they can wait. I promised you eight miniature replicas for your grand opening. Is the date still the same?"

"Okay. If that's how you want to play it. All business. But if you find you need someone to talk to—"

"Jake, I'm sorry I dragged you into my personal mess. I'm grateful I've had this project to focus on. We're near the finish line, and I'd like to stay focused until we wrap it up."

"Gotcha. And then we'll talk?"

I grinned. I could feel his dimple winking at me from the other end of the phone line. "The date for the opening? Still next Thursday?"

"Sure thing. I have reservations beginning that Friday night, so the Randall Mansion B&B has to be ready to roll for Labor Day Weekend. I meant to ask you, is there anyone you'd like to invite other than your mom and Bella? I just need to give the caterer the final number by the end of the week."

"Gosh, I don't think so. Nissa's bringing David to help out. I'll ask her if there is anyone else and get back to you. But I believe there's just the five of us."

"See you soon."

As Mary Jane and Bella focused on Mary Jane's health and gaining strength so she could attend the grand opening of the B&B, Nissa and I spent every waking hour over the next five days perfecting each piece of furniture and accessory. Nissa touched up the window trim, bascboards, and crown molding in each roombox. To light up the candles, lanterns, and lamps, I pushed tiny wires through tiny holes drilled through the thin veneer flooring out the bottom of the box and attached thin batteries cases underneath.

The day of delivery arrived, and we were ready for the big event. It took several trips for me, Nissa, and Bella to bring all the boxes and black velvet table covers down the elevators and into Nissa's SUV.

"Thank you, Bella," I said as she closed the back hatch.

"And thanks for the delish French toast. The best I've ever had." Nissa blew Bella a kiss as she ran around her car to the driver's side.

"That's the only way my babies will eat it—with my homemade maple syrup butter. Yum. Today's a time for celebrating. I wanted it to start with a treat. You girls have a good morning. Mary Jane and I will be there in time for the show."

"It's not a show, Bella," I said. "What time will the wheelchair van be here to pick you up?" I was happy to be able to contribute something to Mary Jane's care. I couldn't count how many times I had made the same arrangements for Liddy.

"I'm told 12:30. We'll be up at the mansion before your two p.m. show."

"It's not a show, Bella," I repeated with a chuckle. I gave Bella a tight hug and held her for a second more. Despite the experimental treatments, Mary Jane was getting weaker by the day, and Bella's actual work was about to begin. The doctor had said she would get worse before she got better, and he wasn't lying. She had not left the condo unless she had a treatment. Most of the time now, Bella sent Nissa to run her errands instead, which she happily did.

"Don't you worry none, Sweetie. Mary Jane wouldn't miss this for the world. She'll call in the troops if she has to, come hell or high water." Bella patted me on my back, then let me loose.

"I know, I know," I said. I wiped my bottom lids with the back of my forefinger, trying not to mess up my mascara.

When I opened the passenger door, Nissa leaned over and waved. "Thanks again, Bella."

Bella kissed her fingertips and cast her love to us as we drove away.

"Okay, Boss, what's the plan when we get to the B&B?" Nissa asked as she took a left out of the parking lot with care.

"First, help me stay focused. I'm nervous about Mary Jane taking such a long ride."

"Isn't that why you ordered the chair car? So, you wouldn't have to worry?" She asked as she pulled in across the street from SugarBeans and parked the car.

"Yes, but you haven't seen her these past few days. She's so weak. I think anticipating telling me the truth kept her strong. Now, I wish she didn't insist she tell me everything already. I feel she's only fighting to get through this presentation, and then—"

Nissa held up her hand. "Don't say it. Think of the burden that you have lifted since you forgave her. I'm sure she wouldn't miss this event if she could help it. She's guilt-free for the first time in a long time, and she's a part of your life now. That'll make her want to be around for your next big event," she said as she pulled up in front of SugarBeans.

"I hope there is a next one," I said, opening the car door to jump out and get two teas for the road.

"What about a wedding?" Nissa inquired.

"Whose?" I suddenly pulled my legs back in the car and closed the door.

Nissa gave me a sideways glance and pointed a finger at my face.

"Me?" I knocked her hand away and jumped out of the car. How could there be a wedding in the future when there wasn't even another date on the radar?

When I returned with our teas, Nissa asked me about Bobby Canton. "I did a little more research on Bobby Canton to no avail. But there's a lot out there about his father."

I sipped my tea to clear my head. "I'm not sure I want to look for family ties. I bet they don't even know I exist. Mary Jane is all the family I need right now. One thing at a time."

"I get it. Say the word, and I'll dig deeper."

"Thanks, but I think I'm good. Just want to get through one day at a time with my aunt."

As we stopped at a stoplight, Nissa said, "Well, would you look at that?" and pointed to the large billboard on the corner advertising the new Randall Mansion B&B and its restaurant, Blue Moon. "What about Jake?"

"What about him?"

"Have you talked to him since the day he stayed for lunch?"

"I'm pretty sure he thinks I'm a basket case. I've kept it to business."

"He hasn't called you since then?" Nissa asked, taken aback.

"I reminded him he was my client. And apologized for dumping on him. Anyway, I think he has a girlfriend."

"I thought you two were good together."

"I want to spend my time getting to know Mary Jane."

"I get it. Your usual tactic. Find something to focus on, so Mr. Distraction doesn't… distract you." Nissa's smile let me know she didn't believe a word about me not wanting to go out with Jake. "Okay, focus. No distractions, no worries about Mary Jane, no more about Jake. I'll be so busy keeping you on track, I won't be able to do anything else. Maybe you should stay in the car."

"Ha. Ha. Hilarious." I relaxed knowing Nissa had my back.

A huge white tent set up in the backyard welcomed us as Nissa pulled around to the back of the B&B. She pulled beside Jake's brand-new truck, the one he had bought courtesy of the last rainstorm.

A gentleman in a tight navy suit adorned with a green-and-navy-plaid bow tie greeted us as we opened the back of the SUV.

"Hi, I'm Charles, the event planner." He held out his hand, palm down.

I hoped I wasn't supposed to kiss his ring. I took his fingertips, adding a light shake. "Hi. Tina Edwards. This is Anissa Fayette."

Nissa nodded as she already had tablecloths in her hands.

"Let me help you with those. We're all excited to see your displays. Follow me." Charles scooped up the rest of the tablecloths and, in a stiff butlerlike walk, waddled toward the backyard.

Nissa turned penguinlike and rocked side to side straight legged, exaggerating his arrogant gait. I backhanded her on the shoulder, holding in my laughter. I leaned into the trunk, lifted out one roombox and followed behind, conscious of taking normal steps.

The tent, fashioned like a wedding reception, provided twelve round tables with white linens, each surrounded by eight white wooden Chiavari chairs. The centerpieces were low clear vases filled with assorted greens and loads of Georgia Cherokee roses, the perfect touch for the event. In one corner, the caterers finished setting up six-foot banquet tables for the afternoon victuals. In the opposite corner, Charles covered a table with one of our black velvet tablecloths.

Nissa joined him and spread her coverings on the other three tables as I approached with the first of the eight replicas.

Charles took the miniature from me and set it on the nearest table. "Here we go. We'll place the boxes two on each of the four tables. Our guests will be able to view each replica from either side." He adjusted the four tables into a perfect L-shape under one corner of the tent.

I approved, as if Charles would have let me do it any other way. Nissa and I headed back to the car to get the rest of the boxes.

Jake called out from the back porch, "Hey, how's it going?" He looked great dressed up in a navy-blue suit with a black V-neck t-shirt underneath. Casual, but classy. And two steps behind him followed the tall blonde.

I tried not to stare. I looked for Nissa, who had stopped dead in her tracks on her return to the parking lot. "See, I told you so," I wanted to shout to her.

The couple approached. Jake hugged me in his usual way and said, "Tina, I'd like you to meet, Elizabeth Garner, my interior decorator."

My gut sought to unwind as she offered me her hand in greeting. His interior decorator. Doesn't mean he's not dating her. "So nice to meet you."

"Me?" Elizabeth's sincere smile and warm tone instantly put me at ease. "So lovely to meet *you*. You made my job so much easier with the furniture you chose from the auction house. I'd love to work with you again."

"Done," I said, knowing deep down I'd love to, but wasn't sure if Jake would mind. "Did all the furniture get delivered and set up?"

"The final piece arrived at 10 p.m. last night. Guess which piece?" Jake asked.

"The Smith and Kentor sideboard?"

"Nope, the newly refurbished chaise lounge you found in the attic," he gloated. "Elizabeth did an excellent job with it. You'll love it. Would you like to see?"

Elizabeth said she'd catch up with both of us later and retreated into the house. I placed a replica in Jake's outstretched arms and grabbed another for myself to carry to the tent.

Charles yelled, "Excuse us. We need space." He shooed away the event staff like flies as they swarmed the tables to glance at the miniature replicas.

As Jake and I placed our boxes on the table, Nissa's David came up behind us with one more.

"Hey, David," we said at the same time.

Charles clapped his hands twice. "Back to your duties. We've got a party to put on." But still, no one moved. They all wanted to peek into the new arrivals.

I beamed from the comments of the onlookers.

"Remarkable."

"Could you imagine making these?"

"Look at the detail."

"You ain't seen nothing yet," Nissa said to the group. "Come back later once we've added the finishing touches."

"The replicas aren't complete," I said to Jake out of the side of my mouth. "We need to set up some tchotchkes and make sure the lights are all working."

Jake looked into the replica of the parlor. "There's my look alike. Did you ever figure out who he was?"

"Nissa did. That's Mr. Phillip G. Randall, George Randall's father. He ran a printing press in London until he was over eighty years old. His two boys traveled to America with money to start new lives. George ended up with his own printing company here in Athens, and his brother went into commercial real estate up north."

"You two are quite the historians."

Needing to explain further, Nissa chimed in, "I found out he had never left England. Which is why he was so hard to locate. You wouldn't believe everything I've discovered."

"Interesting," Jake said, clearly not interested. "Want to go check out the interior of the mansion now?"

Nissa huffed in dismay when he didn't follow up with a million questions about his family. I knew she was armed with information and was dying to share it with him, but she sent us on our way with a double flick of both her hands. "Go ahead. I got this."

I sighed. So much for Nissa keeping me focused on the job at hand and away from Jake.

"Come on. I'll give you a quick tour. Let's start upstairs and work our way down." Jake said.

We fell into a comfortable silence, but as I dragged my hand up the smooth, rich mahogany railing, I relaxed even more. I couldn't wait to see the rest of the refurbished-wood details throughout the house. And I was pleased with myself that I no longer missed Jonathan's presence.

"Have your friends arrived? I saw that you called in with two more guests."

"They're really Nissa's friends, and I haven't seen them yet."

"Well, I'd love to meet them. Any friend of either of yours is a friend of mine."

We reached the old main bedroom, now called the Rose Room. The high ceilings almost dwarfed the Victorian mahogany four-post canopied queen bed and the matching armoire we purchased at the auction. In the corner by the front window stood a sole single-drawer pedestal side table with four splayed scrolled feet on which my miniature replica would be displayed. The pale rose-colored wallpaper with scrollwork and medallions of roses covered the walls, and one wall presented Victorian lace panels framing large windows, which added a touch of romance. The attached en suite glowed with crystal pink marble from Malaysia.

We walked from room to room, taking in the essence of each while Jake explained the particulars. "You and your mother did a wonderful job choosing original wall art," I said, admiring an exquisite reproduction of William Orpen's *The Mirror.*

"We had so much fun. It was something she had never done before, attend an auction. Your guidelines were invaluable and kept us on task."

I regretted not having the time to return to the auction house with Jake but was thrilled he took his mother, and they enjoyed the process.

I appreciated the way he guided the tour. His standoffish professionalism showed he had received the message that I considered our relationship a working one only.

The remaining four bedrooms were all similar in size but smaller than the Rose Room. They each had a fireplace and en suite. Each were full of character with their own color scheme. The two on the other end of the hall were a gentle sage green and, my favorite, plush French grey. The nursery-turned-suite on the third floor was painted in peaches and cream, and the other suite across the hall was a soft vintage lilac.

"They are all so beautiful. I can only imagine waking up in such a charming room," I said as I left the intoxicating French Grey Room.

"You are welcome to stay anytime," Jake said, raising one eyebrow, then mumbled an apology.

I was referring to waking up in my own charming bedroom in my own Victorian cottage one day, but, of course, he wouldn't know anything about that. "Now let me see the lobby and dining area. Then I have to go help Nissa."

The lobby radiated modern Victorian with all its whites, creams, and soft, muted mauves. Three-foot-wide cream-and-white alternating stripes on a wood-grain-textured silk covered the dining room walls. Rose-and-peony woven silk drapes bubbled over knotted cream tassels and puddled on the pine floors in perfection.

"Your designer did a great job," I said. "I might use her."

"For what?" Jake asked.

As easy as it was to talk to him, I reminded myself there was no need to. "I'll explain later. I have to run and make sure we're set before Mary Jane arrives."

"How's she doing? I'm glad she's going to be here, and your other friends." Jake lifted his hand to touch my sleeve but then dropped it to his side.

"Nissa can't wait to introduce you to them. Got to run."

"I understand."

"Thank you for the tour. You've done a beautiful job bringing this old girl back to life," I said, then added, "Good luck today." I ran into Nissa and David as I entered the kitchen.

"We came in to grab water. Want one?" Nissa asked as one of the several waitstaff milling around waiting to begin service handed her a bottle.

"Sure, thanks. Is everything set up outside?" The server gave me a bottle also.

"All set and covered. I put out the name cards while you were having a personal tour."

I shushed her and turned to look for Jake, but he hadn't followed me. "Your fault, you should've gone upstairs with us."

"You're still interested in him. I knew it," Nissa said.

"I'm interested in the mansion."

"Maybe at the moment."

I flicked my wrist at her and returned to the tent, having to work my way through the first arrivals sipping cocktails and admiring the abundant gardens around the bed and breakfast, most discussing what could possibly be under the black velvet cloths in the right corner of the tent.

"I'm going to the parking lot and wait for m… m… Mary Jane."

"It's okay to call her Mom." Nissa squeezed my shoulder and took off with David.

I sat on the back porch in one of the white oversized rocking chairs waiting for the van to arrive. The sunny blue sky and fresh air filled me with contentment. What a great autumn day to have a bed-and-breakfast opening. I rested my head on the back of an old wooden rocking chair and brought forth a past autumn day with Liddy and me trying to count the varying colors of fall leaves that I found in the backyard. I ran back and forth with the leaves, lining them up at Liddy's feet. We concluded the task would never end. There was no way possible to gather all of autumn's spectrum of color. To this day, fall still warmed my heart.

This was the first time I had set up a project without having another client waiting in the wings. A different kind of stress would soon begin, but the rocking soothed my eyes closed. I dreamt of spending time getting to know Mary Jane and adapting my Victorian knowledge from miniature to life size in Liddy's cottage.

I brushed away a tickle on my right wrist and opened my eyes. Jake stood in front of me holding hands with a tall, striking brunette in a green floral maxi dress.

"Tina, I'd like you to meet my mother," Jake said, and I jumped to my feet.

"So nice to meet you, Ms. Martin." I noticed her dimple was as winsome as Jake's.

"Jenn. Call me Jenn. And it's a pleasure to meet you. I adore your artwork."

"And I appreciate what you do. Your style is so refreshing."

Jake excused himself as we two women took to our seats and were far from having a lack of words for one another.

"Jake said you are interested in our family history," Jenn said as we took a seat.

"We dig a little into the family history of the rooms we recreate. You have a large, wonderful family, several artists."

"I'm sorry I don't know much about them. It was taboo to mention anything Randall-related to my mom. I've never met any Randall family members."

"Nissa and I have learned that family is the root of all annals of life. But we're stuck with them, and they're all not that bad." We both laughed.

"Well, enjoy the party. You've earned it. Let's chat after over a glass of wine." Jenn stood up as tires crunched on the gravel parking lot.

I watched the driver open the back door of the van as I bounded off the back porch. Bella looked out of the passenger door and descended as if she had to jump with a parachute. With both hands holding on to the handle above for dear life, she all but fell out, yet managed to land on both feet. We met at the same time at the back of the van and found Mary Jane inside, slumped over in her wheelchair.

"Mom!" I yelled, startling both Bella and the van driver. I would never forgive myself if something happened to Mary Jane on the ride over.

"Hush, Sugar. Let your mother finish her nap. She's going to need it."

We all backed away from the van as the driver lowered the wheelchair lift. He stepped on the platform, raised himself up to retrieve Mary Jane. When the wheelchair reached terra firma, Bella grabbed the oxygen tank from the driver. I lifted Mary Jane's purse and sweater from her lap then reached for her hand.

A groggy Mary Jane looked around, registering the surrounding scene. "We're here. It's so beautiful. You're so beautiful," she said when she saw me.

I smiled at her. "Let's go find our seats. Would you like a drink?"

The coughing started when Mary Jane answered. She looked up at me with apologetic, embarrassed eyes.

Bella turned the knob up on the oxygen condenser, took control of the wheelchair, pointed for me to lead the way with her chin. "Let's get her some water. Just breathe, Mary Jane, just breathe."

CHAPTER 34

The podium stood centered in front of the grand oak front doors flanked with leaded, glazed sidelights on the large front porch. A twelve-inch-wide red velvet ribbon with a multi-looped bow stretched across from post to post. The B&B looked magnificent and regal with her new burgundy tone and pale ochre washed trim.

The front porch overflowed with all the people who had a part in making the B&B happen. Nissa and David joined me, Mary Jane, and Bella on the left of the podium. With the event brochure blocking the lower part of her face, Nissa let me know, "Our guests have arrived."

"Where are they?"

Nissa pointed to a sweet-faced older couple, the man leaning on a cane for support.

"I hope we've done a good thing by inviting them," I said.

"Of course, you did," said Bella as the kitchen staff, all dressed in white Mandarin-collared chef jackets, stepped out of the front doors, and joined the presenters sitting on the right. The vast front yard, even with its long downward slope, boasted well over fifty guests, press, and curious onlookers.

"It's two o'clock. Here we go," I said as Jake approached the podium and adjusted the microphone.

"Hello and thank you all for coming down to see the newly restored Randall Mansion Bed and Breakfast. I am excited to have it all up and running. And, to y'all who know my mama, Jennifer Martin," his mother stood up and waved from her seat on the porch, "I see you out there, Miss Paula—you know this has always been a dream of hers." Jake waved to his grandmother's best friend, Paula, an older woman standing on the lawn wearing a sunny yellow dress and matching hat. Miss Paula waved back, making sure she didn't spill her cocktail.

"Let me know if I made my mama proud. I have a few guests here who would like to have a word or two with y'all, and after that, please feel free to tour the mansion. There'll be refreshments in the back under the tent, featuring samples of what we will offer here at Blue Moon. So, eat up… and then make your reservations."

The audience applauded and snickered at his shameless plug. Jake introduced the mayor of Athens, who, after a few words of congratulations, introduced the deputy commissioner of tourism, who thanked Jake for offering such a great bed and breakfast and restaurant to entice visitors to Athens and provide new jobs for the locals.

Jake introduced an old friend from high school, Elizabeth Garner, his interior designer from Nashville, who stood and waved. Nissa glanced at me with an understanding look and a thumbs up. "Nashville? He's all yours," she teased.

Mary Jane grinned and nodded.

Next stood the editor-in-chief of the *Athens Herald*, Bill Langley, who was also on the board of the Randall Mansion B&B. He discussed its missions, one being the redesigning and maintenance of the public park, which shared the mansion's property lines and used to be part of the Randall's property.

"Eloise Chambers Belkmore was George and Anna Randall's granddaughter. She took it upon herself to make sure this beautiful land would stay free and clear from any building and would offer a place the citizens of Athens could share. Therefore, the newly formed Randall-Martin Foundation will create seventeen acres of public park with Victorian rose gardens and large shade trees, and plenty of trails and family areas. We will bring it back to the way it was when Anna Randall designed and maintained the mansion's gardens."

The audience applauded and murmured its pleasure. Chills of delight ran up my spine as I planned on sneaking in a few fairy doors at the base of some of the pecan trees.

Retaking the microphone, Jake signaled for me and Nissa to stand.

"These two fine ladies from Edwards' Historical Miniatures, Christina Edwards and Anissa Fayette, have put hundreds of hours into research and have created miniature replicas of the original rooms in this 1860s mansion. Details, including the floors, fabrics, and furniture, as well as the flowerpots and portraits, are exact replicas of how the Randall family lived when George built this wonderful home for his new wife, Anna."

The audience applauded, and Jake continued, "Please ask questions as you admire their work. As of tomorrow, each room inside the mansion will display their corresponding miniature replica."

Nissa and I waved and took our seats. Seeing tears in Mary Jane's eyes, I had to look away. It was too intimate a gesture to absorb. I did, however, reach over and squeeze her hand. A tear connected with my knuckles and sent ripples throughout my body. With a shiver, I squeezed her hand tighter.

"Remember, please take pleasure in the food prepared by the staff of Blue Moon and enjoy the Randall Mansion

B&B." Jake held a pair of scissors in the air. The crowd erupted in loud hooting and hollering when both sides of the red velvet ribbon fell to the front porch floor. Jake called out, "Welcome!"

Two of the kitchen staff whisked the podium away as the grand front doors opened, presenting the resplendent foyer. The crowd ascended the staircase. Nissa and David raced to the tent to uncover the miniature rooms and man their stations, allowing me time to spend with Mary Jane. Bella quickly unlocked the wheelchair and rolled her out of the way of the oncoming crowd.

"Do you mind if I push?" I reached in front of Bella for the wheelchair handles. Bella turned over the wheelchair like a baton to a rookie runner.

My shoulders dropped in cadence with my slow exhale as I pushed the chair to the ramp provided off the porch near the kitchen door in the back. I comforted myself with the sureness of pushing Mary Jane in a wheelchair after years of maneuvering Liddy around.

"You take your time, Sweetie. I'll go fetch us some of those edible tidbits Mr. Jake mentioned and meet you at a table in the big tent." Bella pointed as if there was a choice of tents.

"Thanks, Bella." I navigated Mary Jane into the B&B and opened the manual brass accordion door when the modern elevator arrived so we could start on the top floor and work our way down.

After admiring the whole of the interior, we took a stroll through the mansion's gardens along asphalt pathways, taking in all late summer had to offer. Old tree stumps cried out for a fairy house interior, and pecan tree trunks called for fairy doors and gardens.

Mary Jane and I had stopped to admire a bed of apricot-colored roses. As we neared the tent, Bella could be heard brandishing the chef with her idea of how a proper Hot Brown should be cooked. "See here, if you sliced the bread thicker, it would've stood up to your gravy. Plus, you didn't use three-day-old bread. Did you use three-day-old bread? And the bacon's too crispy, you dried up all the juices."

Mary Jane stifled a laugh and signaled me to go in the opposite direction of where Bella stood. One step ahead of Mary Jane, I had already redirected the wheelchair toward our miniatures.

Nissa flagged us over and introduced the lady in the yellow dress Jake had pointed out during his welcoming. "Miss Paula, this is Tina Edwards and her mother. Tina's the brains behind the miniatures. Miss Paula was a friend of Jake's grandmother."

"Did you know the Randall family well?" I asked.

"I've had a house in Athens all my life, and now live part-time in Canada with my husband. He's from there," Miss Paula said in a heavy Southern drawl and raised her eyebrows twice as if she had secrets to tell.

"Miss Paula has an idea for a miniature replica, and she'd like us to come to her home in *Canada* to discuss it," Nissa said. Her tone suggested she'd love to look into it. I was happy for the opportunity to have a new project on the horizon.

"I'm sure we can make arrangements. So nice to meet you." I returned my attention to Mary Jane, and seeing her expression, I knew that I would not be traveling anytime soon.

As we approached the first miniature box, Mary Jane sat at the perfect vantage point to see the roombox through the front glass, the horizontal view. She then sat up as tall as she could to peer into the top of the delicate rooms. I pushed her chair in a little closer as she pressed both palms on the tabletop and tried to stand. The table tilted toward her, sucked in by the soft ground beneath. The miniature rooms slid toward us, and I grabbed Mary Jane under her arms. David jumped in and steadied the table.

Mary Jane's cough erupted as she sat on the edge of her seat, sending an alarm across the tent to Bella, who dropped her plate of food and hustled toward us, almost knocking into a waiter or two. On her way over, Bella called out, "Mr. Charles, there's a mess over by the food station. Best have someone go run and clean it up."

Mary Jane collected her breath and controlled her cough as Bella barged her way in, taking command of the wheelchair.

"No harm, no foul," Nissa said as she straightened the tablecloth and miniature rooms.

"We're all good here, Bella. Wanted a better look, that's all," I said as I squatted beside Mary Jane and rubbed her shoulder. I wanted to show I could care for Mary Jane as well as Bella, but that didn't work out so great. I lost the job once Bella arrived.

With feelings of inadequacy, I stepped back as Bella bent down and spoke to Mary Jane. She grabbed the oxygen tank off the back of the chair and slung it over her shoulder. She hooked her hands under Mary Jane's arms and helped her skootch to the front of the wheelchair. With a count of three, Mary Jane was up on her feet. With loving care, Bella walked her from replica to replica with David following close behind with the wheelchair.

CHAPTER 35

"Your mom has one special friend there," Jake's mother, Jenn, said, and I returned her smile.

"That she does. Miss Bella is the best." I hid my jealousy, determined to be more involved with Mary Jane's care. "I'll introduce you to both if you'd like to join us at our table."

"I'll be glad to join you once you've finished with all these curious people." Jenn left Nissa and me at the replicas to answer people's questions. Nissa was smart enough to bring the box of photos. We delved into all kinds of stories we had discovered along the way as we built the miniature rooms, stories about Emma and Clara, the portraits, and the Baby Jane doll. Before we knew it, we had attracted a crowd. Questions were answered according to our research, and we surprised ourselves with the amount of history we knew.

By the time we finished describing the last room, the kitchen, Mary Jane fought to stand even with Bella's help. It was clear Mary Jane needed to sit down. David rolled the wheelchair under her just in time.

He pushed the wheelchair as Bella and I paraded to a table. "Nobody's sitting here, so these dishes need to go," Bella said, shaking her head as she admonished the waitstaff and handed them dirty plates and cups as they walked by.

"Tina, you sit here with your sweet mama, while I go fetch us some lemonade." By that, Bella meant she would fetch someone to bring over some lemonade. Bella called out commands as if they all served a queen.

"You must be exhausted," I said to Mary Jane as she straightened up the pillow in the back of the wheelchair.

She took a couple of deep breaths through her tube and reached up and cupped my cheek. "I am, Honey. Just give me a minute. I've been looking at the outside walls of this place my whole life. Thanks to you and your wonderful talent, I'm able to see the beautiful insides both present and past. I never thought I ever would."

I laced my fingers in hers and kissed the back of her hand. "I tried to make a dinner reservation in the new restaurant for us next week, but they're booked. They squeezed us in two weeks from now. With a little luck, you'll feel up to it!"

"I'd like that."

Jake's mother approached the table. "Mind if I join you?"

"Please do. This is Jenn Martin, Jake's mother. Jenn, this is my… mother, Mary Jane Edwards." It seemed so natural to call Mary Jane Mother. She was more my mother now than she had ever been. A fierce tiger who protected her cub.

Mary Jane squeezed my hand before she released it to shake Jenn's.

Bella returned with two plates of bite-sized Hot Browns, spread them out in front of us, and said, "I got us a wee bit of everything."

Three waiters trailed behind her. As she sat, she pointed to where she wanted each plate.

"The pimento cheese crackers, the fried green tomato sliders, and the bacon and scallops over there, succotash tartlets and andouille mini dogs over there, the crab cakes and hush puppies right here in front of me," she said, patting the table in front of her with both hands. Then she directed the server with a pile of empty plates to go around and give one to everyone. Somewhere along the line, Bella lost the fact that this was a buffet-style party. But no one, not even the waitstaff, questioned the table service.

Bella asked another waiter to unload his burden of lemonades and iced teas on the table before she took his arm and pointed across the lawn. "Now, would you mind telling Miss Nissa over there to come over here and eat up." She smiled at him and fluttered her eyelashes. He couldn't help himself and broke out in a grin. Nissa was deep in conversations with our special guests. Their interest in the mansion's replica miniatures was evident.

As Bella worked her rear end around to sit more comfortably in her seat, she sent David to the dessert table. "I gathered up a few desserts over there, see 'em on the corner of the table? Could you bring 'em over to us? Thanks, Sugar."

As David set off to collect the piled-high plates, Bella yelled, "Could you hunt down some napkins on your way back, too?"

I busted out a laugh. You've got to love Bella.

"Bella, meet Jake's mother. Jenn Martin, the one and only Miss Bella."

"Bella, you could have organized this whole event," Jenn said as she shook Bella's hand. Everyone at the table laughed and nodded in agreement.

"Next time," Bella said then stuffed a hush puppy in her mouth.

Jake entered the tent holding a brown cardboard box. He placed it on the ground between Mary Jane's and my chairs. He then reached into the middle of the table, grabbed one of the bacon-wrapped scallops, and popped it into his mouth.

"How's it going out here? Bella, I heard from Mr. Charles it would do me good to employ your services. Seems people listen to you around here." Jake's dimple twinkled double time.

"Aw, shucks, Mr. Jake, it's a matter of letting them know what to do and when. All nice and orderly."

Bella blushing?

"What's in the box?" I asked. I leaned over to peer inside, and my mouth fell open.

"Junk one of the construction workers found when he opened up a wall. Thought you might—"

"Junk? It's Baby Jane! I can't believe it." I pulled out the old well-loved one-eyed doll and smoothed down her few strands of long blond curls. The group went silent and looked at me as if I had lost my mind.

Nissa picked up one of the few remaining curls resting on Baby Jane's shoulder. "We think she was Miss Emma's doll. Tina created a tiny replica for her miniature room as well."

"She's beautiful." I smoothed down the filthy pinafore covering the faded and torn dress. She was worn much more than the pictures from years ago. "She was well-loved."

Nissa pulled out a wooden dog with three of four wheels missing from its paws, a packet of turn-of-the-century paper dolls, and an old cast-iron penny bank in the shape of a horse.

"When they tore down the walls, this stuff was found. Someone wanted them saved."

"Which room?" Nissa needed to know.

Jake shrugged. "One of the girl's rooms. The French Grey one."

"So cool," Nissa said. "We'll clean them up. Maybe you could put them on display, part of your family history."

"Great," said Jake. "Aren't you curious at all, Mom?"

Jenn shrugged. "They just don't mean anything to me," she said and picked up Baby Jane. Her forlorn glance led me to feel she wished she had a connection to her great-grandmother's doll.

Nissa poked me in the side to direct my attention to the couple she invited to the grand opening. It seemed as if they were mulling around waiting to leave. "Looks like our friends are waiting to say goodbye." Nissa waved them over.

Jake stood up. "I was hoping to meet your friends." He walked around to greet the couple as they approached.

"Hi, folks. I'm Jake Martin. Thank you for coming today." He stuck out his hand.

"Frances? Hi, I'm Tina. You already know Nissa." I avoided the questioning look from Jake as I seemingly introduced myself to my own friends. "And this is Jennifer Williamson Martin, your second cousin; your grandfathers were brothers.

Jenn slowly stood up, clung to Baby Jane, and took Jake's side. Grabbing his elbow as if holding him back, she said, "Hello."

"Let me make introductions." Nissa took over. "Jake and Jenn, I would like you to meet Sarah and Raymond Jenkins. Sarah is Miss Eloise's niece. She grew up down the street from your mother, Alice." As Sarah spoke, Raymond handed Nissa his car keys and she headed toward the parking lot.

"Alice and I were first cousins. I'm not a Randall, but you and I are still family on the Belkmore side; your grandfather and my father were brothers. I was practically raised in this house. Eloise didn't always approve of the way my father, Samuel Belkmore, raised me after my mother died. So, from the age of seven on, I pretty much lived in this house with your grandmother. I haven't been in the house since Eloise's funeral and Uncle Joe handed me a box of family heirlooms to pass to Alice."

Sarah's nervous prattle was interrupted by her husband as he placed his palm over her hand. "Honey, slow down. It's okay."

It took a moment, but Jenn's handshake turned into a hug.

"I named my daughter Alice." Sarah looked directly at Jenn.

Jenn's eyes softened.

"I named her after your mother. I missed Alice dearly." She turned.

"Why don't you two take a load off?" Bella welcomed the couple to join them at the table and began ordering the staff to bring more chairs, food, and lemonade.

Jenn took a seat next to Sarah then asked Jake if he had anything stronger than lemonade or iced tea.

"Sure as hell do." He jumped up and scurried out of the tent.

"I'll come with," David said at Jake's heels.

Mary Jane, Bella, and I sat in silence as Sarah explained how she had lost touch with Alice once she ran away. Sarah was two years older and was away at college, then moved away when she got married. "A ceremony, I might add, that I put off for several months while we all tried to locate Alice. We had always dreamed of being each other's maid of honor," Sarah said.

"If we only had Facebook or Instagram then," Raymond snickered.

Nissa returned from the Jenkins' car with a small suitcase and placed it between Jenn and Sarah.

Bella pulled on the sleeve of a waiter passing by and asked, "Would you go fetch us some of those special plastic crystal cups there on the drink table? We'll need at least a dozen. Thanks, sweetie pie."

"I never dreamed I wouldn't ever see Alice again after she ran away. It broke my heart. We grew up all but sisters. It crushed me." Sarah's silence prompted Jenn to take Sarah's hand in hers.

"I miss her, too," said Jenn. "All of this is in her honor. She was upset when she found out the mansion sold out of the family. That pretty much sealed the deal with her—she was no longer a Randall. I'm surprised she didn't reach out to you, though," Jenn said, as she sat back in her chair.

"How could she without asking Eloise or someone in the family where I was?" Sarah asked.

"I never knew any of this. It must have been too painful for my grandmother to even tell me about you," Jenn said

"The Jenkins brought along the Randall family bible and some of Eloise's journals," Nissa said as she peeled open the suitcase and handed Jenn a leather-bound book.

Jenn opened the cover to a family tree that went beyond George and Anna Randall. She underlined her grandmother's name with her finger. We met eyes after she drew her finger down the page.

"Time to add your name as well as Jake's." I agreed with what I assumed were her silent thoughts.

"Aunt Eloise wrote to Alice every day in her journals. Uncle Joe asked me to make sure I got these, and the Randall family bible, to Alice if I ever found her once Eloise had passed." Sarah handed over several leather-bound books tied together with a light blue ribbon.

"So, I'd like to give them to you. Your mother was loved and missed so very much. Also, here is Joseph's will. He had left the house to Alice." As she rustled through the papers, she added, "And here's the paperwork from the lawyers. As you see, there were various attempts to find her. After eleven years, they sold the home off."

"Alice, my mother, took my father's name, even though they never married. She melded into the Williamson family. They claimed her as a long-lost cousin. I honestly believe she never knew anyone had spent any time looking for her."

"See melting pots of miscommunication and misperception," Nissa whispered to me referring to her definition of family.

Jake and David arrived with a brand-new bottle of bourbon. "What did we miss?" Jake asked.

Jenn stood up and gave Jake a huge hug. "We have a new family, Jake. And if it's all right with them," she rested her hand on Sarah's shoulder, "I'd like to take the time to get to know them."

I instantly caught Mary Jane's eyes and smiled. We might not have a new family but seeing how easily Jenn put aside her differences—well, in truth, her mother's differences—I realized, now more than ever, one can hide the truth but not the facts. And the facts can set you free.

Jake poured eight drinks, two fingers each.

"I'm not sure what just happened here," Jake said, staring into his mother's smiling eyes, "but I bet a big thanks goes out to Nissa and her research. Here's to what I'm calling a successful day all the way around. Cheers." Jake lifted his glass to the others.

"It doesn't count if it doesn't clink." I reached out and tapped Jake's glass with mine.

Jake winked and tapped each of the other glasses around the table.

Everyone's bourbon went down in one gulp, except Mary Jane's. She took hers sip by sip. With the van driver waiting in the driveway, we sat and listened to Jenn make plans with her newly found family. Mary Jane did not give up her cup until she downed the last drop.

CHAPTER 36

Standing on the gravel driveway as the opening celebration wound down, I waved goodbye to the van after watching Bella scale up the sideboard steps and clamber into her seat. I sent gratitude to a higher being that Mary Jane had made it to the opening of the B&B, grateful to share my success with the woman who had a hand in raising me.

"Great day today," I said, walking arm in arm with Nissa. "Wouldn't have wanted to do it without you."

Nissa laughed. "As if you could have. By the way, we really do have a potential new client. Remember Miss Paula, the lady in the bright yellow dress?"

"With the matching hat, yep."

"Her husband's family is involved in Canadian professional sports. How do you feel about building a replica of a miniature ice hockey arena circa 1912?"

"That could be interesting, and Canada sounds fun."

David and Jake caught up with us girls. "Why don't we talk about it over dinner tonight?" Jake asked. "I'll cook y'all the very first meal served from my Blue Moon kitchen."

"David's got a super-early day tomorrow," Nissa said, pulling them toward her parked car.

"I do?" David asked as Nissa's side glance had him turn to me and say, "I'm always the last to know."

"You do," Nissa said, "and I do, too. I have a doctor's appointment in the morning before work, so I might be late," Nissa insisted, looking directly at me.

I bowed my head and kicked a stone. "Guess we'll have to take a rain check on that dinner," I said to Jake. "I rode here with Nissa."

"I do have a brand-new truck and most likely could drive you home after we ate," Jake said with a shrug.

"Great idea!" Nissa pulled her keys out of her pocket and wiggled them in the air as a goodbye.

"Wait, my purse is in your car," I called out.

"No, it's not, I already put it in the kitchen. And before you ask, I have the velvet covers and the tablecloths in the trunk." Nissa yelled out her car window with a tight-fingered princess wave as David followed in his car.

I secretly welcomed the setup and waved goodbye. Jake's decorator friend didn't stick around much after the formal introductions, and a pointed conversation about her bill assured me she and Jake weren't an item. We headed back to the B&B. He stopped at the base of the steps going up to the back porch as waitstaff passed back and forth to the kitchen. "Oh, by the way..."

"Yes?" I asked.

"Here is your final check." He pulled an envelope out of his breast pocket and handed it to me. "Payment on delivery."

"Well, thank you. But you could've put it in the mail."

"Um... no, ma'am, I am now paid in full. We are no longer in business together. No more excuses." He took a step back, flashed his dimple, and waited for my response.

My plan to take this time to get to know Mary Jane was a priority. I had convinced myself I didn't have time to date. My life was a mess. I had pieces to pick up all over the place, but did I have to pick them up alone? Did I? My gaze met his blue eyes and that irresistible dimple. I took one of his arms and wrapped it around my shoulder and said, "What's for dinner?"

"Whatever Mademoiselle would like."

"Do you have any good wine?"

"You know I do. But to be fair, if we open the good stuff, I'd like to imbibe. So, I won't be driving you home tonight."

"Don't worry. I know which room I want to stay in." I chuckled at my unpracticed sexy voice. "I assume you can supply a toothbrush?"

As a few employees could be heard bustling about the B&B preparing for tomorrow's guests, he diced sweet potatoes and threw them into a hot pan as the remaining staff gathered garbage and wiped down the counters before leaving. I sat on the pristine metal counter, swinging my legs and sipping one of the best wines I'd ever tasted.

"So, all the drama this afternoon?" he inquired as he focused on stirring aromatics in with the sweet potatoes. "Seems like you've forgiven your mother, and you certainly surprised mine."

"And it seems like your mother has forgiven her mother all of her secrets." The smell of sautéing celery, garlic, and onions made my sip of wine all the richer.

"That was a nice thing you and Nissa did. My mother would never have reached out to any Belkmore or Randall family. They were just never part of her life."

"We couldn't pass up the chance once Nissa discovered Alice was wanted, and her family had looked for her. It was worth it to make the connection even if your mother wasn't interested."

"Well, I think my mother realized Grandma Alice had her reasons for not ever reaching out to her family, but finally realized she didn't have to follow suit." Jake clinked his wine glass with mine. "You surely redeemed the family name in her eyes. Again, thanks. But tell me. You and Mary Jane?"

I started from the beginning, unraveling the threads of my childhood. He took the pans off the stove, pausing our meal to listen, and poured doubled the wine already in my glass. He tucked my curls behind my ears and wiped my tears.

"Everything I thought was true from my childhood, isn't. I'm pretty sure having had your project to occupy my mind kept me out of the deep end. Well, at least kept my head bobbing above water."

"Just my project?" he asked with a wink. He turned off the stove and covered the vegetables then placed two sirloins topped with fresh herb butter on the grill.

"Okay, big shot. I'm lucky I met you. You do make a good distraction. If it weren't for you and Nissa, I'd—" I stopped swinging my legs and bent my head.

"You'd what?" He flipped the steaks searing the buttery side and turned down the flame then uncrossed my legs and stepped between.

I rested my hands on his shoulders.

With one finger, he lifted my chin. He repeated, "You'd what?"

I looked into his heartwarming eyes and kissed his fingers. "If it weren't for you and Nissa, I'd be alone. Mary Jane won't be around forever." I choked.

He leaned his forehead on mine and whispered, "You are most certainly not alone." He kissed me on the lips and placed my wine glass on the counter. I melted into him when he said, "Understand? You are not—"

I draped my arms over his shoulders and crossed my legs around his waist, and pulled him in. If I let myself, he could be someone I could depend on, someone who valued honesty, truth, and hard work. Maybe someone I could even love. I kissed him like I had kissed no other man.

Jake broke away, regret in his eyes. "The steaks." He removed the sirloins from the grill and set them aside to rest.

"Okay, where were we?" He swept me off the counter and swung me around, placing my feet on the floor. Kissing me on the forehead, he handed me back my wine.

"Sorry. I got a little carried away," I said, burying my newly found courage.

"I don't mind. Um, dinner's ready. Do you want to eat… or?" Jake wiped his brow with his handkerchief.

"If dinner's ready, we should eat." My practical side, and my hunger, leveled the playing field as my heartbeat sped up. To level the playing field in my mind, I called Mary Jane to make sure she made it home safe and sound. It was good to hear her voice and Bella's in the background. "Now don't you go worrying about us. You go have yourself a good time."

I exhaled to slow down my breath and took a seat at the table. I focused on the meal to quell the heat rising up my back. Dinner was perfect; the food superb, the wine delightful, the atmosphere romantic, and the conversation soul-cleansing. Jake encouraged me to tell him the good stories of my youth, stories involving my mother, Liddy. One story led to another and another. Most of the evening we spent laughing, but sometimes I cried. And I didn't mind.

"What about your birth father's side of the family?"

"The jury's out on that at the moment. One thing at a time." I brought up the information Nissa found regarding my true father.

"I agree you should do more research on Bobby Canton and his family before you attempt any contact. Once you do, there'd be no going back."

"They must not know I exist, or why wouldn't they have reached out to me? It's not like I've moved away or changed my name."

"I find it strange that Liddy never told you she was your mother and Bobby, your father. Even after Jonathan died." Jake poured me more wine.

"I think about that all the time. Why did she not want me to know?"

"Maybe you should just let sleeping dogs lie."

"On that front, I am." I had a lot of processing to do without adding a whole other family to the pile.

After finishing the wine out on the wraparound porch listening to the night owls and crickets, Jake escorted me to my dream suite, the French Grey Room. Clara's room. He opened the door, and to my surprise, the room teemed with fresh blush and pink peonies and roses. On the side table, a tray of chocolate-covered strawberries and a bottle of champagne with two glasses waited.

Jake pushed the door wider. "Dessert?"

I floated into the room and pulled Jake in by the collar. He kicked the door closed with his heel.

CHAPTER 37

I slept in Victorian heaven until 9 a.m. I hid my grin as I snuggled under the covers and burrowed into the pillow Jake had slept on the night before. I must have made it clear that I had fallen in love with the French Grey Room the first time I entered. Jake's forethought of flowers and dessert proved it. Stretched under the thin down comforter, I sank deeper into the lavish pillows. When was the last time I had a morning to lounge, a morning without something scheduled weeks in advance?

I used to be afraid not to have something in my appointment book first thing every morning. But that could change. This was heaven. If I could, I would have stayed in bed all day. But Jake was up and about, dealing with all the preparations for his first bed and breakfast guests checking in for the weekend. I called Nissa and asked her to meet me at the cottage after her supposed doctor's appointment. I'd like to know her feelings about moving the business to the cottage, and her thoughts about what to do with my condo, which brought me to Mary Jane. I had her and Bella to consider too. I sent a quick text to see if all was well. Bella's response was, "We're just fine. Guessing we're not as fine as you." Got to love Bella.

Well, I had tried the bed, now I would try the breakfast—after I try the bath. I threw the comforter off and jumped out of bed to get ready for the day. The luxurious steam shower called my name, especially the Crabtree and Evelyn soap, shampoo, and conditioner.

I spent far too much time drowning in the rosewater scent, romanticizing how comfortable I'd be in Liddy's cottage. I considered putting in a steam shower when I rehabbed the master bath, and my mind raced with colors and fabric ideas.

I wrapped my hair in a cotton bath sheet and covered myself with the rose oil afterbath. Jake's house manager sure knew how to pamper a girl.

As I stepped into the bedroom wearing only my bra and underwear, panic hit. Someone had been in the room. The plate full of strawberry caps and empty champagne glasses, as well as the empty bottle from last night had been whisked away. A bed tray with a vintage Samuel Radford floral teapot, steaming with hot water, and a matching cup and saucer were set up on my now smooth and wrinkle-free bed. My favorite tea, Sweet Tropical Green Tea, rested in the delicate teacup. A small glass of orange juice and a warm apple strudel muffin presided next to a bud vase with a single blush rosebud. I would, for sure, let everyone know how much I appreciated the excellent service.

I carried the bed tray over to the chaise lounge covered in a silvery velvet dusty miller-like print. With my legs stretched out in front of me, I set the tray over my lap and poured hot water into the teacup, inhaling the herbal scent. Pulling the sheers away from the oversized window, I lost myself while overlooking the Randall Mansion gardens.

I imagined my new life ahead. The more I thought of the cottage, the more I wanted to move in, especially as I lounged in this grand excess of ornament. The thought of going back to the cold straight lines of mid-century modern in my condo left me, well, cold. I thought of when Mary Jane moved in and said the apartment didn't look like me and when Jake was surprised by the style of my abode. How had I never seen it? Preserving Jonathan's style, beautiful in and of itself, was just that—his style. I had all but drowned myself in being his daughter, not wanting to lose any ingrained part of him, so much so, I had avoided my sense of self. There really was no separating him from me when it came to our talent and taste, our determination, and our stubbornness, our work ethic, and our love of all things miniature. But could I forgive him for putting into motion the deterioration of my family?

A knock on the door interrupted my reverie. "Shoot." I froze, still in my bra and underwear. "Ah, just a minute."

I jumped up, placing the tray on the foot of the bed, and grabbed the robe off the back of the en suite door. I moaned as I slid my arm into its velvety softness.

I opened the door and invited Jake to enter. "You'll have to give everyone a late checkout. It's impossible to leave this room," I said.

"Glad you like it, ma'am. Maybe you could write a review." He cupped my face with his fingers and caressed my cheeks. "Before last night, I didn't have a favorite room. Now, I do."

I kissed him back, and the rest of our day would have to wait.

CHAPTER 38

Even though the B&B was officially now open for business, Jake didn't mind driving me over to the cottage to meet Nissa. On our way, I mustered up the courage to have him drive by my old childhood home. As we passed by, I held my breath. My eyes blinked as I squelched the upheaval of many mixed emotions seeing the house as Mary Jane must see it. There would be no getting away from Johnathan as it was a clear representation of him—low-lying, hard-lined, and cold. No wonder Mary Jane sold it as soon as she could. As Jake's foot came off the gas pedal, I felt the truck give way. "Please, don't slow down. Keep going."

He did as I asked and continued to Liddy's house down the street.

We pulled up in front of the small white cottage surrounded by a cracked and splintering white picket fence, overgrown lawn, and an emptiness that tugged at my heart. I leaned into the back of my seat as a slideshow of flashbacks flickered. Even though Mary Jane was not in any of my images, every thought circled back to her. The love, despite her guilt, it took Mary Jane to keep Liddy's happiness intact at the expense of her own, and the courage to make sure I was always part of Liddy's life were the flames that will forever keep my heart warm.

Not seeing Nissa's car in the driveway, and not wanting to go in alone, I asked him if he wanted to come in.

"Sure, I'd love to see it."

"If you have a ton of stuff to do today, I understand." I was trying to be polite, but I truly wanted him by my side for this.

"If they can't get along without me at the B&B for a few hours, then I've messed up somewhere. Everyone knows their job, and they'll call if they need me."

"Come on in then," I said, opening the truck door and sliding out.

As we reached the front door, hand in hand, Nissa pulled into the driveway with her window down, shouting, "Hey, wait for me!"

When she caught up with us, I pushed open the door. Liddy's soft rose scent escaped from the entryway as we stirred up the air. Sunlight illuminated the floating dust streaming through the barely opened drapes as if Liddy just sprinkled pixie dust as a welcome. The coffee table in the middle of the living room was on its side. Across the room, the drawers of the antique Dutch cabinet were open. Their contents strewn all over the floor.

"It looks like someone tossed the place." Jake picked up couch cushions and set them straight.

Nissa pulled out her cell phone. "I'm calling the police."

"No, wait. Let's see if there's any damage," I said. "I bet a couple of kids knew the place was empty."

Nissa and I collected the papers, pens, photos, and craft supplies that had been tossed on the living room floor and returned them to the drawers. Jake pulled open the drapes on either side of the large picture window, stirring more sparkling dust in the air, but doubling the amount of sunshine entering the room.

"This place looks more like you, except for the dust and the overturned furniture," Jake said and winked.

"It feels more like me, too," I said as I turned around, taking in the smell of Liddy and her Victorian style. "I can now admit, without any guilt, that this place has always been home."

The old hunter-green couch filled the span of the picture window. On either side stood a marble-topped American Empire side table. To its right, there was a single matching armchair. I swiped my fingers across the cold marble side table and stood in the vacant spot to the left of the couch. Below my feet, I felt the ruts where Liddy rocked in her wheelchair as she watched TV. I squatted down and rubbed my hand over the dents. "Liddy's spot," I said in a low voice. I walked toward the kitchen, "If you couldn't find her there, then you'd find her in here."

I pointed to the scrapes and scratches on the walls behind the kitchen table where the wheelchair left its marks below the Van Gogh *Sunflowers*. "Whatever I do, that picture will stay right there," I said.

Nissa and I washed and put away the silverware and dishes we found dumped out of the drawers and cabinets. It broke my heart to see two of Liddy's Coalport plates with hand-painted lilacs smashed to bits.

"So, what are you going to do?" Jake asked as they followed me through the rest of the house.

"I'm thinking about moving in here." I glanced at Nissa, but she didn't seem surprised.

"No, I mean about the break-in. You can't stay here until we add security alarms and cameras." Jake checked the locks on the kitchen windows.

I picked up scattered papers and a folded newspaper off the linoleum floor. A flash of red caught my attention. I was surprised to find a red circle highlighting my name and age. I looked at the left-hand corner of the newspaper. It was dated months ago.

"Maybe we *should* call the cops. Listen," I said, gesturing for the other two to come closer. "'Notice of deed transfer: Upon the death of Miss Lydia Coretta Edwards, of 35 Cranberry Lane, Bluebelle, GA, to her daughter Miss Christina Ann Edwards, 33, of Floral Ridge, GA...'" I handed the paper to Jake and chewed on the earpiece of my reading glasses. Why did the world need to know about Liddy transferring her home to me?

"You've got to love small-town newspapers. Everything is everybody's business," Jake said. "It's like someone was looking for something because it was your house. I don't like this."

"Well, if I do move back here, I'd like to move the workshop here, too," I said, gaining confidence in the idea. I walked down the hallway clearing a way through my old collection of board games someone had pulled out of the hall closet. It would be a project putting all the game pieces back in their correct boxes. "We can use Liddy's oversized bedroom as the workroom. It has tons of light, its own bathroom, and a door out to the back porch for an entrance. I think this room would—" I pushed open the door and stopped short. Nissa bumped into my back, forcing me into the toppled room.

The back door hung on one hinge, wide open. The mattress leaned saggy and folded against the wall. The box spring cover was torn to shreds and covered with the tattered carpet in a mouse-infested heap. Every dresser drawer hung open, either empty to begin with, or their contents confiscated.

"I really think you should call the cops," Jake said as he walked across the room to close the back door. "This couldn't have been a bunch of kids. Someone was looking for something."

The police arrived within fifteen minutes of Nissa's call. Over the following hour and a half, they took pictures and dusted for fingerprints. They discovered the backdoor had been kicked open and a crowbar was used to pull up floor planks.

"We'll look into this, and I'm taking this newspaper with me." The police officer handed me a card. "I don't like that your name and address were circled. It suggests they came here with a purpose. You really should get a security system. When do you plan on moving in?"

"Well, I haven't really decided," I said, having not yet discussed it with Nissa. "But it will take several months to renovate anyway. You think I should be worried?"

On his way out, the policeman said, "We'll keep an eye out for you, Miss Edwards. My guess is they either got what they came for, or it wasn't here to begin with. Don't worry, and go on with your plans, but make sure you install a security system sooner than later. Call the number on that card if you have any more trouble."

I rubbed my neck with both hands. I didn't need another thing to worry about. But the cop knew the area, and he thought it was a one-and-done deal, so I shook it off and said, "Well, no matter if I move in, rent it, or sell it, I need to update it."

"I'm sure you can handle anything after what you've been through lately." Nissa gave me two thumbs up. "You've got this, girl."

"And I know a few guys who can help you gussy up the place," Jake said, reaching for his phone.

"I bet you do," I said.

"Let me look in the garage for something to board up that back door," he said.

I returned to the kitchen and began inventorying what remained in the cabinets. He came back with a large red-and-black toolbox and set it on the table. "I called one of the guys to bring over some plywood. It won't keep anyone out that really wants to get in, but it'll keep the critters out for now. We'll get you a new door, then install security. It shouldn't take but a couple of days."

While Jake spoke, he wiggled the lock on the toolbox. "Who locks a toolbox?"

We each tried to open it. I took the small gold lock in my hand and pulled. I looked at the keyhole. "Hold on a sec."

I pulled Liddy's pewter rose keyring out of my pocket and tried the littlest key, the one I thought went to a safe deposit box. The lock popped open. As Jake lifted the cover, we peered into the toolbox as if afraid something might jump out.

"A gun?" I took a step back.

Jake grabbed a kitchen knife off the counter and used it to slide the gun to one side then poked around within. "And a bunch of passports and envelopes."

"Don't touch anything." I dug in my purse for the card the police officer had given me and made a call.

As we waited for the officer, I couldn't imagine what Liddy would have been doing with a gun in her house. "But she clearly knew it was there," I said. "The key to the toolbox was on her keyring with her house key."

"How soon can we get security in here?" The cop asked Jake after he checked out the toolbox and its curious items.

"I will call for quotes tomorrow," I answered, letting the policeman know I was in charge here—not Jake.

"I'll make sure she's all secure by the end of tomorrow," Jake said. When I began to object, he said. "I've got the perfect guy to do it."

"The sooner the better," the officer said. "I wonder if this is what your break-in was all about?" He promised to get back to me about the contents of the box.

Jake's buddy brought over some plywood, and they closed up the back door. After returning from seeing him off, Jake held up a bottle of wine and Nissa ordered a pizza to be delivered.

"Quite the prepared Boy Scout." I laughed, looking at the bottle of the same delicious wine we drank last night.

"The wine is a house-warming gift. I had my guy bring it," Jake said as he opened a drawer. "Wine opener?"

Liddy didn't drink, but I had a wine opener in my purse, and I knew not to look too hard for any stemmed glassware. I hooked my fingers into three teacups' handles and set them up on the counter to be filled.

While we waited for pizza, I wiped out the refrigerator, and Nissa swept the kitchen floor. "Nissa, you know you're like a sister to me. I want you to be honest with me. I'm worried it won't be convenient for you if I move the business out here."

"Stop right there. You do what's best for you. It doesn't matter where I live. David's garage is halfway between here and Floral Ridge. I'm good either way. I'm sure we can figure something out."

A weight lifted knowing Nissa had my back.

As the pizza rewarmed on a hot cast iron tray in the oven, Nissa and I talked about colors and fabrics, and all that needed to be done to bring the house back to life. Jake jotted down the phone number of his restoration crew.

"I think I'll go back to the auction house again. I can picture a few pieces I'd like for this place," I said.

"What about selling pieces from your apartment, too?" Jake suggested.

"Great idea. I'll give the auction house a call. No need to rush. It'll take time to get this place ready, plus there's Mary Jane to consider."

"What are you going to do with the condo?" Jake asked.

"Mary Jane sold her townhome, so I have an idea. We'll see." My heart warmed with the paradox of starting a new life in my mother's home, the home I truly grew up in, while my Aunt Mary Jane lived in my old condo. The more I thought about it, the more I liked the idea. I was happy I could provide for Mary Jane and Bella. It was a way I could give thanks to the both of them.

After we chowed down the pizza, Nissa gathered the paper plates and threw them in the trash. She bent over and hugged me from the back. "Gotta go. I'm leaving for Canada in the morning. Going to meet with Miss Paula on Wednesday."

"It feels so weird not going with you," I said, but there was no way I would leave Mary Jane now.

"No worries. David's coming with me." Nissa winked.

"Well, I'm glad you're not going alone," I said, glad my friend got to finally bring her boyfriend on a work trip, something she always pined to do.

"Tina, you take all the time you need to take care of Mary Jane. It'll all work out. As for this house, I've got the measurements, and I'll call around for prices for wide-plank pine flooring. You work on getting the painters in here. Then our canvas will be set, only this time, it won't be in miniature." With a wave, she walked out the front door.

"I guess I'll be driving you all the way home," Jake said.

"She has a way of leaving you stuck with me," I said as he poured the rest of the wine into my teacup and led me out to the back porch.

"It'll be fun fixing this place up," Jake said as he leaned against the railing and regarded the structure of the back porch.

"Hopefully, Nissa will bring back a new commission, and with spending as much time as I can with Mary Jane, this place is going to have to wait."

"Nissa will be fine. Miss Paula is good people."

"And I'm glad David's going with her. She's been dying to mix one of our business trips with sightseeing," I said as he led me by the hand off the back porch into the fenced-in yard.

The pecan trees from my youth glittered in the dappled light of the setting sun. The dancing brilliance illuminated the faded fairy doors and the remains of my fairy houses from long ago. We strolled around the backyard, and I dusted off the miniature doors and brushed the leaves off the flat mossy fairy yards.

"Ouch," I yelped and pulled my hand to my chest.

"What? Did something bite you?" Jake asked as he squatted by my side.

Embarrassed, I laughed. "No. It's nothing. I must have hit a rock or something."

Jake patted the moss, pressing as he scanned the ground. "Here, this is what you hit." He wiggled his fingers in the ground. Trying to pull up the corner of a small box up but failing. He peeled back the moss and dirt like a bedsheet.

"That's weird," Tina said as she watched Jake dig out a small, square black box with gold trim.

Dusting the dirt off the top, he handed it over to me, then patted down the dirt and moss until the fairy garden looked as if it had never been touched.

I fell back from my squat to sitting cross-legged and placed my teacup by my side. Jake joined me, sitting cross-legged in the middle of my decaying fairy village.

With a glance at Jake, I opened the box. Inside were two simple gold wedding bands. "They *were* planning on getting married." Somehow, knowing that Liddy loved Bobby, despite his horrible family, assured me that Bobby was probably a good man. "Liddy knew I would find these if she buried them here."

We turned and leaned our backs on the tree trunk until darkness enveloped us.

I placed the box in my empty teacup when I was ready to go in. Leaning on the back-porch column, he said, "Life is good. Look up at those stars, hold your breath, and listen to the silence."

I snickered. "You can't hear silence." But I looked up and held my breath. The familiar sounds from long ago, crickets and bullfrogs and rustling leaves, were letting me know I was home.

CHAPTER 39

After a quiet week in the condo with Bella and Mary Jane, I entered SugarBeans Café with a *ding*. Marge looked over her shoulder and called out, "Hey, Tina. The regular?"

"Yes, two, please. Iced. Nissa should be here any minute." I tossed my computer bag into a chair and sat with a plop. I would miss this place, but I would visit every time I came back to visit Mary Jane and Bella.

"Here you go, honey." Marge placed two iced herbal teas on the table. In one smooth movement, she rotated and straddled the chair next to me. "Mary Jane?"

"The doctors said it could get worse before it gets better, but this is rough. She doesn't get out of bed much. This last treatment got the best of her. I'm helping Bella with her care. It takes both of us to switch out her sheets and help her change positions. Sad, but I'm glad I can help. I'm reading *Out of Africa* to her, and she seems to enjoy it, that and having her feet rubbed."

"Keep up the good work. I'm sure she appreciates all you do."

Another *ding* from the door and Nissa entered. She opened and closed the door several times for a grand *dinging* entrance.

"Hey! How'd it go?" I asked, sitting down after jumping up to greet her with a long hug. We hadn't seen each other for a week, something unheard of for us.

"Awesome. It was strange not to have you with me, but David loved Toronto and can't wait to go back. We are going to have fun with this job. Totally different than anything we've ever done. You won't believe the pictures of the old arena. Who knew they played hockey way before 1912?" Nissa opened her backpack and flamboyantly pulled out blueprints and photos from her trip. She dramatically smoothed out the papers in front of me and pointed to certain items with exaggerated elegance.

I looked at the blueprints, rubbed my eyebrows, and squeezed my forehead. I hadn't thought to bring my reading glasses with me.

"Are you okay? I'm sorry, I should have asked." Nissa dropped into her seat. "How's Mary Jane?"

"No better, no worse. Just not good. I thought she'd be so much better by now. Thank you so much for going on this trip without me. It was the right move all the way around. The new medicine makes her queasy and she hasn't left her bed since you left town. She has a catheter now and barely eats. I'm glad this was her last round of treatment. Hopefully, it only gets better from here." Tears welled in my eyes.

Nissa grabbed my hand in both of hers and kissed it. "I am so sorry. Why don't you take more time off? I'll start on your cottage, the floors are ready to be installed, and I can work on the hockey rink from there. At the moment, it's all research, anyway. Plus, David and I will look for an apartment in Athens… together…"

"You're moving in with David?"

Nissa held up her left hand with a flourish and wiggled her fingers. A little slow catching on, I raised my eyebrows in question. Finally, her ring caught my attention.

"You're engaged?" I squealed and jumped up from my seat, dragging Nissa's hand with me. "We get to plan a wedding?"

We hugged again, and I almost pulled Nissa out of her chair. I held up Nissa's hand and waved it around, showing everyone in the cafe. Marge yelled out her congratulations.

"Have you set a date?" I asked after sitting down.

"Not yet. But we'd like to have the reception at the Randall Mansion B&B and the wedding in the new Randall-Martin Gardens," Nissa said.

"Perfect. Let's call Jake now so he can save the date."

"I said we don't have a date yet," Nissa laughed.

I picked up my cell phone and called him anyway.

CHAPTER 40

Peaceful, ambient music floated from Mary Jane's room as I entered the apartment and went directly to see how she was doing. I helped her sit on the edge of her bed and together we gave identity to the shapes of clouds floating past as Bella massaged her back with lavender-scented lotion and a tender touch. After Bella fluffed her pillows, I lowered Mary Jane to a comfortable resting position.

"Sugar, would you mind getting the blanket from the dryer?" Bella asked me. "I'm warming it up." Mary Jane's slow recovery had reached the point that Bella seldom left her friend's side, and I had no problem being her gopher.

When I returned, Bella was rubbing Mary Jane's feet. I spread the blanket over her as Bella wrapped each foot in sheepskin heel protectors then tucked the warm blanket around Mary Jane's feet and legs.

"Bella, why don't you take a break. I'll stay and read to… I turned to Mary Jane. "Would you like that?"

"Ya know, you can call me Mary Jane," she said.

"I think I'd like continue to call you Mom," I said and felt strongly about it once the words were out.

"Really?" she asked me, tears quickly followed.

"Are you tired?" I asked as I piled the albums to return to the credenza.

"I am, but…" She pointed at the chest on top of her dresser. "Go get my jewelry box." Resting my hand on the smooth lid, I carried the foot-wide chest over to the bed, recalling the Christmas Jonathan had given it to her.

She had hosted Jonathan's annual Christmas fundraiser the week before Christmas, and of course, everything had to be just right. The Christmas tree decorations glimmered with only gold and silver ornaments, and she had even changed out the living room furniture to match. Weeks before Christmas, Jonathan had wrapped his gift in silver paper. He had tied a gold ribbon around it and added a gold holly branch for embellishment. He placed it under the tree with the other silver and gold-wrapped fake gifts. Mary Jane couldn't hide her surprise when she learned her gift had been hiding in plain sight for weeks.

Jonathan had built the two-tier cherry jewelry chest himself. When I was seven years old, he and I spent weeks rubbing it with tung oil, creating a deep rich finish. Upon opening the extraordinary gift, Mary Jane lifted out a pear-shaped amethyst ring. Even as young as I was, I noticed she didn't place the ring on her finger, but instead, put it back in the chest. It had meant nothing to me then.

Scooching next to her on the bed, I waited for direction. She gestured for me to open the lid. In the top tray, I found the amethyst ring, along with three others: an oval-shaped emerald, a marquis-cut sapphire, and a heart-shaped ruby, none of which I had ever witnessed on my mother's hand.

One more ring, a ring I never saw my mother without, rested in its own distinctive section. Mary Jane's engagement ring, an antique cushion-cut 5.5-carat diamond.

My mother removed the ring and placed it in my palm. "It's for you. Liddy should have received it on her wedding day. It was her mother's," said Mary Jane.

I put the ring on the ring finger of my right hand. Compressed pixie dust.

I lifted out the top tray and found the chest split in half down the middle. My heart raced. There lay a set of 12 mm pearl earrings and *the* pearl necklace, which had haunted my dreams for the past twenty-plus years. The very same pearls that had comforted Mary Jane and kept her calm as she twisted them in her fingertips the day Jonathan died. I grimaced at the memory still.

In the other velvet compartment lay a diamond tennis bracelet with matching earrings and a twenty-inch, white-gold chain with a seven-carat solitaire diamond dangling from it. Every evening in the past, Mary Jane traded in her pearls for diamonds.

"Remember the night you caught me peeking into your room while you were getting ready for one of your famous dinner parties?" I asked.

I was six, already bathed and in my pajamas when I had studied Mary Jane from her doorway as she hooked the diamond necklace around her neck. "Caught by my reflection in your mirror, you called me over to sit beside you. Do you remember what you told me that night?" I asked as I rubbed the large diamond between two fingers.

She said, "I told you your father liked me to wear diamonds at night and pearls during the day."

"But why was that?"

"It was his mother's way. He claimed she felt that pearls brought her good luck and wisdom. She felt diamonds were eveningwear. Jonathan always let his peers and clients know the meaning of the word diamond comes from ancient Greece, where the Greeks would refer to them as 'adamas,' which means invincible. He clearly wanted to send a message to his peers and clients."

I stared at the large sparkling diamond thinking Jonathan just wanted to prove his wealth to his peers and clients by Mary Jane wearing such a gem. When I placed the necklace back onto its velvet bed, the diamond ring on my right hand cast tiny glints of light around the room. I slowly rotated my hand in the sunlight, directing the small round reflections from the diamond to dance on the walls and curtains, just like I had seen many times during my childhood. I had always believed that that tiny, random light dancing and dodging was a fairy flittering around the room. Another truth splintered.

I played with the ring in the light a few more moments then returned it to the jewelry chest, accepting those dreams were suited for another time.

"I've worn nothing in that chest for years. I'd like to see you get some use out of them. You could sell them for all I care," she said.

"We'll see." As long as my mother was alive, I would not accept these gifts. And even afterward, I would think long and hard before wearing any baubles Jonathan gave Mary Jane to quell his guilt.

"Now go in the closet, look up in the corner. The left corner, in the back." Mary Jane nodded me on. "There's a box."

I flipped on the lights. Her bright jewel-toned dresses, from deep amethyst to the perfect gold, not a sunny yellow or a brownish mustard, but the ideal pale saffron, lined the back of her closet. Her pumps, stored in clear plastic shoeboxes and lined up in rainbow order, matched the dresses hanging above. This was the Mary Jane I remembered.

I dragged my hand across the hangers, which clinked as I let each one of them go. On tiptoe, I searched in the corner of the shelf. Under some sweaters, I found a beat-up old shoebox. Pulling it toward me with my fingertips, I slid it off the shelf. Returning to Mary Jane's bedside, I rolled the rubber band holding the lid in place. It snapped and flew across the room, startling us both. We laughed, me much louder than my mother.

I raised the lid in anticipation. I picked up a small, sterling silver rattle with the initials MJC engraved on one side and "Mother's little love" on the other.

I placed it in my mother's hands. She rolled it in her palm, listening to its faint rattle, and said, "This was mine when I was a baby."

I then pulled out an envelope and unfolded a birth certificate… and a death certificate, both dated September 12. Mary Jane Connors Edwards had saved her own sterling rattle to give to her baby daughter, Jacqueline Paige Edwards. Hid in a folded pink baby blanket were several cards, some from a baby shower and some in sympathy.

"Oh, God," I sighed, placing the items back into the box. She placed the rattle on top of the blanket, releasing it only when the rattling sound stopped. I closed my eyes and curled up next to Mary Jane on the bed.

A tap on the door woke us both. Bella stepped in and closed the door behind her. "Tina, Mr. Jake's in the living room with two policemen."

"What?" I said groggily.

"Two policemen want to talk to you. They're out there. With Mr. Jake. In the living room."

"Okay." I placed the jewelry chest and the old shoebox on the shelf in the closet, then kissed Mary Jane on the forehead. Bella held the door open, then stepped in as I stepped out.

Jake had led two gentlemen to the dining table. "This is Officer Lawrence and Detective Peale. They have questions for you about the contents of that toolbox."

The officer placed a manila folder on the table. "Mr. Martin was working at your house in Bluebelle and told us we could find you here. We have a few questions."

The detective explained they would keep the gun they had found for the time being. The 9mm Glock had been wiped clean of fingerprints but had been used in several jewelry robberies and the murder of a French jewelry dealer. "Would you happen to know who it belonged to or why it would have been hidden in your aunt's garage?"

I looked from one man to the other. In no uncertain tone, I said, "No."

"What about these? Have you seen them before?" He spread six passports in front of her.

As I thumbed through them, my stomach sank. Each different name offered the same photo of a balding man, some with a mustache, others with glasses. I recognized him from when Nissa had Googled him and knew it was Robert Canton Sr., my grandfather.

"I'm sorry. I don't know what all this has to do with me. I recently inherited that house. I…" I stumbled on my words, not knowing what more to say.

The detective then slid over a piece of paper. "This is a copy of something we found in a white envelope at the bottom of the box."

The photocopied image of a torn-up check pieced together stopped my breath. I looked at Jake. He slid the paper out of my fingers and studied it. The check was made out to Bobby Canton for $50,000 and signed Jonathan P. Edwards.

Liddy knew.

Liddy knew her brother had tried to pay off her fiancé. She knew everything. She had to have been the one to put it in the toolbox. Bobby had also entrusted her with his father's evidence of guilt. The key to the toolbox on Liddy's own pewter rose keyring was the proof. Did Liddy spend her life protecting Mary Jane from finding out about Jonathan's betrayal when all along Mary Jane attempted to keep it from Liddy? Jonathan's death must have been a relief to both women, while neither grasped the other knew the depth of it all.

Once again, a lifetime of misunderstanding could have been avoided. The three of us could have lived in harmony, save for the bribe from one man, Jonathan.

The red circle on the newspaper we had found in my ransacked cottage flashed before my eyes. As panic reached my face, Jake placed his hand over my tight fist.

"What?" Jake asked.

As much as I didn't want to be involved in any Canton family story, I wouldn't live with any more lies. "The announcement in the newspaper," I said to no one in particular. I ran to my bedroom and returned with a business card and handed it to the detective. "A couple of weeks ago, there was a break-in at my Bluebelle house. This officer took a newspaper we had found that had the transfer of the deed for the house circled in red."

"And you think whoever left it was looking for all this?" the policeman asked as he gathered the evidence.

"Hmmm. They had found out where Liddy lived from the newspaper," Jake surmised.

I sunk into my chair. "They also found out Liddy, Bobby's girlfriend and fiancé at the time of his death, had a daughter born within that same year."

CHAPTER 41

After spending two months helping Bella care for Mary Jane and watching her regain her appetite and strength, we all got to know each other as family. Through playing cards, eating meals together, and appreciating each other's choice of movies, we became intimates and began to heal from time missed.

Between wedding planning appointments, Nissa oversaw the preparations for my new home and office. She had hired Jake's construction team to install the floors and paint the walls, turning Liddy's old bedroom, with its new secure back door, into Edwards' Historical Miniatures' bright, professional office and workroom.

Jake secretly supervised transforming my old bedroom into my new luxury suite, replicating the French grey B&B bedroom I loved so much. As a bonus, next to the steam shower, he added a claw-foot tub to heighten the en suite's spa-like splendor. He had managed to keep me from peeking in over the last few weeks, and I anticipated the surprise.

"I just need you to be safe in your new home," Mary Jane said, dealing out our last hand in a game of rummy. "Are you sure you're not worried about any more break-ins?"

Having asked her if she knew anything, anything at all, about Bobby Canton and his family and her assurance that she knew nothing, I didn't see the need to worry her any more than necessary.

"Jake made sure the state-of-the-art security system was intact, and the police convinced me that the men who broke into my house most likely would never return." Jake and I were relatively comfortable with the news that, unless otherwise notified, my name would in no way be connected to the fifty-year-old Canton case, which in all probability, would remain cold. Most witnesses had already passed, and even though the gun and passports had been found, there were no fingerprints.

"Any absolute proof was long gone," the detective had said.

But he was wrong. For me, absolute proof was in that box, proof of all the missteps my entire family took in trying to do the right thing for each other, proof Jonathan did write that check and did not want Liddy involved with Bobby Canton. As her niece, the Canton's wouldn't be interested in me. But as her daughter...?

Liddy took more than the Edwards' secrets to her grave. She took the Cantons' with her, too. After Bobby's death, Liddy must have kept that toolbox hidden in her garage to help Bobby keep his father's secret. I had a new appreciation for Jonathan wanting to protect Liddy. But then Liddy felt the need to protect Mary Jane and me, and Mary Jane had the undaunting task to protect Liddy and me. What a mess.

After our morning card game, I packed two suitcases with clothes and toiletries and left them by the front door of the apartment. I would live out of them until the Victorian furniture I had bought from the auction house graced the rooms of my new cottage. The mid-century furniture I so painstakingly chose in memory of Jonathan had been picked up by the auction house the day before. My apartment would soon house Mary Jane's belongings, which she had stored when her townhouse sold, along with anything Bella chose to bring.

On a card table set up in the dining room, I had placed a medium-sized cardboard box to collect items I didn't want the movers to pack, keepsakes I would transport myself. Inside I had the framed miniature of Van Gogh's *Sunflowers* Jonathan painted on the piece of bark, and an envelope containing two photographs—a picture of Mary Jane, Jonathan, Liddy, and baby Tina and the picture of my aunt and uncle, the perfect couple, standing on the beach next to my parents on their hands and knees, playing in the sand. I squeezed in a bottle of champagne wrapped in a dish towel and all Liddy's important documents next to the long-saved shoebox from the corner of Mary Jane's closet.

"Knock, knock!"

I jumped up to greet Bella as she returned from recruiting her sons to help me move out, only to have a warm peach cobbler thrust into my hands.

"This here's for your new home. And make sure Mr. Jake gets some. I know it's his favorite."

"Thank you, Bella," I gave her a peck on the cheek.

"How's Mary Jane doing?" Bella asked, not waiting for an answer as she pushed through the bedroom door. "Look at you, sitting up on your own. Are you only sick when I'm here by your side?"

I could hear Mary Jane's improved but labored laughter. It was taking Mary Jane longer to gain back her strength than expected, but with the positive outcome from the treatment so far, the doctors and Bella agreed, Mary Jane would have her strength back soon enough.

The front door, which Bella didn't close, opened wider, and two well over six-foot-tall men entered, dwarfing my entire condo. They each carried a box and pulled suitcases behind them.

"Meet my babies, Anthony and Theodore," Bella said from behind me as each of them reached out a hand. "Since you're family, you can call them Ant and Teddy."

I busted out a laugh, as the two thirty-something, 250-pound-plus, oversized, grown men rolled their eyes and shook their heads.

"She loves to say that," Ant said.

"Nice to meet you." I shook their hands. "You have a great mother. I don't know what we would do without her."

Bella piped up, "Now tell these two what to pack up and bring over to your new home. Teddy brought his work truck so we can get in a big load."

"First, let's put your mother's things into her new bedroom," I directed. "But remember after all my stuff has moved, either one of you can move into the larger workroom."

Bella beamed from ear to ear. "No matter. I think what I'll do is move Miss Mary Jane in there for the view, and there'll be much more room for that big ol' recliner."

"But you can sleep in a bed now."

"My back really likes that recliner." With hands in the air, Bella added an "Hallelujah."

I pointed out the two suitcases in the living room, which were going down to Jake's truck when he got there. Then I led Bella's sons into the workroom. I pointed out all the packed-up supplies, paints, brushes, clear plastic boxes of miniature furniture inventory, books, and files, as well as the oversized workbench with its legs removed and our two desks. It was all ready to go to our new workshop in Bluebelle.

"Bella, I don't know how to thank you for all you do for my mother and me. She's blessed to have you by her side." I hugged Bella with all I had.

"It's nothing, Sugar. I love your mama. We've been together a long time. Anyway, you're thanking us by letting us live in your apartment."

Between trips to Teddy's truck, I grabbed a water from the fridge and hugged Bella again. "I hope you know, Bella, you can stay here as long as you like, even if…" I didn't want to say the words. "Even without my mother. This apartment is yours as long as you'll have it."

"You're a dear," Bella said and pecked me on the forehead.

"But I will certainly miss you and your cooking," I said in all honesty.

"Well, as long as I live here, you and Mr. Jake, plus Nissa and her beau can come to Sunday family dinners. How's that?"

"That would be great," I said, having to catch my breath when Bella released me from yet another hug.

"Your chariot awaits," Jake said from the door with a gentleman's bow and his hand circling in the air.

I responded by presenting Jake with the peach cobbler.

"Where is she?" Jake headed straight for the kitchen, looking for Bella.

I stepped over the threshold of Mary Jane's room as if the floor would fall in from my weight, but I found Mary Jane sitting up in Bella's recliner. The circles under her eyes were still deep and dark, but she offered a big smile. Only time will tell if the positive progress from the treatments will last. I glanced around the room. From now on, this would always be Mary Jane's room, and from here on out, my condo belonged to Mary Jane and Bella. I wished I could do more for them. "Just saying goodbye." I leaned over and kissed her on the forehead. "I'll swing by tomorrow and see how you're doing."

She squeezed my hand and whispered, "You don't have to come by every day. Just give me a call when you have time."

Knowing the doctors felt positive and she was in good hands, the best possible with Bella, I could move on with confidence. "I'll see you Sunday for family dinner."

"I can't wait," she said. The blue of her eyes shined.

"Make sure you nap and take your walks every day," I instructed as I walked out and bumped into Jake.

"Jake?" Mary Jane called out.

I gave him the go-ahead with a lift of my chin, and he handed me back the cobbler.

Having spent my last night in the apartment, I was ready to move on. I placed the cobbler on top of the box of keepsakes, and with both arms, heaved it up to carry away.

The elevator alarm sounded as Ant and Teddy entered the elevator and held the door open for me. They shared the load of the supplies for the hockey arena to place in the back of Jake's truck. "Go on down. We'll be right there," I said.

A minute later, Jake quietly exited my mother's room carrying the cherry jewelry chest I purposefully left tucked away in the corner of her closet. "She wants me to hold on to this for you."

I put down my heavy box and traded the warm peach cobbler for the jewelry box. The beautiful baubles resting on velvet lining represented heartbreak and guilt. Maybe one day, they could express love and forgiveness.

Finally accepting who I was and who I was no longer, I opened the chest and lifted the top tray. I placed one diamond earring in each ear and handed the ridiculously fancy diamond necklace to Jake. With a quizzical look and his winsome dimple, he set down the cobbler then hooked the necklace around my lace collar.

Infused with the strength of the two women who raised me, I lifted the diamond off my chest and gave it a kiss, determined to show Mary Jane's diamonds the light of day.

ABOUT THE AUTHOR

Kyle Ann is the author of "White Picket Fences" and writes contemporary women's fiction that sinks its teeth into families' miscommunications, misperceptions, and the chaos they cause, even in the name of love. After over twenty-five years as a Physical Therapy Assistant and fitness studio owner, Kyle's writing dream of being a "Taylor Jenkins Reid version of Joan Didion" is well on its way as she received her certificate of Creative Writing from Emory University, and is the founder of Embrace Your Muse Creative Writing Workshops.